Marc Johnson

CATALYST

The Passage of Hellsfire
Book 1

Sixth Edition, 2013

ISBN 0-9834770-6-x

Longshot Publishing

PROLOGUE

THE DARKNESS SPILLED into the world, waiting to engulf, waiting to consume, waiting to fulfill its purpose. The light, though weak, was there to stop it as it always was—as it always would be. The battle had gone on since the beginning. This time, the light wrapped itself around the darkness, trying to enlighten it. It was only a matter of time before the light failed.

Luckily, it was not alone.

Fierce winds howled through the winter sky. A snowstorm had swept through the tiny village of Sedah the night before, smothering everything with a white blanket. With the dawn, the storm had turned into an unrelenting rain. The sudden runoff flooded low-lying areas, damaging homes and farmland.

On the outskirts of Sedah, the storm crashed against a rickety longhouse where a young woman struggled in labor. To her, the wind sounded like a horde of dark creatures trying to tear their way in. She longed for her husband's strong arms and steady presence, but he was forever gone from her. The searing pain of that memory matched the pain in her body. Now she had to be strong for herself. And her child.

"Push," the midwife said. "Push."

"I can't," Damara said. Sweat rolled off her body with each heavy breath. Her labor had dragged on for thirteen hours, and she had already endured more than she thought possible. She had nothing left.

The sharp, tight pain encircled her hips. Each breath felt like jagged glass stabbing her belly. She bit down on her lower lip, too tired to even cry out. With her husband gone, the miracle of life felt like the strain of death. "I'm...exhausted."

"I know you are, but you must get through this. Just one more good push and it'll be done."

Damara stared through the midwife as if she wasn't there, trying not to dwell on the pain. Despite the cold, winter weather, she was drenched in sweat. Her clothes clung to her skin, and the heat and humidity in the room weighed heavily on her.

"I don't understand it," the midwife murmured. "It's the dead of winter and it feels like we're in the Burning Sands."

Damara ignored the midwife's words. Ever since she had become pregnant, she had felt the unusual heat residing in her. The cold hardly bothered her any more. Warmth wrapped constantly through her body, sending enough comfort to remind her she wasn't alone. Damara gathered her remaining strength. She closed her eyes and pushed past the throbbing pain, taking fast, shallow breaths. She looked at the midwife, wasting no energy on words. She gave one brief nod.

Damara took a deep breath and screamed, matching the fury of the storm outside. Her anger and determination cut through the weariness, loneliness, and pain. As if the release of her emotions freed her muscles, her body gave one final heave, and there was a violent, rushing pain. It was done.

Damara let out a sigh, letting her emotions drain out of her. The pain in her sides faded. Both the agonizing birth and the emptiness in her life were now over. The midwife held up the baby, and for a moment, Damara could see her dead husband's face in the child's. They finally had the family they had wanted. She smiled through her tears, wishing he could have been here with her. He would have loved seeing so many of his own features reflected in his son.

Exhaustion overcame Damara, and her body cried out for rest. She went limp, letting her eyes close for a moment, a smile still on her lips.

The midwife cut the umbilical cord and slapped the baby. He wailed in chorus with the wind, and a swell of heat covered the women. The shutters slammed and a tree's branches raked against the house. The midwife jumped and glanced uneasily at the window before she finished swaddling the baby and handed him to Damara.

"What are you going to name him?" the midwife asked, wiping her forehead with the back of her hand. It seemed that the strange heat had permeated the room, for the midwife was as drenched in sweat as Damara.

Damara studied the only man in her life. She traced his slimy form, tiny hands, and squinty eyes. Then she clutched him tightly to her, as if she had been bestowed with the most priceless treasure in the world. Unbeknownst to her, she had.

Damara worked her mouth, trying to speak through the dryness. "I'm not sure. I was thinking of naming him after his father, but we always said that if we had a boy we'd name him—"

The wooden door to her longhouse was suddenly flung open. The wind blew cold droplets of rain through the room, a jarring contrast to the muggy heat. Bits of parchment flew, pots and pans clashed against each other, and candles guttered. A shadow shrouded in dark blue robes loomed in the doorway. The midwife cried out and fainted. Damara clutched her baby tighter, fearing that the dark monsters she had imagined had somehow been conjured from the storm. She watched the stranger warily, her free hand sliding under her pillow to the dagger hidden there.

The shadow stepped into the longhouse—not a monster but an old man with a twisted, golden staff. The staff seemed to move on its own, pulling the man into the room. It swung like the needle of a compass, then steadied, pointing straight at Damara and her child. The fist-sized pearl on top of the staff glowed bright fiery red. He had finally found what he was looking for.

CHAPTER 1

Fourteen Years Later

I SAT IN FRONT of the fireplace, trying to get lost in the fire the way I had countless times before. This time I wasn't able to. I kept fidgeting and stealing glances at my mother as she got ready to go to the village church. She wore her finest clothing—her only decent dress. It was also the only piece of clothing we had that wasn't heavily mended and faded from long wear.

"Hellsfire, can you help me with this?" my mother asked.

I went to her, attaching her butterfly headdress to her hair. She fiddled with it, making sure it would stay on, and smoothed out the light wrinkles in her dress.

"You look very fine," I said, looking past the worn fabric at her elbows and cuffs. She looked as fine as we could afford. If I had the money, I would have given it to her to spend on looking as grand as possible to honor her god, even if I didn't believe in him. There were many in town with more elaborate clothes, but in my mind she outshone them all.

My mother looked at me, her light green eyes filled with hope. "Are you sure you don't want to go with me to church?"

I sighed and bit the inside of my lip. I did not want to have this argument again. "I'm sure." If it weren't for most of the people that went there, I might go sometimes. But not today.

Her sigh was full of disappointment. I hated to see her like this, but I held firm. "All right, son," she said, "If you change your mind, the doors are always open."

"I know, Mother."

"Goodbye, Hellsfire. I'll be back later tonight. Be good and don't get into any trouble." She walked out the door and headed for the church.

"I won't." I loved my mother, and I hated arguing with her. Every week, the holy day gave me the quiet solitude I needed. The town shut down while almost everyone went to church. It was a day where I didn't have to work on our neighbor's farm, straining my back, carrying bales of hay, or wallowing knee deep in dirt, feeding the pigs for a pittance that couldn't even keep us decently clothed.

I waited a few minutes until I was sure my mother would be out of sight. I had learned that if I rushed out and she saw me, she'd think I'd changed my mind about going with her. I'd always feel bad saying no and seeing how hurt she was. Sometimes, I'd end up going because of it. Every time I went, I regretted it.

Finally, the oppression of our small longhouse got to me. It was only my mother and me—my father died before I was born. My mother had always told me how he had planned on building a bigger place so they could have a big family. I wished he was around to teach me carpentry and woodworking. But if he was around, I wouldn't be thinking about a bigger home. We would have had one.

A draft picked up and forced its way inside, up near the roof. That was just one of many places that needed to be repaired. The breeze made our dented cooking pots sway on their hooks and clang lightly together. As hard as I scrubbed them clean and tried to repair them, they never seemed to shine. And the metal was worn so thin, I always expected our meals to fall through the bottom.

The roof I could fix. Tomorrow, I would do just that. We weren't in any danger of it raining tonight. I got up from the creaky, wobbly chair and left, not wanting to dwell on how poor we were.

As I walked out of town, I kept getting the evil eye from all the well-dressed townspeople on their way to church. Some were polite and greeted me, but all of them looked at me as if I were doing something wrong.

In the entire town there was only a handful of people who were like me and believed in many gods, instead of one. I learned and celebrated with them. My mother let me go to their services, even though I never told her why. When I was younger, I had made up my mind to be closer to my father. Since he was dead, this was the only way. Unlike my mother, he believed in the four gods. When I died, I hoped I walked with my father.

I reached the edge of town, breathing easier because I didn't believe I would run into anyone else. That's when I saw them.

A group of older boys surrounded Corwyn, who was a year younger than me. They were laughing, taunting him and pushing him back and forth like it was a game. He looked terrified—too terrified to fight back. He knew that would bring him far more trouble than he was in now.

I could see Corwyn trying not to cry and quickened my steps. Fighting back wasn't the only thing that would push the bullies further. If Corwyn cried, they would beat him mercilessly.

If I wanted to I could have slipped by them, but I couldn't let them pick on Corwyn. He was one of the few people near my age who didn't judge me based on what their parents said. They wouldn't let him be friends with me, but that wasn't his fault. In spite of the consequences, I rushed head-long towards them.

"Leave him alone, Nathan," I said. They all turned and focused their attention on me. The younger boy slipped through the group. I didn't take my eyes off the bullies. "Catch up to your parents and go to church, Corwyn."

"Thanks, Hellsfire."

I nodded but didn't say a word.

Nathan and his three cronies spread out and surrounded me. With my speed, I thought about trying to make a break for it, but they were equally as fast, and I didn't want them to know they scared me.

"You'll pay for that, Hellsfire," Nathan said, scowling at me. "Why are you such a killjoy? We were just having some fun before church. Not that you would know anything about church. I wonder, does it have to do with your name, *Hells*fire?" He grinned when he said my name, trying to bait me. I hated when people teased me about my name. When I was younger, I used to get into a lot of fights because of it. A lot of the fights were with him.

I clenched my fists, but stood firm and held my anger in check. Anything I said now was going to earn me a beating, and my mother would want to know what happened. I couldn't tell her the truth. Fighting my battles would only make it harder for her to be accepted by our neighbors.

"I don't get you, *Hells*fire. You're always butting into things that don't concern you." Nathan shoved me—hard. I crashed into the boy behind me. He too, shoved me, but with less force.

"Why do you feel the need to pick on everyone smaller than you?" I asked.

"Not everyone. Just you." Nathan's blue eyes shone with hatred. He smiled like an animal baring his teeth. "Luckily for me, your friend Dorian's not around. This time, it's going to be you and me."

I raised an eyebrow and glanced at the other three boys around me.

"You know your parents will be mad if you dirty your doublet before church."

Instead of my comment having the intended effect, Nathan's face twisted with rage. The relationship between him and his parents wasn't a good one.

Nathan grabbed my collar, not caring that the undertunic underneath his doublet became exposed. The other boys pinned my arms behind my back. I struggled, trying in vain to break their grasp. Nathan balled up his fist. I turned my head, bracing myself for the blow about to follow.

"Nathan!" a voice yelled. "Come here, boy, or we're going to be late."

They let go of my arms. "Damn," Nathan said.

I smiled, relieved that Nathan's father had been of help for once. Nathan took my smile as an insult.

He balled his hand into a fist. Before I knew what had happened, he hit me hard in the gut. The pain forced me to my knees in the mud.

"Now!" Nathan's father yelled.

A look of fear passed over Nathan's face. It was brief, but I saw it clearly. "Another time, Hellsfire," he said. "I'll kiss Kat for you."

Nate leered at me and made kissing noises. I forced myself to be calm, but I couldn't do it. My chest started heaving. Even though it was over between Kathleen and me, I couldn't believe she was now with him. Him, of all people!

I readied myself to rush him. I didn't care anymore about the beating I would get from fighting the four of them, or the chastising my mother would give me. Kathleen shouldn't be with him. *Anyone* else but him. Images of him kissing her, touching her, angered me more than I thought possible. She and I were still friends, cordial, if no longer as close as we once were. I had told myself all romantic feelings for her were gone. I was wrong.

I waited, still crouched, for Nathan to pass by me so I could attack him from behind. He must have sensed my intentions, or maybe he was just being his usual bullying self, but as he walked by, he kicked me in the face. The blow sent me to the ground, into the mud. The humiliation washed away all my anger.

I could do nothing but watch as they walked away. Their laughter rang in my ears. By day's end, I would be the gossip of the entire town.

I resigned myself to this while lying in the mud. I prayed that people would at least have the decency to not tell my mother. I tried to wipe the mud off my face, but all I managed to do was smear it around.

When I finally stopped feeling sorry for myself, I got up. I had wanted to head to my hideout in the forest, but now I *needed* to go. I needed the one place where I could have peace and quiet, and wouldn't have to deal with the townspeople or people like Nathan—the one place where I didn't have to worry about everything we didn't have.

Despite the mud clinging to my tunic and face, it was a beautiful day. I picked up a fallen branch as I walked, brandishing it as if it were a sword. My imaginary opponents were Nathan and his cronies, and I defended other boys my age and younger from them. I dispatched them easily, like the heroes in the tales, and everyone praised me and liked me.

I flung the branch from my hand when I reached my destination. It was a small pond filled with all sorts of creatures: ducks, turtles, fish, and frogs. I called it Peaceful Pond because whenever I was here, my mind felt at ease.

I splashed water on myself, cleaning off the mud as best I could. It felt good to finally get it off. I wished I could wipe Nathan's smug smile off his face as easily. But not even the fresh, cold water could scrub off the memories of the humiliation I felt.

I picked up a few flat pebbles and caressed them in the palm of my hand. I wound my arm and skimmed them over the surface, watching them create little footsteps on the water as they hopped. The cool, wavy grass and pine-filled air invited me to join them. *Become one with us,* it said. I lay down on the soft grass and gazed at a dog-shaped cloud. I tried to go to sleep, but I kept thinking of Nathan.

"Godsdamn him!" I ripped up a handful of grass and flung it, angry at him for disturbing my one place of solitude, and even more angry at myself for letting him.

I got up and stretched my legs. If lying still wasn't going to relax me, maybe running would. I jogged around the pond, heading towards the forest, leaping over exposed roots and fallen branches. I leaped over deep impressions in the earth. And then I saw the girl.

She darted through the forest, dark hair flying, chased by three men. She was wearing some kind of fancy gown, and its full skirt kept catching on snags and underbrush, slowing her down. One of the men was gaining on her. I had to help her. If I could get her away from the nearest one, we could lose the others in the forest.

I used my speed and knowledge of the terrain, staying out of sight of the girl's pursuers as much as I could. I also prayed that their attention would stay on the girl, and they wouldn't notice me.

I hid behind a large oak tree and picked up a fallen branch. Cradling the rough wood in my hand and trying to ignore the pounding of my heart, I waited until the girl ran past. A second later I swung the branch as hard as I could, releasing all the pent-up emotions I'd felt earlier when I couldn't do anything against Nathan. Just as I'd hoped, my weapon smacked into the pursuer's face. The half-rotted branch shattered and splintered, and he fell to the ground. He didn't move again.

The girl stopped and stared at me. Her eyes were purple—a shade I'd never seen before. They seemed to see right down into my soul.

"Run!" I yelled.

The girl broke her gaze and ran. I went after her, confident we could lose the other two and go for help. This was my forest, and I knew every inch. Just as I caught up to her, she leaped a log and went down, giving a muffled cry.

She had tripped and fallen into a shallow ditch. I hopped the log and slid down next to her.

"Are you all right?" I asked.

She grimaced while I helped her up. "It's my ankle. Just a sprain, but it's going to keep me from running."

I looked over my shoulder, but I couldn't see the men from where we were. I was thinking furiously.

"I don't suppose you can use a sword?" I asked, half-joking. By the looks of her clothes, she'd never done anything more taxing than embroidery. I couldn't use one either, but if I went back and took the unconscious man's weapon, we might have a chance.

The corner of her mouth curled. "Yes."

I stared at her. She looked serious. "Good. As soon as we get to the top, I'll get you that man's sword. If you can take one man, I'll look for another branch and try to hold off the other one as best as I can. We'll have to fight our way out."

I boosted her up and climbed out after her. "That's not a bad plan," one of the men said, stepping out of the brush. "Shame you won't get the chance."

They converged on us, pinning us between them and the log. One was small and wily-looking and the other was huge with angry eyes. They both had swords, and looked like they knew how to use them. We were in big trouble. Without weapons, we couldn't fight, and with the girl's ankle, we couldn't run.

Sweat trickled down my forehead. I wiped it aside and said, "Leave her alone."

The smaller, wily one said, "Relax. We're not going to hurt her. She's far too valuable. If we wanted her dead, we would have already killed her."

I glanced at their shortswords. He was right. One quick thrust and we would both be dead.

He pointed a long and dirty finger at me. "You, on the other hand, are a far different story. While I thank you for giving us this breather, my partner is going to be very upset when he wakes up. The mark on his face and the sting of it…well, let's just say I wouldn't want to be you." He gave me an oily smile.

"What do you want?" I asked.

"The girl. What else? Does it look like me or my partner enjoy running through some forest in the middle of nowhere?"

"What about money?" I asked, trying to buy some time and think of a way out of this.

"Negotiation? I do so love negotiations!" He clapped his hand against his thigh with glee.

The big one with the angry eyes never stopped staring at me and the girl.

"We don't have time for this, Rowe."

"Quiet, Bruno. There's always time for a little negotiation. As my father once taught me, 'Everything has its price.'"

I cleared my throat, trying to regain Rowe's attention. He must be the brains while Bruno was the hired muscle. I was going to have to outsmart him. "I could pay you. More than what you're getting now."

Rowe's blue eyes scanned me. They went over my face, my hair, even my fingernails. His eyes didn't miss the mud on my clothes or the holes and tears in them.

"I wish I could believe you," Rowe said and sighed. "It would be so much simpler. But judging from the way you look, I doubt you have enough money to buy me a good meal. And I don't eat as much as Bruno."

The girl moved away from me and closer to Rowe. She shifted into a fighting stance. I didn't know how well she could fight, and her ankle was going to hinder her.

Rowe's face became serious, and his relaxed air vanished. "Not this again. Enough talking." He sheathed his sword. "Bruno, watch the boy while I take care of her."

Even with the bad ankle, the girl fought Rowe. Her attacks were quick and precise, and though she couldn't get the upper hand, Rowe could only fight her to a standstill without hurting her. I was in awe, watching her. If her ankle wasn't injured, she might have taken Rowe. Several times she almost had his sword out of the scabbard, but each time he kept it out of her grasp.

Rowe finally got hold of her, but she kept squirming like a fish out of water.

"Bruno!" Rowe said. "I need help here. Take care of the whelp and let's go."

Anger coursed through my body, replacing my fear. If the girl wasn't going to give up, neither was I. I needed something to even the fight. There were no more hefty branches nearby, but there was a rock the size of a child's head about a step away. If I could just get to it.

I lunged for the rock, but Bruno was there just as I reached it. Despite his monstrous size, he was fast. Before I could grab the rock or put up my meager defenses, Bruno swung. His fist smashed my right cheek. I toppled, spun, and fell to my knees. My cheek throbbed as if it were on fire. Bruno hovered over me, smiling. I went for the rock again, but was met by Bruno's blade just inches from my face.

The cold steel was ready to open the gateway and send me into death's embrace.

"No!" The girl struggled against Rowe, trying to break his grasp. "Leave him alone! You've already got me."

"Silly girl!" Rowe kicked her, and she fell to the ground. He stepped on her bad ankle and she screamed out loud. "I hate to damage the merchandise, but you leave me no choice." He struck her. Blood trickled down the side of her mouth. "Finish the boy, Bruno, and let's be on our way. This is getting tiresome."

My eyes met the girl's. I didn't see any fear, just concern for me. Deep in those shimmering wells, I found the strength I needed. My safety didn't matter. This was for her. It would always be like that.

I growled. "Leave! Her! Alone!"

Everything around me slowed down. Their laughter died; the girl's face froze; a dandelion puff hovered in the air; a fly's wings stopped; the wind ceased. My eyes bore into Bruno. My heart pumped and heaved my chest, trying to leap out. The pain in my cheek faded. My eyes were on fire.

I buried my face into my hands, trying to stop the pain.

"What in the Underworld?" Bruno's eyes grew wide. He started to back away.

The pain left me in gouts of fire, spewing from my eyes to engulf Bruno. The flames crawled over his body, searing every inch of him. He screamed like a hawk, trying to put out the fire with his hands as he ran to the pond. He didn't make it. His hair incinerated, and his skin peeled off. The charred corpse collapsed on the ground, steps away from the cool water. The fire died out.

I turned my gaze on Rowe. He stood for a moment, unsure of what to do. He stared from me to his former partner's blackened body. Then he sprinted away as fast as his legs could carry him. He stumbled and tripped in his panic, but kept going, never looking back.

The girl rose and came over to me. "Thank you."

"I'm…I'm…" I couldn't get the words out. My legs gave out, and I collapsed on the ground. Before I blacked out, I used the rest of my strength to smile at her.

CHAPTER 2

I'M TRAPPED in the heart of the flame, white-hot and eternal. There's no escape, nowhere to run, no place to go where it isn't there before me. When I step, it's there. When I sway or turn, it's there. When I move my hand, it's there. It pulsates with each breath I take. I hold my breath. The flames move with a life of their own, twining around me. They bend inward, as if to whisper a secret. I strain to hear, but the roaring fills my ears and I can't understand.

The flame dances, pulling me into its rhythm. We move together, closer, closer. I am not afraid.

Without warning, it leaps at me.

The fire fills my mouth and pours into my soul, filling my essence with its own. I fall to the floor, feeling my body burning to ash, consumed. And yet I'm still whole, stronger than before. The flame is in me. It is both power and comfort. It speaks, and now I understand.

I am no longer alone.

I opened my eyes to the night sky. There was a small fire burning nearby; its warmth reminded me of my dream. The pain in my head and my belly reminded me of the fight in the forest. And what I had done.

The girl placed more branches on the fire. Her once fine clothing hung awkwardly on her, exposing the curves of her body. She was beautiful, even with her tattered clothes and the streaks of dirt on her face. The soft glow of the fire accentuated her high cheekbones, and she seemed to shine faintly in the moonlight. She was like no girl I had ever seen. I forced myself to remember to breathe again. I had no idea what to say to her. I shook my head and struggled to sit upright.

She turned when she heard me move. "You're awake," she said. "Are you all right?"

"I am now." I couldn't draw my gaze away from her.

"Why do you continue to stare at me?" Her voice and face hardened.

I turned my head away. "I'm sorry."

There was a brief silence. "It's quite all right. Just don't let it happen again."

Who was this girl? She had to be of high rank if I wasn't even allowed to look at her. I bowed my head. "I won't."

She crouched down by the fire and warmed her hands.

I remembered the man I had knocked out with the branch. I nearly jumped up then fell back and grunted from the pain. "The third man! He's still out there. He might—"

"I took care of it."

"What do you mean?" Just then I saw Bruno's sword lying next to her. I strained to see if there was blood on it, but couldn't make it out. "Oh."

I tried not to gaze at her, but it was hard. I wanted to know more about her. She looked angry as she stared into the fire, and the anger grew as the silence stretched out. She was one of those rare women who grew more beautiful the angrier she became.

"How's your ankle?" I asked, trying to break the silence.

"Fine."

I had no idea how to treat this stranger. There were so many questions I wanted to ask. I was more nervous now than I had been when facing those men. I moved closer to her and squatted in front of the fire. She didn't look at me, seemingly lost in her angry thoughts. I blew on my hands before holding them out to the flames.

I tried to get lost in the fire like she seemed to be, but I couldn't do it. While her mind appeared focused, mine was confused and jumbled. I wanted to know how I did what I did, but I also wanted to know more about her.

The oppressive silence overwhelmed me and my curiosity won out. "So…what are you doing out here and why were those men chasing you?"

She said nothing, continuing to gaze into the fire. I thought she hadn't heard me, and then she turned her head so fast her sun-streaked brown hair whipped her face. Her fierce eyes settled on me. "Do you always ask so many questions?"

My body stiffened. I wasn't going to back down from this stranger. She should be grateful that I risked my life for hers. "Are you always being chased by men who mean you harm?"

"What I do is none of your concern."

"It is when it almost gets me killed!" I tried to jump up but stopped when the pain in my side stabbed me once more. "Unbelievable! Ungrateful," I muttered under my breath.

Forget her. As much as I wanted to know about this mysterious girl who wore fine clothing and could make a fire, fight, wield a sword, and had no problem killing people, I wasn't going to beg her to talk to me.

I turned away from her, grabbing a twig. I poked at the dirt with it, trying hard not to think about her or feel her presence near me.

She held her breath for several long seconds before letting out a sigh of surrender. Then she placed her hand on mine, stopping my dirt drawings and taking my breath. I felt my cheeks grow hot.

"I'm sorry," she said. "You're right. I shouldn't have been so rude to you. You did save my life. Forgive me?"

I glanced at her hand before looking at her. I was unsure if I could trust what she said. I relaxed when I saw the sincere expression on her face. I nodded. "There's nothing to forgive."

She removed her hand and smiled. "I'm glad." I couldn't help but smile back.

Her violet eyes settled on me, and, for the first time since I woke up, she looked at me. I mean, really looked at me. As before, when our eyes had met in the forest, the intensity of her gaze made me feel as if she saw straight into my soul, assessing my worth. A power that might have come from the gods themselves.

"Tell me, hero," she said, "do you always go out of your way to save strangers?"

"No," I said in a quiet voice.

"You didn't have a weapon, and yet you went up against armed men for me. Did you know what you were getting into? Did you think before you acted?"

I shook my head, feeling smaller.

Her purple eyes narrowed. "Then why did you do it?"

I answered without hesitation. "It was the right thing to do. You needed my help."

She nodded. "You're either very brave or very foolish." She thought for a moment while deciding which. "Brave."

"Thank you, but I was going to go with foolish."

She laughed, but shook her head. "Never doubt yourself, hero. You're brave."

I turned my head away, hoping she wouldn't see how red my face was.

"I'm sorry," she said. "I've forgotten my manners. I'm Krystal Cambridge of Alexandria."

Alexandria. I knew of the Guardian City far to the north, but I had never met anyone who had been there. All I knew was that it bordered the Wastelands and protected all of Northern Shala from the creatures that dwelt there. I couldn't imagine what she could possibly be doing out here.

"Thank you for saving me," Krystal said. "I'm in your debt." She waited.

"Are you going to tell me your name, hero, or do I have to guess?" Her tone was serious, but she smiled to show she was only teasing.

"Oh, sorry," I said, shaking my head. "My name is Hellsfire."

"Hellsfire? What kind of name is that?"

I winced. She probably didn't mean to mock me or make fun of me. But she sounded like all the people in my village.

She must have read the hurt on my face. "I'm sorry. I didn't mean anything by it. Where are you from, Hero Hellsfire?"

Hero. I couldn't help but smile. "Just Hellsfire. I live not far from here, in Sedah. It's a small village. I'd take you back to my mother's house, but I still feel a bit woozy."

I rubbed my throbbing forehead before glancing at the shadowed sky. I knew I had slept for hours, but I could barely keep my eyes open.

The darkness surrounded us. It was as if we were the only light in the entire world. "Sorry, I don't have a cloak or blanket for you, Krystal. It looks like you could use one."

She tugged at her torn clothing, trying vainly to piece it together where a huge rent exposed her bare shoulder. "I know," she said. "May I ask you something?"

I nodded, knowing what the question would be.

Krystal leaned in close until I felt her breath. Her eyes were filled with fascination. "How were you able to do that? How were you able to shoot fire with your eyes?"

I turned my gaze away, blinking as I remembered the intense heat that had come from my eyes. They still felt itchy and sore. I poked the fire with my stick. I didn't want to talk about it, but I had to. She had already seen me do it.

"I wish I knew. I just…felt it inside of me. Before I knew what happened, the fire came bursting out. I've never experienced anything like that in my life." I looked back at her, reminded of the teasing I always got about my name. My eyes stung, but not from the after effects of the fire.

"The fire just—came out?" she whispered, putting a hand to her mouth. "Before today, I didn't think such a thing was possible."

"It seems that it is."

"Do you think you can control it?"

That thought had never occurred to me. I tore my gaze away from her, fearful of what I might do. I closed my eyes. "You're not scared of me, are you?" I asked, deathly afraid of the answer. Why should her opinion mean so much to me? I barely knew her.

"Hellsfire."

"Yes?"

"Look at me."

"I don't think that's such a good idea. What if you're right and I can't control it? What if I roast you like that man?" The heat in my eyes began to build. I wasn't sure if it was the fire or my emotions.

"Hellsfire," she said in a far more commanding voice than I thought possible for someone so young. "Look. At. Me." I had no choice but to do as she said.

"What?" My voice was a croak.

"I'm not afraid of you. I never will be."

I released the breath I didn't know I held. Thank the gods.

"Why would I be? You risked your life to save mine, knowing nothing about me, hero." Her stern expression disappeared and was replaced by a beautiful smile.

I smiled back. Since I was being so honest, I thought she might possibly open up herself. I risked the chance of facing her wrath.

"Krystal, what in the Inferno are you doing out here and why were those dangerous men chasing you?"

Krystal didn't say anything, absorbing herself in tying her hair up in a bun. "You're so worried about me, Hellsfire, and you don't even know who I am." She said it as if her identity was a burden.

"I'd like to know you, if you'll let me."

She finished with her hair and seemed to weigh my request. She nodded. "I owe you that much at the very least. I was on a...sightseeing trip, when they kidnapped me. I think they wanted to hold me for ransom. I was with them for four days, until I escaped."

"How did they get hold of you?"

"I'm not used to being questioned." She looked furious again.

I didn't understand her. One minute she was kind to me, the next she was angry. It was infuriating.

"I'm tired of having you yell at me," I said. "If you don't want to talk, you don't have to. We can just sit here until morning in silence."

"I don't want that," she whispered. "I'm sorry, Hellsfire. I'm not angry with you; you saved my life. I'm angry with myself for letting it happen and for almost getting you killed. I won't get upset with you."

I raised an eyebrow.

"I promise," she said.

I nodded.

Krystal continued her story. "I went off without my guards. That's how the men took me. I knew it was foolish to do so, but I did it anyway. Sometimes

I need to be alone and clear my head. I don't know if you understand that."

"I do. More than you think."

We shared a tentative smile, understanding passing between us for the first time. I wanted to capture this moment, just the two of us in the firelight. From the softness in her smile, she wanted the same thing.

But, like all things, it couldn't last forever. My curiosity got the best of me and shattered the peaceful moment.

"Who are you, Krystal? Really."

Her eyes filled with pride and sadness. "Krystal of Alexandria, only child and heir of King Furlong, defender of the Northlands."

I gasped. "You're the princess!"

She nodded. "I'm afraid so."

It all made sense now—the clothing, the fighting, the way she could weigh and judge a person, but what was she doing here? I had no idea what to do now. Should I bow to her, kiss her hand, not sit so close to her? I was lost. I never thought I would be sitting next to a princess.

"Hellsfire," she said, snapping me out of my thoughts. "You've been quiet."

"I'm sorry, Krystal—Your Highness—Princess. I'm not sure what to call you anymore."

She sighed. "Just call me Krystal. You don't have to walk on eggshells around me when it's just the two of us. In fact, I would rather you didn't."

I grinned. "Is that an order?"

"A suggestion."

"All right, Your—Krystal. I can't promise you that I won't be nervous, but I'll try."

"Thank you."

"So what do we do now?"

"Go to sleep. It's been a very long day. Tomorrow, will you help me find my guards? I know I ask too much of you. If you don't want to help me, I understand. You'll be well rewarded, of course."

I shook my head. "I'll help you, but I'm not doing this for the reward." I stared into the surrounding darkness. "Should one of us keep watch?"

"I'll sleep with my sword. And you have your powers."

"How do you know I'll be able to use them again?"

"I know. Now get some rest. Until we find my guards you can be my protector, Hellsfire of Sedah."

"As you command, Your Highness."

I lay down, still stunned that I had met and rescued a princess. The stories about her were wrong. She was beautiful, to be sure, but they failed to mention how radiant and strong she was. And she was a lot more approachable than I would have thought any princess would be.

My heavy eyelids closed. My body was exhausted, but I didn't find a restful slumber.

I dreamt of fire and death.

CHAPTER 3

I WAS AWAKENED by the thunder of hoofbeats shaking the ground beneath my head. I rose to my knees and peered through the underbrush. A dozen well-armed men rode out of the fading mist and rising sun. They pulled up near where I had hit the man with the branch, talking excitedly. They must have seen the body. At a sign from their leader, they dismounted and started a search. They would be on us in a few minutes.

I crept back and woke the princess, telling her what I had seen.

"Are they my guards?" she whispered, her voice full of hope.

"I'm not sure. I hope so. But it could be the men Rowe and Bruno were going to take you to." I hesitated, then took a deep breath. "If they're not your men, we can't fight our way out. There are far too many. I'll try to draw them off while you escape through the forest. Make your way northwest to Sedah and look for a woman named Damara. She's my mother. She'll help you."

The princess gripped my arm. "Let's hope it doesn't come to that. But your bravery honors us both."

She found a vantage point where she could catch a glimpse of the searchers. Her purple eyes blazed with intensity, and she gripped the handle of her sword so tightly her knuckles grew pale. If I didn't know better, I'd think she wanted a fight.

The men had fanned out, moving in and out of view through the trees. I held my breath, praying to all the gods that I wouldn't have to risk my life again, but knowing I would, to save her. I searched for the fire inside of me, holding it ready.

A man moved into view. The princess drew in her breath sharply, and I poised myself to run. Then all the tension went out of her, and she rose to her feet, in full view of the searcher. The man's face lit up, and he raised a shout. "I've found her! Thank the gods!"

I let out my breath, letting my emotions and the flame go with it. "Thank the gods," I echoed.

Krystal went to meet the man, me trailing behind her. At the sight of me, he drew his sword. The princess raised her hand. "Put up your sword, Captain Ardimus. He is a friend." The man gave me a hard, suspicious look, but obeyed her. The men poured out of the woods, gathering around us. Now I could see that they had the fabled Dragon of Alexandria emblazoned on the breasts of their tunics. They knelt before her.

"Princess," the leader said. "I'm so glad we found you safe." He rose, and his copper eyes met mine before he looked at the princess again. His face softened with relief and love, and he allowed himself a small smile. The princess didn't return it, but I saw the same emotions in her eyes. His face became somber. "I see you're favoring one ankle."

"I'm fine, Ardimus. Thanks to Hellsfire, here, who saved me from the ruffians who captured me." She motioned toward me. "Hellsfire of Sedah, these are some of my finest guards, and this is Ardimus Hadee, my personal protector."

I felt nervous, surrounded by all these armed, battle-hardened men. While they looked relieved to find Princess Krystal safe, they all viewed me with the same suspicion as their captain. Now she focused their attention on me. I squirmed and tried to avoid looking at their eyes.

"Thank you," I said. "I—"

Ardimus interrupted. "Then you have done immeasurable service to Alexandria. We bow to you." They all rose to their feet, put their right fists over their hearts, and bowed. It made me even more nervous. "Had any harm befallen the princess, it would have been a disaster for Alexandria and the Northlands." He turned to the princess. "We have failed in our duty, and our lives are forfeit. When we have returned you safely to Alexandria, we will turn ourselves over to the king's justice for punishment."

I gasped. Surely they wouldn't just walk in and allow themselves to be executed. The princess spoke. "What you say is true, Ardimus, but I will take it upon myself to tell my father." She stood with her head high and shoulders back, giving her the appearance of stature even though Ardimus and the others were bigger and taller than she was. "I will remind him of your years of loyal service and persuade him to find another punishment fit for all of you."

I stared at her, wondering how she could say such a thing, especially to a man she obviously cared about. She had told me herself that it was her fault she got kidnapped.

"But now is not the time for that," the princess said. "We must return to Alexandria. The time of sightseeing is over. Ardimus, come here." He did as he was commanded. The princess whispered in Ardimus's ear and he nodded. A small leather pouch was handed over to her. "For your troubles, my dear Hellsfire." She handed me the small, heavy pouch.

"Thank you Krystal,—I mean, Your Highness."

"It's the least I could do, for all you've done for me."

"I'd do it all again." I said. "Goodbye, Your Highness. Take care of yourself and please don't get into any more trouble." I grinned. "I may not be there to rescue you."

Krystal returned the playful smile. "I'll try not to. I'm sure our paths will cross again, hero." Our eyes met. In that moment, it was like we were the only two people in the world. I would give anything to see her again, although I knew that would never happen.

The princess got on Ardimus's horse. He nodded at me and mounted behind her. The other guards mounted up, and they trotted their lathered horses through the forest, heading north for Alexandria. Krystal glanced at me one last time. I waved. I waited until they disappeared before I opened the pouch. It was full of coins, more money than I had ever seen in my life. I was thankful for her money and prayed for her safety and that the gods would guide her home.

Suddenly, I realized how worried my mother must be. I'd been gone all night. She'd understand, though. Maybe not about what I'd done with the fire, but about me helping the princess.

The second I arrived home, my mother ran up to me and squeezed the life out of me. Her eyes were red from weeping. She should have already been at the farm where we worked, but she still had on her good dress, now wrinkled and crumpled. Her black hair was all askew, sticking out of the headdress. And I was the cause of her distress.

She held me away from her. "Where were you? I was worried sick."

"Mother...I'm...please...hold on while I try and..." I sat down on the nearest stool and leaned over, sweat pouring off me, breath labored from running so hard.

"Let me go and get you some water." She shook her head and left me, quickly returning with a wooden cup.

"Thank you, Mother." I took the water and downed it. I wiped my mouth on my sleeve.

I relayed the whole story to her, not leaving out anything, with the exception of the strange dream I'd had. Her eyes never wavered, and her face was set in stone. I'd never seen her with that stout, serious look. She was always cheerful and smiling. The creases around her mouth and eyes showed that. She was the most caring person in all of Sedah, and quite possibly the world. At least my world.

I thought she'd at least be surprised to hear that fire came out of my eyes. I mean, who wouldn't be? I had a hard time believing it myself. But she wasn't surprised. My mother wasn't even afraid, and that kind of scared me a little bit. She stood there, hearing everything I had to say, asking no questions. Her head bobbed as she constantly nodded, as if confirming something to herself. When I was finished, she sat down next to me. Her shoulders straightened as if I had lifted a huge weight off of them.

My mother took a deep breath. "Son, I have something I must tell you."

She told me the story of the angel that had appeared at my birth. I had heard it plenty of times, but what she told me afterwards stunned me.

"The angel wanted you to leave Sedah when you showed a sign," she said, with great reluctance.

"Why didn't you tell me this before?"

"Because years passed and you never showed such a sign. I watched when you were a baby and a child. It never came."

"Did the angel tell you why I was supposed to leave?"

She shook her head. "He just said that it was of the utmost importance that you did."

My mother didn't have the answers I sought. That left only one choice if I wanted to find them. But I didn't want to leave. This was the only life I knew. Sure, it was hard. We didn't have any money and the townspeople didn't care for me. But I had my mother, and we loved each other very much. I couldn't leave her all alone. And I wasn't going to. She needed me, and I needed her.

I shook my head. "I'm not leaving you, Mother. We'll just have to keep this between the two of us. If the town gets word of it they'll run me out—if I'm lucky. If they think I'm a danger, they'll kill me for being a demon."

Her voice was quiet as she said, "No. You should go."

"But—"

My mother put a finger to my lips. She knelt down in front of me and grasped my hands, her calm face contrasting with the tears streaming down her cheeks. "You have to go. You must learn more about yourself and find the answers you need. The angel wouldn't tell me any of that. You must also learn how to use your gift so you can help people."

"But I don't want to," I said, sounding like a small child.

"Then what are you going to do?"

I bit my lip. "I don't know. All I know is, I don't want to leave you. You need me."

"I'm an adult, Hellsfire. I'll get along fine, just like I did before you were born and after your father died."

She had a point. With one less mouth to feed, things would be a lot easier. "Can't things go back to the way they were?"

She kissed my hands. "Things will never be the same again, Hellsfire."

My emotions raged against one another. I cried, seeing my mother's face. She was willing to put her only son in danger. She had a lot of faith—not just in the angel, but in me.

"Mother, I—"

My inner anguish over staying or leaving spilled over. The heat within me rose again. This time it didn't release through my eyes. It went to where my mother held me tightly—my hands.

"Mother!" I released her hands as quickly as I could. I wasn't fast enough. Flames exploded from my hands. She screamed in pain. My mother was on the floor, squirming, blowing on her hands. I wanted to rush to her, but I couldn't while my hands were on fire.

I tried my best to concentrate and extinguish the flames. I couldn't do it. I kept thinking of my mother and what I had done to her. I closed my eyes, doing my best to think of something else. I visualized water, ice, snow, the lake. Slowly, the cool pictures helped the fire disappear.

When my hands were back to normal, I rushed to help my mother up. I bent down to touch her, and she flinched away from me. The look of fear in her eyes cut me deeper than any sword could. I took a few steps away from her.

"Mother, are you all right?"

"Yes. Please help me up."

I was relieved, but didn't move. The image of her being afraid of me was burned into my mind.

"Are you sure?"

"Yes."

I did as she asked. She stared at her hands, checking to see if they were burned.

"I'm fine. There's no more pain. It was like touching a hot stove for a second. See?" She held her hands in front of me. After inspecting them and seeing no marks, I breathed easier.

"I'm sorry," I said. I cried like I had when I was a small child—loud and bubbling. I couldn't believe I had hurt the one person I loved more than anything.

"It's all right, son. Shhh."

Whatever fear my mother had of me earlier was no longer there. She swept me into her strong arms and held me. Her warmth overcame me as I continued to cry and apologize. She reassured me that I had done nothing wrong, but I was never going to be able to forgive myself.

Finally, I pulled away from her. She wiped my tears with her thumbs. "I'll leave, mother. I have to. Just tell me where I have to go."

She went to her bed and reached underneath, where she kept a box with her few treasures. She returned with a scroll, handing it to me. "You're going to need this to get where you're going." It was a map, showing a path to the dangerous and mysterious White Mountain.

I gasped. Out of all the places in the world, I had to go there? I might as well go to the Wastelands while I was at it. "The White Mountain? You're joking right?"

"You must."

"But how in the world am I going to survive with no help? I've heard the tales. No one has climbed the White Mountain and lived. How can I possibly make it to the top? I'm only a fourteen and—"

My mother put a finger to my lips. "I believe in you, son. You can do anything you put your mind to. If you weren't meant to survive this journey, the angel wouldn't have told me to send you there. Have faith, and you will find the answers you seek. He *will* guide you. You have the power of fire. Use your gift and it will protect you from the cold…Hellsfire." She teased me, but not in the way some of the others did. My mother smiled, and, despite my nervousness, I couldn't help but do the same thing.

"Help me gather your things," she said. "You're going to have to buy some supplies and warmer clothes. These just aren't going to do you any good." My mother tugged at my clothes, making me feel like a child again.

I futilely tried to shoo her away. "Mother."

"And buy food that can survive the cold. Use the money Her Highness gave you. But don't waste it. Only buy what will help you on your journey, and make sure you can carry it all."

"Are you sure you won't need any money?"

"The princess gave it to you, son, and you're going to need it. I can manage just fine on my own." She studied me for a moment. "And take this. You'll need it more than I."

In one fluid motion, she pulled a dagger out from under her clothing. My own mother went armed, in our quiet, peaceful town! And this was no shoddy, nicked peasant dagger. The blade was fine quality, and the hilt was inlaid with gold. It was balanced and lightweight, yet strong enough to kill a man. Flawless. Even someone with my limited fighting skills could use it. There were some markings on the hilt, but I couldn't read the language.

"Where did you get this?" I asked, my eyes still tracing the dagger.

"Your father got it in the Burning Sands and gave it to me before he died.

He would have given it to you in time. The ancient inscription says 'I will be with you, always.' You never knew your father, but I'm sure he's watching us from heaven. Keep the dagger close. It will protect you in your time of need, as it has protected me many times."

Why would she have needed protection? I stared at my mother, seeing a completely different person from the one I'd known my entire life. She wasn't just my mother and someone who took care of me. She was a woman with a past.

She handed me the dagger. I slid it into its scabbard and squeezed it inside my girdle. The dagger felt like it had an unexplainable energy to it—as if it completed me in some way.

"Goodbye, Mother," I said, and embraced her one last time. I made sure to hug her longer than usual, not only because I was going to miss her and it might be a while before I saw her again, but also to slip some money into her pocket. "I'll miss you and I love you."

"I love you too, son. Remember what I've taught you, and please be careful."

I sniffled back some tears. "I will." I let her go and grabbed my belongings. I stopped at the doorway and took one last look. I wondered if she'd be all right without me. What would happen to me before I next saw her? I had to find out why I had power over fire and learn to control it. I couldn't stay and hurt my mother again.

I went into Sedah, buying the necessary supplies while people were just opening their shops. I was grateful for the money the princess had given me. My mother and I could never have afforded all the things I bought. I got plenty of strange looks from people, more so than usual. They thought it was a bit peculiar to be buying winter gear in the middle of spring, but I didn't care.

I bought a cloak, leather gloves, and, most importantly, a fur coat. I also needed a pair of leather boots and some sheepskin blankets. After the clothes, I bought some food, preserved meat, and a backpack to carry everything in.

The shop owners tried to make conversation with me. I was careful to bring out the exact money I needed, and not show them my pouch, but it was as if they knew I had money. Some even tried to raise their prices on me. When the items I bought started to pile up, I had to start lying. I told everyone I was buying things for Farmer Andrick, the man my mother and I worked for. It would be common knowledge that I was gone soon enough. No need for the gossip to start now.

My biggest expense was an aging horse. We had never been able to afford one before. Even after that, I still had quite a bit of money left. I wished I could say goodbye to what few friends I had, but if I saw them, I might never have the courage to leave. I loaded my supplies on my horse and walked her northwest, towards the White Mountain and my strange, unknown destiny.

Before I reached the edge of town, I saw the one person I didn't want to see. The only thing in my favor was that he was alone. Normally I would have cut through the woods, but because of the horse and the direction I needed to go, I had to stick to the road. I avoided looking at him and tried to use the horse as a barrier. It didn't work.

"Going somewhere, Hellsfire?" Nathan asked, sauntering up to me.

"No."

"Then what's with all this? Did you steal it? Where could *you* have gotten the money from?"

"That's none of your business."

"I'm making it my business." Nathan said, blocking my path.

I met his eyes. "I don't want any trouble. Not today."

"That's too bad."

Nathan grabbed the reins from my hands and shoved me hard. I fell to the ground, landing on a rock. My cloak shielded me from the worst of it, but I was still going to have a bruise on my back.

Nathan loomed over me and laughed. "At least it wasn't mud." From the look in his eyes, he wished it was.

He started walking off with my horse. I scrambled to my feet. "Stop!"

He turned around and gave me a quizzical look.

"It ends here," I said.

"It does, does it? It ends when *I* say it ends."

Nathan stormed over to me. I balled my fist, but he was too big, strong, and fast for me. I was knocked to the ground again, grunting in pain.

My hand went to the dagger secured at my waist. I wanted to get revenge for all the pain Nathan had caused me over the years. For a moment I thought about drawing, but then I let go of the hilt. That wasn't why my mother had given me the dagger. I wasn't going to let her down. All I wanted was my horse and supplies. I wasn't leaving without them, and he wasn't taking them.

I tried to get up again, but he yelled and hit me as hard as he could. I fell to the ground once more, breathing dirt instead of air.

"Why won't you stay down?" Nathan asked.

Blood trickled from the left side of my mouth. I ran my hand over my bruised cheek, feeling how bad a mark I was going to have.

"Please," I said, gasping for air. The fire within me roared. The heat boiled against my body as I struggled to contain it. "Stop. I don't want to hurt you." That was a lie. A part of me did want to hurt him for all the times he had beaten and humiliated me. All I had to do was let go. But I was afraid of my uncontrollable power. I didn't want to kill him.

"Hurt me? That's a joke."

Nathan bent down to hit me again. I put my hand up to try and stop him. All the pent-up emotion—the frustration, the anger, the pain—poured out. It became fire and funneled towards him.

Nathan's eyes widened in surprise. He was quick enough to turn at the last second. The flame still scorched the right side of his face. He fell to the ground, howling.

I rushed to him, smothering the lingering flame. His once handsome face was scorched and blistered. I reached out, trying to see if there was anything I could do to help him.

He slapped my hand away. "Get away from me, you freak!" His expression, normally full of so much anger and hatred, had changed into something I'd never seen before on his face. I had recently seen it on my mother's. "You really are a monster!"

Nathan forced himself up, wincing in pain with every movement. He ran, stumbling and falling because of how often he looked back at me.

I checked to see if anyone had seen what happened. I breathed easier when I saw no one. I thought of returning to my mother and warning her of what had just happened. There were bound to be plenty of questions and accusations. I had no idea what she would tell them. If she was lucky, no one would believe Nathan. They all knew what he did to me, even if they didn't stop it. They might even interpret it as me besting him.

The only thing I knew was that I couldn't stay here any longer. If an outburst like this happened while other people were around, they could be seriously injured or even killed. Afterwards, they would want to hang or burn me and my mother as demons. We'd both have to flee. No, it was best I go now, before things got worse.

Things did get worse. And in the way I most feared.

CHAPTER 4

SHORTLY AFTER LEAVING SEDAH, I met a small group of travelers heading north. They were suspicious of me at first, but when they saw how young I was and that I was alone, they allowed me to travel with them. They were a nice family, heading north to look for work. They wanted to know more about me, why I traveled by myself, and where I was going. I didn't tell them anything except where I was from and that I headed north for part of the way. I wasn't sure if they would want to travel with someone who could shoot fire out of his body.

"Still not telling us where you're going?" Mara, Kenneth's wife said, while we finished up our evening meal by the campfire.

"I should only be with you for another day or two," I said. "Then I'm heading west."

"Can't believe that before we picked you up, you were traveling by yourself," Kenneth said in his deep voice.

I shrugged. "It's not that bad."

"That's because you're young. Ah, you'll learn. I traveled a lot in my youth, and I learned it's always best to have someone who'll watch your back and if worst comes to worst, make for another target. Young and alone, you'll be easy prey. When you get older, you had better be handy with a blade." He patted the dagger lying on the ground next to him. He looked at my waist, eyes narrowed. "I see no blade on you, Hellsfire." I kept my mother's dagger hidden.

"Kenneth!" Mara said, glaring at her husband. "Stop scaring him. You make it sound like you traveled where there were nothing but bandits. I'm going to put the children to bed."

Kenneth put out the campfire and said, "I may have exaggerated a little, but you should still be careful when you leave us. You've got first watch tonight. Wake me in a few hours."

I nodded. "I will. And Kenneth—thanks for letting me travel with you."

I took up a position against a strong oak tree, where I would be able to see everything around us. For the last two days, I had been getting used to taking a watch, but it still bored me. Only the sounds of the crickets and the occasional owl kept me company. There was nothing to watch but the stars and animals that hunted in the night.

While I liked Kenneth's family, being with them didn't allow me to practice my gift—or my curse, depending on what you wanted to call it. Before I met up with them, I had been practicing when I could, though it drained me. I needed not just to be able to access the fire, but to control it. While I still didn't have complete control, I was beginning to understand some of what I could and couldn't do. But I would have to make much more progress before I reached the White Mountain. I needed the fire to battle the cold.

Tonight's watch gave me the first opportunity to practice in days. I had chosen to take my watch in a spot that was partially screened from where Kenneth and his family were sleeping. Between the underbrush and the partially clouded moon, they shouldn't notice me as long I didn't try anything too big.

I moved behind a nearby bush and held my hands out, letting go of the pent-up heat inside of me. It coursed through my body, and I concentrated on directing it to my hands. In my earlier practices, my hands had glowed and felt warm, as if I were holding them in front of a fire. Sometimes I had spurted a few flames. But tonight was completely different.

The fire spewed out of my hands, setting the bush on fire. I tried to stop it. I couldn't. The fire wouldn't obey me. I was afraid to close my hands, in case that made it spread out in all directions.

The fire seemed to have a life of its own. I watched in horror, fighting it while it hopped from bush to scrub to grass, until everything burned. The deadly and relentless light illuminated and devoured everything.

Finally, the fire stopped coming out of me. I concentrated on the flames, trying to put them out, but I knew that even extinguishing a small flame with my mind made me collapse with a splitting headache. This was impossible.

And then I remembered I wasn't alone.

I rushed over toward Kenneth and his family, jumping over the small fires, dashing around the big ones, yelling to wake them up. The rising smoke made me cough and gag, but I put my arm over my mouth and kept going.

My shouts had awakened the family. Kenneth was trying to gather all the supplies and animals as quickly as he could, but some of the animals had scattered, and there were far too many things for him to carry. The two children were clinging to their mother, staring at the flames and crying.

Kenneth glared at me with cold eyes. He looked like he had plenty of questions, but all he said was, "Take care of my family. I can trust you to do that, right?" He disappeared through the flames without waiting for my answer.

My eyes stung. Whether from the smoke or his words, I couldn't tell. This was all my fault.

I grabbed my backpack, bedroll, and one of the children. Little Clara hung around my neck, squeezing so tight it was hard to breathe. Mara ran alongside me with her child and an armful of blankets.

When we were safely away, I put everything down and took off my singed cloak. "Stay here."

I ran back into the flames, lifting my tunic to my face to block out the smoke. I did everything in my power to help Kenneth save what we could. Before the flames engulfed the campsite, we managed to save the cart, one mule, one cow, my horse, and a few caged chickens. More than half the food and water was gone.

The flames burned themselves out relatively quickly—too quickly to be natural. I stood with Kenneth and surveyed what was left of our campsite. His clothes were scorched and tattered. He coughed to get the smoke out of his lungs before turning to me, his eyes as ferocious as the flames.

"What happened, Hellsfire?" he yelled. "You were supposed to keep watch!"

I put my hands up. "I don't know!"

"How can you not know? Where'd the fire come from? What'd you do?"

After what I had done to him, I realized I owed him part of the truth. "I…started a fire and it got out of hand." When my eyes met Mara's and saw her terrified children clutching her, I looked down in shame.

"You started a fire? You were supposed to be on watch! And how could it have gotten out of control like this?" Kenneth threw his hands up in frustration. "You could have gotten us all killed! Our supplies and half of our animals are gone. What are we supposed to do now?"

"I know. I'm sorry. Here." I reached into my purse and withdrew some money. A lot more than was necessary to replace what he had lost. He eyed the coins in my hand, but didn't make a move to take them.

"Thank you, Hellsfire," Mara said, coming up and taking the coins. "But I think it's best if you left now."

I opened my mouth to say something, but closed it. The fire was my fault. I looked at the little children, whose eyes were full of fear. I had almost killed them.

"You're right." I picked up my belongings and slung them on my horse. "Thank you for letting me travel with you. And thank you for letting me be a part of your family, even if it was for a short time. I'm sorry."

"We hope you find what you're looking for," she said.

I sighed, taking one last look at the family I had almost destroyed. "Me too." I left them, leading the horse.

After that, I tried to avoid people whenever I could. Not because I feared bandits, but because I feared for regular people like Kenneth and Mara. I was far more dangerous to them than any sword, arrow, or axe.

I saw the White Mountain days before I reached it. The closer I got, the fewer people I saw, as if they were avoiding it. Soon there were no roads or people—only myself and my ability.

I had to get control of the fire. I slowed my pace so I could practice. It always drained me if I practiced for too long—like doing a hard day's work. Summoning it was easy enough—far too easy—but I needed to restrain it. I couldn't let what had happened with Kenneth's family ever happen again.

I made small fires at first. Just stopping them from flickering gave me a headache. If I tried to move the flames with my mind, my head throbbed until blood trickled down my nose. But I wasn't going to give up. My fear of what I had done to Kenneth's family and the look on my mother's face drove me. Gradually, my body adjusted not only to summoning the fire, but controlling it. I no longer ached from it, nor did I want to pass out.

But I still wanted to know why I could do this. Why me?

Whenever I had such thoughts and frustrations, I would lose control. My anguish and anger fueled the flames. I tried not to dwell on such thoughts, but it was hard, especially on those days when the fire wouldn't do what I wanted.

While I heeded Kenneth's warnings about what could happen while traveling, I didn't run into any trouble of the normal sort. That left all my energy for worrying about climbing one of the most treacherous mountains I had ever heard of.

I tried not to look at it at first, but the closer I came to the mountain, the bigger it grew, until it dominated the landscape. It never seemed to stop growing. I eventually stared at it while walking, wondering how I was going to survive such a monstrous and desolate place, and what waited for me at the top.

Why was I supposed to come here?

In its own way, the mountain was quite wondrous. It stood alone, surrounded by flat land, smothered in the winter season. It was forever frozen in time. No one knew why. There were stories, of course, yet unlike the Wastelands or the Great Barrier, which were remnants of the War of the Wizards, this mountain's origins were mysterious. But its winter had lasted for centuries.

I reached the mountain at midday. While I was anxious to start the climb, I made an early camp so I could rest. I was going to need all of my strength, and more, to reach the top.

A shiver rode along my spine as the towering mountain looked down on me. There was no mistaking it. This mountain was my enemy—a far more dangerous enemy than Nathan, Rowe, or Bruno. I had to find a way to do what no one else had ever been able to do—defeat it.

I scouted the base of the mountain, sizing it up. Everything had a weakness, even the White Mountain. Heavy, smothering snow concealed most of the slopes, but exposed rocks occasionally poked through like unsheathed blades. Cold air enveloped the mountain in an icy shield, seeping across the plain. Its peak shot through the clouds like an arrow. I squinted, trying to see the top of it. It seemed to go up forever. I shook my head. No. It had a summit. I had seen it when I was still a week away from here. I would get there. I had to.

As I explored the foot of the mountain, something began to bother me. The coldness felt wrong—as if it wasn't real, or as if something lurked behind it. I couldn't shake the unnatural feeling, but there was nothing I could do. I had to go on and stay alert for danger.

Finally, I found what I was looking for. It wasn't a fatal flaw in the mountain's armor, but it was something to help me climb it—a faint path. It would make the first few days of my climb much easier.

That night, I ate well and enjoyed the warm food. It would be my last for a while. I didn't bother to practice with the fire. Judging from the look of the mountain, I would get plenty of practice.

When the sun rose, I gathered my belongings and put on my heavy cloak and gloves. I jumped up and down, shaking my fingers and rolling my neck. In tune with my nervousness, the fire started to surface. I didn't let it rise, as I didn't want it to burn my gloves. I would need them. The fear of what I was about to do made it hard to control the fire. When I saw the horse staring at my movements, though, I couldn't help but laugh. It relaxed me a little.

I rubbed the horse's neck and scratched behind her ears. She made a soft sighing noise. I smiled, glad I had her along. She hadn't been as scared as the other horses during that wildfire I caused, and she never seemed bothered by the fire I created. She also was a very good listener. I frowned, remembering why I bought the old girl, but I pushed the thought out of my mind. I just wished I had an apple to give her.

I walked her to the path. I craned my neck, gazing up at the White Mountain—my enemy—and whispered, "Gods help me."

The trek wasn't too bad at first. The snow was at a comfortable level, and the wind soothed my overheated body. What surprised me was that there were more paths etched in the mountain. You had to look hard, but they were there. I couldn't imagine what had made them, or how far they would take me, but I didn't have long to focus on my curiosity. I had far bigger things to worry about. The mountain fought back.

The wind picked up until it wailed like a crying child. I grasped my cloak's hood tighter to shield my face. The wind tore the cloak from my hands until it struck my face with such cold and ferocity it felt like a thousand bee stings. Breathing through my mouth helped with the cold a bit. I focused on my frozen breaths leaving my body. I held onto my horse's reins while she neighed and bucked against the wind and cold.

We tried to find the easiest path, but each time the ground became too slippery with ice, or the deep snow crawled up my leg. My feet slipped every few steps, and twice I went down hard on my knees, grunting in pain.

Towards the end of the first day, I reached the end of the path I followed. On one side, the cliff reared up beside me; on the other was a steep drop to the valley below. It seemed odd to see the green of spring down there, while the bitter wind threw ice crystals at my face.

I found a sheltered spot and dug a campsite out of the snowdrifts. It was a cold and lonely night, and I knew I was in for many more, if I survived.

The next few days were the same. Sometimes I found a path; other times my horse and I scrambled over the rocky ground with no guide but the need to keep going up. I didn't understand why I had heard tales of people trying to climb the White Mountain. Who would do this unless they were compelled to, like I was? I had to latch on to my inner fire to stay warm, and I hugged my freezing horse from time to time for even more warmth. Finally, I got to a place where there would be no more paths. I would have to scramble over fields of shale and tumbled boulders. There was no way my horse could make it. I had been putting off this moment, but I knew what I had to do.

I grabbed the horse's reins and nuzzled my head against hers. She whickered and returned the gesture. While I was used to killing animals on the farm where I worked, this was different. I had never killed an animal I owned before, one that had given me brave service and companionship.

I took out my father's dagger, exposing my body to the harsh elements when my cloak unfurled. The old girl looked at me with calm, black eyes. I slashed her jugular vein with as much accuracy, speed, and strength as I could. Her blood painted the snow. She gave a weary neigh, saying her goodbye to the gods as she collapsed to the ground.

I spent the rest of the day working on her in the freezing weather. I skinned her and cleaned up her hide as best as I could, using the snow and melting it with my power. I cut and packaged as much meat as I could carry. The hide would help keep me warm.

More days passed, and the wind never stopped flinging snow in my eyes. I went to sleep cold and woke up freezing. I had to constantly use my power to keep myself warm. I wondered how people who didn't have my power climbed the mountain. They must be crazy. Or dead.

My power waned, and my body became numb from the cold. It seemed there were limits to what my inner fire could do. I forced myself to trudge along. I was damned if I was going to let the White Mountain defeat me.

By the end of the week, I couldn't feel my fingers or toes. I found a crevice out of the wind and kindled a fire with my sputtering power. I hoped I had enough left within me to thaw out some frozen meat as well as warm my toes. I didn't want to choose between starvation and frostbite.

The next morning, I hauled myself to my feet and kept on. The longer I spent on the mountain, the more the cold, thin, frosty air pained me. With each deep breath, it felt like my heavy feet wouldn't move again. I managed to lift one foot after the other out of the deep snow and plop them back down. I never looked up at how far I had to go. I only focused on the crunchy, white snow in front of me.

I went on, despite how much the howling wind taunted me. I hunched my shoulders in a futile attempt to keep the sharp wind from hitting me.

From the foot of the mountain, this place was beautiful and magnificent. Up high, it was devastating, cold, and lonely. The only thing I could find comfort in was my fire.

It hadn't taken long for my water to freeze through, but I no longer needed it. I would grab a handful of snow or ice and warm it up with my hand. The snow melted even though I had a glove on. It was pure heaven to open my mouth and let the water trickle in. However, the water wasn't enough.

Using my fire and climbing this godsforsaken landscape forced me to eat more. I needed the energy. I began running out of the food I had bought, as well as the meat my horse had given me. I had thought there might be other animals like elks, rabbits, or mountain goats so I could hunt, but I saw none. I was going to have to ration my food. I couldn't tell how long it would be until I reached the top. The mountain stretched on forever—to the stars themselves.

I lost count of the days. They all ran together. I rose when the sun shone and rested when the sun disappeared. I couldn't feel its heat. All it did was allow me to see where I was going and what obstacles to avoid. The snow and wind did their best to obscure it.

It seemed as if I had been climbing for weeks when I reached a steep, icy wall. It looked insurmountable—far worse than any of the walls I had encountered before. Just looking up at it gave me a crick in my neck. There might have been a way around, but it would have added days to my journey. Judging from my now-light backpack, I didn't have days. I chewed on some dried horsemeat, thinking about what to do. No. There was only one way to go—up. It was there I'd get the answers I needed.

I said a heartfelt prayer to the gods, and clapped my hands and rubbed them together. Then I started the strenuous climb, hoping my luck hadn't run out.

My muscles screamed at me not to climb. I ignored them as I slowly made my way up. My fire-warm hands made it easier to grasp handholds on the wall, but the jagged ice tore into my hands and ripped my clothes. I bled across the clear surface, but I couldn't let go.

The weight of my horsehide, sheepskin, bedroll, and other supplies strained my back. I grunted in pain, but continued inching upwards. Finally, I came to the end of my strength. I lost my footholds and one handhold, and hung with only one numb arm supporting all of my weight. Muscles ripped with searing-hot pain, and my scream tore through the thin, icy air. My agony echoed off the mountain.

As I dangled over the thousand-foot drop, I thought about my death and mediocre life. I felt shame, thinking of my mother and her hopes that I could use my power to help people. If I fell to my death, I would let her down. What good would I be and what good would I do, if I died? I wasn't going to give up, for her sake and for the sake of others like Krystal, if not for my own.

And I wanted answers. I wanted to know why could do what I did. It wasn't normal. I wasn't normal. I couldn't—wouldn't—die without knowing.

My rage and determination swelled and exploded violently. In my mind flashed a brilliant light, brighter and hotter than I had ever pictured before. "I won't give up! Do you hear me? I won't give up!" Shattered shards of ice shimmered down on my head.

The heat boiled inside me, aching to be released. I reached out with all of my might, ignoring the searing pain of my arm giving way. I grabbed hold of the side of the wall with my free hand. My arm nearly came out of its socket as my back screamed for release. The fire blazed through my hand, destroyed the glove, and burned through the side of the obstruction. With renewed strength, I struggled towards the top, leaving holes in the glacial fortification. I hurried, not wanting to be on the wall of ice if the fire caused it to come tumbling down.

It did.

Cracks spread through the ice like spider webs. The once impenetrable wall started to give way. First, small bits came apart in my hands and slid down the icy face. Then more of it broke away beneath me. My heated hands tore chunks from the wall, and my feet had nothing to hold them up. I felt like a spider on the wall, scurrying to make it to the top as more of the ice slipped away. I pushed through the biting pain in my shoulders, arms, and back, focusing on each grip and handhold my fingers dug into. If I stopped, I would slide down with the ice and be buried with it.

I reached the top and pulled myself over. The cold ice slid under my belly, cutting into my clothing and my stomach. I crawled away from the edge, pulling myself to safety. The huge slab of ice I had been climbing bowed, groaned, and went crashing down in slow motion, landing at the bottom with a great echoing boom. I lay on the ground, panting. My gashed stomach left a small trail of blood behind me.

I crawled to a safe distance and collapsed on the ground. My angry muscles moaned. Every bit of energy was gone. The weight of all my supplies held me down. I let my muscles relax, thankful for the breather, and even for the snow and ice freezing against my cheek. I was alive.

But if I stayed on the ground, I would become part of the landscape, with the snow piling up on me. I flexed my stiff fingers, then dug my palms into the snow and pushed myself up, yelping from how sore my body was and how heavy my light backpack felt. I stood up on wobbly legs, looking at the cuts the ice had made on my stomach. The wounds weren't deep, and I was no longer bleeding. I limped cautiously towards the edge and looked over.

The weather wasn't as bad up here. I could see through the mountain's shield of snow and wind to the landscape below. Sharald's Forest was a large green spot, and the Daleth Mountains were nothing but brown smears on the horizon. I looked up. I still had some ways to go before I reached the top.

My brief reprieve passed. The wind picked up and started howling once more, intertwining with the snow. I had to find some shelter. I couldn't stay on the ledge waiting for the weather to try and finish me off. My head pounded like drums and my vision swirled. I looked around for some place to camp for the night. There was a cave not too far away. I dragged my worn, bruised body towards it.

The cave's mouth was as tall and wide as a large pine tree. Inside, the cave was even larger. It looked like it could swallow me whole, but I wouldn't satisfy its hunger. I was thankful for its enormous size. If it was cramped and small, I don't know if I could have gone in, no matter how tired I was. Enclosed spaces terrified me.

I entered the mysterious cave, wanting a reprieve from the freezing chill. What I got was a lot more than I bargained for.

CHAPTER 5

I HAD EXPECTED to use what little power I had left to light the cave. I didn't have to. There were burning torches attached to the walls.

I stopped dead. Torches meant people. Who could be living at the top of this godsforsaken mountain? Was it the angel who had visited at my birth? Someone who had the answers I sought? Or something more dangerous and hostile?

I put one hand against the rough rock wall, leaning against it and breathing heavily. I listened to see if there were people in here and if they were nearby. Several long moments went by, and all I heard was the trickling water from the melting ice.

My body wouldn't let me go farther. I didn't take off my bedroll and backpack. It was more like I couldn't support their weight and they rolled off me and crashed to the ground. I followed suit. My teeth chattered and I couldn't stop shaking. The cave was warmer than outside, but the cold still permeated me. What really unnerved me, though, were my swollen, blue and purple fingers. I needed some kind of warmth. I did my best to latch onto my inner fire, but all I got was a small spark of flame. I couldn't get my power to work.

I decided to do it the old-fashioned way and crawled into my bedroll, trying my best to avoid looking at my damaged hands. I covered up with my sheepskin and horse's hide, feeling the warmth creep back into my body.

I unsheathed my dagger and clutched onto it. I wasn't going to drop my guard now. My mind and emotions may not have wanted me to sleep, but my body screamed for it. It didn't take long for my body to win the argument and I drifted off to sleep.

A low rumble like an earthquake vibrated throughout the cavern. I struggled to open my eyes. I moved my fingers and toes, no longer feeling frozen and stiff, even though my body was still exhausted and aching. I needed more rest.

The sound became deeper and louder, and it headed in my direction. I woke all the way up and scuttled behind a huge boulder, dagger in hand. I flexed my battered fingers and found that their color had returned to normal.

I peeked from my hiding place. From the long tunnel at the back of the cave came a billow of smoke. The ground trembled. There was something coming, and it was huge. Then the smoke cleared—and a dragon emerged.

He was slim and snaky, longer than Farmer Andrick's barn, and the color of fire—bright red with hints of yellow and orange. He loomed above me, as awe-inspiring and as fearsome as the mountain I had just climbed. The smoke came from his long and pointed snout, as if he had swallowed a forest fire. The stench of sulfur filled the air. He could kill me with a flick of his razor-like claws or a twitch of his tail. And his bloodshot, hungry eyes were the most fierce and frightening of all.

"Who goes there?" he thundered. The cave shook around me.

I clutched my useless dagger tighter and held my breath. I didn't want to give him a sign where I was. Sweat rolled down my temples and splattered on the ground. I prayed he didn't hear the loud sound it made.

"I know you're here. I can see your belongings, and I can smell you." He inhaled and thrashed his fiery red and orange tail. "Since you won't come out, I'll blast you out!" He veered in my direction and flames spewed out of his mouth in a spiral funnel. I leaped out of the way just as the boiling fire melted the boulder. "Well, there you are," he said. "I was wondering when you'd come out and say hello."

I had heard stories of dragons being protectors, but this one was far from it. This powerful creature wanted to kill me.

"Stay back! Stay back!" I said. "Don't come any closer, I'm armed." I brandished my father's dagger.

"Oh no, I'm scared. Look, the little human is armed. Are you going to pick my teeth with that thing? They could use a good cleaning." The dragon grinned, showing me his rows of pointy teeth. There were bits and pieces of meat in between them.

There was nothing I could do to defeat this dragon, so I tried to reason with him. "Please don't. I'm just a boy."

"If you're just a boy, then how did *you* get up here? Prepare to be roasted like a cow." His predator's eyes gleamed. "Moo. I hope you taste as good as the last human that was up here." He slurped his tongue in delight.

The dragon breathed in, and smoke seeped out of his flaring nostrils. He opened his mouth and blew the flame towards me. In a panic, I dropped my dagger, and instead of running or dodging the flame like someone who had half a brain would do, my hands flew out in front of me. It was a futile attempt to shield myself from the danger that came my way.

The intense heat flew towards me. I pushed with my mind as well as my hands. It was similar to all the times I moved my own fire with my mind, except it was far harder. My head throbbed, and blood flowed out of my nose. My eyes pierced the dragon's fire until I saw it in my mind. It dwelled in him like mine did in me. I could touch it, but I couldn't extinguish it. I changed it, pushing the fire aside.

The deadly blaze never touched me.

It turned upwards and struck the ceiling. The dragon stopped his fire breathing, his face contorted with confusion. I didn't care how it happened. I hadn't even known I could control fire that wasn't my own. At least I was still alive…for now.

The dragon said, "How did you do—" A huge block of ice fell from the heated ceiling and landed hard on his head, interrupting my would-be eater.

The dragon's body crashed heavily to the ground, causing tremors. I fell to one knee, gasping for air. I rubbed my temples and wiped the blood from under my nose. Then I stared at the dragon, waiting for him to rise. If he did, I was finished. There was no way I could have done what I did again. I stared at my hands, amazed I had done it in the first place.

The dragon's body twitched. My body jerked in response. The dragon didn't rise. The only thing that continued to move was his giant rib cage as he breathed. He was unconscious.

I glanced up to the heavens, seeing only cave ceiling and the icicles that hung from it. "Thank the gods."

I thought about killing the dragon. Surely, he could die like any other animal. But when I saw the tough scales along his huge throat, I knew I couldn't do it before he woke. I also didn't want to take the chance that he would wake when I touched him.

I gathered my belongings in my arms and circled wide around the slumbering dragon, praying he wouldn't wake up and kill me. When I was past him, I rushed down the cave. There had to be somewhere where there wouldn't be enough room for the dragon to follow. I thought about going back outside to hide, but the cold would finish me off as surely as the dragon would. From the looks of things, he had no problem with the weather.

I scurried along by the light of the dancing torches, looking for some kind of safe haven. I kept glancing behind me, expecting the dragon to wake up at any moment and chase me. I listened for the tremors that signaled his earlier advance. The only noise in the quiet caves was my breathing.

I passed several other tunnels, but my pursuer could easily fit. Finally, the long tunnel ended in a human-sized room, too small for the dragon even to get his head inside.

The moment I entered the room, something tugged at me, yet I saw nothing. There were two doors in the room, one on the right and one on the left, and a fireplace in the opposite wall, though there was no fire burning. I picked the door on the right, hoping I would at least find a place to put my belongings if not to hide and rest. I didn't want to get lost exploring the place before I was ready.

I grabbed the handle and pushed at the creaky, wooden door. It didn't budge. I pushed again, but the door stood fast. That strange tugging feeling I'd had when entering this room felt even stronger against this door.

"Why is this damned door being stubborn?" I turned to go through the left door instead. Behind me, the right door opened. I spun, dropped my things, and drew my dagger. I didn't know if I could handle any more surprises.

An old man stood in the doorway, holding a gnarled wooden staff. "Do you need some help, young man?" He stepped toward me with a warm, genuine smile on his aged face, ignoring the fact that I was holding a weapon.

I hesitated for a moment, unsure whether to trust him. But it was either trust him or face the dragon, and he was less likely to help me while I waved a weapon in his face. Considering the choices, I put the dagger away. I kept it close on my waist where I could draw it easily. "Please, you must help me. There's this dragon and—"

"Calm down," he said, putting a hand up. "Calm down, young man. You're not in any trouble, but by the time we begin, you will be." He chuckled, his face gleaming like the fist-sized pearl on top of his staff.

I raised an eyebrow. What was he talking about? "What do you mean?"

"Don't worry, I'm not going to harm you. Hold on. I'll be right back and explain everything." He disappeared into the doorway and came out with two stools. "Please have a seat. I've been expecting you, Hellsfire."

I was stunned. Even though I'd come to the mountain for answers, I hadn't expected to find someone who knew me by name. "How do you know my name? And what do you mean, expecting?" I backed away from him and put my hand on the hilt of my dagger. He stared back at me and said something in a language I'd never heard. His blue eyes flashed, and calmness overcame me. I let go of the dagger, sat down, and listened to him.

"I will explain everything. Where should I begin?" He fiddled with his long white beard. "I suppose I'll answer your first question. I know your name because it was *I* who named you. I was at your home the second you were born. I'm sure your mother must have told you?"

I couldn't believe this was the so-called angel my mother told me about. The story was true, but he didn't seem like an angel. No wings, no special glow, no heavenly voice, nothing. He was merely a strange old man with an unusual staff.

"She told me," I said, barely finding my voice. "She's told me the story countless times. She called you an angel."

"Believe me, I'm no angel. I'm better than that." He laughed, then frowned, seeing the sternness and shock on my face. "I certainly hope you have a sense of humor, Hellsfire, but I guess now isn't the time for jokes. I had made it in time for your birth and decided to name you Hellsfire. The name came to me, and I knew that it would be the right name for you."

I leaned forward. "You named me?"

He nodded. "I did."

"Did you also give me these powers I can barely control?" My anger rose, and the fire began to surface on my hands. "Were you responsible for this?" I thrust my hands out to him.

The old man didn't flinch. In fact, his eyes sparkled with delight. "You're further along than I thought."

"Is that all you have to say?"

I was filled with anger. I thought of the dragon and the climb up the mountain, both of which had almost killed me. But it was the memory of what I had done to Kenneth and his family and to my mother that caused me to lose control. Fire shot out from my hands. My eyes widened in horror as the flames headed towards the old man. I was too slow to warn him. There was nothing I could do.

An invisible force parted the flame. Instead of enveloping him, the fire went around him. The flames hit the wall and dissipated.

"I-I-I'm sorry," I said. "I couldn't control it."

"It's all right, my boy. I wasn't in any danger."

I studied him, checking to see if any part of him was singed or burnt. He was fine. "How did you do that?"

"I'm a wizard."

I gasped. "A wizard?"

It all made sense now. Why I was able to do what I did, who made it winter on the White Mountain, and why he had a dragon. But there weren't supposed to be any more wizards in Northern Shala. The Great Barrier and the aftermath of the war had destroyed most of them. The others had disappeared long ago. I stared at the wizard, seeing him in a new light. No wonder my mother had mistaken him for an angel. According to the stories, the power at his command was incalculable.

The wizard leaned closer. "I can see in your eyes that you understand."

I nodded and whispered, "You want me to be a wizard."

"Yes."

I looked away from him. Out of all the things I had expected to learn or to happen, this wasn't one of them. I thought about all the stories I had heard while growing up. There were a few stories of wizards being heroes, like Shala. He had been mainly responsible for defeating the evil wizard, Renak, during the War of the Wizards—a war that had devastated and divided the land. But most stories weren't like that. Most stories I'd heard had to do with the dangers of a wizard's powers. The dangers I knew all too well. I didn't want to hurt those I cared about, and I didn't want to be another Renak.

"Can you teach me to control this power?" I asked, staring at my bruised hands.

"I can. I must warn you, though, that being a wizard is far more than learning to control your powers. It's a serious undertaking, Hellsfire."

I didn't want to be a wizard. All I wanted was to not hurt anyone with my power. "What if I say I don't want to be a wizard?"

"You don't have a choice."

I opened my mouth. Was he going to trap me? Was this his goal all along? What did he want me for? I couldn't escape from a wizard. I was a prisoner here. Tears crept into my eyes.

"What's wrong, Hellsfire?"

"I'm stuck here."

"No. You're here for a reason. You've a destiny to fulfill. You're the One who was prophesied long ago. I'm here to guide you."

"What do you mean?"

"I'm sorry. I can't say any more."

I grimaced, angry that he would tell me that much, but not completely explain himself. I didn't feel special. I was just me. I could do things with fire, but that was more of a burden and a problem than a gift. I couldn't see myself doing anything great, nor did I want to. I considered pressing the wizard for information, but, judging from his stern gaze and hunched shoulders, he wasn't going to tell me any more right now. If I stayed with him, I was sure I could get those answers. But his so-called prophecy wasn't my concern at this moment. I had more immediate questions to attend to.

"How do I know I can trust you?" I asked. "I don't want to be like those wizards in the war."

He seemed a bit taken aback by that. "I can assure you I will do everything in my power to make sure that won't happen."

I ran my fingers through my hair, trying to decide what to do. I sat there in silence for many minutes. He didn't interrupt me or say a word. He knew there was only one decision I could make.

I nodded. With a somber face I said, "All right. I'll do it."

The old man's grin was as wide as the horizon. "Excellent. Now come and get some rest. You look like you need it."

I rubbed my bruises and moaned. He was right, but more important matters had to be settled. I had come to the White Mountain in hopes of finding answers. Now that I could get them, I was going to. I needed to. "What about—"

"There'll be plenty of time for questions later, my boy."

"But—"

"Hellsfire, please," he said, putting a hand up, but barely raising his voice. "You'll have to trust me."

I stared at him, not truly believing that, but not in a position to do otherwise. I could use some rest. "All right."

The wizard smiled. "I'm glad you have patience. It's one of the essential components to being a wizard."

"Master." The dragon's big head appeared near the entrance to the room. I jumped at the sight of him.

"Yes, Cynder?"

"I'm sorry. I've failed." The dragon didn't seem as scary as he had before. He looked sad, his scaly face dragging on the floor. I relaxed a little.

"Failed? I don't believe you've failed in your duty. This is the One I've been waiting for. How did he get by you?"

Cynder turned one of his red eyes toward me and snorted. "He doesn't look like the One. He *luckily* turned my flames upward and they hit the ceiling. The ice came down on my head. I should have grabbed him and ripped his head off like the last human that came." Cynder eyed me hungrily. I had to look elsewhere.

"It's good you didn't, though I'm sure he would have found a way past you."

Cynder blew a stream of smoke.

"I'm quite impressed," the old man said to me. "Do you know how you did that?"

"Not really."

"Doesn't matter, we'll have time for that later. Come now and get some rest. When you wake up, we'll have something to eat."

He took me through the left-hand door, down the hall, and to another room with a bed and a sturdy oak desk.

"Lie down, and come back to get me when you wake up," he said. "Take the same way we just came, and don't go any farther down this tunnel. Eventually, I'll give you the grand tour of the place."

He opened the door and turned to leave. I stopped him. "Wait!"

"Go ahead, my boy."

"You never told me what your name is."

"Stradus. No more questions. Get some rest. I'll tell you more when you wake up."

Stradus left and closed the door, leaving me by myself. My body was relieved to be someplace dry and warm. For the first time in weeks, I was safe from the snow, wind, cold, frost, and loneliness. I didn't have to worry about going to sleep and not waking up. I didn't have to fret over making one wrong step, slipping and plummeting thousands of feet. I didn't have to worry about starting any more fires and getting a family killed.

Yet I had a feeling the dragon and the wizard were far more dangerous than the hazards I had already faced.

CHAPTER 6

I **WOKE UP** in a sea of sweat, feeling like I'd slept a long time. I yawned and rubbed my eyes. My body was stiff and sore, as if I had slept so deeply I hadn't moved throughout the night. As soon as I moved, my back and leg muscles seized up, and my body went rigid. I clenched my teeth against the searing pain, clutching my blankets desperately. For several minutes I could do nothing but stare at the rocky ceiling, afraid to move lest it cause more pain.

Finally, my muscles relaxed and I could move again. The pain was still there, but much less intense.

When I pushed back the blankets, I saw every cut, scrape, and swollen muscle. Without the numbing cold, I could really feel how bruised and battered my body was. The cuts on my stomach, hands, and legs throbbed like a heartbeat.

Miraculously, none of my wounds were serious. I hadn't broken any bones, and I wouldn't lose any fingers or toes from frostbite. I just looked like a mess. Now that I was in a warm, dry place, my body should heal on its own.

My belly begged for food, and I wanted some more information from Stradus. I made my way back to the room where I had met him, my nose following the sweet aroma of food cooking. When I got there, Stradus stirred a pot over a small fire in the hearth. A small round table had been placed before the fire, along with two tools and two bowls. The idea of non-frozen food made my mouth water, temporarily banishing the pain from my body.

"You must have smelled the food," Stradus said. "Sit down and I will explain some things while fixing this lovely dinner of ours."

Dinner? I was stunned I had slept so long, yet my stomach told me it was true. I took a seat across from Stradus and tried to prepare myself for whatever he was about to say. I knew it was going to change my life.

"Like I said before, you're going to be a wizard, my boy. I'm going to train you in the Arts, under my aged wing. You'll be my apprentice." He inhaled the steam from the cookpot. "Finally. It's almost done."

"I know you want me to be a wizard. I still don't understand why or how, though."

"I can only tell you *some* of what I know. As I told you, you are destined to be someone of great importance to the world, but to do that you must first learn to be a wizard. Being a wizard is a great responsibility. You need to utilize the gift the gods have bestowed upon you. There. It's done."

Stradus ladled stew into the two bowls, then went through the left-hand door and came back with some bread. I ate right away, trying to soothe my famished stomach and eat my tensions away.

Stradus eyed me with an astonished look. "Quite an appetite you've got there, young man. As I was saying, you're going to have to be able to use your gift of fire, and I'm here to teach you that. It's going to be tough work. Any questions?"

"I thought all the wizards were dead?" I lifted my eyes from the now empty bowl, shaking my head. I still found it hard to believe I had just met a wizard, not to mention that I was to become one and fulfill some grandiose destiny. I ladled some stew into my bowl, shoveling it into my mouth before it even had time to cool. Even at home, before I started my travels, it was seldom that we could afford for me to eat as much as I wanted.

"Wizardry is far from dead, Hellsfire. It will always be here in one form or another. We're old perhaps, ancient, forgotten maybe, but not dead." Stradus's laughter bounced around the small room. "Those of us who were stranded in Northern Shala after the Great Barrier went up did what we could to clean up the mess that was made during the War of the Wizards. After that, we went our separate ways. I did some exploring, like most of the other wizards, in and about Northern Shala, the Wastelands of Renak, the Burning Sands, and everywhere in between. After all my adventures and exploring, I decided to settle here, continue on with my studies, and wait."

Wait for me? It seemed unbelievable that anyone would spend his whole life waiting for me. Especially a powerful wizard. "Why here?"

Stradus's blue eyes clouded over. "I was drawn here. It was as if the gods themselves called. They guided me here and they guided me to create the cold, harsh weather all year long."

I gasped at his words. I hadn't thought such a thing was possible. The stories I grew up with didn't mention wizards other than Shala and Renak having the power to change the landscape. Others helped, but such stories were always about those two. Having used my own powers for a while now, I could see how to directly affect something using your own body, but not how to alter or freeze the whole environment permanently. To create something like that he must be very powerful. I stared at him, trying to see past his frail, wrinkled body to who he truly was.

I couldn't see anything but a simple old man, yet his words made something in my mind click. There was feeling that had been bothering me since I first got near the White Mountain and saw how it stood out like a white moth against black smoke. I didn't feel the pull of the gods like he did, but I felt something.

"This place feels…unnatural," I said, trying to find the right word.

Stradus put down his tea. "I see. What do you mean by that, Hellsfire?"

"I don't know, but I've been feeling a strange sensation ever since I came to the mountain. It's like when you know someone's watching you, but you can't see them." I shook my head. "I don't know how else to describe it."

"Ah, you're talking about the aura of the place. Magic tends to do that, unless it's subtle, or you want it not to. The more you learn about your powers, the more you'll be able to feel and see it."

"Is it dangerous?"

"By the gods, no!" Stradus chuckled to himself. "It's harmless. Tell me, do you tend to trust your feelings often?" His gaze settled on me as if my answer was very important.

"I don't understand. What do you mean?"

"I'm going about this the wrong way," he said to himself. Stradus played with his beard for a few moments. "You said you wanted to control your power. I assume something happened because of it. Tell me about it, my boy."

I bit my lip, unsure if I wanted to. Then I realized that he was a wizard and would understand the things that confused me, or that I wasn't comfortable talking about. I relayed my entire story from the time I met the princess all the way to now. I told him about the mistakes I'd made with the fire, but I didn't tell him about what I'd almost done to Kenneth or what I did to Nathan.

"You saved the Princess of Alexandria?" he asked in a whisper.

I nodded, thinking about it. While I was scared of what had almost happened to me and her, I couldn't help but remember her smile and violet eyes, and the quiet time we shared together by the fire. I smiled myself, wondering what she was doing right now.

Stradus said nothing while I thought about the princess. He seemed to be deep in his own thoughts, though I couldn't tell what they were. His brow was deeply furrowed, and the globe on his staff swirled and became clouded. I wondered what I'd said to make him so concerned. Did it have to do with the princess, or my powers? Or was it something else entirely?

The wizard brought himself out of his trance, and his staff globe became clear. "You've already learned that emotions can be tied to a wizard's power. That's how you saved the princess. That's how your power manifested." I hoped he would explain more, but he changed the subject. "Come, let me give you a tour."

The inside of the White Mountain was far bigger than I had imagined. A whole network of caves had been dug out and constructed. I thought Stradus had done it, but he said that someone had lived here before him and designed the cave complex, though he never found out who. When the gods led him to the place, it was already abandoned, with nothing remaining but a few torches and some leftover crates of supplies. Whoever it was had left in a hurry.

Stradus thought it might have been dwarves, since they were known to make their homes in caves and mountains. The way the White Mountain was designed seemed to say yes, but not all the stones had been smoothed and carved out in the dwarven manner. Some of the archways were uneven, and holes were not completely filled in. Not signs of a battle or struggle, just sloppy workmanship. The dwarves were many things—sloppy wasn't one of them. Not when it came to building and engineering.

I couldn't tell the difference. I had never met a dwarf or seen what they could build. It amazed me that such a place could exist and be protected from the harsh elements outside.

Stradus took me all the way back to the cave entrance to start my tour. I shivered, glad to be out of the storm, but still too close for comfort. The caves I had seen earlier were where Cynder dwelled. One was his sleeping chamber and the others were where he kept his food. The huge caves had plenty of room for him. He could even stretch his wings and fly in one of them.

After a quick tour of Cynder's domain, we ended up back at the room where we had eaten. The second I stepped through the doorway, the same force tugged at me again. I stopped and looked over my shoulder.

"Is something the matter?" Stradus asked, cocking his head.

I paused and put a finger to my mouth, thinking. "I'm not quite sure. I get a strange feeling whenever I pass through this entrance."

"Your skills are more developed than I thought. I put a web there. A weak and simple web, made to detect someone's presence. It also allows those with the slightest hint of magical skill in them to pass."

"A web? You mean like a spider?"

"Exactly, my boy," Stradus said. "Webs are spells you must create with your hands. They're commonly used as detection systems or shields. By the time I'm done with you, you'll be able to see this web and undo it."

The wizard led me through the left door and down the passage that went past my room. A bit farther on, the cramped tunnel split in two. We stopped and he pointed down the left branch.

"Down here are three rooms: the garden, the spring, and the storage room."

The huge storage room was full of barrels and wooden crates containing various supplies. After that room was a small one containing the spring, which bubbled out of an elaborate marble fountain. I had no idea where the water came from, but it was good to have fresh water easily available, though it was no Peaceful Pond.

The last room was amazing.

Wondrous flowers and plants colored the room. Some shined and glowed, despite having no sunlight. Sweet aromas tickled my nose. There were many plants I had never seen before. I didn't understand how they could survive, considering there was no light except the torches. I shook my head. It must have been magic.

As we walked around the room, I touched the soft plants, feeling the tenderness of their petals and leaves. I bent down, examining a bright purple flower.

"You like plants?" Stradus asked.

I nodded, thinking of all the time I spent in the forest.

"Me too. I'll include some things about them in your training."

I turned my head to see a wooden workbench with flasks containing different colored liquids. Stradus explained to me that he used the space to develop and distill various plant-based potions. I wanted to stay and marvel at his garden, but Stradus tugged me along.

"Don't go through this door," Stradus said, pointing to another door beyond the three he'd shown me. It looked like it hadn't been opened in ages. "It's a maze past here, and it goes deeper and deeper into the mountain."

"You're afraid I'm going to get lost?"

"That isn't the reason I don't want you to open the door, Hellsfire. I've put a strong web here in case you get curious during your stay, and it could harm you if you try to undo it. It's for your protection as well as mine. Cynder and I aren't the only ones dwelling in this mountain."

"I thought you said you didn't find the people who carved out this place?"

"I didn't. I found something else entirely."

The wizard's words only made my curiosity rise. What else besides a wizard and a dragon could be in this mountain? Maybe I would find out one day, but it wouldn't be anytime soon, since I couldn't even see the web, let alone undo it. We made our way back to the fork in the road, and he told me what other rooms lay in wait.

"There are four rooms down here," Stradus said. "There's the exercise room, the practice room, the library, and the latrine. You'll be spending most of your time in the first three rooms. When you advance enough, then you'll be able to come into my garden and concoct some potions. Come."

We made our way into the exercise room. It was huge, with a long circular track carved into the floor around the perimeter. In the center of the room was a pile of iron bars with round rocks attached to each end.

"You must train your body while you're here," the wizard said. "As you know from climbing this mountain, external forces are going to take their toll on you. Every other day, you will work in the library."

The library contained many books—far more than I had ever seen. There were shelves marching down the room, all full. The peculiar smell of old books hovered around me. There was also a reading table with a couple of candles on it. I imagined what stories lay in those books, waiting to be awakened.

"Tell me, Hellsfire, do you know how to read?"

"My mother taught me when I was younger. She thought I'd need the skill, even though books are hard to come by where I live. I'm not the most proficient reader, but I can manage." I stood staring at the rows and rows of information. To think what kind of knowledge a wizard had, and what I could learn.

"That's good, my boy. Now I don't have to spend my time teaching you to read. That reminds me, is there any particular skill you're good at?"

I shrugged. "Not really. When I was younger, I tried taking an apprenticeship with a blacksmith. He was reluctant to take me on, but did it as a favor to my mother. I could never get things right with the metal. Nails were bent out of shape, and pots came out bulbous instead of round. Now I spend my time helping my mother out at a neighbor's farm. I can herd, feed, and take care of animals with the best of them."

"Did you at least go to school?"

"When I was younger I did, but as I got older I went to work. It's not as if we're wealthy, and I had the option of getting a better education by going to some far-off school. Don't worry, though. My mother taught me a lot of things." I stood even straighter, as if I had something to prove to this wizard aside from magic.

"That's good. What else did she teach you?"

"She taught me how to ride a horse, sew, and slaughter an animal as painlessly as possible. But the most important thing she taught me was about people. She taught me to judge a person by what's in them and to trust my instincts. And to help people because it's the right thing to do and that it'd come back to me. She even allowed travelers to stay at our house, and I heard lots of stories about other parts of the land. It was amazing, the stories they and my mother would tell me. I always wished I could go somewhere."

"Don't worry, you're going to go far in life."

"That prophecy of yours."

"No. It's more. You're going to be a wizard now, my boy. One of the first things you need you learn is that you will only be limited by your imagination and will."

I nodded, thinking about what he said. I made a silent promise to myself, never to give up or give in to those limits.

"Your mother sounds like a very good person," Stradus said.

"She is. She's well liked in town."

"I am curious though, Hellsfire. What happened to your father? I didn't see him the night you were born."

"He died in the Burning Sands before I was born. Mother told me he died a hero, protecting everyone, but she wouldn't tell me any more than that. She'd always get teary eyed and couldn't go on. This is the only thing I have to remember him by." I pulled out my dagger and handed it to him.

"'I will be with you always.' This is a fine dagger, Hellsfire." Stradus made some thrusting moves. "Sharp and strong, and the hilt is well crafted. Where did your father get it?"

"The Burning Sands."

"You should always cherish it." Stradus handed the dagger back and I secured it on my belt. "You have a fine family, my boy. You would do well to remember that."

"I will."

"I suppose we should get back to the tour," Stradus said. "This library is where you will train your mind. These books have a lot, and I mean *a lot* of information. They contain spells, incantations, summonings, prophecies, and histories—among other things. Of course, many of these books aren't written in the language we're now speaking. Hence, you'll have to learn the most common language amongst us magical folk. It's called Caleea. It's the one on your dagger, as a matter of fact. It's an ancient and mostly forgotten language, but you will learn it nevertheless. Now, let me take you to the practice room."

The practice room was the most plain and boring out of all the rooms. All that was in it were some candles, rocks, and wooden sticks. But the room had an eerie sense about it that bothered me. All the other rooms had some sort of life and sound in them, but this room had the feeling of being a noiseless void. It didn't seem to belong to this world.

"I guess you could say this would be the most important room," the wizard said. "You'll be practicing your magic in here. Don't get me wrong, all the other rooms are important, but here is where you'll hone your skills and abilities." He stepped a few feet away from me and turned to face me. He cleared his throat. "Let me see what you can do."

I hesitated. "What do you mean?"

"I need to see where you stand with your power. Do what you can with your gift."

"But—"

"Don't worry about what you think you can or cannot do."

I shrugged. There wasn't much I could do. "All right." I showed him my ability to make fire and maintain it with my mind, and my ability to heat up my hands to varying degrees.

I started to let go of the magic when he said, "Don't stop. Tell me, do you know how you're doing it?"

I stared at him. I never talked while using my magic. Magic. It still felt funny to say that.

"I know it's hard, Hellsfire, but try not to focus too hard on the magic. It'll be like walking and talking once you get used to it. Please tell me if you know how you're doing it."

I nodded, struggling not to feel like the weight of the magic was crushing me. "I kind of do. It's like I'm touching some kind of inner fire and I'm able to pull it out. It gets easier when I become angry or stressed, but I also learned to focus and use it to a certain extent." I released my magic and started panting. Talking and performing magic was something I wasn't used to.

"I see. Hmmm, I wanted to save this until later, but we might as well get to it. We haven't much time." Stradus sat cross-legged on the floor. He patted the ground for me to join him. "I guess I should start from the beginning and explain to you how magic works. You know of the four gods, correct?"

I smiled. "Of course. Who doesn't? With the exception of those who are like my mother and believe in only one god."

"I didn't know your mother believed in just one god." He stroked his long, white beard. "I'm going to tell you some of what you already know, but please bear with me, because it ties in with magic.

"Each god represents one of the four elements of nature. You have one for air or wind, one for water, one for earth or land, and one for fire." As he talked, the globe on his staff changed colors to suit each god. I marveled at it, but I didn't think he noticed he was doing it.

"What you probably don't know is there are actually six gods."

He stopped, letting the information sink into my head. Six gods? How could there be six gods? To think that my own mother and most of the people in Sedah worshipped one of the six gods and chose to ignore the other five. It made no sense as to why anyone would not acknowledge the other gods, but then again I thought there were only four gods.

I cupped my head in my hands, remembering what the others had told me when I was younger. I tried to see if I had missed something. While I might have forgotten a holiday from time to time, performed a ritual in error, or dressed wrong, I couldn't remember two missing gods.

I had always thought those in town who worshipped one god were ignorant. It just seemed like the world and the heavens were far too much for only one god to handle. If I was wrong about the gods, what else was I wrong about? What would happen when I died? What had happened to my father?

"If what you say is true, then why don't people worship all six gods?" I asked.

"I'm not a priest, Hellsfire. I won't be able to answer the truly deep questions you have about your faith."

"But—"

He raised his staff in front of him. "We can go over this later. You need to pay attention to what I'm going to tell you."

I bit my inner cheek and pursed my lips. I guess he was right. The gods weren't going anywhere, and I had a more immediate problem to deal with—my powers. The wizard stared at me, waiting to see what I'd do. I nodded and relaxed.

"As I was saying, the other two gods don't quite represent the elements of nature, but at the same time, they do," he continued. "One represents death and destruction while the other represents life and healing. Like the other four gods, these are neither good nor bad, just a fact of life. No one worships these gods in most of Northern Shala, but I guess those in Sedah do. They worship the life god."

"Magic," the wizard continued, "works, more or less, the same way as these six elements. Inside everyone and everything lurks a magical force. What separates us wizards from everyone else is our ability to access this force called mana. There's a mana for each of the six elements, and it can be represented by color. You have blue for air, red for fire, black for death, white for life, green for earth, and a blue-green for water. Water always was a tricky color." Stradus laughed.

"Inside everyone, there's always one mana that's dominant—one mana that outshines the others and which people have the most ability to use. Even though most people will never in their lifetime be able to look inside themselves and use it directly in its purest form, they'll still access it. For example, you have people who are good with nature or able to take care of the earth with their green mana; or people who are good at sailing and fishing, which uses the blue-green mana; or people who are able to understand poisons, death, and decay, which are linked to black mana. *You* have the power of red mana, but, more precisely, of fire. Do you follow me so far?"

I stared at him wide-eyed. I wanted to say no. Instead I scratched my head and said, "Sort of."

"What don't you understand?"

"You said yourself that your…mana, was that of the air, and yet you're able to keep a beautiful garden without any sunlight, and you're also able to keep the torches consistently burning. How? Those have nothing to do with air."

The wizard rubbed the globe on his staff. "I started out like most people do in all walks of life, with something I was naturally good at. It just happened to be air magic. It's not all that different from you with fire."

When he reminded me of what I could do, I realized I had forgotten about using my power. I closed my eyes, concentrating on keeping the flame lit but not doing anything with it. It rose near the surface, where I could release it quickly with but a thought.

"As I advanced," Stradus said, "I learned other things. I learned to tap into the other mana that were inside me and in the world. I'm not as skilled with the others as I am with air, but I can use them well enough.

"The only real trouble I have is with white and black mana. Even in my day, they were very elusive and hard to control, and only a few have mastered them. The only wizards I knew who had mastered them to their fullest— besides those on the Wizards' Council—were Renak and Shala." He whistled. "And *no one* could compare to those two. The things they did baffled even the Council.

"You will learn, just as I did, the skills and knowledge you'll need to use the other mana and you'll experience just how difficult it may be. Lastly, when you master using mana, your eyes will reflect that."

To prove his point, the wizard's eyes lost their pupils and solidified into each of the colors in turn. I felt the intense power, even though he didn't do anything with it. It reminded me of being close to a powerful storm. I couldn't see it, but I knew it was there. I nodded in understanding. He let go of the mana, and his eyes returned to normal.

Stradus was going to say something else, but stopped when he saw the look on my face. "If you have any questions or don't understand something, you shouldn't hesitate to ask. One of my old teachers used to say, 'When it comes to the Arts, there's no such thing as a dumb question.'"

I paused and exhaled. "No, we can move on. I think I understand the basics of magic and mana." Meanwhile, my mind tried to absorb his words. I understood the idea of starting out with something you're good at, but I didn't understand how one could branch out with mana. I felt no mana other than fire, but then, I didn't know what to look for or how to go about it. I had to experience it firsthand. I guessed I was going to be here awhile.

"That's good, my boy," he said. "Magic can be broken down into three main categories: spells, incantations, and summonings, but there are many more." Stradus grinned at me. I let out a quiet sigh, but he didn't notice.

"Remember, all these things can be great or small, and you must tap into a mana or energy of some sort." He waved his hand. "We'll get into that later. As you've already learned, some spells don't have to be spoken to be used. However, spells have to at least be pictured in the mind and latched onto the mana or energy. The stronger the spell, the more things you'll have to do to raise sufficient power. Like making a sacrifice of some sort, using a potion, doing some physical action, and so on. Do you understand?"

"I think so."

"Don't worry. I promise you'll know this by heart when we've completed your training. Next are incantations. Incantations involve words. You'll have to pronounce *precisely* the exact words you're going to need and, as always, tap into the mana or energy you'll need. Some incantations can be said right now in the common tongue we're speaking. They're rather weak, but they still work. The stronger incantations have to be said in the ancient language and, like spells, may involve a potion or sacrifice to be used at the proper moment. Next are summonings." He opened his mouth, then paused to look at me. I guess he could finally see how lost I was. "I'm sorry if I'm moving too fast, but I'd like to get through the basics as soon as possible. You'll understand as soon as you start practicing." The wizard ran his fingers through his white hair. "I just don't know how long I'll be here, Hellsfire."

Something struck me. How old was Stradus? He talked about Renak and Shala as if he had known them. By the gods, that was nearly a millennium ago. I thought of asking him how he was able to live so long, because I was curious as to how a person could extend his life. I decided against it. I should learn the basics before trying that, and he would probably just tell me that I should focus on the current lesson. And I could only imagine how much my headache would grow from listening to how to do something so powerful. There was so much I could learn from this ancient wizard.

"Even the most basic summoning is quite difficult and complex," Stradus said. "They all require a ritual of some sort. Rituals will require you to do any or all of the things I'm about to tell you. You either have to dress a certain way, tap into a specific mana, have a set number of people present, make a sacrifice, use tools, draw symbols, perform them at the right time and place, and so on. The reason you would want to perform a summoning is that you may need the power it can grant to perform something very great. For example, you can summon a powerful creature, be able to keep the weather in place like I do on this mountain, or even create a powerful barrier."

I leaned forward. "You mean like the Great Barrier? The barrier that separates Northern and Southern Shala?"

"Yes."

"Someone was able to create that through a summoning? How was that even possible?"

"It was very complex, and it wasn't one person that did it. One day I'll explain what I know about it to you, but now is not the time." His blue eyes deepened in color, as if remembering that tragic time of a land torn in two.

"I understand."

"I don't think you do, but you will. What I told you are the basics of magic; everything is built upon that. There's much more, like prophecies, veils, the Netherrealm, and the intricacies of alchemists and visions and a million other things, but I'm not going to get into those now."

My mouth gaped open, dry air pouring in. How much more could there be? A lot, it seemed. I rubbed my temples. No wonder wizards lived for a long time. They had to, just to learn everything their masters told them.

"The three categories I told you about aren't set in stone," the wizard said. "Summonings, incantations, and spells are usually interwoven. When you're doing one of the three, you're often involving two or all of them. For example, you can do a spell and recite some kind of incantation to strengthen it. A summoning will always involve all three when you're performing the ritual. Do you understand what I've just told you about summonings?"

"I think so, but summoning something sounds very hard," I said. The pounding in my head became louder.

"It is, but over time you will learn how to do it. Do you have any questions on what I've just said?"

I had a lot of questions. Who wouldn't? How to grasp onto the different types of mana, what type of sacrifices would have to be made, what other kinds of energy existed, was I already experiencing visions, and so many other things that I suspected would take years for me to comprehend. But out of all the questions running through my head, there was one that piqued my curiosity the most, though it was probably the least important.

"Why do you have a dragon?" I asked. "I thought there were no more."

Stradus's wrinkled face grinned. "It seems people think everything is dead, just because they haven't seen us in awhile. When it comes to dragons, they don't live in these parts. Most of them live west, past the Burning Sands, and haven't been around since the war."

"Why is that? I thought they protected humans. Alexandria uses their symbol."

"There was a time when dragons watched over and protected us, but that was a very long time ago, during different times. Each wizard gets a guardian sometime in his life. Mine happened to be a dragon, that's all, but he was a friend before that. Guardians could be anything: a dragon, turtle, eagle, fish, unicorn, and so on. Usually it's something you least expect."

"How do I get a guardian?" I asked, bright-eyed. I knew I would need one.

"You're not handed a guardian, if that's what you're thinking, and you don't get to pick your guardian, either. It's not like going to the market." Stradus stroked his long beard. "One day, you're going to meet an animal. There's going to be this special bond between the two of you. You may not see it at first, but it's there. Kind of like when you're in love, but it doesn't compare to that." His voice got dreamy and distant. "Then again, what does?"

My heart sped up as I thought about Kathleen, my first love. I nodded. I understood how that bond felt, despite the fact that loving Kathleen had been mostly confusing and painful.

"Something significant will happen between the two of you, and you'll know you were meant to be together," the wizard said. "Odds are you *will* find it, or it will find you. You've just got to have patience. Not all guardians will be able to verbally communicate, but you'll understand each other nevertheless. Come, and let me show you the last room on this tour. Sorry for trying to cram so many things in your mind at once, especially on your first day. I remember when they tried to do that to me in school, and I hated it. To rub it in, they gave us all a test."

We got up and exited the practice room. Stradus showed me the privy and afterwards said, "My young Hellsfire, we are done with the grand tour and with your first lesson. I suggest you retire to your chambers and get some rest, and think about what I've just told you. Or you can go and talk to Cynder. I think he's glad to have someone besides an old man around."

Cynder? Glad for me to be here? I massaged my damaged shoulders, wincing at the mind-numbing pain.

"You can let go of your mana now."

My eyes widened. I had forgotten about it. It truly had become a part of me. When I let it go, there was an empty, gaping hole where it once was.

"Tomorrow, we begin another step of your journey. I'll be in the garden if you need me."

I went back to my chambers. I needed to be alone to digest what the wizard had said. There was far too much to think about. I had thought I was just going to learn how to control my fire. Being a wizard entailed far more than that. It was a great responsibility. One I had to learn to handle.

I failed the first chance I got.

CHAPTER 7

Months Later...

THE DRAGON GRINNED, exposing rows of sharp teeth. He blew his fiery breath. The flames rushed in my direction, trying to burn me. I put a hand out and pushed. The fire split and went around me, crashing into the cave walls.

The dragon released another stream of fire. This time it twisted and twirled. Instead of misdirecting it, I willed it to extinguish before it touched me. Cynder snorted before spewing more fire. I held it in front of me with my mind, creating a wall of flame that rose to the ceiling.

"I'm not impressed," Cynder said. He peered down his nose at me.

I winked at him, then began to manipulate the wall of fire. The fire mana within me stirred, transforming the flames into my own flying dragon. My dragon wheeled and darted towards Cynder.

"You're supposed to be working on defensive magic only," Cynder said. His tail swung out to disperse my magic. My creature's form melted, and it almost disappeared into the air. I held onto the flames and pumped my own magic into them. The fire burst through the cave. I closed my hands and merged the flames, once again imagining and shaping a dragon. I sent my creature diving after Cynder.

We were in the biggest cavern of the entire mountain, so Cynder had plenty of room to move around. He ran, dodged, and stomped, trying to avoid my creation before it got him. My dragon burped small fireballs at Cynder. They splashed against Cynder's scaly side. Each time he swiped at it with his tail or talon, it dispersed, but I kept remaking it.

Cynder growled. "I grow tired of this, little one." He stopped running. "If that's how you want to play."

Cynder rose to his full height, puffing his chest out and stretching his enormous wings. He flapped his wings, summoning a sudden gust of wind. It smashed into my magic, dissipating it. He flapped again, and the wind attacked me and knocked me to the ground. I strained to rise, pushing against the wall of air. I tried to use wind magic against him, but with the weight of his powerful body behind him, he was too strong. My air magic did nothing, and every time I tried to summon other magic, the wind squeezed me harder against the ground.

"Enough!" I yelled. "I yield!"

Cynder stopped. He furled his wings, a smug expression on his face.

I rose and stared at the dragon. Since I'd come to the mountain, he and I had become friends, so that sometimes I forgot exactly what he was and what he could do. I stretched my arms, back, and neck, hearing cracking noises. I massaged my left shoulder. Stupid dragon. I was going to be sore the rest of the day.

"Never send a human to do a dragon's job," Cynder said, blowing smoke out of his nose. He raised his foot and stomped hard on the ground, causing me to stumble. Cynder grinned, showing off his pointed teeth.

I saw a head-sized rock near him. I reached out to the earth mana I was now able to feel. I drew energy from the mountain, channeling it through my hand. I focused on the rock, trying to use the magic to lift it and fling it at Cynder. The rock trembled and jumped before I tired. I gasped for air, feeling the sweat drip down my face.

"You're getting better at earth magic," Cynder said.

I raised an eyebrow. "I am?"

He stretched his long neck until his eyes were right near the rock. "Yup. I believe it moved an inch that time." Cynder erupted with laughter, his booming voice pounding in my ears.

I gave Cynder a sour look.

"Don't be so dour, Hellsfire. You're improving, at least in your use of fire magic. Everything else needs work. If we fight again, I won't use my fire. I'll just use my jaws." Cynder's head snaked over and he snapped his teeth in front of me. I jumped, causing him to laugh again.

"I hate you."

"You lower species tend to do that. Listen, how much do you want to test your magic?"

"What do you mean?"

Cynder's red eyes swiveled from side to side, and he lowered his voice. "How good are you at webs?"

"You mean making them?"

"No, I mean unmaking them."

It dawned on me what he meant. "You mean you want me to try and undo the web that Master Stradus made on the forbidden door?"

"Shhh! The air can carry our words."

"He can't hear us all the way from his garden, can he?"

"He's a master air wizard. These days, I'm more surprised by what he can't do."

I peered over my shoulder and lowered my voice. "Didn't Master Stradus say the web was in place to protect us because we're not the only ones in the White Mountain?"

"In all the years I've been here, I've not seen any sign that that's true."

"You do realize your big head can't fit down the corridor to that door?"

Cynder blew smoke at me, enveloping me in it. I coughed and gagged before summoning wind to carry it away. "I realize that," he said. "Which is why I'm asking *you* to do it. I'll keep him busy."

"What if I get in trouble?"

"Our master will be impressed that your skill has come along so far that you could undo his spell. If you can."

I nodded. I would love to be able to impress Master Stradus by showing him all I'd learned since arriving. But I still wasn't sure. "What if he's right and there *is* something dangerous down there?"

"So what? Think about it, little Hellsfire. What could harm one great dragon and one and a half wizards?"

I stared at him.

"If you get into trouble, you can blame it all on me."

"I was going to do that anyway." I glanced away from him. "I don't know, Cynder."

"I'll take you for a ride."

That got my attention. If a dragon gave you a ride, it was a huge honor. It meant they trusted you and you were their friend. And he knew I was dying to ride him, after hearing Master Stradus's stories of how it made him feel like part of the wind, soaring and watching the way the ground looked like patchwork below him.

But Cynder could be tricky. "Do I have your word?"

Cynder snorted. "Do I look like a human? I'm a dragon, the most trustworthy and honorable of all the gods' creations."

I just stared at him.

"All right," Cynder said. "If it pleases you, I give you my word." He lifted his foreleg and held out a massive talon. I grabbed it with both hands, shaking it until he flung me off. I landed on my feet near the tunnel entrance. "Get going and let me know what you find."

Later that morning, when I was sure Master Stradus had left the garden and was well away from me, I exited the library, cutting my studies short. I tiptoed down the hall, looking over my shoulder as if Master Stradus was going to appear at any moment.

I got to the door and let out a breath I didn't know I held. I forced myself to take deep, normal breaths. Master Stradus had taught me to use my magical senses to peer beyond what a person normally saw. Up until then, I had been sensing magic by instinct, such as feeling the webs in his chambers and the magic of the mountain.

The strong web held the door in place, shining with the brightness of multiple manas. I gazed at the bright colors, watching them move and glisten across the door while I tried to figure out how to begin. There were so many strands, and they were so intricate. They overlapped, and the colors kept shifting.

And there was something else. Something about the web that bothered me and made me hesitate to undo it the way I had planned. I had learned that the strands could be woven in many ways. The more you took your time with them and created complex patterns, the stronger they were. Most webs were rushed and easy, since the magic wasn't intended to be permanent, not like an enchantment. But this web was different. Master Stradus had taken his time with this one, and the weaving was more complex than any I had ever seen. It was meant to last a long time, and keep almost anything out. Or in. I didn't know if I believed that we weren't alone in this mountain. Master Stradus clearly did, judging by this nearly impenetrable safeguard.

Getting rid of all the magic that bound this web was going to take a lot of time—far more time than even Cynder thought. I only hoped he would be able to keep Master Stradus's attention.

I started with the magic I knew best—fire. I extinguished the fire mana in the web, making sure not to accidentally touch any of the other manas. The other manas called out, trying their best to entice me. I ignored them, not tapping into any of their power. If I did, it would set the web off.

The fire in the web dimmed until it disappeared. I smiled, thinking I was finally getting somewhere. The problem was going to be with the other magics. While I could access them, my ability to use them was still limited. But I thought about impressing Master Stradus with my progress, and riding Cynder through the autumn sky, and I kept going.

I thought I had finished with the red mana in the web. I was wrong. The fire reasserted itself, flaring once more into life. The rest of the web brightened in response, and the magic came alive. The colors swam and danced. It moved so fast, I couldn't get my defenses up.

The magic leapt from the web. Pain raced up my arm, as if my bones had turned white-hot. A force struck my chest, like a blow from a dragon's tail. It hurled me into the air, and I slammed into the wall, the rough rock gouging into my back. I slid down and collapsed, my face smacking against the cold floor.

I tried to move before Master Stradus found me. I couldn't. The magic seized control of my muscles, forcing them in place. My whole body went numb, like when I had climbed the mountain to get here. Only my eyes weren't affected. I stared at the web, seeing the colors lessen from their bloom until they were dim again. Their ferocious movement stopped. The magics went back to their designed places, traveling in their methodical ways.

My jaw loosened, and I muttered, "I knew this was a bad idea. Stupid dragon."

"Quite right." Master Stradus towered over me. His beady blue eyes glanced at the door before resting on me. "I warned both of you we weren't alone in this mountain, and that it's dangerous down there. Did you think I was lying?"

I shrugged, still slumped on the ground. "Cynder convinced me he hasn't seen anything while he's been here."

"Is that all?"

I hesitated. "He also promised to give me a ride on his back."

"Did he now?"

I nodded.

"It's a wonderful feeling, soaring high up in the clouds." Master Stradus's face became wistful, and he gave a half-smile. When he looked back at me, he became stern again. "Instead, what you're getting is punishment."

I frowned.

"The both of you. Cynder should know better. Let me help you up."

Master Stradus helped me, but I still had limited movement. My body had trouble responding to my commands.

"How long will I feel like this?" I asked, dragging my right leg as I limped alongside him.

"A few more minutes," he said. "Thank the gods you didn't bypass the first barrier in the web. That one was a warning. The second defense would have been far worse."

I didn't get to ride Cynder that day or for a long time afterward. Master Stradus made me and Cynder scrub the entire cave complex clean, and I had to prune every plant in the garden. For the next couple of weeks, he also watched while I worked on my exercises with Cynder. But the biggest punishment was that I practiced and trained harder with magic. The sessions were far too long, pushing me to exhaustion by day's end. The few breaks he allowed were shorter. Master Stradus also made me read stories in the library out loud to him about the consequences of undisciplined magic. He questioned me more after each spell I performed.

Despite all that magic, I never got to practice a ritual or summoning. I only read about them. It wasn't until a year later that I did the most basic summoning ritual.

After going through it, I understood why.

CHAPTER 8

WHILE THE CAVES of the White Mountain had started to be a home to me and I had accomplished what I set out to do in controlling my powers, there were times when I felt trapped. I had been confined here for over a year. I didn't know what was happening in the world or to my friends and family I cared deeply about. Were they all right? Did they even think about me?

During my studies in the library, I had read about one of the easiest rituals, in which a wizard could summon a creature from the Netherrealm called a maleika. Maleikas were used during the War of the Wizards to spy on places and people. I asked Master Stradus about it, to see if I could summon one. He said I wasn't ready. That was reasonable. I wasn't sure if I was either. Then I asked if he would summon one, so I could check on my mother.

"No," Master Stradus said, continuing to grind leaves with a stone pestle in preparation for making a potion.

Now he was being unreasonable. I normally didn't push him, but this time I did. "Please."

"I said no, Hellsfire."

The flames within me rose, pressing against my body, aching to be released. I forced the magic down and calmed myself. Being angry would get me nowhere. "Please, Master. I just want to see how my mother's doing. It shouldn't take long. I'll cook for the rest of the year or tend to your garden. Please."

"No."

My temper snapped. "Why not?"

Master Stradus stopped halfway through grinding. He exhaled, put down the stone, and walked out of the garden.

I stood by the workbench, poking angrily at the half-ground leaves. It wasn't fair. It wasn't as if I wanted to watch half-naked slave girls dancing in the Burning Sands. I hadn't seen my mother in over a year, and she was all alone. I just wanted to know if she was all right. Didn't Master Stradus know how much I worried about her? And he wouldn't even dignify my request by giving me a reason for refusing. He'd just walked out without even bothering to answer, like my mother didn't matter at all.

Fine then. If Master Stradus wasn't going to help me check on my mother, I would do it without his help.

I waited a week before making my move. During that time, I studied the ritual until I knew it backwards. I didn't even tell Cynder what I planned to do, as he might feel obligated to tell our master.

I did it at night, when Master Stradus was well asleep. I took the ritual book from the library, and then made my way to the garden to prepare the potion I needed.

I cut pieces of the plants I needed, taking a leaf here and petal there. I upended one plant, taking its roots. My shaky hands made the cutting difficult. So many things could go wrong in a ritual, and potions weren't my best subject.

While cutting and grinding the plants, my attention was divided when it should have been completely focused. I kept re-reading the book, making sure I did everything right, yet I also kept glancing at the door, expecting Master Stradus to barge in. The noise of the grinding stone seemed ear-shattering in the quiet caves, no matter how slowly I did it.

I cooked everything down, motioning with my hands for it to hurry up. I was just pouring the finished potion into a flask when I heard a noise outside that made me spill some of it. The hot liquid splashed on my hands.

"Godsdamn it!" I yelped.

I froze, listening for Master Stradus opening the door. When I heard nothing, I sighed in relief and wiped off the spilled liquid. I finished pouring the potion into the flask and was about to leave when I remembered the mess I had created. Bits of leaves were in the grinding stones. The knife I had used for cutting needed to be wiped down. The potion clung to the bowl I had used to heat it. Everything had to be put back in its place.

I cleaned everything up, hurrying as best I could. I had already used too much time in preparation. The salty smell of the potion still lingered in the room, but I hoped it would dissipate in time.

I took the potion and rushed out of the garden, heading straight to the practice room. The practice room was a lot more ominous when I was by myself in the dark. The torches were out, to simulate nightfall outside. The Nexus of the White Mountain almost felt like a ghost. It was hard to deny its presence. Like Master Stradus had told me, magic was a lot more powerful here. I had to remember that, lest the ritual get out of control.

I grabbed some of the candles that were lying around the room. I created a candle-composed circle big enough for me to sit in, and used my magic to light them. The circle of fire swayed when I stepped inside.

I sat cross-legged and re-read the ritual one last time. I practiced the motions before checking with the book to see if I was right. I had spent my punishment time last year reading Master Stradus stories of the things that could go wrong if you didn't perform a ritual perfectly. I didn't want to end up entombed in the rock floor or with my head twisted backwards.

I ignored the loud thumping in my chest and took a deep breath, trying hard to calm myself. It was time to begin.

I latched onto the necessary mana, which was a dash of each, and then in the ancient language of Caleea said, *"Being of the other plane, I call you forth. Being of the other plane, I call you forth. Heed my words. I seek a maleika to come into this world and be my ears and eyes. Come, oh maleika."* I drank the potion and spat the horrible, salty stuff out. I winced. *"Come, maleika, and obey me!"*

The potion moved and vibrated in the places where I spat. The puddles moved faster and faster. Wisps of sour aroma seeped into my nose. The pieces of potion solidified and came together, floating above the ground. A ghastly, foggy, ghost-like face appeared. It had no nose and a wicked grin. Its right eye stared malevolently at me. There was a scar where the left one should have been.

The creature's voice sounded like rocks grating together. *"Who dared to summon me?"*

"I did."

"And who might you be?" Its eye pierced me. It said something in a language I had never heard before.

"I am Hellsfire."

Its hollow laughter numbed my ears. *"I've never heard of you. What is it you want?"*

"I want you to go to a town called Sedah and check on my mother. She lives in a longhouse on the outskirts of town."

Nothing happened. It floated there, in my circle. A bit of irritation showed on its transparent face, if such a thing were possible.

I concentrated, picturing the forest I used to romp in and the home I was raised in. I saw my mother's warm, smiling face and the hot corn bread she used to bake. The apple cider we made for Winter Solstice was clear in my mind. I recalled the animated stories she used to tell about the strange creatures in the Burning Sands she called camels.

"I see it now." The maleika fizzled and disappeared.

A terrible pain hit me in the stomach. It churned and roared. I clutched my aching belly. Something was wrong. I wasn't sure what. It could have been the potion, but the ritual had worked. I was tempted to look in the book, but knew to stay focused on the ritual.

The maleika shimmered back in front of me. *"I have done as you asked, Hellsfire,"* it said.

"My mother, how is she?"

The maleika's ghostly form faded and rippled, much like a pond when a rock was thrown into it. My mother appeared. She was bent over the stove, cooking. Next to her was one of our neighbors. My mother smiled, and laughed at something the other woman said. I reached out to touch my mother. The vision disappeared, replaced by the one-eyed maleika.

"Satisfied?"

I wasn't. I missed her. I wiped tears from the corners of my eyes.

"Would you like to see something more interesting? How about a girl or an enemy?" The maleika had a slight grin on its ghastly face.

"No, I wouldn't." Sweat trickled from my forehead, splattering on the ground. I breathed more deeply, but I felt like I couldn't get enough air.

"Is there anything else you wish, then?"

"No. *Maleika I summoned thee. Now I banish thee.*" It didn't move. It floated there with its one eye and crooked smile.

I summoned more mana. *"I said, I banish thee!"*

"How dare you try to get rid of me! I have done you this favor and now you must do something for me."

It came closer, and even though I sweated, a chill overcame me. My skin froze in response. I traced the hardness of my arm with my fingertips.

"You haven't any choice," it said, floating closer.

I tried to draw in magic to stop it, but I was too weak. All the pieces of mana I'd used to summon it slipped out of my hold. My body let me down as much as my magic did. I blinked my heavy eyes, trying to bring things into focus.

"You have a lot of power in you. I'm going to enjoy this."

The creature smothered my head in its hazy body, engulfing me like a duck eating a fish. The mist-like being surrounded me, blinding me. Little surges of lightning emanated from it, pummeling me. My body jerked in response to each sting. Those prickles of its strange magic transmitted bits of my power to it. I could feel it taking it. I roared, thrashing and flailing like a bird struck down by an arrow. My hands went right through it. No matter how much I rolled or contorted my body, the damn thing wouldn't come off. The longer it stayed on my head, the more of my magic it stole, and the weaker I became. I couldn't keep up this fight forever.

I stopped trying to use physical force and used my brain. The creature's intense burning magic increased. I bit the inside of my cheek to keep from crying out with the pain. I focused and did the one thing Master Stradus told me to do when all else fails—use your strongest mana.

I let go of all the magic I was trying to hold. The creature laughed in response, sucking all the incredible power into it. I seized the one magic I wasn't letting go of—my fire.

My anger and frustration took over. It surged through my body, growing stronger than the agony this creature visited upon me. Flames shot out of me. The scorching inferno encircled me until it became my aura.

My fire assaulted and battered the maleika. This was no spell, just raw magic waging war. The creature's magical attack halted, and its grip loosened, granting me a chance to breathe normally again.

My brief reprieve passed. The maleika screeched in rage. The creature backed off slightly and spoke in a weird language, casting another spell. Its magic wove and flew, passing through my elemental magic and hammering me. A blinding agony seized me. The pressure from all the magic being cast in the Nexus made my head feel like it was about to rupture and explode, but I couldn't stop. If I did, I was dead anyway. My skin tightened against my face as I yelled. My veins felt like they were popping out. I knew if my magic reached the creature, it would die. I just had to concentrate and keep pushing.

Yet the fire within me slowly wavered. My shoulders slumped and my body swayed. My mind and body couldn't take the crushing magic anymore. Blood ran from my ears.

The door crashed open. Master Stradus arrived, bringing the winds with him. They doused my already exhausted fire, and the maleika wasted no time in reattaching to my head, draining the life force from me.

The force of a storm tore at my head while Master Stradus tried to get the maleika off me. The creature struggled to stay on. Master Stradus increased the winds, strong enough to cut me or tear my head off, but using such skill that they never touched me—only the maleika. My master's winds wrapped around it until its grip loosened. The maleika let go of my head and slammed into the wall. I fell to the ground, barely getting my hands up in time to keep my face from striking the floor.

"Hellsfire!" Master Stradus rushed to me. "Are you all right?"

I shook my head. My sweat poured to the ground, and I gasped for air.

"How nice to see you after all these years, Wizard," the maleika said, glaring at my master with its one eye.

"You?" Master Stradus said. *"I remember you. I owe you."*

"You owe me?" it said. *"You owe me? It's I that owes you. I have only one eye thanks to you. Time hasn't been kind to you, old man. Remember what happened last time? Let's see how well your pupil fares now."* The air in the room thickened as the maleika gathered in power.

"No!" Master Stradus said. He conjured a gust of air, pushing the maleika back towards the wall and keeping it in an invisible cage of air. It fought against the cage, unleashing wisps of power at it. "Hellsfire, finish the ritual quickly. This is no ordinary maleika. Drink the potion and say the words while I hold it back. You must use a great deal of energy on this one. No matter how strong it is and how hard it fights, it's still a maleika. You summoned it here, and it must obey the rules of magic."

Master Stradus struggled against the maleika. He used his staff to focus his power. The inside of the globe swirled. Dark blue, spinning round and round.

"Do it quickly!"

I mustered what reserves of strength I had left. I forced the potion down, focusing on all the parts of mana I used to summon the creature. What was left of my fire blazed, heightening the spell. My body swayed, and stars appeared in front of my eyes. The room spun. I couldn't tell if it was because of what I saw, or my master's spell. The maleika resisted my mana, but Master Stradus kept it occupied. I cried out, *"Maleika, I summoned thee and now I banish thee. Go back where you belong!"*

A bright hole tore into this world. It laughed as its transparent body began to fade. *"It's not over yet, Wizard. I'll have my revenge."* Master Stradus roared and sent a whirlwind of lightning at it. The maleika's ghostly face smirked at Master Stradus before it dissolved like fog on a summer morning's day.

Master Stradus came over to me and put a hand on my shoulder. "Are you all right, Hellsfire?"

"I-I don't feel so good…Master."

The pain flared into my head and sides. I shivered and wrapped my arms across my body. My stomach growled until it erupted and I spewed up my dinner, heaving all over the floor. The fire within me disappeared, replaced by coldness. Chills overtook me, and I curled into a ball, unable to stop shivering.

Master Stradus bent down and turned me over. He placed his warm hands over my forehead and chest. His pupils became white, and his hands glowed, filling with the power of white mana. The warmth melted into me until I stopped shaking and tasting my own vomit.

"Thank you," I whispered. I closed my eyes.

"Don't sleep. Not yet." Master Stradus extended his magical senses. Magical needles pricked me. "That damned thing. It put a curse on you. You'll live, but we must hurry before the spell gets worse. Let's go to my garden."

Master Stradus helped me up. I wiped drool and vomit off my face with the sleeve of my tunic. We made our way to the garden, me using Master Stradus as a crutch. He gave me his staff while he prepared a potion to counteract the maleika's spell. I leaned on the staff, using its power to help stabilize me.

"Master…how did you know-w-w that ma-ma-maleika?" My teeth chattered and I couldn't stop them.

Master Stradus looked up and away. When he didn't move or say anything for several long moments, I let the subject drop. I had pressured him before when I asked to do the ritual, and he got angry with me. Considering the line I had crossed by doing it anyway, I had no right to expect him to talk about it again.

His voice was quiet, but his words had the weight of a storm. "I'm only going to tell you this once, Hellsfire, and not because I want to, but because I must. You need to learn that when I tell you not to do something, you must not do it."

I opened my chattering mouth to say something, but it was as if he read my mind.

"I know being here is very hard for you. I know you've left your loved ones and you sometimes feel trapped in this place. I understand that and know what it's like to be away from them. But unlike me, you weren't dragged away and forced to become a wizard."

I stared at him and raised an eyebrow.

"But that's a story for a different time and not one I'm going to tell you now."

His voice got quiet and small. "In my arrogance, before the Great Barrier, I thought I was skilled enough to take an apprentice even though my training wasn't technically complete. Tara said she always wanted to be a witch, and she wanted to protect her mother in case the war came to them. Against my better judgment, I decided to teach her what little I could before I left for the war. What harm could there be in teaching someone basic magic?" Master Stradus sighed. "I was a fool.

"I suppose the real reason was that Tara looked up to me. I didn't want to let her down. She was much younger than you are now—about ten or eleven—with beautiful blond hair. She often came to see me, constantly smiling and asking questions. She was like an annoying little sister, but I sensed there was a great power in her waiting to be released." He created a flame and boiled the pieces of a plant in a liquid over the fire.

"What…happened…to her?" I looked with fascination at my now-pale hands.

"Don't worry, my boy, I'm almost done. As I was saying, I had her perform the same ritual you did just now. It went quite well, but in the back of my mind, I sensed something wasn't completely right. I should have listened to myself." Master Stradus picked up the bowl and said, *"Oh spirits, please alleviate the curse that was put upon the boy. Bless this potion.* Here, drink this."

The potion was warm and sweet, and I guzzled it. It was far better than the potion I had drunk earlier to summon that one-eyed freak. It took a few moments, but I stopped shaking, my body warmed up, and my stomach and head stopped swirling. I smiled and took a deep breath, watching the goose bumps disappear from my arms.

"Thank you, Master."

"I'm just glad you're better," he said. "If that maleika had had more time it would have done worse." Master Stradus sighed. "I suppose I should get back to my story."

I handed his staff back to him and said, "You don't have to."

He grabbed it with a shaky hand. "No. I want to. I should." He gazed into the distance. "After the ritual, we ate and went to sleep. During the night, the maleika attacked me, draining me of my life force and taking my magic. It was much stronger than any maleika I had encountered before. I was able to get that cursed thing off but I couldn't banish it." His voice became hoarse and his face tightened. "As I should have.

"I told Tara to run for cover while I worked on a stronger spell. But she was too stubborn. She thought we'd be able to finish it off together. The thing was too quick, and smothered her head."

Just as it had done to me. I shivered. I had a feeling this story wasn't going to end as well as mine.

"I was afraid to attack it while it was on her, so I tried to finish the ritual again." Master Stradus's focus rested on me, his blue eyes piercing me. "If something goes wrong, retrace your steps, use your strongest mana, and finish the spell again."

I nodded.

"Good. I said the banishing words, pouring all my strength into them, and it loosened its grip. I used the rest of my strength to summon a holy lightning bolt, nailing it right in the eye. The maleika howled and howled until it vanished. I hoped it had died when it went back to the Netherrealm, but I was never sure." Master Stradus was quiet for a few moments. He stroked the globe on his staff, staring off into the distance. I could see the muscles in his jaw working as he tried to contain his feelings.

"I rushed over to Tara to check if she was still" –he paused and swallowed— "alive. She looked one last time into my eyes, and then she was gone. I tried desperately to heal her with my magic. I had none left."

Master Stradus's cloudy eyes were heavy with regret and remembrance. I now understood why he was so hard on me in lessons, and why he got upset when I tried to undo his web. He didn't want anything to happen to me. I was a fool to keep disobeying him. I had needed a reminder that magic, no matter how simple it may seem, was a great responsibility and should be taken seriously. No matter how badly I wanted to see my mother and how much I missed her, she would be disappointed to know the risk I took to do it.

"After I buried Tara," he continued, "I became so enraged that I summoned maleika after maleika, trying to find the one that killed her. I never found it. The other maleika either couldn't, or wouldn't, tell me what I needed to know. I...lost my temper and killed dozens of innocent maleika. It wasn't their fault she was dead. It was mine." The globe on top of Master Stradus's staff darkened. His hands reddened as he tightened his grip. I watched as the globe swirled and his power continued to build. The air around us became heavy and violent.

Master Stradus took a deep breath. His power dissipated as he calmed himself. "I continued to summon one every year on the anniversary of her death in hopes I'd be lucky. I never saw it again until now."

Master Stradus's blue eyes focused on me again, and his voice became firm. "While you're in this mountain and under my tutelage, I expect you to do everything I say. It's not because I enjoy telling you what to do. Magic is very dangerous, Hellsfire. Even if you think you're doing everything right, things can still go wrong."

"But I wanted to see my mother." I bit my lip and looked down in shame when I saw how exasperated he looked. "I'm sorry. You're right. I shouldn't have performed the ritual after you said no."

"Quite right." His eyes softened. "I was terrified when I saw the same maleika doing the same thing it did so many years ago." He placed his hand on my shoulder. "I'm glad to see you're all right now, my boy."

I nodded. "Me too." I couldn't resist the impulse to hug him, burying myself in his sky blue robes.

Master Stradus's muscles tightened in surprise. He relaxed and returned the hug. We embraced for several long moments before he broke it. He cleared his throat. "I don't want you to do anything like that again, Hellsfire."

"I won't."

"I'm serious."

Our eyes met, and I said, "So am I."

"Good. Now, all things considered, you did a good job."

"I did?"

"Yes. You successfully summoned a maleika. If it hadn't been that one, things might have gone better. I promise you, you'll get to summon more to check on your mother and those you care about."

"Thank you, Master."

"Now go to bed. It's late."

I yawned and put a hand to my mouth. I left him and walked to the door. "Good night, Master."

"Good night, Hellsfire. One last thing."

I stopped and turned to face him, holding the door open. "Yes?"

"Sleep well while you can. Tomorrow, you have to get up early and sweep the entire cave."

Before that day, I never knew Master Stradus had a pupil before me, but I suppose it was natural. He had lived for a millennium, or close to it, and I never fully realized all the things he must have gone through. He must have had some great adventures, yet he also must have witnessed many tragic events.

Coming to the White Mountain, I had thought I was only going to learn to control my powers so I wouldn't hurt anyone again. But as I mastered it, I found I enjoyed using my gift of magic. I no longer thought of it as a curse.

I understood the basics of magic and what it could do, but I had never thought of the pain it could bring. Not just in hurting someone, but in *not* being able to do something. Master Stradus's lesson taught me that. No matter how much power I had, it might not be enough. I might also live longer than those I cared about, powerless to do anything except watch them grow old and die. Being a wizard was a far grander undertaking than I originally thought, but also far more daunting. And there was still that prophecy about me, which he never gave me any more details about.

After my mishap with the maleika, I read more about other types of beings who existed in the Netherrealm, or at least I tried to. The very few books Master Stradus had were either vague, or a bunch of dry theories on how, what, or why. After sifting through a lot of information, I realized that all the books came to the same conclusion: if you wanted to know about other worlds and beings from those worlds, you'd have to summon a creature from there, which might be very hard to control, and might kill you—or worse. Or you could cross over yourself—if you were able to, and lucky enough to make it back; or find a rare crosswalker, who could go into the Netherrealm with ease. In the end, I gave up. I had no plans to go over into the Netherrealm. However, if I ever saw that one-eyed monster again, I was going to finish what my master started.

Another year passed. A side consequence of my becoming a wizard was that my appetite for meat soon vanished, until I could no longer eat it. Master Stradus told me it was a consequence of being able to access mana.

I learned more magic and read a lot more. I studied more of the plants that were in the garden. Master Stradus was true to his word, and we regularly checked what happened in Sedah by using maleika. I wished my mother could have seen me or that I could have talked to her. Not even magic could help with that. I also got to practice other rituals.

As much as I enjoyed being around Master Stradus and Cynder and performing magic, there was something missing. No matter how many times I summoned a maleika or went outside the caves, I still felt confined. Every day, the walls and ceiling moved an inch closer. If that wasn't bad enough, the books I read, along with Master Stradus and Cynder regaling me with stories, made me wish I was outside of the White Mountain to experience all the things they had. I often thought about leaving, even though my training wasn't complete.

Just to make sure, I asked both Master Stradus and Cynder about how my skills were progressing. Master Stradus was pleased with my progress, while Cynder thought I was merely adequate. I knew I still had a lot to learn from them, but being cooped up in the mountain wasn't going to help. All of my lessons suggested that people learned from the situations they encountered, not from being in a classroom. Even back when there was a wizard's school, students were deliberately put into dangerous and stressful situations. There was nothing like that here. I didn't know if Master Stradus designed it that way on purpose, or to shield me.

It had been centuries since Master Stradus last took on an apprentice. While his last pupil hadn't come to as tragic an end as Tara, things went sour. Maybe he just wasn't good with apprentices.

These questions and thoughts filled my head for months. I tried to weigh the cost of staying versus the cost of going. As I had found out the hard way when I first used my powers, it was a perilous world out there. Like poison, the doubt and introspection seeped their way into my everyday tasks, until they were all I could think about. Unfortunately, my lessons and studying were affected. I couldn't even talk to Cynder because he wouldn't understand. Being here was his honorable duty. He was our master's guardian, and, because of conditions amongst his own people, he had nowhere else to go.

I tried to overlook these things. I tried to remind myself I could still be killed if I left without the proper training. But little by little, those sensible thoughts were drowned out until they no longer mattered.

And then, I had a vision.

CHAPTER 9

I SAT CROSSED-LEGGED on the edge of a ridge near the peak of the White Mountain. Nightfall engulfed me and the snow swirled around me. Often, after a day's training, I would find myself out here, escaping the confinement of the caves. It had helped at first. I breathed a little easier seeing the blue sky, the green forests, and the brown earth far below. But lately, being trapped so high above it all, I found those same sights depressing. The world's changing seasons reminded me that time moved on, while I was stuck in unending winter. The only way I knew time had passed was that Cynder teased me about my deepening voice, my sleeves exposed too much of my wrists, and I no longer had to look up at Master Stradus to meet his eyes.

Being outside also served another purpose. At first, I used practicing my power as an excuse to be outside. That's what I told Master Stradus I was doing. As time went on, my lie became the truth. Without my power, the weather would have torn me apart. As when I first climbed the mountain, I accessed my power and held onto it, letting it seep into every pore and warm my body. At first, it tired me just standing there. The more I went outside, the easier it became, until I sat on the ledge in the cold storm for hours.

I closed my eyes, ignoring the cold and frost that surrounded me. My breathing and heart slowed until I drowned the growl of the weather outside my body. I journeyed inside myself, heading towards the inner fire. The red and orange flame danced, moving and twisting like a firefly in the moonlight. It filled my very essence with its own. It was a strange yet familiar sensation, like we belonged together, as if we'd always been one. The flame changed colors, from a natural red and orange to an intense blue and black. The power surged within me. I knew I could do anything. But I was afraid the power would overwhelm me if I tried.

I held it for as long as I could. I got lost in it, and it became something else.

A baby eagle stands by his mother on the edge of a cliff. The mother nudges the baby with her beak, encouraging him to abandon the ledge and fly. The eaglet squawks in protest, but his mother forces him over the edge, sending him plummeting toward the ground. The baby eagle falls fast, flapping his wings in vain. The momentum is too great for him to handle. He's going to crash into the ground. At the last second, his little wings catch the wind. He soars higher, higher into the open sky. He circles once, taking a last look at his mother, then heads off toward the horizon.

The eaglet changes shape. He's no longer a feathered bird, but a bird made of fire, igniting the entire sky. His trail spells out my name as he soars towards me. He stares at me and gives an ear-shattering cry, shaking the heavens and the afterlife. He darts at my chest, burrowing and burning his way inside. I cry out as he fills me with power. Fire spews out of my eyes and mouth until I'm forced out of my trance.

I gazed up into the night sky, unsure of what I had seen. Everything I'd read about visions raced through my mind. Was I the eaglet? What was the vision telling me? A bright star streaked across the sky, and it looked like the baby bird.

I was still pondering over the meaning of my vision when another one flooded my mind. It was so forceful and strong I toppled over, face in the snow, and I blacked out.

The inferno erupts in front of me, gliding and floating in mid-air. I open my hand, and the fire leaps into it. I can sense its immense power, its scorching heat, and yet to me, it only feels warm. The flame rolls over me and caresses my skin. Its movement matches my breathing. I force my hand to remain steady. The fire disappears, melting into my body, adding its strength to my own. My inner-mana swirls with exultation. I no longer feel cold and alone. I feel alive and powerful. I can do anything.

My hand explodes. I hiss and turn my head to shield my eyes. A flame frees itself from my body and ruptures into a ball the size of my head. I stare at the renegade flame. It shifts and transforms, slowly changing into something recognizable. It looks like a human head but with wild, swaying hair.

The longer I gaze at it, the slower it burns, revealing itself piece by piece. The outline of a face appears, two gaping holes for eyes. The intense reds and oranges soften, peeling back until their colors change to flesh. The eyes burn hotter, hotter, until their centers grow blue, then purple.

And I recognize the face. It is her. She has haunted my dreams since the day we met. Drifting through my mind, planting herself into my thoughts until she gained a foothold. She has guided me in my most stressful times, helping me when I struggled with grasping a mana or saying an incantation. I have used her memory as fuel for what I have to do lest people like her get hurt. I have never known if I would never see her again, but I could never forget those soft violet eyes.

"Krystal," I whisper.

The darkness crushes the fire's light. The flame fights, burning as brightly as it can, but it's no match for the darkness. The princess's face disappears. The fire changes, burning with dark flames. It contains hulking, ferocious monsters. They're drenched in blood, with bodies strewn around them. Innocent people run through the smoke, screaming to get away, but they're cut down by the creatures. I close my hand to get rid of the images, and the fire burns my skin.

I can't shake it off. When I move, it sears my unburned skin. I hold it still, fearful of the pain. It forces me to watch murders and mutilations, death and destruction. My anger increases with every child chopped down. I'm powerless to stop it.

Those images vanish, changing into a small figure cloaked in black robes. The fire in my hand no longer burns with warmth, instead turning as icy as death. A small flame splits off from the larger one. Two purple eyes stare from the small flame to the darker flame. The bigger fire swirls around her until it douses her.

"Krystal!" I shout.

The ink-black flames turn towards me. Two icy eyes peer back at me.

I woke up to find my cheek buried in the snow. I peeled myself from the ground and wiped the frost from my cheek. There was red on my fingertips. Blood—leaking from my nose. I forced myself to stand, head pounding.

I stared into the darkness, towards Alexandria. My bones ached with dread. The princess was in trouble, but I wasn't sure how or why. If Alexandria had fallen, we surely would have heard about it, even cooped up in the White Mountain. Wouldn't we?

I thought about leaving the mountain to see if everything was all right, but what could I do to help the princess and her kingdom? I wasn't combat ready. I needed to finish my studies. I tried to dismiss what I'd seen as an unhealthy obsession with that beautiful girl, but as soon as I did, the pain in my head returned and the images from my visions flooded my mind. I collapsed to my knees, blood from my nose splashing across the snow in front of me. I cried out in agony, clutching the snow. What was wrong with me?

I crawled towards the cave entrance. Each time I tried to get up, the pain shoved me back down into the snow. It wasn't until I let the visions flood my mind once more, and thought of going to the princess, that my jumbled mind became clear. The pain disappeared. I breathed easier. The agony was replaced by a moment of perfect clarity. I knew what to do. The vision was a sign.

I had to trust it. I had to leave.

Where I came from didn't matter. Who I was didn't matter. I was going to help the princess if she needed my help. I prayed to the gods I was wrong, and that my fears were for naught.

I went back to the warm comfort of the caverns, making my way to the little dining hall to tell Master Stradus. I took my time, because as much as I had longed to leave, I was going to miss the place. Assuming Master Stradus would let me leave. With his obsession about the prophecy he had never explained to me, he might not.

As I walked through the huge tunnel, memories raced through my mind. I remembered when I first met and ran from Cynder, times we'd played hide and seek, and when he took me for a ride on his scaly back. He liked to sprint through the tunnels, making me clasp onto his scales lest I go flying off. I learned to always hang onto him, even when he walked slowly, because he'd suddenly speed up again, sending me to the ground with a thump. And the sensation of soaring over the earth while he flew like a giant eagle was something I would never forget. I would never have dreamed that the vicious White Mountain that I knew had killed so many would become a home to me. A dragon and a wizard were strange company, but they had become family.

When I arrived at the entrance to the dining hall, I saw the web's invisible strands and smirked. I could easily undo it with a touch of my power. How things had changed in the past three years. I walked in and found Master Stradus busy fixing dinner. My thoughts went back to the first meal I ever had with him, learning about the path I was to walk, but we each make our own decisions in life. He had even told me this in his wizardly way.

"Hello, my son," Master Stradus said as he leaned over the black pot and inhaled the stew's aroma. "Dinner will be ready in a second. Pull up a seat while I make you a bowl."

I took the stool beside him and waited for my food. Normally, there'd be some kind of conversation during the meal, unless I was extremely hungry. This time I was quiet. I was the baby eagle. The need to leave was a gut feeling, boiling inside of me. The problem was, I wasn't sure if I had completed enough training for what might be in store for me. If I didn't know enough, I could be killed—or people could get hurt.

Master Stradus must have sensed the disturbance and conflict in me. He didn't say a word, and he didn't scrutinize. He once told me that it's a wizard's job to wait, but he must also know when to take action. After we ate, I took a deep breath and let it all out.

"Master, I've something to tell you," I said.

He gave me a quizzical look, then smiled. "I thought you might. I'm ready when you are."

I told him about the visions I saw on the ledge, and about how Alexandria might be in trouble. I told him about the pain I suffered when I thought about staying.

Afterwards, I said, "I…I believe I must leave this place." I turned my head. I couldn't look at him. What if he said no? What if he wanted me to stay because he was lonely?

He was silent, weighing my every word. I didn't know if that was good or bad, but then he said, "No. You cannot—you must not—leave."

My eyes met his. "But why?"

"Because your training is not complete."

"What about the visions I had?"

"What about them?"

"They're warning me about something." I threw my hands up in frustration. "The pain won't go away. The more I think about staying, the more intense it becomes."

He shrugged. "I can give you something for the pain, but what can you do about the danger you sense? You're *not* a wizard. You still have much to learn, Hellsfire. You can still lose control of your powers. What if you hurt those you try to help? By going, you could make things worse."

"I—I…" I hung my head as I thought about his words. He was right. I could do more harm than good.

Master Stradus's blue eyes continued to bore into me. He didn't say one word.

I shook my head. No. I had made my decision, and I was sticking to it. I raised my head and looked at Master Stradus. "I'm leaving, Master. This is something I must—no, need to do. I hope you understand, but I'm leaving whether you want me to or not." I stood. I was now taller than he was, but if I had to fight him with magic my height wasn't going to help.

Master Stradus didn't stand. He didn't even draw any magic, which I was thankful for. He reached for his tea and took a sip.

I clenched my hand while I waited for him to say or do something. When he finally spoke, his words surprised me.

"Would you like some more tea?"

"No."

"Then please sit down," he said in a calm voice.

"All right." I did, but I was still tense. I expected him to do some kind of spell on me, and I had to be ready for it.

Master Stradus put his tea down and leaned forward. "Are you absolutely sure about this decision, my boy? It's a big decision to leave without having completed your training."

Without hesitation I said, "Yes, Master, I'm sure. Something's happening out there. I don't know what it is, but people are in danger. The gods sent me this intense vision for a reason."

Master Stradus stroked his beard. "None of this has to do with how enclosed you've felt lately?"

I tugged at my collar and fidgeted. "You've noticed."

He nodded. "It's been affecting your studies."

This discussion was going nowhere. If he thought I wanted to leave because of that, he wouldn't let me. "But Master, it has nothing to do with that. Don't you believe me?"

Master Stradus hesitated. He caressed his staff as his blue eyes searched me. I wanted to turn my gaze away, but couldn't. I guessed he didn't believe me. He wouldn't let me go. I was a fool to think I could leave without completing my training. But I didn't think the gods would let me stay, if the throbbing pain they sent me was any indication. I couldn't stay here no matter what Master Stradus said. I had already started planning my escape and my climb back down the White Mountain.

Master Stradus did something completely unexpected. He smiled.

"I believe you, Hellsfire." His blue eyes told of the sadness in him. "I've tried my hardest, yet I know I've not taught you everything you need to know. But if the gods call upon you, I cannot hold you back."

I was relieved that Master Stradus had relented, but it also dawned on me that I wasn't going to have his help if things went wrong. If I messed up, it would be on my head. All I had were the lessons he had instilled in me.

"How ironic that the prophecies that guided you to me now send you away."

I perked up. This was something he never talked about with me. He thought anyone who knew too much of their own future would try to influence things. Cynder wouldn't say either. The dragon feigned ignorance. I listened to my master, hopeful that he finally was going to enlighten me.

Master Stradus gazed into the distance. "When it comes to prophecies or visions, most of the time you can interpret them in any way you choose. It's all a matter of perspective. Remember how I told you I came to your house because of a prophecy?"

I nodded, but he wasn't paying attention.

"Before you, I looked and looked for children who could be the One. They were promising and had some of the signs, but they weren't it. I didn't get the feeling from them that I get from you. I even took on an apprentice, thinking he was the One. But it wasn't true. So you see, you *are* the One. You must be. I can't be wrong after all these years."

The desperation in his voice was frightening. To think that one man thought so much of me. I hoped he was right and hadn't made another mistake. His borderline obsession might be wrong, but I didn't want to destroy his dream even if I didn't believe in it. The prophecy wasn't important to me. What was important was protecting people and controlling my power.

"I remember your birth well," he said. "It was a most unusual night. It happened in the middle of winter and it was extremely hot. I didn't think the prophecy would be so literal. 'In the dead of cold, the spark will burn,' indeed. I followed the trail and it led to you, my boy. You are the One, Hellsfire. But it's not I who needs to believe, it's you."

I let his words sink in, but I still wasn't sure if he was right. A potential wizard, yes. But the One? I brushed those thoughts aside. Since I was never going to know about my own prophecy, there was no use dwelling on it. I had to make my own choices and pray they were the right ones. The only thing I was sure was right was leaving.

"I trust you'll leave in the morning? Unless you want to go right now?" Master Stradus asked.

I remembered the cold and darkness and how oppressive and scary it could be. "I can wait until the morning."

"That's good, my son. Now, do you want to break the news to Cynder or shall I?"

"I will."

Master Stradus woke me early the next morning. He had fixed me a light breakfast. I could barely sit still. I kept fidgeting, anxious to be on my way. I also wanted to leave before he changed his mind and forbade me to go.

When we were finished with our meal, my master said, "I have a surprise for you." He went into his room and came back with something that made me gasp.

A wizard's robe.

He handed it to me. I gently took it, careful that I might wake up and this would be a dream. I stroked the ancient fabric in my hands. The magic contained in the robe responded to my touch. A tingling sensation spread from my hands through my entire body, immersing itself in me like a greeting. I gasped in amazement, letting it say hello and not fighting it.

I was shocked that Master Stradus would give me such a rare and valuable thing. While wizards' robes might look like other robes, they were far more. They weren't simple fabric. A lot of care, work, and magic were put into them.

There were stories of wizards' robes protecting their owners, and those that couldn't be worn by anyone but the wizard. Even with their owner dead, ordinary people couldn't put on the robes. Some even believed they had a will of their own and were alive. I didn't know what to believe. I was just amazed and thankful to be given this immense gift.

"Thank you, Master," I said in a hushed tone. "But I thought a person only received a wizard's robe when their training was complete?"

"That's true," Master Stradus said. "But I thought you might need it. It once belonged to a good friend of mine. Do the robe justice."

"I will."

"Go ahead. Put it on."

I pulled the loose robe over my head. The power it contained intertwined itself with my inner fire until it accepted me and we became one.

"I have something else for you," Master Stradus said.

"You do?" I put a hand to my mouth. He had already given me so much.

Master Stradus handed me an ancient leather-bound book, small enough to fit in a pocket, but surprisingly heavy for its size. I flipped through the pages. It contained spells, incantations, and rituals. Entries were written both in the common tongue and Caleea. Diagrams and pictures were drawn in for the more complex spells. Lists of ingredients were given. There was a huge amount of information for a book so small. I had never seen some of this magic before, and some it was very powerful.

"I was given that book a long time ago. My former teacher thought it would be of great help, and it was. I no longer need it. I'm giving it to you for the same reason she gave it to me."

I held back tears, touched that he would allow me to go, and give me so much. "Thank you, Master."

"You're welcome, my son. Come, let's get you packed."

We went to my room. I took my dagger, purse, bedroll, and goatskin pouch. I left my blankets because I knew I wouldn't need any as long as I had my snug wizard's robe. I also left my backpack. My purse could hold enough supplies and I still had money from the princess. I would buy the extra supplies I needed, along with some new clothes, when I got to a village.

Next, we headed to the garden. Master Stradus gave me several small potions in magically reinforced glass that he thought might also come in handy. They were basic growth, revitalization, stabilization, and entrapping potions. We filled up the rest of my purse with food, and my goatskin pouch with water. My heart dropped into my stomach as we made our way to the exit and the waiting cold.

My eyes welled up as memories of laughter, frustration, joy, hardship, and love flooded my mind. Cynder came out to join us, and the fires in the caves danced sadly as if to say goodbye.

"Are you sure you don't want to wait until we've finished your training?" Master Stradus asked.

"If I don't go now, I may never go."

"And that would be a travesty," Cynder said. "I agree. You should go now."

"Anything to get away from you."

Master Stradus laughed.

Cynder snorted smoke.

"Cynder will see you off the mountain so you don't have to needlessly tire yourself."

I breathed a sigh of relief. I didn't know which was harder—climbing up the mountain or climbing down it.

"Hellsfire, I want you to be very careful while you're out there."

"I will, Master."

"That's not what I mean. Use your power sparingly. Don't flaunt your magic and don't tell people you're a wizard-in-training if you can help it. The world might have changed since I was last in it, but there might also still be people upset over the War of the Wizards."

I nodded.

Master Stradus smiled and laid his hand on my shoulder. "Hellsfire, take care of yourself and remember your training. This is just the beginning of the long journey the gods have laid out for you. Come back if you need anything."

"I will, Master. Thank you for what you've done for me. I really appreciate it."

"You've made an old man proud." Master Stradus embraced me. "I'm going to miss you, my boy."

"Me too."

"Well, I'm not going to miss you," Cynder said. He broke our embrace by craning his long neck between Master Stradus and me. "You've been a constant pain in my tail ever since you got here."

"You're still not going to let me forget that bump on the head I gave you, are you?"

"Dragons never forget, little one."

"That's because you're too stupid to forget."

"You little runt!" Cynder's tail slammed against the ground. I readied myself for what was going to come next.

"Enough!" Master Stradus said. "I'm not going to miss you two bickering. Cynder, take Hellsfire down the mountain."

"I don't see why *I* have to take him down," Cynder said, glaring at me with his red eyes. "He got up here fine by himself. Why can't he get down by himself? It's not that far of a jump. I can give him a push if you like." He flicked his claw.

"Cynder."

"All right, I was only joking. Come on, I haven't got all day." Cynder lowered himself, and I climbed onto his scaly back. "Sure, have the dragon do all the work. I don't see why humans can't learn to build flying machines. You already have a catapult. You'd think you could take it one step further. Some kind of winged contraption."

I looked at my mentor one last time. "Goodbye, Master. I know we'll meet again one day—and thank you. For everything." I waved as Cynder took off with a sweep of his giant wings.

"Remember your training, my boy," Master Stradus called through the rough wind. "Don't forget, I'll be here if you need anything. Take care of yourself!"

I had no doubt that I would see him again. The question was, would I survive that dreadful feeling in my bones?

Cynder flew me down the mountain in no time, soaring through the winter weather like an arrow in flight. He came to an abrupt stop. The backlash of wind almost unseated me. I yanked back hard on his neck scale, nearly peeling it off. He grunted, and I laughed. That's what he got for trying to send me flying off of him. I wasn't falling for that trick again. I hopped off his bumpy back onto the dirt-covered ground.

"Thank you, my dear friend," I said.

"Friend? An illustrious, noble dragon a friend to a simple human? Ha!" Cynder rolled his eyes, pointed his snout in the air, and blew smoke.

"Yes, friend. It's been a pleasure getting to know you. Thank you for teaching me the ways of the dragon and for helping me with my magic." I bowed to him.

"You should be so lucky, little Hellsfire. But I must say it was fun getting to know a human who is young and bold, rather than one who is tired and old." Cynder and I laughed at his joke, glad Master Stradus wasn't around to hear it. "It has been fun trading quips with you, even though you were outmatched by a far superior being."

I grinned at him. "Yeah, right."

"Try and take care of yourself. I know how fragile you humans are. Don't bite off more than you can chew. I'd hate for you to die before our next fight. Next time we meet, it will be I who will get the best of you, oh Chosen One."

"I'm sure our paths will cross again, you pretentious, arrogant smokestack."

"Bye." Cynder blew a puff of smoke in my face, causing me to choke and gag. I hated when he did that. I summoned a gust of wind to dissipate the smoke. He raised his mighty wings and flew back up towards the cave before I could get my revenge on him. He soared through the harsh, freezing weather as if it were nothing to him.

For the second time in my life, I realized I was alone and about to set out into a world I knew little about. Images of my vision burst into my mind. I dropped to one knee from the overwhelming force. The pain eased up and passed. I stood up and peered off in each direction, trying to figure out which way to go and praying I was not too late.

Then I remembered the shooting star.

CHAPTER 10

AFTER A COUPLE of days of traveling in the direction of the shooting star, my journey brought me into the middle of Sharald's Forest.

It was strange to be in a forest again. It had been close to three years since I'd last been among the trees, but my body hadn't forgotten how much I loved having moist dirt under my feet and the smell of pine in my nose. The air wasn't stale, as it was in the caves. It was alive and moved of its own will, constantly changing its currents.

I made camp, and a chorus of crickets surrounded me. A family of spiny hedgehogs scurried past me, just out of reach of the light of my campfire. An owl's big eyes settled on me before she turned her attention to more manageable prey.

After settling in and eating, I went to sleep. In the middle of the night, a loud rustling noise woke me. It sounded like a large animal, maybe even a boar. The hairs rose on the back of my neck. It was close. The swaying of the forest ceased, and a tense silence surrounded me. I knew that silence could mean only one thing—danger.

I was too used to the safety of the caves, and so I was caught completely off guard. A strong, sturdy net was thrown over me. I grabbed onto the net and grasped the red mana inside of me. My hand glowed crimson, causing the net to burst into flame and incinerate. I got up and pulled my hood back. Three small, shadowy figures moved towards me with blinding speed. I readied a spell just as I caught glimpse of a sword's blade glistening in the moonlight.

"Wait!" one of them yelled. "He's not one of them."

"Who are you?" I asked, squinting my eyes and keeping my guard up.

One by one, the trio came into the thin moonlight, and my eyes adjusted to see them. I gasped, taken aback.

They were elves.

Elves were legendary. I had seen one or two in my life, from a distance. I'd never met any until now.

"We're from Sharald," one of them said, his voice light and polite. His light green skin and dark green tunic blended in with our surroundings. It was no wonder I hadn't seen them before they netted me. "My name is Prastian of Meridian." Prastian lowered his longbow and bowed his head slightly. "Sorry for the misunderstanding. The big one is my trusty companion Behast of Olyn, and the little one is my younger brother, Demay."

"I'm Hellsfire." I bowed in return, but never took my eyes off the muscular Behast.

"Unusual name for a human," Behast said.

I opened my mouth to say the same, but decided not to when I saw his hand tighten on his sword hilt.

Behast glowered at me.

Prastian stepped in front of him. "He was honored enough to be raised by dwarves, so he's different from the rest of us. What are you doing out here at this time of night, Hellsfire? Judging from the way you look and the fact that you're away from the main roads, you aren't a bandit or part of a caravan. You don't look like a simple traveler."

"I was sleeping."

"I could see that. Where are you going?"

I glanced up at the direction I had seen the star fall and shrugged. I didn't want to tell him that I was on my way to Alexandria so I said, "I'm not sure."

"You realize you're in elf territory," Prastian said.

I nodded.

"While we don't mind your kind being here, we want to be sure there's not any trouble."

"Are you saying I'm going to do something?"

"No," Behast said, eying me. "You're the least of our problems. Vile Wasteland creatures are about."

"Is that why you ambushed me? You thought I was a creature of some sort?" I felt a deep foreboding at his words. The Wastelands were far from here, and the army of Alexandria had always stopped them from getting this deep into Northern Shala. Unless my vision was true and Alexandria had already fallen.

I stared past the elves into the forest, willing myself to see all the way to Alexandria. I saw nothing, of course, but clenched my fists in frustration until I left marks in my palms. Maybe I was too slow and had failed to leave in time. If anything had happened to her...

"What are you hunting?" I asked.

"Ogres," Demay said.

"What are ogres doing here?"

"We're not sure," Prastian said, "but we've been finding more and more creatures from the Wastelands in our forests." He grasped his bow even tighter. "Unsuspecting people have been dying. Animals have been slaughtered. We've sent out hunting parties and have been searching for days, trying to find them. Yet, we've found nothing."

The elf's voice was quiet, but the rage was evident in his words. It must have been hard to contain his frustration at the thought of his people dying. I was worried too. Not for the elves or what was happening in Sharald's Forest, but for what might be happening in Alexandria. Did Alexandria still stand? Was the princess slain?

"What about Alexandria?" I asked. "Shouldn't the Guardsmen of Alexandria be stopping them?"

The trio of elves shared a look and didn't say anything. I pressed them. "Does Alexandria still stand?"

"We haven't time for this," Prastian said. "We must leave and get back on the trail."

"Quiet!" Behast said. His long ears swayed back and forth. "We're not alone."

Before we could respond, two gigantic ogres crashed through the trees. One hit Demay with his rock-sized fist and sent him soaring through the air until he crashed hard into a tree. Before the ogre could finish Demay, Prastian drew his bow and loosed arrows into the ogre's arms, enraging him. The ogre charged Prastian.

The other ogre went after Behast. The elf drew his sword and sliced the ogre's long, scarred arms when they came into range. Instead of rushing at Behast, the ogre ripped up a small tree by the roots and used that as his club. Despite the ogre's monstrous strength, Behast held his own.

Prastian had more trouble. While he had managed to strike the ogre with two arrows, he couldn't get enough room or time to draw his bow again. He tried to keep the ogre's attention from his unconscious brother. He drew his short sword, using it much like a snake, with quick cuts and slashes. That did little to harm the ogre—just enraged him further. Luckily, Prastian's speed and quickness kept him out of the ogre's reach.

I ran to help Prastian, summoning mana along the way. Master Stradus had taught me offensive spells, but I had no idea what to use, or where to begin. I had only used my magic in this way in practice. Real combat was completely different, and I couldn't think straight. I readied my fire, thinking I was out of the ogre's reach.

I was wrong.

The ogre's long arms swung hard and fast. His monstrous fist knocked me against a tree. I grunted from the pain in my back. Leaves rained all around me. I scrambled up and began a spell.

Before I could say the incantation, the ogre grabbed me by the throat. He lifted me high into the air, looking at me with angry eyes. His monstrous hands closed around my throat. Spit flew from my mouth. I fought the urge to attack his arm, and instead stretched my arm towards his face, summoning red mana. His hands crushed my throat; death loomed in his eyes. Before that could come to pass, a bright crimson fireball formed in my hand. It flew into the ogre's rotten mouth and back through his head. Brains and blood splattered the trees.

His grip loosened, and I fell to the ground. The ogre's oversized body swayed and tumbled down, crashing next to me. I put my hand around my throat and gasped. The cool night air soothed my sore throat. I stared at the ogre's half-head, with his glazed, stony eyes, taking in what I had done. It was the first time I had consciously used my magic to harm something. Then reaction set in, and my hand started shaking. I felt like I might faint.

Behast had finished off his ogre, and came over to me. "You fought well," he said. I clenched my hand to stop it from shaking. He stretched his ogre-blood-stained hand towards me. The black blood stuck to him like honey. I nodded, taking his hand, and he pulled me to my feet. I put my hand to my side and stretched to see if my body worked properly. Except for a few bumps and bruises, I was fine. We walked over to where Demay lay.

"Fight it, little brother," Prastian said, leaning over him and checking his body with a gentle touch. "Please, wake up." Demay was in far worse shape than any of us. Pale green blood trickled from his mouth, and his breathing was erratic. He looked as if he might have injured his spine when he hit the tree.

"How bad is it?" Behast asked.

"Bad." Prastian said. "I think it's internal. I need some herbs or a good healer, but it's too far for either of those right now. I'm afraid we won't make it to Sharald in time."

"Let me try," I said. I reached into my purse and pulled out one of the stabilizing potions. "Give him this."

Prastian didn't hesitate. He poured the translucent liquid into Demay's mouth, and Prastian leaned over until he heard Demay's steady, rhythmic breathing. "Thank you. How long until he's better?"

"I'm not sure. It's designed to keep the person alive until proper help can be found." I almost offered to try to heal Demay, until I thought about all the times I had practiced using white mana. It was very elusive and difficult to use, and if I messed up, things could get worse. Plus, I wasn't supposed to tell anyone I could perform magic.

"I would never be able to forgive myself if something happened to him." Prastian started to pick up his brother.

"Let me," Behast said. "I'm much stronger than you, and can make the journey back to Sharald without any loss of speed."

"Thank you, my friend. Hellsfire, if you don't have important matters to attend to, you should come with us to Sharald."

I thought about his offer. I had always wanted to see Sharald. While it lay to the north, in the general direction I headed, it would still be a couple of days out of my way. I needed to reach Alexandria and see if the princess was all right. The elves' stories of the Wasteland creatures filtering into Northern Shala had made me even more worried about her. I was going to tell him no, but then I realized that the thought of going to Sharald gave me no headaches or nosebleeds. While traveling, I had occasionally had thoughts of going to see my mother, but every time I did, the pain struck me. There was no pain now.

I decided to trust my instincts and go to Sharald. Since the elves were Alexandria's closest neighbors, they would have more information about what was going on. If Alexandria had fallen, they would know.

"I'll go," I said.

"Good," Prastian said. "Then let's leave."

We ventured deeper into the forest. Prastian led the way, Behast followed, and I trailed. The two moved fast and with ease, even in the dark. It was hard to keep up with them. I made enough noise to wake the whole forest, while they barely made a whisper.

Because of the ogres, and what the elves had said about seeing other Wasteland creatures, my eyes constantly darted around, alert for an attack. The elves did the same thing, but with their ears. I carried mana with me, hovering near the surface, ready to be released.

We reached Sharald as the sun rose and the early morning mist faded.

Some said the elves were birthed from the forest. I almost believed it when I saw them. They startled me, appearing without warning out of the oak and maple trees surrounding the city. They eyed me warily as they talked to Prastian in the elf tongue. I had a feeling there were more guards in the trees, but try as I might, I couldn't see them. Their green skin blended in perfectly with the leaves. They also wore brown tunics to match the bark of the thick trunks and branches. I lowered my guard only when Prastian took leave of the sentry posts and guards and we were let into the city of Sharald.

I had heard stories of Sharald when I was younger, but seeing it was something else. The huge city was literally at one with the forest. The elves built most of their homes and some shops in the trees. The foliage decorated and covered the airy buildings. Some were even built in the trunks of the larger trees. Long wooden bridges connected the buildings. They looked thin and insubstantial, but the elves seemed at home on the swaying structures as they went about their daily duties, carrying bundles and supplies across them with ease. Elf children ran across the bridges as if they were on the ground, or simply swung from branch to branch.

The elves didn't clear the ground like most people do. There were paths wide enough for carts and horses, but most of the city was covered with trees, scrub, and bushes. I had to push aside some stray branches that stuck out into the road.

As we made our way towards the center of the city, people smiled and waved at my elven companions. Their bright faces sagged and dropped when they saw the injured Demay. When they noticed me, the older elves whispered amongst themselves. I found that strange, because humans go regularly into Sharald for business and sightseeing. Unlike some other races, they didn't close their borders to outsiders. I put my hood up, trying to hide my face from the elves' scrutiny, though their looks weren't ones of malice or anger. I couldn't tell what it was, but they wouldn't stop looking or whispering.

Some of the elves I saw looked exhausted, wearing bandages or slings. Others were at work making arrows, and we passed an open space where a group practiced with their bows, faces intense as they hit their targets.

The children ran freely through the city, playing with other children or with animals. There were many animals, and none of them had restraints. Deer, rabbits, and raccoons moved among the elves, unafraid. They even held still while the children fed or petted them, though most of them shied away when I came near. I knew that elves never harmed an animal unless they had to, but I hadn't realized they lived in such harmony with the forest creatures. I had never seen such a thing.

We finally reached the center of the city, where the king's palace lay. The aura of the ancient building nearly forced me to my knees. Green mana radiated from it. The magic was ancient and very powerful, thumping with every breath I took. It felt like the heart of the forest. I relaxed, trying not to fight it. I let the magic flow around me so I wouldn't be crushed by it. When I did that, I saw what normal people did.

The castle wasn't in the trees like most of the other structures, but it was part of them. Hardened vines and trunks made up a gigantic dome. There wasn't a hint of decay or withering anywhere. The combination of different plants was far more wondrous than I could have imagined. They composed a beautiful chorus, producing a harmony so beautiful my heart understood it even while my head didn't.

I shook off the wonderment and followed Prastian and Behast inside.

People came and carried Demay away. Others led us down a long corridor and into the audience chamber. The inside of the dome was just as strange as I'd thought it would be. The vines had hardened so much that they were like stone. There were no insects or holes in the walls. The magic was ingrained in the structure, keeping everything perfectly preserved.

In the audience chamber, the first thing that caught my eye, besides the emerald throne, were the paintings. Dozens of them surrounded us.

I walked around, taking them in. It was like walking through time. Most of the portraits showed the elven family tree, starting with Sharald. The family tree wasn't long, because elves live longer than humans and don't have as many children. I stopped at one of the last paintings, amazed. It was a portrait of a young elf and what appeared to be a young Master Stradus. He had the same sky-colored robes and wise smile, but I couldn't tell if it was him. He looked so youthful and was without his staff.

With all my gawking and the fact that I was dead tired from being up all night, I didn't notice the ruler of the elves come in. Prastian cleared his throat, and I looked up to see an elf of great stature with long, dark green robes, sitting on the emerald throne. His wrinkly, pale green skin, along with the way his ears drooped down, betrayed his years. I'd noticed that the younger elves' ears pointed up. The older they got, the lower their ears became, as if to signal their return to the earth. The elf king smiled at me.

"Hello, Your Majesty," Prastian said, and knelt. Behast and I followed suit.

"I'm glad to see you've returned, dear cousin," the king said. "I was worried what would become of you. Don't fear; my best healers are working on Demay as we speak. I wouldn't let anything happen to family." His wise, light green eyes turned on me. "I see you've brought a guest."

"Forgive me, Majesty. This is Hellsfire. He helped us defeat the ogres that troubled the area. Hellsfire, this is our king, Sharald."

"Majesty," I said. My eyes darted from him to the paintings as I tried to suppress my confusion. I had read of the great Sharald, but he had died many years ago, not too long after he established the city. This elf, while having similar features, didn't look like the one in the portrait.

King Sharald laughed. "Please, Hellsfire, call me Sharald. Everyone does. I am actually Sharald the Fourth, descendant of the great Sharald. Rest easy. I saw the look of surprise on your face. I must say I take great pleasure when people think I'm him."

I smiled. "As you wish, Your Majesty. I mean Sharald."

"Good. I know you must be tired, but let's have breakfast. After you three clean up, come to the dining hall. I can tell by the looks of you, you have much to tell."

Guards escorted me to another room where I cleaned myself up. They offered me a new tunic and breeches. I was thankful, glad to have some clean clothes that fit, even if I wore them under my wizard's robes. When I was ready, they led me to the dining room. Flowers decorated a long oak table. An elf led me to the head of the table where the others waited for me.

Sharald motioned for me to seat myself, then said to the servants, "Please bring us our food. We're all famished."

Breakfast consisted of fruits, nuts, vegetables, grains, and cheese. There wasn't a single piece of meat. The elves thought it wrong to kill animals unless it was absolutely necessary. That suited me fine, since wizards didn't eat meat either.

After breakfast, Prastian told the story of what had happened to him. His words danced on air while his tongue provided the music. His yarn-spinning refreshed me. I didn't even yawn, despite how tired my body was.

"This is very alarming," Sharald said. "Very alarming indeed." He sat in silence while he pondered the elves' story. His emerald eyes rested on Prastian. "Things are getting worse. We're having to send out more hunting parties, and people are dying."

Prastian nodded.

"Yet the gods have given us hope and a sign." King Sharald turned his fading green eyes on me.

"Sire?" Prastian said.

"I'm delighted to have the services of a wizard among us again." Sharald's voice was kind and inviting, if not accurate. "It's been ages since I've last seen a wizard. Not since I was a young boy and my father sat on the throne. Despite all that's happened, this is a great day indeed."

"That's how you were able to cast aside our net and defeat the ogre," Behast said. "Magic."

My two companions stared, boring holes through me.

"I have never seen or met a wizard before," Prastian said.

I opened my mouth to counter his statement and say I wasn't a wizard yet. Master Stradus's words and their expressions told me not to. I remained quiet, not offering any answer and praying that King Sharald wouldn't push me further on the matter. If he did, I'd have to tell them.

After a few awkward moments, Behast said, "The attacks are getting worse. We need to do something."

"I know," Sharald said, frowning. "We need to go and find out what has happened to Alexandria and to the earlier expedition."

My ears pricked up at this. I wanted the conversation to go this way, but didn't know how to get it there. King Sharald might question why I wanted to know about Alexandria, and why I, an outsider, should be a part of their plans. Thankfully, Sharald seemed willing to let the conversation continue.

"Perhaps we can send another group, cousin," Prastian said. "And I can lead that group?"

"You called me cousin," Sharald said. He smiled. Prastian's cheeks turned a dark green. "It has been a while since I heard that." Sharald laughed. "I take it you must really want to go." He took a heavy breath. "I'm going to miss hearing that more often before I return to the earth. You may go to Alexandria, Prastian."

"Thank you, Sire."

"While I trust your expertise, something up there's amiss. You're going to need a little more help. Maybe help of a wizardly kind." Sharald put up a finger and smiled. "Hellsfire, I already owe you for what you've done, but I have one more favor to ask of you. Could you please accompany my elves to the kingdom of Alexandria?"

My eyes widened. I was already going to Alexandria, but going by myself to check on things and being a part of an envoy were far different. Something was clearly wrong in Alexandria, and as yet I had no idea what it was. While the monsters were getting by Alexandria's defenses, the city hadn't fallen. Otherwise, there would have been refugees in Sharald, and I hadn't seen any. If I went alone, I could move freely. As part of Sharald's envoy, there would be a lot more politics to deal with. Whatever I did, for good or ill, would reflect on King Sharald. On the other hand, as a royal envoy, I would have a better chance of getting an audience with the princess. If she remembered me, I was sure she would see me.

I felt I should heed Master Stradus's words. It was bad enough the elves knew of my abilities, but I didn't want those in Alexandria to know. Even if I wasn't a wizard yet, my power could sway things and make them a lot worse. I didn't want to be like Renak during the War of the Wizards, when he defied the Council and took matters into his own hands, thus starting the war that divided the land. Lastly, the elves in Sharald were friendly to wizards. The people in Alexandria might not be.

"I'll…have to think about it, Your Majesty," I said. "If that's all right."

"Of course." Sharald was obviously disappointed, but his fading emerald eyes twinkled. I knew he wouldn't let it go.

Sharald dropped the discussion of sending a team to Alexandria and changed the subject to more personal matters. He dismissed me and said I was free to roam the city if I liked. I did want to explore Sharald, but I also felt like being alone. I needed to decide whether or not to go with the elves to Alexandria.

I took leave from the others and went outside to get some fresh air. I stood in a beautiful garden. Hedges cut in the shapes of animals surrounded me. There were large ones, like elk and horses, along with smaller sculptures of grasshoppers and pigs. In the middle of them all was a small pond. I stood at the edge of it, watching the turtles, fish, and frogs. Waterfowl dove beneath the water, gulping down food. The place reminded me of Peaceful Pond, and more importantly, of home. My heart ached to return there. Fresh footsteps approached me from behind.

"May I speak with you?" King Sharald asked.

I turned around and bowed. "Of course, Your Majesty."

"Sharald, Hellsfire. Please call me that."

"Forgive me Si—Sharald."

"It's all right. I need your help, Hellsfire."

"I'm flattered, but I haven't decided anything yet.

"Please, you must listen to me," Sharald said, grasping my shoulder with his soft hand. He looked up at me, green eyes pleading, while he waited for a response.

I nodded.

"I may look healthy to a human's eyes, yet I'm not. I'm getting on in years, though I do my best to look well in front of my people. Although some suspect the truth, they don't acknowledge it. I'm sorry to say I have no natural successor. I'm barren and the line of Sharald ends with me. Prastian is to succeed me. He's skilled at dealing with those both in and outside this forest, he's excellent with words, and he's good in combat. The problem is, he's a bit too adventurous. Instead of remaining here, he prefers to travel, to better understand people. He may get himself killed before he is able to become king. I need to find out what happened in Alexandria, so I'm going to have to send my best elves. But if anything should happen to them…." Sharald rubbed his hand across his wrinkled ear and stared at me, reading my face. "I can see you do not understand, Hellsfire. Let me tell you what's been happening lately.

"I don't know if you are aware, but things have slowly been getting out of hand here in the north. The creatures of the Wastelands have been sighted more and more often. We were used to occasionally getting a few, though even that was a rarity. Yet for the past six months, we've had to send regular patrols to kill the creatures. The thought did cross our minds that Alexandria had been taken over, though word of that would surely have reached us, and the creatures would come in greater numbers. Nevertheless, something is terribly wrong up there. It's as if creatures are regularly walking by Alexandria's defenses. I *need* to find out what is happening, and your services would be greatly appreciated. Like in days past, we need a wizard."

That was the problem. Master Stradus had taught me a lot about being a wizard. He taught me how to perform spells, how to use my powers correctly, how to access and use mana. But what he didn't teach me, what he didn't have time for and what I might have to learn from experience, was how to be responsible. How was I to use my powers with non-magical people, but not overdo it or have them rely on me?

"This isn't just for me or my people, it's for all Northern Shala," King Sharald said.

I raised an eyebrow. "How so?"

"The things that come from the Wastelands aren't just a threat to us, Hellsfire, they're a threat to everyone. Look at it this way. Why did Shala beat Renak? Renak had the better wizards, more resources, the element of surprise, was more aggressive, and was better organized." Sharald swept his hands across the pond. "But it was Shala who came out on top. Shala won because he was able to pull together the different peoples of the land. If he had not, we all would have lost. I see the same thing happening now.

"We are all different peoples, but unlike then, there's no one to lead us. If the creatures get through and Alexandria falls, we will all fall—one by one. Hardly anyone in the land will be safe. Our first defense is and always has been Alexandria. That's the reason why it was built in the first place, and that's why it must always stand." His voice grew louder and stronger. "We must find out what's going on there."

I cringed at the thought of my homeland being overrun by the foul creatures and my mother and friends dying because of that. "Even Sedah will fall?" He stared at me, confused. "It's my hometown, Your Majesty."

Sharald nodded. "Sedah will most assuredly fall. It's just a small agricultural village. It holds no significant importance, but the creatures will destroy all in their way. That's just the way they are—the way they have always been. Will you please help me and, in turn, save those you love?"

I took my time before making a decision. Sharald was kind and didn't interrupt me or stare at me while I thought. He looked out over the pond and animals just like I did, but my mind no longer paid attention to what I saw. My training was incomplete, and I could still make things worse with my power. I could also make them better and help people *if* I made the right choices.

The stories I had learned growing up played through my head, and starring in them was Shala. He didn't want to go to war with Renak, but soon realized he had no choice. Shala did it because Renak had to be stopped. There was no one else to challenge Renak, and a lot more people would have died if he hadn't come forward to do what he could.

I wasn't Shala. I wasn't a hero. The elves needed my help, and I needed theirs. It would be better if we worked together.

"I'll help you," I said.

"That's exactly what I wanted to hear." His old ears twitched in delight.

"But before I help you, Your Majesty, there's something you should know."

"I'm all ears."

I couldn't help but break my serious expression and smile at that. "I'm not a wizard yet. I haven't completed my training."

I held my breath and stared at him, waiting to see what his reaction would be. The great elf glanced away and looked at the pond. His eyes followed a turtle as it finished its basking and dived back into the water.

"I can see why you don't want to go," Sharald said, keeping his eyes on the water. "Thank you for telling me." He turned his attention back to me and smiled. "None of that matters now. You've done well in helping the others. I still want you to go with them."

"Me too." I surprised myself by saying that, because it was true.

"Good. Even though you might not be a wizard yet, your expertise will come in handy."

I nodded. I could only hope he was right.

"Now that that business is over, you must help us prepare," Sharald said.

"Prepare for what?"

Sharald's smile was as wide as the horizon. "A celebration."

I yawned and put a hand to my mouth. "Forgive me, Your Majesty, but I don't understand."

"Tomorrow, we will celebrate. According to my healers, Demay should be well by then."

"Are you sure we should have a party? Shouldn't we get ready in case Alexandria is in serious trouble?"

"We're not at war, Hellsfire. Not yet, anyway. We're as ready as we can be until we find out what's happening up there." Sharald took a deep breath and his body seemed to melt. "I'm about to send my heir and an apprenticed wizard into a possibly dangerous situation, my younger cousin almost died last night, and I, myself, am dying. So yes, a celebration is exactly what we need. When I was younger, someone once told me to enjoy life because you never know what tomorrow may bring. That's what we're going to do. It's an order." Sharald smiled.

I smiled back at him. "As you wish, Your Majesty."

"Excellent. Come, I will get you a room so you can rest. No one deserves it more."

"Thank you, Your Majesty."

We left the serenity of his garden, and I finally got some sleep. I spent the next day setting up for the party. Demay was even helping, although he would wince and complain whenever we had to do hard work. We lined each home with flowers and made flower necklaces, hanging them around everyone's neck.

I enjoyed the flower necklace. It had a festive feel to it, smelled good, and stood out from my dark robe. The elves also had a leaf in each ear.

That night, there was plenty of dancing. The exotic, fast-paced music kept me moving. Even though I couldn't keep up with the elves and their style of dancing, I still had a lot of fun. I danced with all the pretty young elves who'd come up to me. But elves weren't the only ones there. All travelers and traders were invited to stay and enjoy the festivities.

A great bonfire was erected, stretching into the sky. It moved and swayed with me, though I wasn't using any magic. In the midst of everything, the mana of earth radiated from the elves. It had the power of an earthquake, far more powerful than even their domed castle, and yet it felt gentle. It was no wonder the elves were close to the land and were good harvesters. I hadn't been able to sense the magic from Prastian and the others before. It was too small, and worked without them knowing it. But with so many elves together, I felt it. People always said the trees talked to the elves. It was true. I heard their whispers, although I couldn't understand what they were saying.

During the celebration, Sharald told me the team to Alexandria would consist of Prastian, Behast, Demay, and myself. Sharald thought it best he should keep the group together, since we had already proven we worked well together. He had tried to keep Demay out of it, but Demay wouldn't take no for an answer.

Time flew by. I think I drank a little too much, as I passed out somewhere on the ground. At dawn, someone's foot nudged me. He told me where the others were. I wiped the drool and dirt off my face and scurried to find them. My head pounded, but it had been worth it.

When I found my newly acquired friends, they had all the provisions and horses ready. They smiled at me as if I had made an ass of myself the previous night, but I shrugged it off. I couldn't remember much from my drunken haze, nor did it matter. Sharald came to see us off and wished us luck.

We needed all the luck we could get. There was something wrong with Alexandria, and whatever we found wasn't going to be good.

CHAPTER 11

BETWEEN THE URGENCY of King Sharald's mission and my worry over Princess Krystal, we pushed our horses on the way to Alexandria. What normally would have been a six-day trip, we made in four. We arrived at the Guardian City at mid-afternoon on the fourth day.

I breathed a little easier when we neared the outer walls that surrounded the city. I had been worried that Alexandria might have fallen and would be overrun with Wasteland creatures. That clearly wasn't the case. What did concern us, though, was the sparseness of the guards walking the walls, and the fact that we had met no patrols on our way to the city, which Prastian said was unusual. Had the king pulled guards from the south wall because of the increased attacks from the Wasteland creatures to the north? There was no way to know until we got inside and spoke with Prastian's contacts.

In the meantime, I gawked at Alexandria like the farm boy that I was. It was huge—far larger than Sharald—and built of wood and stone. The city spread uphill from the south wall, up to the towering castle that rose at the far north side of the city. From that height, the guards could get a magnificent dragon's-eye view of the city, the Daleth Mountain Range, and the Wastelands of Renak. It was from those towers that the forces of Alexandria had kept watch and guarded Northern Shala since the War of the Wizards, when Renak's evil creatures had been driven into the Wastelands. The castle reminded me of the White Mountain—without the freezing weather and strenuous climb. Up close, it was both magnificent and intimidating. Unlike King Sharald's castle, I sensed no magic emanating from it. Knowing that men had made it with their own hands, with no magical help, only enhanced its beauty. I hoped I would get the chance to explore its halls and see the views from its parapets.

The south gate of the city was open, manned with two guards. That seemed like a small number, when so many monsters appeared to be wandering the countryside. We dismounted and led our horses through, expecting to be questioned, but the guards gave us no more than a cursory inspection. I saw Prastian and Behast glance at each other, eyebrows raised, ears twitching. Apparently, it seemed strange to them too. None of us said anything, but I felt uneasy. Something was wrong here.

We passed through a short stone tunnel that ran under the city wall, and found ourselves in a crowded marketplace. I had always heard that Alexandria was a prosperous, peaceful city, but many of the stalls and shops were closed and boarded up. As we walked, I noticed that most of the crowds were gathered around the ale shops and bawdy houses, or in tight, sullen-looking knots. The shops that were open had men standing outside with clubs or daggers, as if they expected to be besieged by thieves, and few people were buying. We passed by a butcher shop where a thin, hollow-eyed woman with two children clinging to her skirts pleaded with the proprietor. "No credit!" he snapped at her. "Coin only."

I moved closer to Prastian. "Is it always like this?" I murmured. He shook his head, a frown growing between his eyebrows. Behast walked with his hand on his sword hilt. Even Demay's high spirits seemed dampened.

We found stabling for our horses, wanting to keep them near the gate in case we had to leave quickly. Prastian paid the hostler well to keep our mounts safe, though I began to suspect we'd be lucky to find them still here when we returned.

We were in a poorer district of the city, and there were beggars on nearly every street corner. Scrawny women and children tore at my heart. I moved to loosen my purse strings.

"Don't," Behast said, placing his hand on my arm.

"What do you mean, don't?" I asked. "They need our help." My eyes fell on a mother who cradled her crying baby. She tried to quiet him, but failed. The baby was so gaunt, it might not live past tomorrow. Tears welled up in my eyes. My mother and I were poor, but we always had food on the table. I couldn't believe King Furlong and Krystal would let things get as bad as this. It wasn't as though the city was besieged; clearly supplies could go in and out, just as we had. My inner fire rose, aching to be released. I didn't know what made me angrier: Behast for telling me not to help, or my fear that the darkness from my dream had already crushed the princess, and Alexandria was falling apart.

"We don't have time for this," Behast said.

"He's right," Prastian said. "Something's wrong here, and we've got to find out what it is and what happened to the previous team that was sent here."

"I was just trying to—"

"I know what you were trying to do, Hellsfire. In normal times, I would applaud you for it and even be as charitable as you. We haven't that luxury now. In all my visits to Alexandria, I've never seen conditions this bad. King Furlong wouldn't allow it. We can help the most by finding out what's behind this."

I let go of my purse and sighed, feeling my anger and flame subside. He was right. This wasn't why I came here, and my money would only help a few people for a short time. My vision had sent me here, but it was going to take more than magic to figure out what was wrong in Alexandria. I was suddenly very glad to have the elves with me.

"What can we do, Prastian?" I asked.

Prastian kept his eyes in front, trying not to dwell on the misery around us. "We do what King Sharald sent us to do. If the opportunity arises, we do more."

"All right. I'll follow your lead."

I glanced one last time at the mother and her child. Our eyes met, and she cried out for my help and some coin. I shook my head and said I was sorry. She spat at my feet. I bit down on my lip and turned my head away.

We continued on. As we moved up toward the castle, our surroundings became more prosperous—clearly the homes of merchants and craftsmen. The buildings were square and utilitarian, as if everything had to be useful and practical, and no one had time for frippery. Maybe that was what life was like when your whole reason for being was to fight a war that never ended. Even here, though, there were signs of decay and disrepair—crumbling mortar, sagging roofs, and peeling paint. As we passed a tavern, Prastian said softly, "I don't like this."

"Don't like what?" Demay asked.

Prastian lowered his voice even further. "The taverns shouldn't be full at this time of day. And many of these men are soldiers—you can tell by their bearing and the way they move. They should be on duty—either here in the city, or out on patrol. Why are they out of uniform, with nothing to do?"

I stared at the patrons at the courtyard tables. Most of them looked drunk, though it was still well before sunset, and they were not happy drunks. They held onto their mugs too tightly. They nursed their drinks, staring sullenly into them instead of buying more. No one joked; no one laughed.

"Should we go talk to them, Prastian?" I asked.

"Later, if we have the chance. I want to see the castle and the condition it's in, and hear what King Furlong will say."

The closer we got to the castle, the better things looked. The homes were taller, stronger, and sturdier, as most of them were made of stone. Gates surrounded a few of them. When we passed a portly man with hired guards in tow, I realized we must be in the wealthy section of Alexandria, where the nobles lived.

We walked through a large square. In the center was a statue of Alexander, the city's founder, fighting an ogre and two goblins. It was an amazing sculpture, showing the fierce determination that had characterized Alexandria and its people ever since. But the surrounding grass was yellow and overgrown, and bird droppings decorated Alexander's face, as if no one cared any longer about upholding his legacy. My stomach felt cold, and my fear for Krystal increased.

Right outside the castle gates, one more building caught my eye. It pulled at me, forcing me to stop. It was the temple of the four gods. The low rectangular building looked ancient, as ancient as the castle, but it was the only clean, sparkling thing I had seen in the entire city. The sun reflecting off its shining alabaster walls nearly blinded me. Etched into the white pillars lining the entrance were the gods' symbols, representing the different kinds of mana. While the temple was beautiful in its own right, no one but a wizard would sense the magic beating in the symbols. I took a step forward, drawn to the god Emery's symbol of fire. Someone tugged on my sleeve.

"Hellsfire," Demay said.

"What? Oh." I snapped out of my trance. Before I turned away from the temple, I saw that the brothers and sisters who served the gods were on the steps, handing out bread. I smiled, glad to see that there were still those trying to help.

When we approached the castle gates, we were challenged by the Castle Guard blocking our way.

"State your business," one of them said.

"We're here to see King Furlong," Prastian said. "Sent as a delegation from King Sharald."

The guard glowered at Prastian, and for a moment I thought they would refuse us entry. Then one of his companions stepped forward. "Prastian! It's been a long time since I last saw you."

"Hello, Jerrel. How's the family?"

Jerrel's jaw tightened for a second. "Fine, thanks for asking." His face relaxed. "I'm sorry not to give you a warmer welcome. Please enter. I'll just let the King know you're arriving." He nodded to another guard, who ran towards the castle.

"Thank you," said Prastian. He paused. "Have any other elves passed through here lately? I was hoping to meet some of my kinsmen here."

Jerrel shook his head. "Not in the castle. There haven't been any since the last time you were here."

"Thanks, Jerrel. I'm sorry I didn't bring any goodies this time around. Next time I see you, I promise I'll bring something for your children."

"Thank you, Prastian. Always a pleasure to see you." He waved us through the open gates. As we passed through the portcullis, the guards eyed me, probably wondering why I was with a bunch of elves.

"Jerrel said he hadn't seen the other elves Sharald sent," Demay said. "Think he was telling the truth?"

"Unfortunately, yes."

"Which means we have bigger problems," Behast said.

"Yes. Keep your ears sharp."

As we headed up the hill towards the inner keep, we passed by the royal stables, barracks, and workshops. Eventually, we ended up in a large courtyard. Hedges outlined paths for us to walk. In the center was a large marble fountain. On top of it stood a crouching dragon, reminiscent of Cynder. Water poured constantly from his mouth. I smiled, wondering what Cynder would think of this. Dragons were creatures of fire, not water.

We were just outside the keep. It rose into the skies like a giant, the setting sun turning its white walls a delicate pink. But there was nothing delicate about the heart of Alexandria. Its towers seemed to pierce the clouds.

Although there weren't many guards on the outer walls of the city, the castle ground crawled with them. Guards blocked our way at the entrance to the keep, challenging us. Prastian negotiated our way in, showing them a special seal given to him by King Sharald.

My heart began to beat faster. Not because of the guards who stared suspiciously at us, but because of the princess. Was she all right? Would I be able to see her? I had no doubt that Prastian would get us an audience with the king, but would Krystal be there?

"You'll have to leave your weapons here," a guard said.

"Is something wrong?" Prastian asked. "Normally, we would relinquish our weapons outside the audience chambers."

"New rules. If you want to enter the keep, you'll have to go unarmed." The guards' bodies tensed, as if they expected us to oppose them. Maybe even hoped we would.

Behast's hand moved to his sword hilt.

Prastian smiled at the guards. "As you wish." He took off his weapons, and Demay and Behast followed suit. I left my dagger where it was, under my wizard's robe. The guards didn't find it when they patted us down, and I breathed a sigh of relief. Prastian would not be pleased if I caused an incident. I was sure I wasn't the only one with a hidden weapon.

With our entrance into the castle achieved, our journey had finally ended. However, the mystery and danger had just begun.

CHAPTER 12

THE GUARD ESCORTED us down a long hallway. My feet didn't make a sound on the thick red carpet. My heart beat so loudly it drowned out Prastian's conversation with the guard. I wiped the sweat from the sides of my cheeks. I was so close to Krystal, but would I be able to see her? If I could just see if she was all right, I would breathe a little easier. I didn't know if I would get to talk to her. I hadn't told the elves that I had once met the princess, or that she owed me a debt. I wasn't sure I wanted them to use that for their own political advantage.

I shook my head. I had to remember I wasn't here just for her. King Sharald had sent me here for a purpose, and I had agreed to help his cause. Something was wrong with Alexandria. The creatures from the Wastelands should not be getting through. There were also the missing elves to think about. I flexed my fingers until my knuckles cracked. How in the Inferno was I going to handle all of this?

The hallway ended in the throne room. There was no one sitting on the great throne.

"Wait here," the guard said. "The king will be here shortly."

Behast grunted, standing with his arms crossed. "I don't like this. Something has smelled bad since we entered the city, and I don't mean the sewers."

"I'm excited!" Demay said. "I've never been here before. I wish it was under better circumstances, though." His face grew sober for a moment, but he couldn't remain serious for long. Almost immediately his eyes sparkled again, taking in the stained glass windows, the tapestries depicting famous battles, and the alabaster of warriors.

The sun set and twilight deepened, and still we waited. Demay soon grew tired of paintings, stained glass windows, and statues. He shifted and fidgeted. Behast was as still as a statue, but his fingers kept trying to grab a phantom sword. I looked at every servant and guard who walked by, hoping it was the princess. I prayed she would recognize me, smile, and say everything was all right. She never came. Prastian was the calmest one of us all. He stood still and politely greeted everyone who walked by. He struck up a couple of conversations, trying to get information, but no one wanted to stop and chat.

"You're getting nowhere, Prastian," Behast said.

Prastian smiled at the bigger elf. "That's not true. I've learned plenty of things. I've learned that everyone here is tense, and they're looking over their shoulders as if they expect to be punished at any moment. More importantly, I've learned that no one's seen the other elves, and Jerrel hasn't lied to us."

"Then where are they?" Demay asked.

"I wish I knew, little brother. I wish I knew." Prastian took a deep breath. "I can only pray to the gods the king knows and is able to help us."

"And where is the human king?" Behast asked. "Does he normally keep you waiting this long?"

Prastian shook his head. "No, and that worries me. Even if the king were detained by a crisis, one of his advisors would normally come and greet us, offering refreshments. To ignore a direct envoy from another monarch is a grave breach of protocol."

As time passed, my empty stomach rumbled from the lack of food. All of us were so tired of waiting we didn't even have the energy to speak to each other anymore. Prastian gave up trying to talk to the people that came by. We just stood there, absorbed in our own thoughts.

Finally, a guard came up to us and said, "The king will be here shortly."

Behast snorted.

Before Behast could say anything, Prastian said in a pleasant voice, "Thank you. We know how busy kings can be."

The guard nodded and left.

"Prastian," an aged, sickly voice said. "It's good to see you again." We all turned to see who it was.

The king had entered through a door near the throne. He was dressed in white velvet, jewel-encrusted robes that flowed behind him in a train. The robes made him look small, and he walked as if he were weak and frail, not like a man who controlled the most vital pass between the Wastelands and Northern Shala. The king came forward and sat upon his throne. Dark purple circles surrounded his eyes. A dark form followed him through the door and stood obscured in the shadows.

"Your Majesty," Prastian said. We all dropped to one knee.

"Prastian, my friend," King Furlong said. "It's good to see you again. It's been a long time. Too long. I've missed your company." He managed a weak but sincere smile.

"And I've missed yours, Your Majesty."

The king opened his mouth to speak, but a coughing fit seized him. He looked like he wouldn't be able to stop. Servants moved in to help, but he got hold of himself and waved them away. He rubbed a silk cloth over his forehead. One of the servants brought him a cup of water.

"Forgive the interruption." King Furlong drank the water and sighed in relief. "There's nothing like water to cure what ails you." He took a deep breath before squinting at me. "Who is the human with you, Prastian? He's strangely dressed for spring."

"He's a friend and advisor of King Sharald's, sire. Our king thought it best that he should come with us."

The king nodded. "Why are you here, Prastian?" Though he spoke to the elf, the king never took his eyes off me. Despite how sick he looked, his blue eyes were like a hawk's.

"Our king sent us here to follow up on a delegation that was sent here before us. It's been weeks, and we've heard nothing from them."

The king leaned forward. "I've not seen any elves lately."

"Are you sure, Sire? They should have been here."

"I'm positive. I've not seen any elves." The king glanced around the room, meeting the eyes of each guard and servant. They all shook their head no.

My eyes met the king's, and I believed him.

"Why did King Sharald send his elves here?" King Furlong asked.

"Your Majesty, as of late we have encountered many creatures from the Wastelands in our forests, and have heard reports and rumors throughout the land of many more, wreaking havoc. We know some creatures are bound to get through into Northern Shala, but there haven't been this many incidents since the War of the Wizards."

King Furlong inhaled, his wispy breath echoing through the great hall. An expression of worry came over his face. "I don't understand, old friend. I've not heard of such reports."

A voice spoke from the shadows behind the throne. "That's because there have been none, Sire."

The king gestured. "This is my advisor, Premier."

The man stepped out of the shadows and nodded. Premier wore robes similar to mine, though his were deep black. Not just black like mine were, or like someone's hair or eyes. It was the darkest black I had ever seen—like it was made from the night and shadows. Our eyes met, and he feigned a smile. I did the same. There was something about him that made my hackles rise.

Even though his skin was aged and hung from his body, Premier somehow didn't look old. His body was as frail as the king's, but there was an air of power about him. He looked as though he could remain alive and vital simply because he wished it.

I extended my magical senses to see if Premier was a wizard. I closed my eyes, focusing on my power and trying to make it subtle, lest he deflect it and put his guards up. My mana brushed up against his skin, trying to detect some hint of power or see if he would block my attempt. I picked up nothing. That disturbed me. Unlike the elves, there wasn't a wisp of mana there. Cynder carried red mana and Master Stradus blue. Even ordinary people carried a tiny hint of mana—their life force. Premier was like a void. If I didn't know better, I would say he wasn't even there. Or he was dead.

I wished Master Stradus was here. Premier had too great an aura of power to be an ordinary human, but if he was a wizard, he hid his mana. I would need to see him perform some kind of spell to be sure.

But wizard or no, advisor or no, vision or no, I didn't trust him.

I opened my eyes, and Premier smirked at me.

"If he's an advisor, he hasn't been doing a very good job," Behast said in a tone low enough for only us to hear. I had to strain my ears, though the elves had an easy time hearing him with their long ears.

"Premier, is there any truth to what our forest friends say?" King Furlong asked, turning an eye to his advisor.

Premier leaned in and whispered in King Furlong's ear. The elves' ears twitched, but from the look of frustration on Demay's face, they heard nothing. The king started coughing again, but I still sensed no magic. I needed to know more about Premier.

Then, from the corner of my eye, I caught movement that distracted me from Premier and King Furlong. I turned, and saw her. She took my magic and my breath away.

Her sun-streaked hair had grown, flowing down her back from the small jeweled tiara she wore. She had grown up, as I had, as her snug blue satin dress made clear. She held herself upright, with an aura of strength as her shield. I stared at her, drinking in her face and body. She seemed physically all right, thank the gods. But that didn't mean there wasn't anything wrong.

Behast elbowed me, bringing me back to the present. I remembered where I was and what we were in the middle of. My face heated up. Not only had I gotten distracted from our mission, but I'd been staring at the princess like a loutish farm boy.

The king's intense gaze fastened on me. "This young man seems to have forgotten that we were speaking. It seems the princess is much more interesting than our conversation."

Now my face burned like fire. I'd insulted the king and the princess both, with one look. Had everyone noticed me gawking? My first impulse was to glance at the princess. I stopped myself. I wasn't going to find any help from her or my friends for my mistake. She might not even remember me. We had only met once, and it was years ago. I was a nobody from a village no one had even heard of. I knelt on one knee, staring at the seams in the stone floor.

"Forgive me, Your Majesty," I said.

Prastian rescued me. "The princess's beauty is legendary, but it cannot compare to the reality," he said smoothly. "It seems that Hellsfire was temporarily overcome."

The king still did not look pleased. The princess stepped forward.

"Prastian," she said, "how good it is to see you again."

"Princess," Prastian said. "It's good to see you too." He bowed to her, and the other elves followed suit.

"I was just telling my father the other day how we've not seen any of our friends from Sharald in ages." Krystal touched me lightly on the shoulder. "You may rise, Hellsfire. It's good to see you again as well. I didn't know you were a friend of Sharald's." I smiled up at her, pleased and surprised she recognized me.

I got to my feet and bowed, much more clumsily than the elves. "Your

Highness."

The king's angry expression melted into one of confusion. "Krystal? You know this man?"

"Yes, Your Majesty. He once saved my life."

The king leaned forward. "Really? When was this?" I noticed that Premier seemed interested as well.

"Several years ago, when I traveled Northern Shala."

King Furlong nodded and sighed. "Ah. I remember." He looked at me. "So you're the one who saved my precious daughter from those bandits?"

"Yes, Your Majesty," I said.

"Then I'm in your debt." The king forced a smile. It wasn't exactly in appreciation. He still looked suspicious of me. He coughed again, gasping for air. When he recovered, he said, "I must leave you now. The guards will show you to your rooms. I will see you tonight at dinner." Premier whispered in the king's ear. "I will have to ask all of you to wait in your rooms until then."

"Father, would you like me to accompany you back to your room?"

"No, Premier is here."

Krystal turned to us. "I will show you to your rooms," the princess said. "If you'd follow me."

We were silent as we followed her from the room. It was not until we were halfway down the corridor that I ventured to speak.

"I'm glad to see you again, Your Highness," I said as I walked alongside her, flanked by guards. I recognized Ardimus, from that day in the forest.

"And I you." She smiled at me. "I see the years have been kind to you. You look well, Hellsfire."

My eyes devoured her. She had grown taller and her body's curves had deepened. "And so do you, Your Highness." Ardimus flicked me a quick warning look. "I mean, you look better than when I last saw you. I mean—"

"I know what you mean, and I thank you." Krystal's lips curled in a little smile. "I'm glad to see you came to Alexandria. I just wish it was under better circumstances."

"What do you mean?"

"I—" The princess stopped herself, glancing quickly at the elves. "So what brings you here, Prastian and Hellsfire? I assume this isn't a social call."

"No, Your Highness," Prastian said. "We came because our king ordered us to. We're looking for elves who were sent here a few weeks ago. We've not heard of them since."

Krystal looked surprised, then concerned. "You're the first elves I've seen in months."

"Are you sure? They should have been here."

Krystal's voice turned icy. "I'm positive, Prastian. I have no reason to lie to you."

"Forgive me, Your Highness," Prastian said.

She nodded. "Why would King Sharald send elves here?"

"He's worried about the Wasteland monsters," Prastian said. "Increasing numbers of them have been getting through your patrols and wreaking havoc near Sharald. We've had to send parties out to kill the creatures. We needed to know if things in Alexandria were as bad as they appeared."

Princess Krystal's face didn't change, but those of the guards around us did. Their faces hardened, and a few gave each other worried looks.

"As you can see, Alexandria still stands," the princess said. "As long as the bloodline of Alexander exists, it *will* stand."

"As you say, Princess."

"But Princess, something's wrong," I said. "Surely, you of all people could find out what it is."

She stopped and measured me with that royal gaze of hers.

"Forgive me, Your Highness," I said, bowing. "Could you please help us out, if you have the time?"

"I'll do what I can, Hellsfire."

"Thank you."

We reached our rooms. I was the last to enter mine.

"I'll be back in a few hours to escort you to dinner," the princess said. "You may want to rest. I know how tiring traveling can be. Though you may find a formal dinner even more tiring."

"Where will you be?" I asked.

"I have duties to attend to."

"What about the guards?" I glanced at one of the stoic guards from the corner of my eye.

"As father normally puts it, 'the guards are here for your protection.'" Krystal smiled. "I'll see you in a little while, hero." For a brief moment, she melted my worries and hunger away.

But the moment didn't last. I shut the door, then cracked my neck and shook my shoulders, trying to relieve myself of the stress that had built up over the day. I wished that I was visiting Alexandria under more normal conditions. I would have loved to see the city and talk with the princess.

There wasn't time for that now. We needed to find out what had happened to the elves and what was wrong within the city. Alexandria hadn't fallen yet, but it looked like it was getting ready to topple.

I took a look around. I couldn't believe the size of my room. It was almost as big as my old longhouse in Sedah. The bed was big enough to hold three people, and the pillows were stuffed with feathers instead of hay. There was a large wooden dresser and three cushioned chairs. The bed's covers were made of satin. The only downside was that the door couldn't be barred from the inside.

I walked over to a window that overlooked part of the courtyard. It was full of servants, guards, handmaidens, and pages all going about their business. Across the courtyard, from the shadow of a darkened doorway, I thought I saw someone staring up at me. I blinked and rubbed my eyes, then took a closer look. Nothing was there.

I drew back. My lack of food might have made me see things that weren't really there. Who would want to spy on me? Maybe Premier, or a concerned guard. Or maybe just a curious servant. I went to the bed and lay down. I had never slept on anything so soft. Maybe I would take a nap. I had a feeling it was going to be a long, tiring night.

I woke up when I heard a chain rattle. Footsteps crept across the stone floor. It was a servant with a candle and hot water, so that I could wash and change before dinner. I had just finished when Ardimus appeared at my door.

"I have come to take you to the dining hall."

"Where's the princess? I thought she said she'd come and get me."

"Her Highness is busy." His expression said I had a lot of nerve questioning anything the princess did.

"I can't wait to eat!" Demay said when we were all in the hall. "I'm starving. I hope these humans can cook as well as us."

"Demay, please," Prastian said. "I'm sure the feast will be enough to fill our starving bellies. My younger brother meant no offense, Ardimus."

"None taken," Ardimus said. He turned to me. "Hellsfire, I never got the chance to properly thank you. I owe you what my people call a 'debt of honor.' I will not rest until I fulfill it, although my first duty will always be to the princess and the king."

I opened my mouth to argue, but stopped. I knew it would be pointless to argue. My mother had once told me about debts of honor. They were unbreakable unless one person died or the debt was fulfilled. They were common among those from the Burning Sands, but many people had their own variations—those from places where honor and duty were paramount. I nodded to him and hoped that he wouldn't need to fulfill his debt. If he did, then that meant I was in serious trouble.

When we entered the dining hall, I froze. It was filled with powerful, well-dressed people. Men wore gorgets with slight patterns along the bottom edges. The bright reds and oranges contrasted with the browns I was used to. The women wore slim and modest gowns. Necklines were high and white or black gloves covered their arms.

"We should be as sociable as we can," Prastian said.

Behast grunted.

"Even you, Behast. We need to see if anyone here knows what happened to our people."

"But the princess said she hasn't seen any elves," I said. "And I believe her."

"I know, Hellsfire. I believe her too. That doesn't mean that no one else knows anything. Someone must have seen something."

"I'll do my best."

"Good. Also, please try not to cause any more incidents."

"Incidents?" I asked. "What do you mean?" Prastian had already left the group. He smiled and greeted some people he knew.

Demay went off to try and be like his brother, talking with nobles. He walked right up and complimented the women on their choice of dress. Behast went to talk to the one group of people he could—soldiers.

I stood there trying to figure out who to approach. As I scanned the room, I realized there was no one I could relate to. I wasn't a soldier, so I couldn't talk about weapons or fighting. I wasn't a noble, so I couldn't talk about ruling or ordering people around. I had the most in common with the servants, and they were too busy with their duties.

"You look like a statue," Princess Krystal said, from over my shoulder.

I turned and bowed. "Your Highness."

"Why are you standing here all by yourself?"

All the other people were engaged in conversation. They laughed and smiled at unfunny jokes or told battlefield stories. Some whispered lies I'm sure were far deadlier than any sword or magic. "I honestly didn't know who to talk to."

"Are you enjoying yourself, at least?"

I gazed into her violet eyes. "I am now."

She smiled. Although she was schooled in not showing her feelings, her color heightened faintly. It was not quite a blush, but it was close.

I grinned back, happy that I could bring such a lovely smile to her face. "I wish you could show me around Alexandria, Your Highness."

"Me too."

"You did promise me a tour all those years ago."

"I wish I could give you one now, but I can't."

I was going to ask her why, but I remembered what I was there for. "Did you find out any information about the other elves, Your Highness?"

The princess frowned and shook her head. "You're far too direct and honest. You would be terrible at politics."

I hung my head, trying to conceal my embarrassment. I was going about this the wrong way. "Sorry."

She threw her head back and laughed. "Don't be. It's refreshing."

I bowed. "Glad I could be of service, Your Highness."

"I'm sorry. I haven't found out anything about those other elves. Are you sure they came up here?"

I shrugged. "I'm not, but King Sharald is and so is Prastian. They set out to come here, and no word has been received that they went anywhere else."

"Do you think something might have happened to them along the way? They might have been attacked by bandits."

"Maybe." My eyes widened. "Or maybe it was something worse? The Wasteland creatures."

"Hellsfire, things—" Krystal stopped herself. She glanced around and lowered her voice. "Since you've been so honest with me and you've saved my life, I'm not going to lie to you. Things aren't as they seem."

"What do you mean?"

"That's all I can say right now."

There were far too many people around us. They didn't seem to be paying attention to our conversation, but that didn't mean they weren't. "I understand. Thank you, Princess."

The princess's violet eyes looked worried, and she lowered her voice even further. "Listen, there's something else I must tell you. I—"

The princess didn't get to finish her sentence. A footman announced that dinner was ready. Krystal hesitated, then moved off with dignity to take her seat. I raised an eyebrow. What could she tell me that was so important, if it didn't have to do with the missing elves? Prastian disturbed my thoughts by touching my elbow. He led me to the great, rectangular table. We were given seats close to the king and princess, as befitted a royal envoy.

When the servant came with the first course, I had to stop him. I told him I wanted to have what the elves ate. I no longer ate any meat because of my powers.

"Are you sure, sir?"

"Yes, please, and thank you."

"As you wish."

As I ate each vegetable-filled course, Prastian kept the king and others engaged in conversation. Instead of trying to find out more about the missing elves, he tried to find out more about Alexandria, so he could get a feel for how things were beyond what we had observed. However, people kept dodging the subject, no matter how subtle his questions or comments were. I was glad he kept the conversation going. I didn't want to talk, and the king's eyes kept straying towards me, making me nervous. Premier kept glancing at me too. His cold eyes held a hint of amusement.

People might have been starving in the city, but those in the castle had no problem getting food. Strangely, though, Premier didn't seem to eat or drink anything. It was during my third course when the king turned his full attention to me.

"Hellsfire," the king said.

I lifted my head from the delicious bean and onion soup. I swallowed and wiped the insides of my mouth with my tongue, tasting saffron. "Yes, Your Majesty?"

"I'd like you to explain something to me." His words were innocuous, but his tone wasn't. The room suddenly became very quiet.

I swallowed, even though I had no food in my mouth. "I hope I didn't do anything to offend you, Your Majesty."

"Years ago, my daughter told me you saved her from bandits. When she told me her story, I found it difficult to believe. After all, she was young, and had just gone through an ordeal. It seemed impossible that someone so young and outnumbered rescued her singlehandedly. A few years later, I now find you, of all people, in my audience chamber—sent by King Sharald.

"For the past few hours, I've wondered why." The king placed his hands under his chin in a thoughtful manner. "My daughter told me where you said you were from. It's nowhere of importance. Now, during dinner, you've not eaten any meat. Why is that? Is our food not pleasing to you?"

"The food's perfectly fine, Your Majesty. I don't eat meat anymore."

"Were you raised by elves?" Everyone chuckled at his joke, but I saw how serious his question was.

"No, Your Majesty," I said. "I've lost my appetite for meat."

The king looked hard at me for a moment. He weighed me like he must have weighed countless subjects, soldiers, and diplomats. "Are you a wizard?"

Everyone stared at me. I glanced at Krystal, and saw she tried not to look embarrassed. "Well, it's kind of hard to explain, Sire. I'm actually a…" I thought about lying, even though I was never very good at it. Master Stradus had said not to say anything, fearful of what might happen. But when my eyes met Krystal's clear, violet eyes, I knew I had to tell her the truth. If I lied to her father, even to protect myself, I would lose her trust. I didn't want that. "I'm a…wizard-in-training, Sire."

A gasp went around the table. Everyone appeared horrified, with the exception of the elves, some of the guards, and Krystal. And Premier. He simply looked curious.

"So you are a wizard," King Furlong said, not paying attention to the "in training" part. "I don't believe I've ever seen a wizard before. Do you know why?"

I shook my head. "No, Your Majesty," I whispered.

"Because wizards have never been welcome in Alexandria. We built this city with our own hands, out of the ashes of what the wizards destroyed. We've fought Renak's evil legacy for a thousand years, with nothing but our swords and our honor." His blue eyes narrowed and darkened. Luckily, they didn't focus on me. They settled on Prastian. "Why would King Sharald send a wizard to accompany you?"

"He thought it prudent, Your Majesty," Prastian said.

"Prudent?"

"Yes. As in the days of old."

The king had no response for that. Instead, he turned his gaze on me once more.

My hands heated up with inner fire. Premier watched me, like a cat watches a mouse. I began a breathing exercise—slow, rhythmic breaths. I wanted to close my eyes, but couldn't, lest the king think I was ignoring him.

The fire in my body began to dissipate.

"You will cause no trouble here, Wizard Hellsfire," King Furlong said. "King Sharald has long been a trusted ally, and you have done my daughter great service in the past, so I will allow you to remain. But I will tolerate no magic. If you use your infernal power within these walls, I will have you imprisoned."

"Father, please!" the princess murmured.

"Krystal, I am the king and will do as I see fit!" He slammed his hand on the table. Trays, plates, and cups jumped. So did the nobles. They looked startled, as if they weren't used to the king behaving like this. Princess Krystal's eyes darkened with worry. The king rose. "I will be in my chambers. Come, Premier. This dinner is over."

The room remained silent while the king withdrew. Then everyone started talking at once. The princess leaned across the table to me. "It would be best if you went back to your rooms. He should feel better in the morning." She left in the same direction the king had gone, with Ardimus following on her heels.

"We should do as the princess advised," Prastian said, keeping his voice to a whisper.

We all got up and headed out of the hall. I felt people's eyes on me and heard the whispers in my wake.

When we were well away from the dining hall, Prastian spoke, sounding worried. "I know the king," he said. "I've never seen him chastise a guest in public that way."

Master Stradus had told me that humans were distrustful towards wizards, but I had never thought anyone would imprison me because of what I was. King Furlong wasn't himself. He was sickly and under the stress of what was happening to his kingdom. But still, no one but the princess had seemed to object to his threats. And without magic, the odds were stacked mighty high against me helping anyone here.

"What did you do?" Demay said, peering up at me, his light green eyes blinking in confusion.

"He didn't do anything," Prastian said. "A lot of people still blame wizards for what happened during the War of the Wizards, especially other humans. Since Hellsfire's a wizard, they think he has some kind of connection to the war. In their minds, they think he caused some part of it."

"That makes no sense at all. Hellsfire's completely innocent."

"That's not true," I said. "I wish it were, but it's not."

"Hellsfire, you did nothing to provoke the king," Prastian said. "I would have told him so myself, but that wasn't the time or the place, and he is ill. I'll get him to see reason."

I looked at my elven friend and said, "No, Prastian you are wrong. My simple presence gives people the right to question my motives. You heard what the king said. Alexandria has been cleaning up the mess from the War of the Wizards for a thousand years."

Prastian opened his mouth, but I stopped him. "You don't understand. In a way, I *am* responsible for the destruction that happened before, during, and after the war. I get my knowledge just as you or anyone else gets their knowledge. It's passed from generation to generation. My magical abilities come partly from the wizards in the past. It's from them I get my power, and my beliefs about how it should be used. And they did a lot of things in the war. Some of them terrible."

Prastian stopped and turned to face me. "Hellsfire?"

"Yes?"

"If I stabbed you with a sword, would you get mad at me?"

I swallowed some saliva, not seeing where he was going. "I suppose I would. And then I'd probably die."

"Why wouldn't you get mad at my mother, who gave birth to me, or my teachers who taught me how to use a sword?"

I raised a finger, but I couldn't think of anything that would counter his argument. He was right. I couldn't be responsible for what had happened all those centuries ago. The best I could do was not repeat the same mistakes.

"I see you finally understand what I'm saying," Prastian said, resuming our walk. I nodded. "My point is, we're each responsible for our own decisions in life. The first Sharald taught us that. Sharald knew, from the first time he saw Renak, that the power Renak sought would corrupt him. It wasn't the power itself, but the path Renak took. Renak chose that path."

"Thank you, my friend. You're the wisest elf I know."

"Aren't we the only elves you know?" Demay said.

We all laughed at Demay. It was good to laugh, considering what we'd seen throughout the day. Tomorrow was going to be even harder. Between the king's suspicions of me, the lack of information about the missing elves, and the terrible state Alexandria was in, we were going to have a hard time getting any answers. We said our respective good nights and entered our rooms.

I thought I might get a peaceful night's rest before we continued our investigation the next day.

I was wrong.

CHAPTER 13

I WAS AWAKENED by the sensation of being dunked into cold water. The web I had placed over the door had served me well. A shadow crept across my room. I stayed perfectly still, continuing to breathe slowly as if I still slept. I readied my mana, letting it rise to the surface.

The shadow leaned closer to me. In the dim moonlight, something gleamed. I grabbed his wrist and twisted, dislodging the weapon. Then I created a fireball in the other hand, raising it to illuminate his face. I caught my breath.

"Forgive me, Your Highness," I said, letting go of her wrist and squashing the fireball in my hand. "I thought you were an intruder."

"It's quite all right. I understand and appreciate your…readiness." She rubbed her wrist.

"I'm sorry, did I—"

"I'm fine," she snapped. Krystal motioned to a candle holder on the dresser next to my bed. "Could you please?"

I waved a hand and ignited the candle. "It's good to see you, but what are you doing here, Your Highness? Especially in the dead of night?"

"We haven't much time. I don't know how long the drugs I gave the guards will last."

I raised an eyebrow. "You drugged your guards?"

"Yes. I needed to talk to you."

"But what if you're caught? Won't you get in trouble?" More likely, I would get in trouble. But I didn't want to say that.

"Leave that to me."

I nodded, and she took a seat next to me on the bed.

"I need help, Hellsfire," Krystal said. Her purple eyes had lost their gleam. She looked really worried.

"Anything I can do, I will, Your Highness."

She gave a faint smile. "You're sweet, but hear me out before you make any rash decisions."

"All right." But I already knew the answer was yes.

"Good." The princess took a deep breath. "I found the elves you were looking for."

"That's great!" I lowered my voice when I remembered she wasn't supposed to be here. "That's great." Her face didn't look thrilled. "It is, isn't it? I mean, they're still alive, right?"

"They're alive, but the news about them was hidden from me—from me!" The princess's eyes darkened with anger.

"Was it your father?"

"No. It was Premier." Her voice was as icy as the White Mountain.

"Premier?"

She nodded. I saw she struggled to remain calm. "Yes."

The princess didn't say anything for several moments. She stared at her hands in her lap. "What is it, Princess? Whatever it is, you can tell me."

"I know. That's why I'm here." She hesitated, then tried to smile. "What did I tell you all those years ago? We're alone, Hellsfire. I'd like it very much if you would call me Krystal."

"As you wish, Your…Krystal."

"Thank you."

Krystal fell silent again, staring into the candle's light. I was tempted to urge her to answer my question, but didn't. Her hand trembled slightly. I took a chance of overstepping and grasped it lightly. She looked at me, smiled, and squeezed my hand.

"When I first met you," Krystal said. "I truly meant it when I said wanted to show you the city I loved. She was…beautiful, Hellsfire. We could have gone to the opera house, listening to music that would make you cry and laugh. We could have gone to the marketplace to meet my people. There's a wonderful stall in the South Market with the most delicious honey bread. The honey's so sweet, it's like a drink of the gods." Her shoulders slumped. "But not anymore. My city's falling apart. And it's all because of Premier!"

Krystal turned to me. "You've seen the city on your way in?"

I nodded.

"Like any major city, we've always had our share of beggars and prostitutes, but it's never been this bad. I do my best, giving out food to the children and women. The guards fear me being attacked by the hungry mob, but they're my people. Visiting them and giving them food is the least I can do. But it's never enough. It's just a symptom of a bigger problem." Her nails dug into my hand. I held on despite the pain. It hurt me far more to see her like this.

"I barely see my father anymore." She reached up impatiently with her free hand, brushing a tear from her cheek. I wondered, when was the last time she had let herself cry? "In the rare times I do see him, he can't make a decision without Premier. Premier has wormed his way into every aspect of government. It's as if he's become the ruler of Alexandria without so much as a fight. The other advisors and I have been blocked at every turn. The worst thing is, Premier's disbanded most of the army and the City Guard. We don't have enough men to repel the Wasteland creatures if a strong attack comes."

The princess faced me. In a whisper, she said, "If I don't get rid of Premier and take back the city, Alexandria will fall."

I gasped. My vision and King Sharald were right. I thought of the people in the marketplace, the starving mothers and children, all of them butchered by Wasteland creatures. Like a fire, it would spread from here. It would be as uncontrollable as an inferno, raging throughout all of Northern Shala until it finally spread to Sedah. No one would be able to stop the creatures if they weren't stopped here. Alexandria needed help. The princess needed help. What could I do? The gods had guided me here, but I hadn't even completed my training. I didn't know what to do.

Tears streamed down the princess's face, and I forgot everything but her pain. All she wanted to do was help her people and keep them safe. I reached out to wipe the tears away. My hand stopped when I remembered who she was.

"Forgive me," I said.

She moved slightly away from me, regaining her composure. "I'm sorry. Here I am coming to you in the middle of the night asking for your help, and I start crying, looking like something the horse dragged in." She let go of my hand and used both of hers to wipe the tears away. She sniffled. "I'm not usually like this."

"Why did you turn to me, Your Highness?"

"There's no one else. You're an outsider, and not bound by the trappings of politics. That was one of the reasons wizards were used as intermediaries before the war. I know you've said you're not a wizard, but I believe you are."

"Oh."

"And I trust you, Hellsfire." The princess gave me a brief smile before she hardened her face, hiding any vulnerability behind her royal mask.

I couldn't speak. She trusted me so much that she was willing to risk her kingdom—and show me her true emotions.

The princess's quick eyes caught the movement of my hand flexing. She stared at the nail marks in my hand. "Did I do that? I'm sorry." She placed her hands over mine and rubbed it lightly, as if trying make the marks go away.

"There's nothing to forgive, Princess." I put my other hand on top of hers.

"Oh." She stopped. Her face relaxed, and she blushed.

"What do you need me to do, Princess?"

She took a deep breath. "It's my father, Hellsfire. You've noticed how ill he is?"

I nodded.

"I've had the best healers working on him, yet they've been unable to find anything wrong. I thought he might have been poisoned, but there's no trace of that. All this happened not too long after Premier arrived. In all my research, trying to help my father, I found mention of some of the things wizards could do using potions. How they could incapacitate a person, or make them sick. Not just sick in the body, but in the mind. I believe that's what's happening here.

"All of what's taken place can't be a coincidence. Remember how I told you our defenses are weakened? Well, strangely enough, there's not been a major attack in months. The smaller attacks have been harder to fend off, with fewer men, but it's like they've been testing our defenses. I have no proof or evidence, but I believe Premier's controlling the creatures. Much in the same way Renak did. There will be another—"

"War," I said.

"Yes. Only this time there will be no Shala or Wizard's Council to stand against Premier. With the Great Barrier up, there will be no help from the south. We're all alone."

I let her words sink in. She was right. Premier had to be stopped now, before another bigger, more devastating war took place. "You think Premier's a wizard?"

She nodded. "I do. I've not seen him use any sort of magic, but there are too many unanswered questions. Too many coincidences. And no matter how ill my father is, I can't see how he could be persuaded to disband our troops. It's who we are."

"I understand." I squeezed her hand, and she returned it.

"Can you tell if Premier's a wizard?"

I exhaled, slumping my shoulders. "No. I tried to when I got here. I didn't sense any magic, but there's something about him. Something wrong. If my master were here, he might be able to help us."

"That's all right." I could tell she was disappointed, but she immediately moved on to the next issue. "All right then, if we can't get proof against Premier, I need you to rescue the elves and convince King Sharald to send his army here before the attack comes. It *will* come. Trust me. And we must win, or all of Northern Shala will be overrun."

"I will do as you say, Your Highness. I am yours to command."

She smiled and brushed aside a lock of her hair.

"But are you sure King Sharald will listen to me? What if he wants to fortify his forests?"

"He might, but he won't. He sent Prastian up here, and he sent you with him. King Sharald *trusts* you, Hellsfire. We have an alliance, but more importantly, a friendship. He'll help us."

"What if he won't?"

"Then all is lost."

I thought of Sharald's words to me near his pond. He had wanted me to come because he was worried about the creatures of the Wastelands trickling down into Northern Shala. But was he worried about Alexandria and the people here? I searched my memory for any hint of it. I couldn't find one. He had seemed concerned about Sedah, but I believed that was more to entice me to come here. But elves cared about all life. He would help. I had to do all I could to persuade him to.

"I'll do my best, Krystal. Bringing the missing elves back to him should help." I paused, thinking. "You know, I don't understand why Premier didn't just kill them."

"He is. Slowly. Painfully. That is his way. He's methodical, a planner, an observer. He feeds them and gives them water, but without the sunlight, fresh air, and forest, the elves will die. The elves tried to cross him, and he wants to make them suffer for it.

"Whatever happens," Krystal said, "I want you to rescue the elves and leave Alexandria. It will no longer be safe for you here, once they escape. I will do all in my power to protect you, but Premier has far too many of Alexandria's resources at his disposal. He'll kill you if you get in his way, and I'm afraid my father would let him. Get back to the forests, and you'll be safe."

"What about you, if Premier finds out what you've done? You'll be in harm's way. I don't want you to get hurt. Come with me. We could flee the city together and come back with Sharald's army."

Krystal's eyes shone with tears. "Still trying to save and protect me, hero? No. I couldn't leave my father and my people. This is my city. I will not leave it while it's in danger."

I wanted to convince her to come with me, but her face was set like stone. She wasn't going to be swayed. "All right. Just don't get in harm's way, Princess. I can't protect you if I'm not with you."

Krystal's face softened. She was about to say something when we heard a noise in the hall. She jumped.

"I must get back to my room before I'm discovered," Krystal said. "The elves are in the southeast dungeons. Prastian should know the way. Please convince King Sharald to help me." She turned to go, and then came back and leaned in close, kissing me on my cheek. "Thank you again, hero. Please be careful." Krystal moved noiselessly to the door and opened it a crack. It seemed that the hallway was clear, because she vanished through the door, not looking back.

I watched her shadow disappear, and put my hand to my cheek, letting it linger. "You too."

I closed the door. There was no turning back now. Whatever she asked of me, I would do it. Whatever help she needed, I would give it.

We had found the information we needed about the elves. There was one last question, and it was about Premier. I would get my answer, but I was pretty sure I wouldn't like it.

CHAPTER 14

I DRESSED, grabbed my belongings, and left the room. The guards outside our doors still slept, slouched against the walls. One of them stirred as I passed. We didn't have much time. Behast and Prastian were wide awake and holding their daggers the moment I entered. I waited until we had collected Demay and were far away from our corridor before pulling into an empty reception room and explaining what the princess had told me.

"They're as good as dead if we don't free them!" Prastian could barely contain his anger.

"At least they're alive right now," Demay said. "Let's go rescue them and leave this place."

"I do not like the idea of a rescue attempt without our main weapons," Behast said. "If we should encounter resistance, I'm not sure how much of a fight I can put up with this little thing." Behast held his dagger in the air with his fingertips.

"I'd like my bow and arrows at my side," Demay said.

I turned to Prastian. "What do you think we should do?"

"Our weapons will still be stored in the guardroom at the entrance to the keep. The dungeons are located on the east side, near where we are now. We should rescue our follow elves, get our weapons, then leave. Don't worry, Behast. We have a mighty and powerful wizard with us."

I forced a smile. "Thanks."

"I'm going to take the lead, using my ears to guide us. There won't be many guards around at this hour; however, servants may be about. Keep your ears ready, but don't harm anyone who's not armed."

We left the room and disappeared into the darkness of the castle, moving as fast as we could without making noise. The elves took the lead. I tried to keep up with them and move as silently as they did. It was hard. The only places where there were lights also had guards or servants.

The elves had no problem moving around in the dark. Prastian knew the area well, and they let their ears be their guides. I couldn't use any magic to help me. A weak spell would do no good, and anything stronger might be detected by Premier. I had to pray my black robes concealed me in the shadows.

After many turns, stairs, and long corridors, we reached our destination. Prastian put his hand up to tell us to stop. We huddled against a wall, near a statue. Prastian peeked around the corner, his long ears quivering. Finally, he waved us forward.

Prastian whispered, "There are two guards in front of the entrance to dungeons. From the sound of it, they seem bored. They're obviously not expecting any trouble."

"Good," Behast said. A gleam shone in his eyes. "I will deal with them."

"No, we must not kill any of them," Prastian said.

"No? What do you mean no?"

"Shhh! I mean no. These are good people, following orders they believe come from their king. What's happening is Premier's fault. We will only kill people in self-defense. No more, no less. They're our allies, Behast."

Behast bowed his head in agreement. He looked disappointed. "As you wish."

"As I was about to say," Prastian said, "we need some kind of distraction so they don't have time to alert anyone else. Hellsfire, I don't suppose you could extinguish those candles over there?"

I peeked around the corner, then slid back to where the others were. "No problem."

"Good. The moment you do that, we go and knock the guards unconscious." Prastian looked back towards Demay and Behast. "Are you both ready?"

They nodded in unison.

"And remember, no killing."

I poked my head around the corner and drew the element of wind around me. In Caleea I said, *"May the God of Wind carry my breath and extinguish those candles."* I opened my mouth and blew. My breath divided, streaming towards each of the candles. The strands of air brushed against the guards. They looked around in confusion before the wind crushed the light.

As soon as the light was gone, the elves became a blur. The three elves, though smaller than the guards, were able to surprise and take down the first one easily. Prastian used the hilt of his dagger to hit him in the temple, knocking him unconscious before he could respond. The second guard reacted fast enough to almost draw his weapon. Behast was on top of him before he could. Demay helped Behast contain the guard while Prastian hit the man in the neck, then in the head. The guard grunted before falling to the ground.

"Let's go and get your friends," I said, walking towards them.

"Hellsfire," Prastian said and gestured to the candles.

I waved my arm and the flames re-lit.

"Wow," Demay said. "How'd you do that?"

"Come on, we haven't much time." Prastian took the keys from the guards. One by one, we went down into the dungeons.

The dungeon's mouth seemed to open wide and swallow us. The stairs were cramped, enclosed by the damp, mildew-covered walls. I shuddered. Even after spending almost three years in the caves on the White Mountain, I still hated enclosed spaces. As we descended into the blackness, the stench that crept into my nose was unbearable. It smelled as if a carcass had been left to rot in the baking sun. When we reached the almost pitch-black dungeons, we were in a hallway lined with cages. There were no windows. Luckily, there were also no other prisoners to deal with, although the dungeons were big enough to hold a hundred people. There were only the elves.

Two were slumped against the wall. One of them had open wounds on his arms. Flies hovered around the blood-encrusted cuts. The other's face looked like it had been slashed with a knife. A third elf lay on a thin layer of hay. His breathing was erratic, and his green skin was covered with welts where it showed through the rents in his ragged clothes.

But things were far worse than their physical wounds.

When I extended my magical senses, I felt that their green mana was fading. I barely sensed anything in them. They were dying inside, piece by piece, withering until they were nothing. Even their ears pointed down.

I grasped the steel bars in anger, letting their rough surface scrape my palms. Premier was responsible for this. How many other people had Premier destroyed? I concentrated, trying not to lose control of my powers.

"Prastian, hurry up and open the gate," Behast said, the anger in his voice rising. "I can't stand to look at this. This is no way to treat an ally."

Prastian unlocked the gates, and the three elves rushed to their fallen comrades. "My friends, we've come for you," Prastian said. "Get up. We must get you out of here and back into the forest so it can heal you."

"What's going on here?" The oldest elf slowly opened his eyes. "Am I dreaming again, or is Premier tormenting us once more?"

"You old fool. It is I, Prastian. I've come to rescue you."

The elf's eyes widened in surprise. He blinked several times and stared at Prastian. "Prastian? Is that really you?"

"Yes, Marlese. But if you really like it here, I can leave you."

"I'm sorry. My eyes are sore, but it must be you. Only you would have such terrible wit." Marlese struggled to rise, and Prastian helped him up.

"Dashion, Wintrop, we must get a move on. They've finally come for us. I knew Sharald wouldn't let us down."

Behast and Demay helped Dashion and Wintrop, while Prastian explained the situation to Marlese. Marlese and Prastian walked over to me after their conversation was done.

"So you are the one to thank," Marlese said, smiling at me. "I have a feeling my people are going to have a hard time repaying you for all the good you've done."

I shrugged. "I haven't done anything yet." I glanced up at the stone ceiling, imagining Premier out there. He had to be stopped.

Marlese grasped my arm. "I thank you nevertheless."

I nodded. "Why were you thrown into the dungeons, anyway?"

"It was probably something Wintrop said. I think he angered Premier and was insubordinate."

"Me?" Wintrop said. "I believe it was *you* who accused Premier of being a simple-minded fool."

Marlese coughed. "As I was saying, things got out of hand, and a slight misunderstanding arose. I don't think it mattered. Premier seemed eager to throw us in here before we could talk with King Furlong and, more importantly, before we could return to our king to tell him what we saw."

"Marlese, we don't have time for this," Prastian said. His ears twitched.

Marlese's ears rose. "You're right."

"Wait," I said. "Before we go, did Premier do anything when he visited you?"

"Aside from having the guards beat us, no. He took a perverse pleasure in watching and studying us like we were an experiment. From his interest, I don't think he's ever seen elves die in captivity before."

"What's wrong, Hellsfire?" Prastian asked.

"I don't know. It's just something about Premier." I exhaled. "I wish we knew more about him, but not even the princess knows all that much. He's dangerous. I know that."

All the elves nodded.

Prastian's ears perked up. "We have to go. Now. Someone's going to find the guards and we have to be past the city walls before sunup. Is everyone ready to go home?"

The elves' faces lit up with joy and relief.

"Good. Everyone follow me and stay close behind. Trust me, we're going to get you home."

The rescued elves had to lean on the others as we climbed the stairs. "Are you going to be able to make it, Marlese?" Prastian asked, supporting him.

"I'm fine, Prastian. We'll make it. Just get us out of here and into the forest."

As we made our way up the flight of stairs, I couldn't help but think about Premier. What would happen after we made it back to Sharald? Even if I convinced King Sharald to send his army up here and help, he could run into some serious resistance if Premier was a wizard. It was bad enough that Premier had weakened Alexandria, but if he was a wizard, he could destroy Sharald's army as well.

There were entirely too many variables, and they all hinged on Premier. I had to find out more about him so we could plan our next move. There was no one else who could handle it. I couldn't put any of them in danger. I was the only one with magic. It fell on me.

Marlese was winded and breathing heavily when we reached the top. Prastian gave him a questioning look. "Oh, don't look at me like that. As long as there's no more stairs, we'll be fine."

"Is everyone ready?" Prastian asked. "As the story goes, fast and quiet wins the race."

"No," I said. "I can't go on."

"Why not?" Prastian asked.

"I've got to know more about Premier. He's the key to all this."

"You could always come back."

"It might be too late then."

"But—"

"Let him go," Marlese said. "He's right about his instincts." Marlese's green eyes burned with hate. "Premier's our true enemy." Dashion and Wintrop nodded.

"I understand," Prastian said.

"I'll try to catch up with you if I can," I said. "One last thing." I took a deep breath. The problem with staying behind was that I was the best one to convince King Sharald. "I need you to talk to King Sharald. He has to send his army here. Krystal—I mean, Alexandria needs his help."

"We shouldn't involve ourselves in their politics," Dashion said, grimacing. "Let the humans die to the Wasteland creatures."

Dashion's words angered me, until I remembered what Sharald had said. "I know you elves were wrongfully imprisoned, but if Alexandria falls, we all fall." I turned back to Prastian. "There are good people here. They need your help."

"I agree, but I don't want to risk my people's lives."

I sighed. "I won't push this issue any further. There's no time for that. At least promise me you'll relay my words to King Sharald."

Prastian bowed his head. "I will, but I hope you will be there to present your case to our king yourself."

"Me too."

"Good luck," Prastian said before the elves disappeared into the darkness.

I hid in the shadows near the entrance to the dungeons while the elves made their way out of the castle. To buy us more time, I dragged the guard's bodies to the stairwell. Hopefully, by the time they woke up or were discovered, I'd be long gone and have found out what I needed to know.

But to learn more about Premier, I first had to find him.

From what my master had told me, wizards were a secretive folk. At least, post-war. They wanted to be left alone to work on their magic, and not be hunted down. If Premier was a wizard, he'd want the same thing. I kept that in mind while I wandered the castle's dark halls.

As I went, I tried to imitate my elf friends. I moved on the balls of my feet and crouched low. I relied more on my ears than my eyes, in the dim light between torches.

There were far too many rooms in the castle, and I couldn't search them all. Premier was someone of importance. He would have his own space, probably away from everyone else. My mind flashed back to the first thing I had seen of Alexandria—the towers.

That had to be it.

I ran as quietly as I could to the base of the towers. The light inside the castle wall grew brighter as the sun prepared to make another day's journey. It was only a matter of time before everyone awoke, instead of the mere handful of servants and guards I had to avoid right now. Unfortunately, the first tower I tried was guarded far more heavily than the rest of the castle. I bypassed it and hoped the others weren't. The second and third towers were guarded like the first. I pinned all my hopes on the last tower, praying my reasoning would be right.

I peered around a corner at the entrance to the last tower. I let out a breath. There were no guards at all.

I moved silently to the wooden door. On one side was a sconce with one candleholder and one unlit candle. The matching sconce on the other side hung sideways, as if it had broken and no one wanted to repair it.

This had to be it. Premier might have acquired power in Alexandria, but most of the people still wanted to avoid his dark aura. And if he really was a wizard, he wanted to avoid them even more.

With my magic by my side, I lifted my shaky hand and pushed the door open.

CHAPTER 15

I OPENED THE DOOR and peered through the crack. Barely any light shone through. I imagined Premier standing there, waiting for me, and shivered. I took deep breaths, trying to gather my courage. Someone did it for me. I heard heavy footsteps coming across the stone courtyard. Quickly, I slipped through the door and closed it. I leaned against it, hearing the footsteps approach, pause, then fade away.

I didn't move until I was certain he was gone, and I could no longer hear my heart pounding. Then I was able to focus on my surroundings. I was in a large, circular stone room that took up the whole base of the tower. There were no torches on the walls, but the morning's dim light shone faintly through the arrow slits on the far side of the room. About halfway across were two staircases—one leading up, the other down. I felt faint magic tugging at me from the lower level.

As I descended the stairs, following the trail of power, I knew something was wrong. There wasn't any feeling of life in the tower. In the other parts of the castle, there were always faint noises—people snoring or making love, servants getting ready for the day's work or running to do their master's bidding. And always, like a faint hum underneath everything, the life mana of so many people. This tower had a dead, oppressive feel to it—like the feeling I'd gotten when I tried to probe Premier. Awareness with no life force behind it, just malevolence. The tower's eyes were on me, and they weren't friendly. I rubbed the goose bumps on my arms and kept my magic at the ready. I didn't draw on it, in case Premier could sense it.

The lower I went, the hotter it felt. The humidity and dampness crushed me, reminding me of being enveloped in Cynder's breath. I wanted to rip off my wizard's robe.

I reached a landing on the staircase—and the magic that had drawn me. I sucked in my breath when I saw a light gray web shimmering at the top of the next set of stairs—a simple detection web. This was the evidence I was looking for. Premier was a wizard. But what was I going to do about it? I couldn't accuse him publicly. The princess would believe me, but we couldn't prove it to anyone else. No one else could see the web. I needed more evidence, and the only way I was going to get that was by venturing deeper.

The web was like the first one I had passed through when I met Master Stradus. This time, I was equipped with the knowledge of how to dissipate it.

I rolled up my sleeves and began to unmake the web with my fingers. Little wisps of magic danced on my fingertips. I moved the opposite way the web was formed. It was easy to follow, because all webs left little traces of how they were made. The simpler the web, the easier it was to see. The gray web lost all its color, then collapsed to the ground and faded away. I made my way down the stairs. Torchlight flickered up from the bottom, and I moved carefully, not wanting to alert anyone below. When I got there, I was in a small open space, faced by a wooden door.

I exhaled all the breath from my body. There was a web in front of this one too. It was much more complex than the first, stronger and interwoven with more strands. It shone bright crimson. I paused for a moment to figure out how to bypass it. I could see that it was set to cause excruciating pain to anyone who passed through it. Interestingly, it was specifically designed to affect only humans, with the exception of its maker. Other life forms, like animals, could pass through unharmed. And so could creatures.

As I studied the web, I realized it was slightly out of alignment, as if something had passed through it. As I watched, it settled back into its proper place, which meant that whatever had passed through had done so recently. And since it wasn't lying on the other side of the door screaming in agony, it wasn't human. I didn't know what it was, but I had no choice but to press on. It was too late to turn back now.

Since the web was designed to cause pain, a counterbalance must be used. Life was that counterbalance. Normally, I could use the life force of a nearby plant, but there were none down here. There was an alternate way to get rid of the web, but it was much more dangerous to me. No mistakes must be made.

"Gods help me," I whispered.

I let a small portion of my fire trickle into my finger until it lit up with a tiny flame. I sprinkled it with dirt from the floor, igniting it with earth mana as I recited a brief incantation in the old language. I glanced at the door, half-expecting Premier to feel the magic I was using. I waited several minutes, just in case, but he didn't appear. I took a deep breath and retraced the web, using the greenish/red flame to disintegrate it, strand by strand.

It was slow and tedious work. If I rushed and messed up, the spell could backfire and magnify the web's power a thousandfold. I could die from the backlash.

A sudden howling noise from above made me jump. I went perfectly still, hardly daring to breathe. If I had to stop this in the middle, I was doomed. Then I felt a breeze, and realized the noise was the wind, blowing across the arrow slits in the base of the tower, making its way down the stairs. It came again, and I relaxed, letting my breath out again.

Too late. The web glowed, and I felt its magic gathering force. I cursed myself. My flame had accidentally touched the wrong strand. The flames raced along the web, with me trying to extinguish them with my magic before the web could alert Premier. I finally got it out, but Premier could appear at any moment. The web hung in tatters, and it was only by luck that it hadn't exploded in my face. At least the gaps in the web should make it easier to get rid of.

I had relaxed too soon. The web's crimson color deepened. I had a second to register what was going to happen, and got off an incantation just as the web unleashed its magic. A blinding, searing pain flashed up my right arm. I clenched my teeth so as not to cry out in pain. I worked a counterspell with my left hand, as the pain worked its way across my chest. The color faded from the web.

My arm hung numb and useless. I used my left to destroy the last remnants of the web, worried that Premier would come through the door at any second. I couldn't put up a defense with one arm.

I finished demolishing the web, and Premier still had not appeared. I hesitated to open the door, once more picturing him standing behind it, ready to destroy me. But I hadn't come this far to give up now. I carefully opened the door, staying behind it. A horrible stench hit me, and I bit my tongue to keep from coughing and gagging. There was no one behind the door, just an empty stone room with two more doors and more stairs. These doors didn't have webs on them, and I couldn't sense any more active magic. I picked a door and opened it slowly. One torch lit the gloomy hallway beyond. I was going to take a look around when I heard voices from downstairs.

I tip-toed down the stairwell, trying not to make a sound. Sensation returned to my right arm, although it still felt like it had been stuck with a thousand needles. I flexed my fingers, ready to cast spells again.

When I arrived at the bottom, I was in a short hallway. A few feet down on the right was a half-open door, from which voices came. Light spilled into the hallway from inside the room. I slipped down the hall as quietly as an elf, peeked around the corner, and froze.

In the corner of the room was a stone workbench strewn with chopped ogre limbs. Black blood overflowed the bench, dripping on the stone floor. At the end of the workbench sat an ogre's head, forever frozen into a horrific, silent yell. Its skin was peeled back and the eyes were empty holes. Hanging against the wall above the workbench was the ogre's massive torso. It had been cut open and the skin spread wide, revealing its enormous ribcage. The belly cavity was empty of organs.

Something moved in the shadows next to the workbench, and I realized it was another ogre. He was clothed in brown rags, and his tough, blotchy skin looked like a gray rock with lichen growing on it. At his feet was an enormous wooden club the size of a small elf. As I watched, the ogre reached into a bucket on the workbench and pulled out a long, slimy piece of intestine. He tilted his head back and lowered it into his mouth, smacking his lips like he ate a great delicacy. I turned my eyes away and pinched my nose, gagging.

I heard the ogre swallow his snack, and then he spoke. "Are you all right, Master?" I moved so I could see further inside, steeling myself for more disgusting sights. Instead, the rest of the room was perfectly clean and meticulously tidy. There was a wooden workbench with candles, rocks, chalk, a jug of water, and wax lined up on a tray. One wall held shelves of books, supplies, and containers, all in neat rows and organized by size.

Premier sat cross-legged in the middle of a chalk hexagram drawn in the middle of the floor. His eyes were closed and his face blank—his only movement was the rise and fall of his chest as he breathed. I sensed him gathering magic in his meditation, but I couldn't tell what he was doing with it. I saw no spell.

Premier slowly opened up his dark eyes. "If you disturb my meditation again, Baal, I will hang you on the wall and let your comrades eat your entrails out of your live, twitching body." His voice was calm and pleasant, as if he discussed the weather.

The ogre stopped chewing and turned a slightly lighter gray. "Yes, Master."

Premier rose from the floor and sat down on the only chair in the room. He put his hand on the chair arm, and then lifted it again. There was black blood on his fingertips. "And if you must have your… distractions…please confine the mess to the workbench." He glanced toward the disembowelment in the corner of the room, then pulled out a snow-white handkerchief and wiped his fingers. He held it out and waited for Baal, who rushed over and took it from him.

Baal bowed. "It won't happen again, Master."

"I wouldn't expect any less. There will be plenty of time for you and your kind to have your fun. In the meantime, this should be the last time I see you until you bring the army to Alexandria."

The ogre perked up. "Is now the right time to attack, Master?"

"Yes. I've invested enough time in this city. Alexandria lies weakened. You had no trouble getting in here?"

"The city's defenses are nonexistent. There was no trouble."

"Excellent. The sooner we take over this wretched city and begin the next phase of our project, the better." Premier sighed. "I'm tired of dealing with the people. And I want to move quickly. That boy that came with Sharald's elves may pose a problem."

"Because he's a wizard?"

"Quiet," Premier said, turning his cold eyes on Baal. "Hellsfire is only an apprenticed wizard."

"Then how can he be any threat?"

Premier drummed his fingers on the arm of his chair. "I never said the boy was a threat. But where did he get his training? His presence means that other wizards might be in this part of Northern Shala, and they might be able to thwart my plans."

"But Master," Baal said. "Even if they do exist, they can't stop you from taking Alexandria."

"Fool!" Premier said. "I have bigger plans than Alexandria. Far bigger plans. Alexandria is a means to an end, no more." He fell silent. The ogre fished an eyeball out of the bucket and ate it. Premier went on, "I wish I had more time to interrogate Hellsfire and learn who and where his master is. Unfortunately, I will have to have him killed before he alerts anyone to my true nature. Especially that annoying little princess."

I tensed. I had to leave. But first, Krystal had to be warned. She was in far greater danger than she realized.

"The question is, how to do it?" Premier mused. "The princess is constantly hovering around him. She's been trying to block my every move for months. If I kill Hellsfire, her suspicions of me will be confirmed. She could take drastic measures to stop me." He sighed. "I'm going to have to make it look like an accident. Maybe I can—"

"Master?"

Premier narrowed his eyes at the ogre. "Another interruption. Do not let there be a third, Baal." His voice was still pleasant, but the ogre went pale again.

Baal bowed lower, his head nearly touching the floor. "Of course, Master, but I think I smell something." He sniffed, moving toward the door. "We might not be alone."

According to the stories, ogres could see like cats in the dark. Now it seemed they could scent like dogs. I slid back against the wall, feeling like my collar choked me.

Premier's chuckle echoed through my ears. "Baal, don't be a fool. The only smell is you and that mess over there. I placed two webs in the tower."

"Master, what about the one you were talking about?"

"He's just a boy. He hasn't the knowledge or power to undo the webs." Premier paused. "However, in case you're right…" He flicked his hand, sending Baal off to investigate.

I scurried from my hiding place, trying to make it back up the stairs before the ogre saw me. I had to pray that the ogre wouldn't track my scent or pursue me any further. Just in case, instead of going back up to the door that had held the crimson web, I went to the door I had been about to explore earlier, which I had left ajar. I closed it just as I heard the ogre get to the top of the stairs.

I didn't summon my magic, in case Premier sensed it, but I was ready to use it if the ogre or Premier came through the door. I felt the massive ogre walking around on the other side. He sounded like an earthquake. He came closer and stopped outside the door. I clenched my fists. I saw his shadow through the crack between the door and floor, and I stopped breathing.

He didn't open the door. The shadow disappeared and I heard him go through one of the outer doors. It slammed shut.

I wiped the sweat from my brow. I prepared to open the door and escape, half-expecting a trap.

"Hey!" a ragged, coarse voice called from behind me.

I spun around. There was another door with a small barred window set into it. The handle was chained and padlocked. I crept cautiously up to the door, despite my better judgment screaming at me to leave. If Premier kept an ogre, perhaps he kept some other kind of dangerous creature in this room that he planned to unleash upon the land. I peeked inside the room.

"You must help me!" the voice said. A hairy face popped up from nowhere, in front of the little window.

I stumbled backwards. My feet became tangled, and I fell to the floor. I mumbled a curse, hoping Premier or Baal hadn't heard me fall. I got up, composed myself, and held my fire mana ready.

I moved closer and looked in the window. The prisoner was small, about the size of an elf, yet broad and muscular. His bushy, gray beard hung down to his waist. Through the rents in his ragged clothing, I saw his skin was scarred and bruised. He smelt like Marlese and the others, though not as bad as the ogre. Astonished, I finally realized what he was—a dwarf.

"Quickly!" he said. "You must get me out of here! We're in grave danger and we haven't much time!"

I wasn't sure whether to trust him. Then I realized that any prisoner of Premier was probably a friend of mine.

"I will set you free, but you must stand back," I said, looking over my shoulder. The spell I had ready was going to be fast, but crude. It was also going to hurt.

I grabbed the lock and heated it, forcing it to pop open. I had to bite my tongue; the lock scorched my hand when I yanked it off the chain. The dwarf shot from the room and grabbed me with iron strength.

"Thank the gods you rescued me, lad," he said. "I'm grateful you did while there's still time."

"Time for what?"

"I'll explain later. We must make haste and flee the city."

I nodded. I didn't want to stay down here longer than I had to.

I took the lead. When we got to the door, I put a finger to my lips. The dwarf nodded in understanding. I opened the door and peered out. No one was there. We walked quietly but quickly.

As we passed through the door that held the crimson web, I heard a slight sound behind me. I whirled, mana at the ready, and saw Premier at the top of the stairs, the ogre right behind him. Premier's dark eyes met mine, and he smiled.

CHAPTER 16

AS SOON AS I met Premier's gaze, I reacted without thinking. I performed a quick spell, releasing my fire mana at Premier in a funnel of flame. He caught the fire with his hand and absorbed it. He moved closer. Confident. Not hurrying. I had to think of something to distract him. I looked at the door and came up with an idea.

I pushed the dwarf through the opening, and used wind mana to yank the door off its hinges and send it across the room, smacking into the ogre and Premier. The pair staggered.

"Run!" I yelled to the dwarf.

We ran up the stairs and through the second door. I paused, hearing heavy footsteps behind us. I summoned more mana to shatter the door, and the pieces spiraled at the approaching ogre. He crossed his arms in front of his head as the wooden shards struck like arrows, embedding themselves deep in his flesh. He roared with anger and pain. I didn't wait for Premier to catch up. I ran up the remaining stairs. The dwarf waited for me at the top.

"I'll lead," he said.

I followed him through the castle. He didn't go straight for the main entrance like I would have done. He seemed to know the castle well, and took a route that avoided most of the guards. I kept listening behind us for the ogre and Premier, but we seemed to have lost them. However, we couldn't avoid the people starting to rise for their daily business. We didn't give them time to ask questions as we ran by.

I thought we would have to contend with the guards at the keep's entrance, but there weren't any. Their unconscious bodies were off to the side. The elves must have taken care of them. We dashed out of the keep into the dim morning light. We slowed to a fast walk as we headed down the hill, so as not to attract too much attention.

We just had to pass the portcullis, and we would be out of the castle grounds where I could breathe easier. I prayed that Prastian and the others had taken care of the guards, because I had no idea what we were going to do if they hadn't. I didn't want to hurt anyone. Unfortunately, when we got near the entrance, we could see the guards were on full alert. They lined the entrance, weapons at the ready, and unconscious and possibly dead guards were being carried away on stretchers.

"Do you know of another exit?" I asked the dwarf, glancing at the walls.

The dwarf stroked his beard. "I'm sure there's another one, but we not only would have to find it, but the guard there will probably be just as heavy."

"The front it is."

We strolled towards the guards with confidence. My plan was to walk right past them, praying they wouldn't ask any questions and that I wouldn't have to use my power on them. As we approached, the guards readied their weapons.

"What do you think you're doing, Wizard?" a guard asked, gripping his sword's hilt tightly.

"Leaving."

"You're not leaving. You're under investigation for what's happened here."

The men atop the walls aimed their crossbows at me. The guards on the ground stayed out of their line of fire, but drew their swords. I summoned the wind around me, ready to use it to disperse the crossbow bolts.

"I didn't do anything," I said.

"No, but your elven friends did." One guard looked up from bandaging a wounded man. It was Jerrel.

I raised my right eyebrow. "I can't believe my friends would harm anyone. Sharald and King Furlong are allies."

"Most of my men suffer arrow wounds, and only elves could loose their bows so quickly and accurately."

"Accurately?" I asked.

"Yes. Prastian made sure he didn't kill any of them."

"That's good."

Jerrel glared at me. "Some suffered broken bones from falling off the wall, and one will never lift a weapon again."

"I'm sorry about that, but we need to leave."

"You're not going anywhere," the other guard said, eyeing me.

"Please," I said, ignoring him and focusing on Jerrel. He was the only guard who hadn't drawn his weapon. Maybe he could be reasoned with. "I don't want to hurt you or your men."

Jerrel's hard eyes stared at me, then moved to my companion. He saw the wounds on the dwarf's body. Jerrel's eyes settled on me. His gaze never wavered, and neither did mine. I was leaving one way or another. I couldn't be caught. If I was, not even the princess could help.

Finally, Jerrel said, "You may go." The guards around us lowered their weapons. "You obviously weren't responsible for the attack, and we have no orders to detain you."

"Premier won't be pleased about this," the glaring guard next to him said.

"We serve King Furlong and Princess Krystal. No one else. Understood?"

"Yes, sir," the man said, sheathing his sword.

"I suggest you hurry, Wizard Hellsfire," Jerrel said.

I nodded. As we passed him, I said, "Thank you, and—you're not the only one who serves Princess Krystal."

"I know."

The dwarf and I hurried out of the castle, disappearing into the marketplace, doing our best to blend in with the people there.

"Nice work, lad," the dwarf said when we were well away from the castle. "I was afraid we were going to have to fight our way out. And thanks for rescuing me."

"No problem, although we're not safe yet." I glanced over my shoulder, expecting to see Premier come bursting of the castle, or at least see riders chasing us down. "We've got to leave the city. I'm not sure if Jerrel's given us enough time."

"I agree." He fiddled with his beard. "We're going to need horses."

"I have my own. I can buy you one and new clothes, and then we can go our separate ways."

"You're not coming with me, lad?"

I raised an eyebrow. "To where?"

"Erlam. I could use your help."

I shook my head. I had to get to the elves, and stop Premier. "Can't. I've got important things to do."

"This concerns all of Northern Shala."

I paused and looked down at him. "What do you mean?"

"There's an army of Wasteland creatures coming to Alexandria. They must be stopped!"

I saw a contingent of guards running up the street. I pulled the dwarf around the corner of a building and readied my magic. However, they went past us.

"I agree with you," I said. "I was just going to go to Sharald to get help from the elves."

The dwarf's bushy eyebrows went up. "Very wise of you, lad, but Alexandria's going to need more help than that. I've seen the creatures. There's far too many for either Alexandria or Sharald."

"And you can vouch that Erlam will send its army here?"

He nodded. "Aye."

I glanced back at the castle, worrying about Krystal. "I'll go with you, but first I need to warn the princess. Now that we're past the castle walls, if I have any problems, you can and should escape."

"You can't. The guards will arrest you, and Premier will have you executed."

"I'll use my magic to get by them."

"What about Premier?"

"I don't care!" I clenched my fists, doing my best to control the wildfire storming inside. I couldn't get the picture of Premier's mocking smile out of my head. "She needs to be warned. Things are far more dangerous than I thought they'd be—than she thought they'd be."

He placed a strong hand on my shoulder and said in a calm voice, "I wish we could warn her, lad. I tried to tell the king, but it was Premier who imprisoned me before I could do so. Do you honestly believe you could get to her and then get away?"

The fire inside me subsided as I realized the truth. "I suppose not." I sighed, and my shoulders slumped. "I don't even know who you are."

"Jastillian of the Rammalong House." He grasped my forearm.

"Hellsfire."

"Good. Now's let get out of here, lad."

I took one last look at the castle and prayed to the gods that Krystal would be all right and that I'd see her again. If anything were to happen to her...

"I'll be back." I promised to Krystal.

I retrieved my horse and bought one for Jastillian, as well as some clothes that were far too big for him. We trotted out of Alexandria, but as soon as we were past the city walls we broke our horses into a full gallop. We didn't slow down until we were out of sight of the city. After that we alternated between trotting and walking the horses.

I kept glancing over my shoulder, expecting to see a cloud of dust as a horde of guards galloped after us. Luckily, there wasn't. Either Jerrel or Krystal had bought us time, or Premier didn't want word of the dwarf and our escape to get out to anyone. Either way, I was thankful.

As tough and strong as Jastillian looked, he couldn't keep up the pace we were going. His body finally gave out on him, until he could barely hang onto the horse's reins or sit up straight when we rode. I couldn't either. I rubbed my eyes, remembering I had been up half the night. We decided to stop for a rest. Our bellies needed to be filled, and the horses needed to graze.

"I'll try to scrounge up some kindling and firewood," Jastillian said.

"And I'll go and try to get something to eat."

I walked around for a bit, looking for anything edible on the barren plains. It took me awhile to find something to eat, and when I did, the roots I pulled weren't exactly the tastiest. Thank the gods I had some dates and dried fruit in my purse. I was about to walk back to camp, but then I thought of Jastillian. He must be terribly hungry, and I knew dwarves loved meat.

I had hunted years ago in Sedah, and finally I flushed a brown hare out of the scrub. He stared at me with his liquid brown eyes, unmoving. I created a quick fireball and flung it at him. By the time he decided to run, it was too late. He died with a shriek. I slung the dead animal over my shoulder and went back to camp. I plopped down near the roaring fire and gave Jastillian the hare.

"Good job, lad," Jastillian said. "You wouldn't happen to have a knife on you, would you?"

I nodded and gave him my dagger. Jastillian skinned and cooked the rabbit. What would have smelled delicious to me a couple of years ago now made my stomach churn. It rumbled, and I had to force my tongue to remain still. Jastillian tore into the rabbit, leaving nothing but bones. I ate the food I had gathered along with what was in my purse. I was more tired than hungry anyway.

"That was delicious!" Jastillian said and licked his fingers. "Thank the gods for good food! It has been weeks since I last had anything more than bread and water. I would have offered you some, since you were the one who caught it, but I know wizards don't eat any meat."

I sighed and rubbed my furrowed brow. "Are you going to tell me how you ended up in Premier's dungeon, or do I have to guess?"

"I'm sorry, lad. I suppose I've kept you in the dark long enough." Jastillian stroked his beard. "I guess I should start from the beginning. I've never seen or heard about you before, Wizard Hellsfire—"

I blushed at the title. "Please, just Hellsfire."

He tilted his head. "Hellsfire, and I do *a lot* of traveling. But I can say for certain, you're a true friend if I ever met one."

"I've never met a dwarf before."

Jastillian chuckled. "You know about dwarves, lad?"

"A little bit."

"In that case, I don't need to tell you about us. Let's just say, I'm different from most dwarves because I'm a historian."

"A historian?" I said, raising my right eyebrow.

"Don't sound so surprised, lad. We dwarves keep historical records. There are few of us who do it, to be sure, but we do exist. My specialty happens to be the War of the Wizards. I've been all over the land to see what happened during the war. I've read records, talked to other historians and even a few wizards, studied artifacts, looked at bones, and visited landmarks. Before my capture, I was out in the Wastelands doing some research and—"

I gasped. "You were in the Wastelands?" I had never heard of anyone going into the Wastelands so casually. The Guardsmen went out, but only for patrols. And they didn't go out alone.

Jastillian laughed. "Calm down, lad. The Wastelands are like any other place; you have to know your way around, that's all. It's a barren place, and the inhabitants are dangerous. If you don't know what you're doing, you'll definitely be killed. Ah, but it does have its beauty, and more importantly, its stories.

"I hadn't been in the Graveyard for a few years, but I recently received some new information. I knew it was a long shot, but I wanted to follow up on it. You see, lad, it was said that one of Renak's trusted generals had a special medallion. After the war, his wife buried him with it."

"Why would his wife bury him with such a valuable object?"

"It wasn't forged of gold or silver. It was a family heirloom, from what I've learned."

"Then why do you want it?"

"It's a piece of history, lad." Jastillian looked at me as if I was mad. "It deserves to be restored, preserved, studied, and remembered. Sadly, I never got a chance to see if the information panned out. A storm forced me north, and I was too close to the old city of Masep. I came upon a vast army of creatures in and around the city. They looked like they were preparing for battle. That was unusual, because of the size of the group and the fact that they consisted of many different types of creatures.

"I don't know if you know this, but most of the Wasteland creatures don't get along. They like to stick to their own kind. I had to find out what they were up to because with a disciplined force like that, it couldn't be anything good. If the Wasteland creatures were actually able to unite, then that would spell a lot of trouble for us all."

I nodded. "Like during the war."

"Exactly. I captured a couple of goblins and interrogated them. Those small creatures didn't tell me much, but they did tell me one important thing before I killed them."

I leaned in close and said, "What did they say?"

"They were preparing for an imminent attack on Alexandria, led by a wizard. A wizard in these parts worried me almost as much as the rumors." Jastillian's brow creased.

"Rumors?"

"Aye, lad. Rumors about Alexandria having gone soft and the creatures getting by them. I knew I had to go warn King Furlong. I made my way to Alexandria, but I never got a chance to see the king. Instead, I had to talk to Premier. When I told him what I saw and who I was, Premier had me imprisoned. Only afterwards did I learn that Premier was the wizard."

I glanced at the fresh scars on his arms and neck. "Why did he torture you instead of killing you?"

Jastillian snapped a rabbit bone in his hand. "He said he needed my expertise."

"For what?"

"He wouldn't tell me. He questioned me about my travels and where I've been. In normal circumstances, I would be happy to tell anyone about what I've learned. I told him nothing." Jastillian's glare could destroy mountains. "I've a feeling he's looking for something. Whatever it is, it's very old."

"Didn't he use magic on you?"

"Aye, that he did." Jastillian's eyes wandered momentarily, his pain shining through. He raised his head and met my eyes. His voice was loud and strong as he said, "I may be a historian, but I'm also a warrior and a dwarf. I won't succumb to *anyone,* not even a wizard. The whole land's at stake. I've no time for pain."

I nodded. "I could try and heal you."

"I saw the magic you performed, lad. You're an elemental wizard. From what I know, your kind isn't as skilled with white mana."

"That may be true, but I could still do my best to help heal you."

Jastillian shook his head no. "Thanks for the offer, lad. You've done enough already. You freed me, and now you've just healed my belly." He laughed again before licking the grease from his fingers.

I didn't laugh. I couldn't help but stare in the direction we'd come from and worry about the aftermath of our escape. "Are you sure you can get the rest of the dwarves to help? They might not want to get involved." I had a feeling that convincing them would be far harder than the elves. Dwarves could be a very stubborn people. I didn't want to waste my time going to Erlam.

"You needn't worry, lad. I have some sway in Erlam, and I'll do my best to get my people to help you."

"Thank you. That's all I can ask." I relaxed, knowing I had him on my side. "Where have you met other wizards? I haven't met any but my master. If there were more around, we could ask for their help."

Jastillian shook his head. "Unfortunately, there are none nearby. I've seen a couple throughout my travels. Very elusive, you wizards are." Jastillian's eyes gleamed. "But I love the thrill of the hunt. That makes studying the war a challenge. Us dwarves love a challenge, no matter its form."

I guessed I was on my own in stopping Premier.

"What were you doing down there by my cell, lad?" Jastillian asked.

"Spying. I was trying to figure out what Premier was up to. I knew there was something wrong about Premier from the moment I met him."

"You're quite the sneaky one," Jastillian said, and smiled. "I'm glad you're on my side." He rose and stretched. "I feel much better. Let's get a move on before the sun sets. We're wasting daylight sitting here."

We cleaned up our camp and continued our trek, pushing hard with the occasional, shorter break. By the time the sun had finished its journey, we found a spot to rest for the night.

We had reached a nice little clearing on a plateau. It was well away from the main road. From our position we could see anyone who might be following us within a horizon's view. The sky was lit with purple, orange, and red. The colors reminded me of my vision—and of the princess's eyes. I hoped she was all right.

After I tied the horse's reins to a nearby tree, I unloaded my supplies. They weren't heavy, but my body was so exhausted, it felt like the world fell off my shoulders when I put them down. I put a fist to my mouth and yawned.

"Get some rest, lad," Jastillian said. "I'll take first watch. If we're lucky and push hard enough, we might be able to make Erlam in four days' time." He put a few more logs on the fire. "I'll wake you for your turn."

I stared into the growing darkness. I wanted to make a trap, or some kind of warning system, but I was exhausted, and a spell to cover the entire area would be too time consuming and complex.

"May the gods make your dreams pleasant," Jastillian said.

But my dreams weren't pleasant. I tossed and turned, sweating and breathing heavily as I dreamt of Krystal. Premier tortured her. He stripped her of her clothing and trapped her in the stockade. He forced her to watch while her city burned and the creatures killed her people.

I gasped as Jastillian woke me. My sore and tired body cried out for more rest. "What—"

"Shhh," Jastillian said, clamping his hand over my mouth. "We're not alone."

That woke me and pushed the fatigue out of my body. Was it Premier and the ogre? I got up and peered into the darkness. I couldn't see anything—the fire had dimmed to embers. I opened my magical senses to see if Premier was out there, but I got nothing.

"How many?" I whispered.

"Eight. Could be more."

"Any signs of Premier or the ogre?"

"No. Guardsmen."

I let out a breath. That would make things easier. The only thing that worried me was whether they might have items to combat wizards and magic. Would Premier have given them access to such things? I thought no, in fear of them being used against him.

"I'm going to try and circle around behind them," Jastillian said. "You go the other way and try to do the same thing." He cradled a large branch in his hand. "We take them out one by one, before any of them notice. I know you have great power, but it only takes one arrow."

"I have a better idea. You get behind them. I'll greet them and try to convince them to abandon this task."

Jastillian tugged on his beard. "I don't think that's a good idea. We don't know how many are out there for sure. It's best we take them by surprise."

"No. I don't want to kill them. I want to give them a chance. They're no match for me."

"They might not listen to you. They've been given a duty and will do their best to perform it. They wouldn't think twice about killing you."

"I know, but I'm not them. I don't want to kill other people if I don't have to. Jerrel gave us a chance. Maybe these men will too."

"Very honorable, lad. Good luck." Jastillian disappeared into the dark.

I bent down and touched the ground. Tapping into the earth mana, I used it to feel the soldiers out there. I had to focus past the spiders and beetles that skittered in the dark. I had to ignore the heavy weight of the rocks and branches that lay there. The soldiers were quiet and light-footed, but the earth felt every impression they made. Jastillian was right. There were eight. I rose when they were close enough for my purposes.

I fueled the almost-dead campfire with my power until the bright ball of fire illuminated the surrounding area. The eight soldiers stopped and shielded their eyes, blinded by the sudden light. They recovered quickly and drew their swords.

"Lay down your arms and return to Alexandria," I said.

The men didn't move. They stared at me, their bodies tense.

"Don't make me hurt you."

I played with the campfire in front of me. Streams of flame extended from it and moved about as if they were alive. The heat flowed around my body. I sent the fire toward the men. The fire danced in front of them, causing them to drip with sweat, but they didn't move. A few of the younger men squirmed, but that was all.

"Hellsfire, look out!" Jastillian yelled.

I hadn't seen anyone move, but I dropped the fire show and shielded myself in a layer of fast-moving air, as Master Stradus had taught me. Two crossbow bolts clashed against it and turned aside. I created two gigantic fireballs from the campfire and sent them flying in the direction from where the shots had come. One man screamed from the left while the other dropped his crossbow and dodged the fireball on the right.

I dropped my shield, not sensing or seeing any danger. The fire in front of me blazed brighter until it shot up into the night sky. I parted the fire as I walked over it. I took some of the fire with me, cradling it in my hands as I prepared to use it as a weapon.

"Drop your weapons. You have the last warning I intend to give."

The lead man did as I said. The other men followed suit. The archer came into view. I walked up to the group of men and asked the leader, "Who sent you?"

He narrowed his eyes at me and leaned back from the dancing fire. But he didn't say anything.

I raised my hand and pointed it at another man. I didn't want to, but I prepared to send the flame that spiraled around me at him. "Who sent you?"

"Premier. Premier sent us."

I lowered my hand. "And your orders were?"

"To kill you and capture the dwarf."

"Does the king or princess know about this?"

"No, sir."

I glanced at the other men to see if he told the truth. He did. "I want you to go back to Alexandria. When you get there, tell Princess Krystal what took place here and what your orders were." I let the hot fire flow out of my eyes and stared at each of the men. "I'm a wizard. I will know if you obeyed my orders."

"Yes, sir!"

"Now leave!" I swept my hands and sent the fire surrounding me to the ground. A line of fire nearly crossed the men's feet. They turned around and ran.

I bent down and touched the ground again, feeling their heavy footsteps as they ran. It was never a good idea to run around in the pale moonlight. One of them fell, possibly twisting his ankle. The feel of his feet was erratic as two of the others helped him limp to their horses. As soon as I felt the horses' hooves trot away, I released the earth mana.

"You did it, lad. I've seen magic before, yet I'm always impressed. That was amazing."

I didn't say a word. Tiredness struck me. I had used a lot of magic, and it was sloppy and showy. I had done it that way to impress them enough to fear me. A true wizard would have been more precise in his spells.

Jastillian picked up one of the swords. "Are you sure they're gone?"

I sighed and shrugged. "As sure as I can be."

I walked over to the man who had died. Bending down, I was taken aback by how young he was. He was about my age. His face and his left arm were badly scarred. His face was oddly quiet, for dying in such a terrible way. I forced myself to continue to look at him, even though the smell of burnt flesh sickened me. I stared into his lifeless eyes, wishing it didn't have to come to this.

"He died an honorable death, Hellsfire," Jastillian said, placing a hand on my shoulder. "He died in battle and in service to his country. There's no greater honor."

I swept my hand over his eyes and closed them. In a quiet voice I said, "There was no honor in this. He didn't die protecting Alexandria. He died because of Premier. Godsdamn Premier. We've got to stop him before more people die."

"We will, lad. We will."

I got up, and we walked back to the campsite. I re-ignited the campfire and placed some more wood on it to keep the animals away.

"Go to sleep, lad," Jastillian said. "You've got a few more hours before your watch."

I shook my head and sat down near the fire. "You go to sleep. I'll keep watch for the rest of the night."

"Are you sure?"

"Yes."

Jastillian paused as if to say something. "I'll see you in the morning."

When I was sure he was asleep, I hugged my knees against my chest. I glanced towards the direction of the dead body, shivering from a cold that wasn't there.

We continued our long journey, traveling parallel to the jagged Daleth Mountains. We didn't run into any more soldiers from Alexandria. Every time we stopped and rested, we had a conversation of some sort. I got to know

Jastillian well in the short days we were together.

He told me about some of the travels he had embarked upon, and about his children, who traveled as much as he did. In return, I told him some of the information I knew about the War of the Wizards—things I'd read and heard. I didn't tell him about Master Stradus though. I wasn't sure if my master wanted people to know he was next door to them, along with a dragon. The trek was a tiring one, but we did make it to Erlam exactly when Jastillian said we would.

Would coming here be enough? And could I return to Alexandria in time?

CHAPTER 17

WE TROTTED OUR HORSES up the slanted plateau that led to the dwarven city of Erlam. It had been cleared of trees, so there was only scrub, low-cut grass, and a few flowers as far as I could see to either side. Jastillian said that the landscape was very similar to the Wastelands, but this had been done deliberately. The dwarves felt they could win on the field of battle against an invading army if they were able to face them in the open. If things went wrong, they could always fall back to the mountains.

A patrol rode out to us, well before we reached the city. The dwarves' short, stocky, armored bodies on horseback looked awkward, almost comical to me. What didn't look comical were their stern, angry faces. Their beady eyes got even narrower when they rested on me. Their riding style may have looked awkward, but their armor and weapons didn't.

They wore red and black uniforms that blended into the landscape, the faded red ochre of their helms and breastplates matching the loose red dust, while the black of their gauntlets, boots, and helms resembled the cracks that spiderwebbed the ground. The varied browns of their beards and bare, muscular arms were like the rocks that dotted the plain. The dark, aggressive colors made them even more intimidating.

"Greetings, Jastillian," one said.

"Greetings."

"It's good to see you again." The sentry's brown eyes scanned Jastillian. "I heard you were in the Wastelands. You look like the cat dragged you out of the Inferno. Rough time?"

Jastillian smiled. "Aye, you could say that."

"Who's the stranger?"

"A friend."

"We have orders not to let outsiders in."

"Says who?"

"Who do you think?"

"He's coming with me."

The other dwarves looked to their leader, waiting for his response. Despite being beaten, bruised, and outnumbered, Jastillian's fierce gaze didn't waver. It intensified, making the dwarves squirm in their saddles. All except the leader, who didn't falter, either.

Seeing the implacability of the leader made my anger rise, and with it my fire. I clenched my fists and bit down on my inner cheek to control it. I wasn't going to let this patrol bar me from getting help. I would never get into the city if I did anything foolish. I had to trust in Jastillian and let him handle this.

"On your head, Jastillian," the guard said. "So be it."

Jastillian nodded and the dwarves rode off.

"What was that about?" I asked.

Jastillian sighed and scratched his cheek. "No idea. We'll find out soon enough."

At the foot of the Daleth Mountain Range, the plateau dipped into a small valley. The green of the valley contrasted with the stark browns and grays I had just seen. A blue river flowed out of the mountains, feeding the city with life. We dropped our horses off at a stable on the outskirts of Erlam, finishing our journey on foot.

People made their homes and shops in the valley, and unlike in Alexandria, the people and buildings weren't run down. The wood used in construction wasn't rotting or in need of repair. There were crowds of dwarves shopping and bargaining in the marketplace and on the main streets, but there were no guards or starving mobs. The aroma of chickens, cows, and pigs dominated the air. The smell of meat was so strong, it permeated my clothes. I breathed in relief when we passed a baker.

A huge marble scene decorated the middle of the marketplace. A white statue of a dwarven hero battled ferocious monsters that I had never seen or heard of before. His axe was stuck in the middle of one. The carvers had captured the monsters' sharp fangs and claws, and the dwarf's rage while killing them. The inscription beneath the statue said, 'You can achieve your heart's desire, only if you're willing to die for it.'

"That's Eostar, lad," Jastillian said. "Some consider him the greatest dwarf who ever lived. Have you heard of him?"

"Sounds familiar." I might have read about him in one of my master's books, but I couldn't remember anything now.

"You know, lad, if it weren't for Eostar, Shala would have lost the war." Jastillian gazed lovingly at the statue. "He inspired me to become what I am today."

"How so?"

"Eostar wasn't the best or strongest warrior, but he inspired all of us to become more. If it weren't for Eostar, we would have helped Renak win the war."

I turned my gaze away from the statue, cocking my head and raising my eyebrow.

"Don't look so surprised, lad. Before Eostar, we dwarves only cared about fighting and honor. We cared about who was the strongest, and would follow them because it was the honorable thing to do. We learned later that survival of the fittest doesn't necessarily mean those who are physically strong, and that honor can come in many forms.

"We didn't technically enter the war for a long time, but we didn't have a problem with Renak's followers crossing our borders to get at our enemies. When we finally entered the war, we sided with Renak. It was a long struggle for Eostar, but he helped us see there's more to life than fighting and the battlefield.

"Strength and honor can be in ideals—in doing what's right despite the odds or what others think. At Eostar's urging, we joined Shala's army at a pivotal point in the war. That's how the Erlam of today was born. Afterwards, we branched off into other occupations like healing, history, even archery. Even so, we dwarves are still mighty warriors. It's just that it's no longer *all* we are."

I stared at Jastillian, realizing for the first time that he was much more than a simple historian. And I was going to find out what.

We left the marketplace and walked through residential neighborhoods. Most of the buildings were constructed out of slate or sandstone, material easily taken from the mountains. While some of the homes were bigger and had more stories, all seemed to be of the same uniform, blocky shape. The dwarves didn't seem to believe in creativity in design. However, the walls were strong and smooth, with no cracks in the foundations or crumbling mortar.

As we made our way through town, Jastillian was greeted by everyone that walked by. There wasn't a single dwarf who didn't acknowledge him, ranging from the littlest dwarf child to the most scarred, battle-tested one. He smiled and said his hellos. From the greetings of the people and the reaction of the guards, I began to suspect that Jastillian must be someone of importance. Even Premier didn't want to kill him. He wanted to kill me.

I had worried that coming here would be a waste of time. With Jastillian by my side, it might no longer be. Whoever he was, Jastillian had some influence.

I couldn't help but notice that every dwarf had a weapon. The children had mock wooden axes. They ran around, chasing and fighting each other. They fought with intensity, but never cried out, even when they got hit. Most of them smiled and roared with laughter instead.

The adults favored axes of various sizes, slung across their backs, and large enough so that they extended above their heads. How could they carry such a thing and use it effectively? It was no wonder that their arm muscles, and every other muscle, were bigger than my neck. Even the vendors were armed. The elderly dwarves tended to favor short swords, probably because they were lighter than the axes.

As we approached the foot of the mountain, a huge stone wall loomed over us, over twenty feet high. It curved like a horseshoe around the entrance to the underground portion of the city. In front of the wall, for a long bowshot in every direction, was an open space. Just like on the plateau, all the trees and brush had been removed, and there were no buildings. Nothing to provide cover for an enemy. It was a kill zone.

The only entrance was a thick steel gate, flanked by two towers that extended ten feet higher than the wall. Guards paced the top of the wall; they stopped as we approached and eyed us suspiciously, as did the ones on the ground. Just as we got to the gate, we were met by a female dwarf wearing an officer's insignia.

"Jastillian, glad to see you're back," she said, and allowed herself a smile.

Jastillian smiled back. "Me too, Lurlane."

She frowned at me. "Outsiders aren't permitted, though." The guard tensed. "He may wander around the town, but he can't go inside."

"We're going to see the council. It's business."

Lurlane eyed me and Jastillian for several moments. "I'm duty bound."

The guards behind her fingered their weapons, and the ones on the towers raised their crossbows.

My fire slipped again. I was losing control. I balled my fists, trying to hide it, but it trickled along my fingers. I folded my hands into my sleeves, hoping no one saw it, and that I could get control of it before it got worse.

"It's important. After our meeting, you'll know soon enough," Jastillian said. "Everyone will know."

"Please," I said, my voice hoarse. "I've come for Erlam's help."

She stared at me, sizing me up. "All right." Lurlane nodded, and she and her men stepped out of our way. "I suggest the two of you clean up before you see the council."

"Thank you," I said as we passed by.

"You owe me, Jastillian," Lurlane said. "Big."

"I know."

We passed through the steel gate. Immediately inside were barracks, training grounds, and forges for the guards. Groups of dwarves performed training drills, fighting in formations. Others fought one-on-one, attacking their opponents with their axes. Unlike the children, these adults swung with purpose and precision. Farther along, dwarves wrestled each other to the ground, half-naked, with sweat glistening from their bodies. The dwarves hadn't sent out any monster-hunting parties like the elves, yet it looked like they prepared for war.

There were other dwarves working instead of fighting—pushing carts with materials and supplies from the mines to the forges, or making weapons and armor. Everywhere, people were busy. We made our way to the edge of the military zone, up a flight of wide stone steps, and stopped. My mouth dropped open. Jastillian grinned at me.

We stood before the stone heart of Erlam. Because of the dwarves' skill with stonework, the mountains literally opened up, like a giant had taken huge bites out of them. The dwarves used the mountain for their foundation, supports, and construction materials—carving, cutting and polishing the stone into the shapes they wanted. Tunnels, bridges, ramps, and archways connected tier after tier of buildings, disappearing into the darkness of the mountain.

"What do you think, lad?" Jastillian asked.

"Amazing," I breathed, the words barely leaving my mouth. I stood gawking until he clapped me on the back.

"We'd best get a move on."

I liked the Cave City, as Erlam's inner city was called, better from a distance than I did once I was inside. Streets and tunnels were narrow, and buildings crowded together. There was enough room to breathe and move, but it made the space tighter than I liked. The narrow tunnels and low ceilings made my breathing speed up. Even after all my years in the White Mountain, I'd never gotten over my dislike of being closed in.

Deep, low, faint voices echoed throughout the mountains. The sound bounced off the walls and ceiling, so I couldn't pinpoint where it came from.

"What is that?" I asked, straining my ears.

"Singing. We dwarves like to sing while we dig. Makes the work go faster."

We traveled on paths clean of any debris. There were a few staircases, but most of the walkways were carved into ramps so it was easier for the dwarves to transport materials. It did make for a lot of rising and falling, though. Some ramps were steep enough to make me slip.

As we moved farther into the city, darkness overtook us as the enormous cave blocked out the light. Torches had been placed everywhere. With Jastillian's permission, I picked up one to carry. Dwarves had excellent eyesight even in the dark, but I didn't. I could have used my power for light, but I didn't want to draw attention to myself.

Every building we passed was constructed of stone, some carved right out of the living rock of the mountain. The gray, brown, black, or white-veined buildings were far more smoothed and polished than any building I had ever seen before. Because of the way the dwarves dug, using the natural contours of the rock layers, the level of the ground rose and fell.

We walked by one building; I ran my hand over its smooth, cool surface. There were no bumps or uneven grooves. I remarked on that to Jastillian.

"Aye. These buildings need to be strong, in case of earthquakes or falling rocks, though we also take pride in craftsmanship for its own sake. And this city is also a fallback position if we get attacked and can't hold the field. All our important buildings are here, such as the treasury, food stores, historical artifacts, records. You know, Erlam was very different when it was first constructed, all those years ago."

I nodded. "I know. Erlam was originally a small mining town. How in the gods' names did it get like this?" I waved my arms across the expanse.

"We needed more materials, and dug deeper and deeper into the mountains. We also liked having a good defensive readiness, and what makes for a better defense than a mountain itself? We have a saying, 'The mountain won't move, and neither shall we.'"

I smiled. "Good point, but what about earthquakes and avalanches? How do you keep the mountain from collapsing on you?"

Jastillian stroked his bushy beard. "Despite what some of you humans think, we're not just diggers and blood-thirsty warriors. We're also builders, lad. While a lot of the things we create *are* for warfare, some things aren't. This" –he swept his arms out— "is one of them. We've used the knowledge we've acquired over the centuries to refine and perfect how we build things. Some of our engineers used their expertise to make these mountains habitable."

"That's incredible."

"Aye," Jastillian said. "In my travels, I've learned that magic was used to help with the original beams, joints, columns, and frames, but I wasn't able to find any evidence of it in our own records. We lack a wizard's expertise." He twiddled his beard and stared upwards. "Still, if magic were involved even a little bit, it would be a great find."

"If I'm ever back this way, I'll check for you," I said, looking up to see what he saw. Even now, I could make out dwarves working among the buildings. No wonder everything was so clean and in such perfect repair. I wished I was just visiting Erlam, and could sight-see.

But I wasn't.

I couldn't get the princess out of my mind. Had Premier already brought his forces to Alexandria? Had she gambled—moved against Premier and failed? If only there was a way to know what was happening. I wasn't leaving here without securing the dwarves' help. If I had come all this way here for nothing, and abandoned the princess in her time of need, I would never be able to forgive myself.

I looked over my shoulder and whispered, "Krystal. Please be safe."

Jastillian led me to a flat, rectangular building, which he said was the largest building in the mountain. We walked up a long staircase, between polished dark gray columns. There were no windows. It was far too deep in the mountains for windows to be of any use.

"Jastillian," one of the guards said, blocking the open archway.

"Greetings."

"I see you've brought a visitor, yet I've not been notified, which means the human doesn't have clearance. I know it's been a while since you've last been here, but there are no outsiders currently allowed into Erlam." The dwarf shook his head wearily. "Tell me why I should admit you, instead of having your friend locked up."

"It's urgent. We're going to see my mother."

"You may see her. The human stays."

"He's coming too."

The guard shook his head. "He can't. I don't care—"

"He's a wizard."

The guard stared at me, dumbfounded, before looking back to Jastillian. Then he broke into a chuckle. "He tell you that, to get you to bring him to Erlam? Not likely. Everyone knows there are no more wizards in Northern Shala." He shared a smirk with the other guards.

"Hellsfire," Jastillian said.

I nodded in understanding. I released my anger and frustration at being barred at every turn while people's lives were in danger. This was taking far too long. The torch flame in my hand exploded into a fireball twice as big as my head. I dropped the torch, keeping the flame hovering in front of me. It flew towards the guards and stopped, spinning faster and faster. The guards backed away, eyes wide, hands on their weapons.

Jastillian coughed, catching my attention. He shook his head slightly.

I reached out to the fire. My hand reabsorbed it. The warmth flowed through my body as the fire disappeared from view.

The guards moved aside, still stunned.

"It's good to be home." Jastillian smiled and clapped the guard on his shoulder as we passed through the archway and into the building. He looked satisfied, but I had an uneasy feeling that getting the dwarves to help was going to be a lot harder than entering their city.

CHAPTER 18

"**LET'S GO GET CLEANED** up before I take you to meet my mother," Jastillian said.

"Who *is* your mother?" I asked.

"She leads Erlam."

My eyes widened. That was great news. Hope rose within me. Maybe coming here wasn't a waste of time.

"Think she will help?" I asked.

"I'll do my best, lad."

Jastillian led me through the narrow halls. Banners hung all over the place, many depicting a muscular arm wielding an axe. It was the dwarves' symbol for strength and power, intimidating people in battle. Jastillian said that even though they were now more than just a warrior people, they kept the symbol to remind themselves of their past.

Although I was accustomed to living inside a cave, the inside of the castle was far darker than I was used to. Torches burned sporadically along the halls, but didn't provide enough light for me. The hallways and rooms were shorter and more compact than in either of the castles in Sharald or Alexandria, or the inside of the White Mountain, making it far more crowded than I was used to. I also had to duck beneath the arches, because everything was sized for dwarves.

We moved past the common areas, heading to the more private parts of the castle. Guards eyed me, but didn't stop me, since I was with Jastillian. Thankfully, I didn't have to deal with them again. I was afraid I would lose control this time.

All the buildings I had seen, while strongly built and well-constructed, were boring to look at, at least from the outside. But the inside of the castle was a huge contrast to the outside. It wasn't stark and bleak, as I'd thought it'd be. I thought of what Jastillian had said about Eostar, and about the dwarves being more than what people saw on the outside.

Instead of paintings and portraits, the dwarves used little statues made of rocks and minerals to depict great battles. In one gallery, there was a scene where dozens of tiny carved quartz crystals had been sculpted into dwarves. They fought larger Wasteland creatures made from limestone. The crystal dwarves held tiny weapons, and their faces wore perfectly carved expressions of pain or fury.

Statues stood throughout the halls. Instead of dwarves, these were fantastical creatures. There was a topaz dragon with wings unfurled, an alabaster unicorn with front legs raised, and lastly, a gold griffon with a ferocious scowl.

I stopped as we passed another room. It had a large shelf with many separate compartments. In each compartment were different minerals or rocks, all with labels clearly written in front of them. I recognized a lot of them, like gold, slate, clay, bronze, and silver. There were a whole lot more—including some I'd never seen or heard of before. A group of younger dwarves stood in front of the display as two adults tested their knowledge.

"Come on, lad," Jastillian said, jolting me out of my gawking. "I can give you a test later on the materials found in these mountains." He chuckled at his joke.

I tore myself away and ran to catch up to Jastillian. We reached the end of a hall, and there was a plain, wooden door with steam seeping underneath it.

Jastillian opened the door and said, "This is where you can wash up and relax, lad."

Steam hit me and flowed over my grimy face. The warm, refreshing feeling caught me off guard. It seeped its way into my skin, and I sighed like I had just entered the heavens. In a large pool of warm water, a couple of naked dwarves were soaking.

"What is this place?" I asked.

"One of our bathhouses. Most of them are located in this building, but if you like, I can take you to one of the other rooms where you can wash yourself with a bucket and rag."

I chuckled. "No, this will be fine." I lost my breath at the thought of warm water I didn't have to create myself. "Thank you, Jastillian. I've never seen anything remotely like this. How did you create it?"

"We didn't, lad. We found a hot spring deep within the earth and routed the water. We dwarves need a hot bath after—" In a deep, booming voice, Jastillian sang, "'Digging in the dirt all day, digging our own graves. Digging 'til we reach the end, having our bodies lost in a maze.'"

I scratched my head. "What?"

Jastillian laughed. "It's been awhile since I've sung. Let me give you some privacy. I know how some of you humans are with showing what the gods gave you."

"That's all right, you don't—"

"Hey, you two!" Jastillian yelled.

The pair of dwarves opened their saggy eyes and said, "Jastillian!"

"We were wagering on when you'd get back," one said. "I just lost."

"I wouldn't have made it if it weren't for my friend here," Jastillian said, slapping me hard on my back.

I nodded in their direction, and they nodded back.

"I hope you two don't mind cutting your bath short," Jastillian said. "I promised my friend here some privacy."

"He must have faced impossible odds to help you. Especially since you're in those ridiculous clothes." The two dwarves laughed at Jastillian's expense. "We were just getting out anyway."

The two naked dwarves got up out of the pool, dried themselves, put on some clean tunics and breeches, and took their dirty miners' clothes with them. "It's good to have you back, Jastillian. See you around."

"You didn't have to do that on my account," I said. "I would have been fine if those two were in here."

"Nonsense, lad. It was the least I could do. I'm going to get out of these rags and get dressed. We have to look presentable for my mother. I'm sure she'll be on our side and will wish to send help to Alexandria. The problem is getting the others to vote with us."

"How can we do that?"

Jastillian played with his bushy beard. "As a wizard, you're going to have to convince them Alexandria needs more help than the elves. Try to think of something persuasive to say."

I stared at him. I'd figured that he would do most of the talking. "Like what?"

He wiped drops of condensation from his forehead. "The truth. Speak with your heart and you'll convince them. Some of the people that will oppose us will be very vocal. Don't back down from them. We still respect strength. If you speak from that position, people will listen to you more."

I nodded.

"Good. I'll be back in an hour or so. Enjoy your bath. Not many outsiders get to experience these baths, and even fewer get to enjoy them in peace. Hang up the towels when you're done." Jastillian smiled. "Have fun."

I took off my heavy wizard's robe and boots, then my tunic and other undergarments. I crept into the heated pool, savoring every precious moment. I melted and moaned the second the water touched my skin. It was warm and comforting.

I grabbed some sponges and washed myself clean of the trials I'd been through. While I scrubbed the dirt out from under my fingernails, I couldn't help but think of the princess and what she might be going through now. She was strong, but Premier was a wizard.

I was thankful for Jastillian's advice in dealing with other dwarves. Erlam's ruling council was going to be a lot harder to convince than King Sharald. I wished I could have seen more of Erlam. I needed to get a feel for how the dwarves thought and what they cared about. The only thing I knew was that they didn't care about me. That didn't bother me. What bothered me was, did they care about Alexandria or the creatures from the Wastelands?

I sighed and squatted down farther in the water, dunking my head in. I thought about the arguments the dwarves might have and how I could counter them. I wasn't a diplomat or a politician or any good with words. I couldn't do this. It wasn't good enough to try. I had to succeed. I must succeed.

I rinsed myself off. The now-brown water floated by and then circulated away, taking with it my thoughts and frustrations.

When I was done cleaning myself, I leaned back against the edge of the pool and drifted away, becoming lost in the serenity around me. The purple bruises on my thighs didn't bother me, nor did my sore muscles. My exhausted body was at peace in the warm water. It wanted me to sleep, but my mind wouldn't let me.

I kept thinking about the girl who needed my help, the wizard who stood in my way, and the dwarves I had to convince. To calm my nerves and clear my mind, I practiced my magic.

I latched onto the water mana, creating three gigantic bubbles in the pool. I used air to force them to rise out of the water. They hovered in front of me, and then I sent them flying around the room, bringing them to a halt before they hit anything and burst. I summoned them in front of me once more, then raised my hand out of the pool. A stream of fire came forth, popping all three bubbles.

I created five more bubbles. I zipped these around the room while I shot fire out of my hands. It was a simple exercise, but using more than one type of mana simultaneously always was a strain on the user. Often-times, you had to grasp the mana both from inside yourself and from the environment. It would divide your attention and concentration and burden your mind, will, and body.

I crafted both the fire and the water into more complicated shapes as my exercise went on. Water in the shape of cats was chased down by fire dogs. Water flies flew by before being munched by a fiery praying mantis. The magic electrified the room, fire and water splashing and sizzling everywhere.

I breathed heavily, letting the exercise clear my mind, focusing only on the magic and what I had to do to maintain it. I went faster, and my spells became stronger every time I thought of Premier and how he had mocked me and wanted to harm the princess. I got so absorbed that I didn't hear Jastillian come in.

"Lad," Jastillian said.

His voice broke my concentration, and my fire dissipated. The water in the air stopped dead before plummeting to the ground. Water splashed on my head. I wiped it from my eyes.

"Sorry to interrupt," Jastillian said.

"That's all right. I was just performing some exercises." I put a wrinkled hand to my throbbing forehead. The magic must have taken more out of me than I thought. I looked around the room, noticing that water had gotten everywhere. "Sorry about the mess."

Jastillian laughed. "Nothing to forgive, lad. It's only water and it'll dry up sooner or later. That was quite an impressive show you just put on. It never ceases to amaze me, the things you wizards can do."

Jastillian loomed over me, wearing short black breeches. They matched his gorget, and his tight red tunic showed off his muscles. The colors, combined with his size, gave him a commanding presence. His beard was also trimmed, now only down to his chest. But the most notable thing about him was the huge battle-ax strapped to his back.

"You look good," I said.

"Aye, I must say it feels good to be cleaned, shaved, and have clothes that fit. But what really makes me feel good is to have some kind of weapon on me. Even though this isn't my true weapon."

"It isn't?"

"Premier took my weapon!" Jastillian clenched his fist and growled. "I'm going to get it back, even if I have to pry it from his dead corpse."

"What's so special about the weapon? Is it expensive or something?"

Jastillian laughed. "No, lad. We teach that *all* weapons are special. They're used to defend you, your home, and the ones you love. And that weapon was an ancient relic I got from the war and had repaired. It's impossible to replace, and I went through a lot to get it."

"Were your wounds tended?"

"Our healers patched me up well enough. I had to send them away when they wanted me to rest." Jastillian frowned, and his right cheek muscle flexed. "I must warn you. After talking with my mother, it's going to be a lot more difficult than I thought to get our army to help. There will be…resistance. There will be those who oppose us. It's them you must convince. You must secure three-fourths of the table."

I knew I shouldn't have wasted my time coming here, but it was far too late to turn back now. "I'll do whatever I have to do to convince them to help me."

Jastillian smiled. "I know. Now let me turn around while you get dressed."

I was going to protest, but Jastillian was right about humans being bashful, at least when it came to me. Not having any clothes and having someone stare at me made me shy. I wasn't that comfortable with Jastillian yet, and he wasn't a pretty girl.

I got out, dried myself off, and put my not-so-clean clothes back on. When I put on my wizard's robe, I inhaled its scent. It smelt surprisingly clean.

Master Stradus once said a wizard's robe is a part of the wizard, and the two become one. In time, I'd understand. Maybe the robe was clean because I was clean? Although it might have been because of the fact that it soaked up all the steam, and I had been in the room for a long time.

I rubbed my wrinkly fingers through my slick hair and said, "I'm ready."

"Good, lad. Before the questioning, we'll get to eat first. I'm sure you're as hungry as I am."

My stomach rumbled so loud I'm sure Jastillian heard it. "Just a little bit."

We left the quiet sanctuary of the bathhouse. Jastillian led me through the halls. We walked up a broad flight of stairs, passing four guards before we reached a set of large double doors carved out of granite and etched with the dwarves' symbol. Jastillian opened one of the doors.

The room was much larger than those in the rest of the castle. In the center was a large, circular stone table, and about two dozen well-armed dwarves of varying ages surrounded it. The room was surprisingly stark. I had expected it to be as richly decorated as the rest of the castle. There were no paintings, statues, or even banners. The only decoration was the dwarves' symbol carved into the middle of the table, just visible under the platters of food.

All heads turned towards us as we entered, and the conversation stilled. Jastillian led me to a seat on a stone bench, next to an elderly female dwarf.

"Hello, my son," the old dwarf said. Her short, thin hair was as white as snow. When she smiled, her face creased with wrinkles.

"Hello, Mother," Jastillian said. The pair embraced.

Jastillian's mother looked towards me. Her vital, dark blue eyes had that same piercing gaze as King Furlong had. I wondered if all military rulers had the same way of sizing a person up. I inclined my head. Jastillian's mother was the only dwarf present who didn't wear a huge weapon. She chose to carry a short sword, sheathed at her side.

"Hellsfire," Jastillian said, "This is the leader of Erlam, Lenora."

"A pleasure to meet you, ma'am. I'm grateful you allowed me to come into your wondrous city."

"Thank you for helping my son, Wizard Hellsfire."

"Please, just Hellsfire."

"He shouldn't be here," said a younger dwarf with red hair.

"That's right," another said. with a fierce gaze. "There should be no outsiders here in the heart of Erlam at this time."

"He rescued me from a great and dangerous wizard," Jastillian said.

"Your point?" the red haired dwarf asked.

"He's a wizard. There hasn't been one in Erlam for centuries. The least we could do is show our hospitality to him."

"Enough of this!" Lenora said, eyeing Jastillian and the red-haired one. "We will discuss this after we've had something to eat, as is our custom."

They bowed their heads.

Lenora raised her ale-filled mug. Everyone did the same and so did I. They slammed them hard down on the table. Nobody had warned me to turn my head away. I wiped some ale from my eye. The red-haired dwarf smirked.

There was plenty of food on the table, but an overabundance of meat. Everything from boar and deer, to chicken, rabbit, and pig filled the platters. The aroma of roasted pork and grilled rabbit upset my stomach.

I avoided all the meat, eating mostly potatoes, bread, and beans. The dwarves made a little small talk, but most were too busy tearing their food apart. Having traveled with Jastillian for the past few days, I had learned that dwarves ate this way to show appreciation for the food—not with words but with actions.

I didn't get into conversation with any of the dwarves. Most glanced at me often, peering over their food. That was unnerving enough, but the red-haired dwarf, the one who had argued against my presence, never took his eyes off me.

I tried to be polite and not stare back, but it was hard. He was one of the bigger and younger dwarves in the room. His clothes strained to contain his muscles. His red beard and hair added to the fierceness of his gaze. The more he stared, the angrier I grew. My fire started to build.

I did my best to endure it, pretending I didn't notice. I was an outsider, and I needed their help. I couldn't afford to get into an argument. Luckily for me, dwarves also show appreciation for good food by eating quickly, and the food was good enough that the meal was not a long one.

"Mother, if we may?" Jastillian asked.

Lenora looked around the table and saw that everyone was finished. She ate the last piece off a pork shank and put the bone down on her plate. Then she nodded yes.

Jastillian said, "All of Northern Shala is in *grave* danger."

Time seemed to stop as the whole room became quiet.

Jastillian then told all the dwarves of his journey into the Wastelands, his capture, our escape, and of Premier's plans to take over Alexandria. All eyes were locked on Jastillian. He had a teacher's voice, deep and thoughtful. It fluctuated with his emotions, and was never boring. In fact, he made the whole tale sound even more exciting than it actually was.

After Jastillian was finished, one of the slightly older dwarves said, "I feared something was wrong in Alexandria." She glanced to the dwarf who had stared at me through dinner. "We should have sent a party there as I suggested. The elves had the right idea, for once."

"Whatever you want to say, Artesia, you can say in front of Hellsfire," Jastillian said.

Artesia looked at Lenora. She nodded. "We've had problems with the Wasteland creatures, Jastillian. Extra patrols have had to be sent out to deal with them. They haven't been enough of a threat for us to worry that Alexandria has been overrun, but there've been enough to be an annoyance. Now you say they're just a symptom of a much more worrisome problem." Artesia scanned the table and said in a loud, forceful voice, "We must mobilize our army to go to Alexandria and help them."

For a moment I was relieved. They wanted to send the army. This had been much easier than Jastillian had said it would be, and I hadn't had to say anything. But my relief was short-lived. The dwarves started talking among themselves, until it all blended into a low rumble. I tried to get a read on them, but it was hard. All their voices and questions overlapped, and their expressions differed. A few seemed eager for battle and wanted to help. Others appeared worried, nervous, and a few were angry and hostile.

"Quiet!" Lenora said, slamming down her mug. Silence fell. "I'm not opposed to helping Alexandria, but what if Premier has already taken the city? What shall we do then? We can't possibly enter Alexandria with our force alone. It's...tactically unsound."

"Mother, you sound afraid," Jastillian said.

Lenora narrowed her eyes. Anger passed over her face. If you wanted to provoke a dwarf, the best way was to call him or her a coward. Then Lenora laughed and slapped her son hard on the shoulder. "You're lucky you're my son. Otherwise I'd have to drub you with my sword hilt. Sieging a castle takes resources and time. Time we may not have."

"You're not actually considering this," another dwarf said in a calm voice. "It's none of our business. We should fortify our defenses here."

"But what about the people of Alexandria?" I asked. "You're not going to let them die and leave the elves to face the Wastelands alone?"

"If Alexandria has failed in its duty, then the city should fall. I admire the elves' courage, but if they are foolish enough to do this—may they die well."

"They need your help. You're the only country close enough and strong enough to help them." I wanted to throw my hands up in frustration, but restrained myself.

The dwarf shrugged as he reached for his mug. He took a sip and wiped the ale from his black beard. His calmness frustrated me more than the other dwarf's anger.

"Premier and his creatures will run rampant across all of Northern Shala if you don't help them," I said.

Another dwarf said, "They won't breach our defenses." Many of the dwarves nodded in agreement. Even the female dwarf who had first spoken up looked thoughtful.

I looked around the table. I needed something more to convince them. "Alexandria would pay you whatever you ask. They'd owe you for saving their kingdom. Whatever you want, Alexandria would give you."

The older dwarf I had been arguing with raised an eyebrow. "Are you an ambassador for Alexandria, that you could promise such things?"

I wasn't, but hoped the princess would understand. "No, but I—"

"Then why are you promising them? Hmmm?"

"You're forgetting the treaty, Om," Jastillian said, interrupting me before I could respond. Thank the gods. "We're pledged to help Alexandria against the Wastelands if they need us."

"I know the treaty you speak of. It requires our help if they request aid. No such envoy has come. While I appreciate Wizard Hellsfire's desire to shower us with the riches of Alexandria, he wasn't sent here in an official capacity." He put his hand up before others could respond. "This sounds more like internal strife with Premier. We shouldn't get involved in Alexandria's politics."

"You don't honestly believe that?" Artesia asked.

"It doesn't matter what I believe. That's what it is."

Before Artesia or Jastillian could respond, the dwarf who had stared at me throughout dinner said, "What about Premier?"

Jastillian's body tensed, and he pushed his shoulders back to make himself look bigger. "What about him, Gort?"

Gort gave Jastillian an intense look. "How are we to deal with Premier? Whether he already holds the city or not is not the point. We need a wizard of our own to beat him."

"Weren't you paying attention? We already have one." Jastillian nodded in my direction. "Hellsfire already went up against Premier and lived. He's going to do it again."

Gort snorted. "He's young, and you still embellish your stories. Sounds like he got lucky to me."

I almost rose, but Jastillian beat me to it. "Are you questioning the lad's bravery, skill, and *honor?*" He slammed his hand on the table.

Gort stood up too.

"Boys, I will not have you arguing here," Lenora said. Gort and Jastillian slowly sat back down, still glaring at one another. Lenora turned to me and said, "Hellsfire, I need to know if you can defeat Premier."

All the dwarves' eyes turned towards me. I grew hot under my collar from their intense scrutiny. I stared at my empty plate, remembering the spells I had cast at Premier. They were quick and easy spells, true, but they meant nothing to him. He was a fully trained wizard who had managed to insinuate himself into the court of a king who hated wizards, and had influenced the king's mind to such an extent that he had become the true ruler. If I hadn't gotten lucky and caught him off guard with the door, he probably could have crushed me to a pulp.

Now wasn't the time to tell the dwarves that. I couldn't be honest with them the way I could with King Sharald or Princess Krystal. They wouldn't respect that. They'd think me weak. I had everything to lose by being honest. So I tried something I wasn't good at—I lied.

I took a deep breath and looked into Lenora's eyes. "I can and I will." I had to face Premier again and destroy him. Not for my own sake, but for Krystal's. However, many of the dwarves didn't look convinced.

"We've heard the arguments," Lenora said. "I believe it's time to put this to a proper vote. Whether we choose to help Alexandria or not, we must prepare for battle. I prefer to take the offensive and attack Premier rather than be trapped in these mountains when he comes for us." She met each dwarf's eyes, her gaze settling longer on Om. "And he *will* come for us. All in favor of marching to the aid of Alexandria, raise your hand and say, 'Aye.'"

Lenora raised her hand first and Artesia quickly followed. Some of the dwarves glanced at the two women first before raising their hands. I thought this was going to be an easy vote, until I saw a number of dwarves like Gort and Om sitting with their arms firmly crossed. At the end, just under half the dwarves sided with us. Gort smirked again.

"No," I whispered.

"I'm sorry, Hellsfire," Lenora said. To everyone else she said, "Prepare our defenses. Double our patrols. Send scouts to Alexandria to see if it's fallen. Let's get to work."

The dwarves began rising to see to their preparations. Jastillian clapped my back and said, "I'm sorry, lad."

My palms were flat against the stone table. My fingernails dug at the cold, hard surface. I had come all the way out here for nothing. Nothing! The princess, the king, all the people of Alexandria and Sharald were in trouble, and all the dwarves could think about was themselves. The cowards!

I could no longer control my power. The torches in the room erupted, then died, plunging the room into complete darkness. I sensed everyone in the room had frozen, all turning to stare at me. Instead of reigniting the torches, I stood up, letting the fire and my anger flow out of my hands until I became a burning torch. The flames danced on me, circling my body and encasing me in an aura of flame.

The doors flew open, and guards rushed in. The sound of weapons being drawn rang in my ears.

"Hellsfire," Jastillian said. "What are you doing?"

"I came here for your help. I'm not leaving without it."

"My people have spoken," Lenora said. "We're not helping Alexandria."

"What if I can ensure your victory?" My voice was confident, even though I didn't feel that way.

"How could you possibly do that?" Om asked.

"We won't fight alone."

Gort snorted. "The elves."

"No, not the elves." I ignored Gort and gave my attention to the others who had voted against me. "I could get another wizard to help—a powerful and experienced one, and with him, a dragon." I had no idea if I could convince Master Stradus and Cynder to come out of the White Mountain to help me, but I had to risk it. It was the only way to convince the dwarves. They would fight if they knew they could win.

"Could you reach him in time?" Artesia asked.

"Yes," I said without hesitation. "Give me your fastest horse, and I'll get there."

"From what Jastillian has told me of wizards," Lenora said, weighing her words carefully, "since the Great War, they prefer not to meddle in the affairs of the world. Can you convince him to aid us in battle?"

I nodded. "He'll help."

"With this new information, we must take another vote," Lenora said.

"How do we know he's not lying to us?" Gort asked. "It's been centuries since we've last seen a wizard—or a dragon. Now they're in abundance?"

I focused on Gort. The fire surrounding me burned brighter and hotter. "Are you questioning my honor?"

The guards shifted, looking at me and Gort before glancing at Lenora to see what they should do. Gort's eyes narrowed, and he never wavered. This fool was going to cost Krystal the help she needed. I was no ambassador. I wasn't good with words. I could only do what Jastillian suggested—show them strength. I wasn't going to stop until they relented.

Lenora stepped in front of Gort. "You've made your point, Wizard Hellsfire. Allow us to vote. There will be no more interruptions or outbursts in my chambers. You *will* abide by the outcome of the vote, whether you like it or not."

I nodded. "Yes, ma'am."

The surrounding fire flew to the torches. They burst into life, reigniting all at once like stars. The guards lowered their weapons, but didn't put them away. The rest of the dwarves sat back down, and I joined them.

"All those in favor of helping Alexandria, vote 'aye,'" Lenora said.

The same dwarves as before raised their hands. A few more had changed their minds, bringing it to over half the table. Most of the ones who hadn't voted yes held fast. I exhaled, feeling that my show was for naught and that I had let the princess down. I had no idea what to do now.

Then Om raised his hand. "Aye."

The other dwarves looked at Om in surprise. Some of the ones who had voted against me raised their hands, except for Gort. He clearly was having difficulty containing his anger at Om. A little over three-fourths of the table voted in favor of the proposal.

"Then it's settled," Lenora said. "I want the army ready to mobilize by the end of the week. I want the fastest scouts sent to Alexandria as soon as possible. We must know if Premier has already taken the city." Lenora smiled, then raised her fist and roared, "Let's drive the creatures back where they belong!"

Everyone cheered, shaking the hall. The dwarves dispersed to make preparations. My shoulders slumped in relief. I was also tired from that mana-consuming spell. Now, if only we could make it to Alexandria in time.

"Nice work, lad," Jastillian said. "For a second, you had me worried. That's the way to show them strength."

I opened my mouth to tell him that what I did was more of an accident, and that my emotions had gotten the best of me again, but decided against it. "I'm just glad I was able to get their help."

Jastillian had turned to leave, when I stopped him. "What should I do in the meantime?"

"Sorry, lad. I got caught up in all the excitement. I can feel my warrior's blood boiling to the surface, and it feels good." He stood erect, took a deep breath, and clenched his mighty fists. Then he said, "You can look around Erlam if you like. Are you going to leave tomorrow?"

I nodded. "At first light."

"I'll get you one of the fastest horses I can."

"Thank you, and thanks for all your help. Without you, your mother, and Artesia, I wouldn't have gotten the help I needed. I really appreciate it."

"Nonsense, lad. You made your case well. I'm just sorry that Gort made it more difficult than it had to be." He sighed. "But that's what family's for."

I raised my eyebrow. "Gort's your brother?"

"Aye. I take it you have no siblings."

"None."

"You're lucky. Gort and I don't exactly see eye to eye. Never have, never will." Jastillian put his massive hand on my shoulder. "But that has nothing to do with now. Go. Have fun, explore, or prepare if you want, but remember to get some sleep. I'll come get you an hour before sunrise."

"Where will I sleep tonight?"

"Sorry about that, I completely forgot." He burst out with a laugh so loud it echoed in the near-empty hall. "We're going to be busy, so any empty room in this place will be fine."

"How will you know where I'll be?"

"Don't worry, I'll find you," Jastillian said, and left.

A part of me wanted to explore the city of Erlam, as it might be the only time I ever saw it. I didn't. A larger part of me worried and fretted over the upcoming battle, the safety of the people of Alexandria, and how to convince Master Stradus to help me. To calm my nerves, I found a quiet, empty bedroom and spent most of my time in meditation. I tried to focus my energy and get lost in the mana that was all around me. It was hard, yet, as Master Stradus had taught me, that was the point of meditating. So that I could concentrate under any circumstances.

The next morning, Jastillian came right when he said he would. The bags under his eyes were deep. I felt bad because I hadn't worked as hard as him or any of the other dwarves as they prepared their army. I expressed this, and he said not to worry. They expected me to be the magic against magic.

I got on my horse and headed west back towards the White Mountain, wondering if Master Stradus would not only be grateful to see me, but willing to help me. Could I convince the hermit to leave the comfort of his caves and prophecies, to help me defeat Premier?

CHAPTER 19

I ARRIVED AT the White Mountain in the middle of the night. It shone against the dark sky, its frosted surface glistening. I got off my horse and sat cross-legged in front of the mountain. I focused on the fire within until I gathered enough power to perform my spell.

I raised my hands high into the sky, my sleeves tumbling down. I pictured the entrance to the cave. Blocking out all noise, I encased my mind in silence. I said an incantation and let a portion of the fire flow outward, shooting up in the sky. I focused hard on the flaming geyser, pushing my mind against the cold and wind. The stream of fire forced itself closer to the mountain and reached the mouth of the cave, shooting inward. I said a word to disperse it and created a great, flashing, fiery show that hopefully illuminated the whole cave and got someone's attention, even at this late hour.

Creating such a huge spell drained me. I leaned over, breathing heavily. As I waited for a response, I tried to think of another way to contact Master Stradus if this didn't work. Soon enough, though, a monstrous shadowy figure flew down from the mountain. He landed right beside me, hard and fast, causing a wind that almost sent me to the ground. As usual. The horse whinnied and shied in response. I had to hurry over and restrain him before he took off. The horse's large, black eyes became even larger, and his nostrils flared as he sighted the dragon. He pulled against the reins.

"Back so soon?" Cynder asked. He snorted a puff of fire and yawned. "Real world too much for you? I was having a good night's sleep until you decided to perform that little light show. Some of us higher beings need our sleep. What kind of spell was that, anyway? If I had been in the tunnel, I wouldn't have appreciated it."

I didn't have time to trade wit with him. Besides, I had him easily beaten. "Cynder, I must go and talk to Master Stradus. It's of the utmost importance."

He saw the seriousness in my eyes, for once. "Very well. Climb on." He peered down at the horse. "Is this for me? Thanks for the snack." Cynder grinned and wasted no time, snatching the horse before I could stop him. The horse cried out as Cynder's sharp talons dug into his flanks.

"Godsdamn it!" I said. "You overgrown oven. That was a gift—for me—not a snack. If it wasn't for that horse, I wouldn't have made it here as soon as I did."

"Humans." Cynder snorted. I climbed up on him, and he flew me through the stormy weather to the cave entrance. After he dropped off his food, he even took me all the way to Master Stradus's room so I wouldn't have to walk.

"Cynder, you might want to stay for this," I said as I hopped off.

"Since it'll probably take me a while to get back to sleep anyway, I might as well." His red eye went back towards the caves and to the dead horse. "Although, I am a little hungry." He mulled it over. "I guess I'll stay." Cynder groaned and settled his head near the doorway.

I found Master Stradus sitting on a stool, sipping some hot tea. He gave me a warm smile. "Good to see you, my boy, though I'm surprised you're back so soon. That was quite a signal you made, all the way up the mountain. You must be a little tired from it. How about some tea?"

"No, thank you, Master. I came here because I'm in dire need of your help. Northern Shala is in grave danger, and we need you."

Master Stradus stopped drinking his tea and sat straight up. He reached for his staff and stroked the globe on top. It swirled with sky blue colors. "You've got my complete attention, Hellsfire. Tell me exactly what you mean, from the beginning."

I relayed my entire story, trying to go quickly. Every second I talked was another wasted. But I failed. I rambled on and on. Everything was important to me, and so many things had happened since I last saw him.

Master Stradus didn't interrupt me. His eyes never left my face, and he didn't move except to drink his tea and fiddle with his staff. In my time with Master Stradus, whenever I'd had a question or didn't understand something, he'd work me through it by first hearing all of what I had to say.

Cynder, on the other hand, fell asleep midway through and snored. It sounded like countless birds were caught in his nose, flapping their wings. I was used to it, but it was still disgusting.

Master Stradus put his tea down after I was done and said, "Why, that was quite an adventure you've had in such a short period, my boy."

"Will you help me, Master?"

He paused. Then he blinked, slowly, and poured more tea.

"Master?"

He spoke slowly and deliberately. "I've lived in seclusion for a reason, Hellsfire. After the war, I first spent my time trying to help people and repair the land. The outside world grew suspicious of wizards, and rightly so. We caused a lot of damage."

I had thought of Master Stradus in a lot of ways—teacher, wizard, master—but in that second he was a frail old man. His eyes were deep and sorrow-laden, as if he carried a great burden that he could no longer handle.

I stood to get ready to leave. He wasn't going to help me. I saw it in his eyes. If I could wake Cynder up, maybe he would help. At the very least, I hoped he would give me a ride to Sharald since he had killed my horse.

"Where are you going?" Master Stradus asked.

"To Sharald. I gave the princess, the elves, and the dwarves my word. They need my help, and someone has to fight Premier."

"You don't stand a chance against him." His voice wasn't cold or mean. It was stated as a matter of fact.

My power rose. I focused my mind to keep it at bay, along with my anger. Instead of arguing with Master Stradus and wasting my time, I turned to leave.

"Wait."

I clenched my fists. "People are in danger. I don't have time to wait, Master."

"You're going to need help."

I stopped and turned around. I raised my eyebrow, allowing myself a glimmer of hope. "Does that mean you'll help me?"

He sighed, accentuating his age and how weary he was. "I will, but it's not going to be easy. Even with me at your side."

Master Stradus's words hit me, and his body language spoke volumes. He wasn't scared of Premier. Out of all the things he did and witnessed, he couldn't possibly be. He was a powerful wizard in his own might. No. It had to be something else. There was only one possible reason he didn't want to go.

"You sound like you know him," I said.

"I do," Master Stradus said. "It's been many years since I last saw him, but there's only one person who'd be bold enough to call himself Premier." He motioned to the chair with his staff.

"Shouldn't we get ready to leave?"

"You need to know what you're getting into if you plan on facing Premier. Now, sit." He relaxed and smiled. "We have plenty of time, my boy."

"But—"

Master Stradus put a hand up. I stopped talking and sat back down.

"I'm sorry, Master. I'm just worried about them." I looked towards the exit as if I could see Alexandria by willing it.

"I understand, but you must learn to be patient, Hellsfire. It's very important you learn what we're up against."

I nodded. He was right. And anything I could learn about Premier would help me fight him.

"A long time ago, in a different land and time, before the Great Barrier went up and before the war ended, Premier and I trained at the same wizard's school. Before we were wizards, and before we earned our wizard names." He tapped the globe with his fingers.

"The Council was training wizards to fight against Renak. Premier and I shared the same room and were at the top of our class. We were friends, but also rivals. We always tried to outdo one another, whether it be with spells, incantations, potions, or especially, girls. Exuberant youth." Master Stradus showed a wrinkled smile.

"Premier wasn't like the way you describe him now. He was cocky, to be sure, and always wanted to be the best, but his intentions were good. I believe the power he discovered corrupted him. We were the best of friends before I lost him and everything changed.

"Near the end of our training, we became more serious in our studies. We stopped spending as much time with the girls and started sneaking into our teachers' libraries. We were looking for more knowledge, any advantage to keep us from dying in the war. Unfortunately, it didn't stop there.

"Our fear of death pushed us even further. We explored the city outside the school, venturing out at night, talking to people who dabbled in the darker side of magic. We thought we needed any edge we could get, any sort of power they could show us.

"In school, we trained together. Outside of school, we trained apart, only coming together to show off what we'd learned. That was how it happened."

Master Stradus had been grinning, with a look of the youth that had long escaped him. Now his smile turned into a frown.

"One night, we both slipped out and went our separate ways," he continued. "When dawn came, Premier didn't meet me. I waited for him as long as I could before I had to return to our room. He made it back just before our lessons started.

"But something happened to Premier. He was...different. He was battered, ragged, and there was a look in his eyes—as if he had seen a horror no man should ever see. Not even a wizard. It was days before he said more than a few words. Eventually, I learned that he had come upon a book of great power—the *Book of Shazul*."

My eyes widened. I had read about the book and the wizard who created it. Shazul had been one of the most powerful wizards who ever lived—before he went mad and destroyed himself. And to think, I had been throwing my puny fireballs at Premier. No wonder he had laughed at me.

"I can see you know of what I speak," Master Stradus said. "But there's something I haven't told you. Now is that time."

I leaned forward, curious and scared of what he might tell me.

"The *Book of Shazul* is more than just a book of spells," he said. "It also is a book of prophecies. One of those prophecies had to do with you." He reached for more tea while letting the information sink in.

I gasped and stared at nothing. It all made sense now. Why Stradus came to my mother the night I was born, why he named me, why he waited in this mountain. If he read those prophecies in Shazul's book, they would have tugged at him, gnawing at his mind. When I first got here, I had asked him about the prophecy, but he had never answered my questions.

Until now.

"You never told me about this before," I said.

"Would it have made a difference?"

I shrugged. "It might have."

"Prophecies are very dangerous things. Sometimes they can be interpreted wrongly. Other times, by knowing what they are, you'll end up causing them to come to pass."

"Could you tell me more about the prophecy involving me?"

Master Stradus shook his head. "I can't. It's bad enough I'm telling you this much. I'm only telling you so you'll understand what you're up against."

"I understand."

"No, you don't. I hope you will someday." Master Stradus poured himself some more tea before he continued. "I asked Premier what had happened to him, but he wouldn't tell me. Eventually, I stopped asking.

"Premier started acting differently. He was constantly late for class, and he barely paid attention to the lessons. And we were so close to graduation. What bothered me the most was that he was no longer interested in girls."

Master Stradus shook his head, reliving old, painful memories. "My old friend turned into a hermit. Despite not paying attention to our teachers, his powers grew. The spells he did were amazing, and his power became stronger than mine. So I did what any friend would do—I took to spying on him.

"It was then I saw him with that blasted book.

"I saw him practicing the spells in it," Master Stradus said. "I thought he had stolen one of the books we students weren't allowed to use because the spells might be too dangerous. But that wasn't it. He had hidden it in a tiny, unused room in the basement. I snuck in one day while I was certain he'd be away. When I touched the book, I felt the magnificent power it contained. It was also terrifying. But I convinced myself that if Premier could understand and control it, so could I.

"It took ages to bypass all of Premier's protection spells, but I managed it. And when I finally opened the book, it was—it was…" Master Stradus trailed off and closed his eyes. He gripped his staff so tightly his knuckles lost their color. The globe on top of the staff swirled with mana.

"Master?"

Wind blew into the chamber and made the torches flutter. Sweat ran down Master Stradus's forehead and dripped over his eyebrows.

"Master!" I yelled.

The wind stopped, and he opened his eyes. The globe was clear of mana. He wiped the sweat from his face and said, "It was like I was touched by the gods."

He continued his story as if he hadn't noticed anything unusual had just happened. I didn't say anything either. I wasn't sure that reminding him of what he experienced so long ago was a wise thing to do.

"The first thing I saw were the prophecies," he said. "I never had the talent to become a seer, and I sure wasn't a prophet. Ah, but my teachers were right, my boy." Master Stradus chuckled.

"What do you mean?"

"My teachers used to say I always had my head in the clouds. I'm glad I did. You see, son, I was always wondering about the future and what was in store for me, and what would happen when the war was over. If I hadn't been fascinated by things like that, I think the spells in the book would have ensnared me and I'd be corrupted like Premier. Instead, the prophecies became my obsession, and the book never truly took hold of me."

Master Stradus was only partly right. He did let it take hold of him. He created the spell that encompasses the White Mountain, and waited for me for centuries. At least Master Stradus did it after he led a good life and saw the world. It saddened and frightened me to realize that centuries of dreams and hopes were pinned on me.

"You wouldn't believe how accurate the book was," he said, jolting me out of my thoughts. "It told of the War of the Wizards, the Great Barrier, the Burning Sands, you, and maybe even me, I think."

"Really?"

"Yes, but I didn't know it back then. It took years for me to understand a fraction of those prophecies. The more I learn and wait, the more I understand. That's partly why I've been cooped up here so long. Because of that fateful day when I got lost in the prophecies and Premier came back to find me buried in his book."

Master Stradus drank some more tea, then licked his lips. "When we were young, Premier was known for his emotional outbursts. As we grew up, and his training made him more disciplined, he learned to focus his rage, waiting until the perfect time to strike. That day, when he found me with his book, I stared into his dark eyes and felt the powerful magic he was drawing in.

"Despite the angry storm brewing underneath his still face, he summoned the book to his hand and looked down at what I was reading. He didn't say a word. I had a feeling if I moved or drew in any magic, Premier would have struck me down hard—friend or no. But he did something unexpected. He laughed."

"He laughed?" I asked.

Master Stradus smiled and said, "That he did. The magic he gathered around him dissipated, and my old friend returned. Premier closed the book and said I never ceased to amaze him. All those spells at my fingertips, and I was reading prophecies. Sadly, his laughter didn't last. He became silent and stern again.

"He wanted me to join him. He said that with the book, the two of us could take down Renak. We would be unstoppable."

I knew he hadn't said yes, but I couldn't stop myself from asking, "Did you do it?"

Master Stradus fiddled with his long beard before answering. "No, but a part of me wanted to. A rather large part, I'm afraid." He looked up towards the ceiling. "It was so tempting—the power, the prophecies, the hope of saving my friend, and of avoiding the war.

"I tried to convince him to take the book to the Council. With their years of experience, they could help us. That was the wrong move. I had forgotten how much Premier hated the Council and blamed them for the war. He said the power belonged to him, and not those old fools. I looked into his eyes and saw that his lust for power had taken him. I had lost my best friend forever.

"I then foolishly tried to grab the book from Premier, but he cast a spell at me. He was so quick, and I was so surprised he would do such a thing, that it caught me off guard. My muscles locked up, and I cried out in agony. He leaned over me and said, 'Goodbye, my friend.' I thought he meant he was going to kill me, but he spared my life. I could do nothing but stare at him, watching him leave for parts unknown.

"When the spell wore off, I went outside to follow him, but I couldn't see or sense him anywhere." Master Stradus slammed his staff on the floor. "Too much time had passed. After that, I never saw him again. I always thought he might have died or possibly had gone to join Renak, since they seemed to be on the same path. Now I know what happened to him. Poor fool."

"What'd you do after that, Master? Didn't you try to go and track him down?"

"Sadly, I never got the chance to. They were going to send me to the war. With a great deal of persuasion, I did get to see the Council and tell them what had happened." Master Stradus frowned. "But they didn't believe me. I suspect they thought he was just another deserter.

"You know that Renak created the Wasteland creatures, twisting and enslaving them to serve him? I suspect Premier may have done the same thing, with the knowledge he learned from the book. For years, wizards have tried to learn Renak's secrets. None have succeeded until now."

Master Stradus yawned and put a hand to his mouth. "Well, my boy, I would say it's time to retire. We've been talking half the night, and you must be tired."

I yawned too and rubbed my tired eyes. "I am."

"Get some sleep. Goodnight, my son. It's good to have you back." He smiled before heading back to his room.

"Goodnight, Master," I said. "And goodnight to you too, Cynder." The dragon's huge nostrils flared as he snored.

I made my way to my room. I took a moment to enjoy the memories that flooded my mind at the familiar sights and scents. I was so tired I plopped myself on the bed, not even bothering to take off my clothes.

Master Stradus was right about the fact that I needed to know more about Premier. Now that I knew how powerful, methodical, and careful he was, I couldn't underestimate him, nor could I face him alone. I was glad I had come back to the White Mountain, and more importantly, thankful that Master Stradus was going to help me.

I still couldn't believe that Master Stradus and Premier were once friends—best friends at that. Would Master Stradus be able to do what was necessary to defeat his old friend? Since Premier had the book, would we even be a match for him?

I went to sleep with these weary thoughts, questions, and fears on my mind.

CHAPTER 20

I WOKE UP REFRESHED and energized. I hadn't slept that well in a long time. My tranquility passed quickly, replaced by guilt. I couldn't help but think of the others: the elves, the dwarves, the princess. I wondered what they were going through right now, and if we could arrive to help them in time. I said a quiet prayer to the gods in hopes that we could.

I made my way to the little dining hall where Master Stradus had made some soup.

"Good afternoon, my boy," Master Stradus said. "You had a long sleep."

"Good afternoon?" I said. "I've overslept! Master, we must leave. We've got to go and meet the others. We must—"

"Relax, my son, relax. We have plenty of time. I woke up early this morning and went outside to see if your friend had made it to Sharald. He did. It looked as if the whole forest was moving. You see, nothing to worry about."

"Shouldn't we go and join them?"

"We will, but we have plenty of time. It'll take the elves about four days to move an army that size to the rendezvous point. We'll meet them when that time arrives." Master Stradus's face became grim. "We must get you prepared."

"How will we get there so quickly?"

"You forget, Hellsfire, we will have a dragon with us. But first, let's eat. After that, we will go through some more training."

I shook my head and ran my fingers through my matted hair. "Can't wait."

After our meal, Master Stradus led me to the practice room. "Let's see how well you've progressed since you left me."

"But I haven't been gone that long, Master."

"You'd be surprised at how much things can change in a short period of time. Go over and stand on the other side of the room. As the dwarves would say, 'I want you to hit me as hard as you can.'"

"Hit you?"

"Yes, but not physically. I'm an old man, and you'd knock me to the ground." He laughed and leaned on his staff. "I know we've never done this before, but I want you to throw a spell at me, and I will try to counter it. You will keep doing that until I say stop, or until you're too tired. A practice wizard's duel. Understand?"

"I do." I raised an eyebrow. "But are you sure about this?"

"Yes." He raised his voice. "Now attack, and don't hold anything back!"

I raised my arms and engulfed him with flames. He disappeared inside the cone of fire. Within moments, a funnel of wind took its place. I needed another idea.

I grabbed one of the growth potions from my pouch and threw it against the ground, hoping I wasn't going to need it later, and that potions weren't against the rules. But Master Stradus had his staff; it was only fair I had something. And once I was fighting Premier, there would be no rules.

The potion spread over the floor. I spoke an incantation, combining it with earth mana. The ground swayed and rumbled as I poured my energy into the spell. Two green vines sprang from the rock and wrapped around Master Stradus's arms, binding them. A third erupted and grasped his neck. More shot out, holding his legs in place. Master Stradus struggled to free himself, but soon he realized that he would never be able to break free through physical means.

His face became stone-hard with concentration.

The pearl on top of Master Stradus's staff hummed with power. Out of the ground rose a humongous carnivorous plant. I hadn't expected or intended that. It was twice as big as Master Stradus and me combined. Its head thrashed about, teeth snapping, saliva dripping from its mouth. It turned toward Master Stradus and narrowed its hungry, mad eyes. Before I could stop it, it swallowed him whole.

I waited a few tense seconds for him to burst out of the plant monster. He didn't. The plant had gone completely still. I didn't know if that should worry me or not. I took a couple of cautious steps closer, concerned. Suddenly, the plant exploded, spewing green stuff all over the place.

"Yuck," I said, wiping plant goo from my face. Master Stradus stood tall, untouched and unharmed. He had a white glow about him.

"Not bad, my boy. Tell me, are you tired at all?"

"I feel a little light-headed, but I'm ready whenever you are, Master."

"Good. Now, let's see how skilled your defenses are. Prepare yourself!" I took a deep breath and clenched my fists, gathering in mana. I readied myself for whatever came my way.

Master Stradus chanted in the old language, his eyes becoming solid blue gems. A cold breeze entered the room; the candles swayed. A drop of water dripped on me. I wiped my face, still wondering what he was going to do. Another drop struck. When I looked up, I saw a cloud had formed just under the ceiling. I was about to disperse it, when a bolt of lightning shot out of the cloud—straight at me.

I scrambled out of the way just in time. The lightning tore a hole in the floor. I raised my hands to disperse the cloud, and this time a huge gust of wind hit me. It sent me flying against the wall of the cave. I groaned as my back slammed into the rocky wall. Master Stradus continued to channel his power through his staff, the globe ever swirling.

The little cloud quickly grew into a monstrous one. Huge winds knocked me back and forth against the hard rocks. Rain fell so hard it stung with every drop. In the midst of the storm stood Master Stradus—calm, dry, and chanting.

I strained my muscles, pushing my hands against the wind and trying to keep on my feet. *"Just as water can extinguish fire, can fire burn water!"*

Fire exploded out of my hands and rolled over the ceiling in waves, smothering the cloud. Steam blanketed everything, leaving the ceiling scorched and the room smelling like charcoal. With the cloud gone, the rain and wind both stopped. I thought Master Stradus would have come out of his trance, but he was still chanting. The globe atop his snaked staff whirled.

I pried myself away from the wall, wincing from my scrapes and bruises. I circled Master Stradus, preparing defensive spells. It became harder for me to move. At first I thought it was the weight of the water in my drenched clothes, but when I tried to take another step forward, I couldn't. My feet were stuck. The ground had turned into a kind of quicksand or bog.

I struggled to escape, but my predicament only grew worse. The bog sucked me deeper—up to my thighs, then waist. The mountain was eating me alive.

"Need help, Hellsfire?" Master Stradus held his hand out to me. The quicksand was now confined to a small area surrounding me, and his eyes had returned to normal. "Here, my boy, let me help you."

"I don't need your help," I said, with the mountain up to my chin.

"Of course you do. You shouldn't be ashamed of the fact you weren't paying complete attention to everything. You did very well."

I ground my teeth. "It's not over."

"Hellsfire, please. Now is not the time to be stubborn. The ground will soon cover you from head to toe."

"I will get out of this myself!" I gave him a fierce look, then sighed. "You won't always be around to help me, Master." I gulped one last breath and slid deeper into the mountain.

"Hellsfire…"

My heartbeat was the only thing I heard. I wanted to scream, but all I would have gotten was a mouthful of mud. I hated being entrapped in tight spaces. I hated giving up even more.

People were counting on me. They needed my help to fight Premier. I wasn't going to let them down. I thought of all the good people Premier was going to kill if I didn't get out of here, starting with the princess. I concentrated, forcing my mind to take control over my panicky body.

My training took over, and I heard Master Stradus's lessons in my mind. *Focus*, he said. I closed my eyes and calmed my mind. In the quiet solitude of the enclosed ground, I understood what my master had done. He had created the storm as a diversion, albeit a very dangerous one. I had faced two fronts: the storm and the land itself. It was quite ingenious of him. This was how wizards dueled. I'd do well to remember it.

I was quickly running out of air. I had to hurry. I grasped my inner fire and shifted it through my hands into the surrounding mud. I focused on my friends who were willing to give their lives in the upcoming battle. My emotions fueled the fire. I couldn't—wouldn't—let them fight alone!

The ground heated up and dried out, becoming as brittle as rust. I stopped sinking, and dug through the dry, crackling dirt. When I finally broke through the surface, I panted and gasped for air.

As soon as I was no longer in danger of suffocating, I gave a tired smile. "You see, Master? I told you I would get out of that myself."

"Come, let's get you cleaned up."

I washed myself and my clothes. I dried my tunic with blasts of hot air, but left my wizard's robe to dry the usual way. It hadn't cleaned itself, as when I was in the bathhouse in Erlam. Maybe because I was very tired from crawling out of my grave, or maybe it really was the steam that had cleaned it in Erlam. A living robe? I shook my head at the preposterous idea.

I went to the garden, where Master Stradus was kneeling in the dirt tending his plants. My eyes took in every plant and flower—their leaves, petals, and the wondrous colors. My nose was filled with sweet smells. "I almost forgot how beautiful your garden is."

Master Stradus nodded as he overturned some topsoil.

"I still don't understand why you don't use magic to help you. It'd be a lot easier."

"That would *ruin* the point," Master Stradus said. "The only magic I used was in the beginning, to get the plants to grow and for the light. Now, I rely on the skill of my two hands and my knowledge of plants." He stopped digging for a moment. "After everything I've been through in my life, it's the simple things that I enjoy. I hope you'll come to understand that."

"What do you mean, Master?"

He began digging, carefully loosening the dirt around the roots. "Remember all the things I've taught you, that's all. The world's a dangerous place, son. You have to be careful, especially in the upcoming battle."

I took a moment, staring at him. What could have gotten him so frustrated? There was only one thing I could think of. "You don't think I'm prepared, do you?"

He stopped his digging and turned towards me. Sadness loomed in his eyes. "No. I do not."

My anger and fire rose with my frustration and disbelief. "How could you not believe in me?" I yelled. "After all this time, after all you've said, I'm not the One?"

Master Stradus stared at me, not saying a word. The expression on his face was unreadable. He sighed. "You are the One, Hellsfire. I believe that. You haven't fully mastered your powers, and you know not all the dangers that lie in the world. You have started to learn some of these things. But you need to master your powers and learn about the world, or you're going to fail."

"I thought you said I did well in the training room today?"

Master Stradus rose, reaching for his staff. He dusted himself off. "You did, but you could have done better. You should have paid more attention. In battle with another wizard, you must think on your feet. You only paid attention to my cloud, but you never thought of the ground beneath you. You always have to think ahead, Hellsfire. Always.

"In warfare, it's different. You'll have plenty of time to work your spells, and you'll have the support of others. Even then, you must still think ahead. You must see the things that are not there but might be. Think of *all* the possibilities. That's one of the things that makes a wizard. The magic is but a small part of it."

My face sagged, and my anger dissipated. He was right. I had a lot to learn, but I thought I was doing my best so far. If my best wasn't good enough, then perhaps I wasn't the One he thought I was? Perhaps he was wrong. Perhaps I had wasted my time and his.

Master Stradus walked over to me and placed his hand on my shoulder. "My son, you came to a great realization today when you knew I wouldn't always be here for you. I'm sorry I've placed so much pressure on you, Hellsfire. Remember what I've taught you, and most of all, follow your heart." He smiled at me. "You've grown a lot over the past three years. I'm proud of you. But you still have a lot to learn, and so do I. For a wizard, the learning never stops."

Master Stradus walked out of the garden. A hot, stinging sensation crept into my eyes. I wanted to be alone, so I went out on the ledge, staring down at the landscape below. I tried in vain to imagine what was happening in Alexandria. Because I was exhausted from today's duel, I didn't last more than a couple of minutes in the weather. The cold pierced into my skin. I went inside to the library to read some stories, in hopes I would be able to laugh and lighten my mood.

We ate later in the day, but little was said during the meal. I went to bed earlier than normal. I wanted to think about the things Master Stradus had said to me in the garden. Fighting Premier was going to be even harder than I had thought. I had little hope of standing against him alone. I was glad my master would be with me.

We spent the next three days in practice duels and making potions to take with us. Each morning I woke up sore. My first thought was always of Krystal and the others. I wished we had a way of seeing if they were all right, but Master Stradus had hesitated to use a maleika for fear of conjuring the one that had almost killed me.

On the fourth morning, I woke earlier than usual. The elves should be nearly to Alexandria by now. We should be leaving soon.

Master Stradus had breakfast prepared. He waited until I had taken a bite of freshly baked bread before he spoke. "You should know this. Premier has taken Alexandria."

The bread dropped from my hand. "No," I whispered. I immediately thought of Krystal. Pictures of Premier doing unspeakable things to her formed in my mind. The flames grew still like my heart. "Master, how do you know this?"

"I used a maleika."

"But you said—"

"I know what I said, Hellsfire. It had to be done. Precautions were taken."

I didn't care that he took a risk in doing it, and that he did it without me. I jumped to my feet and paced, fists clenched. "Godsdamnit! If only we had left sooner! I knew I should have stayed behind. If only—"

"Hellsfire, there's nothing you could have done. Premier captured Alexandria long before the dwarves or elves got there. By the time you arrived here, it was already too late. And if you had stayed behind, he would have killed you."

I stopped pacing and perked up. "The elves and dwarves are there?"

He nodded. "I've sent a messenger hawk to tell them about our arrival. We fly out later today."

"At least the armies are there. But I still wish we had done something to prevent this." My initial burst of emotion faded. The flames resumed their normal burn. I sat back down on the stool and slumped over the table, ignoring the food.

"I know how you feel."

I looked up at him. "You do?"

Master Stradus set down his cup of tea and cradled his staff in his hands. "I never told you this. I never got a chance to enter the war."

"I always thought you did."

He shook his head. "We arrived after the last battle had already taken place. I was…frustrated. Friends had died, and I wasn't there for them."

I let his words sink in. That's exactly how I felt. So many people were putting their lives on the line, and I was sitting in here in safety. *Book of Shazul* or not, I shouldn't have left the princess by herself. I should have taken her away from Premier. I should have done something—anything!

"After the war, peace was tenuous at best," Master Stradus said. "Old debts were remembered, and new alliances were formed. Countries used this time to expand their lands or resources. I foolishly got involved in a dispute between two principalities over mining rights in the Daleth Mountains.

"I wanted to help the people involved, but I also wanted to prove something to my dead friends. The situation turned into a pitched battle, and I blindly rushed into it, making things far worse."

Master Stradus reached for his bread, then decided against it. He went for some tea but his hand shook. He clenched his fist. "People died because of me, Hellsfire." Tears filled Master Stradus's eyes.

"Because you were late?"

"No!" He pounded his staff on the floor. "It was because I was young and foolish and rushed into things. I didn't understand the situation or what would happen when I charged in."

I nodded in understanding. Despite how much I wanted to help Krystal and the others, it was foolish of me to rush into things. I knew that in my head; however, my heart kept going out to them. Especially her.

"My biggest mistake," Master Stradus said in a hoarse voice, "was that I forgot my training in the heat of battle. Battles are tricky. Time doesn't move, and then it moves far too fast. Your emotions, the sights, the smells, and the sounds will panic and confuse you. It did me. It was as if everything I had ever learned left me in the most critical moment. People died because of it." Master Stradus wiped away some tears that had fallen down his face. "I train you so you won't make the same mistake I did. Remember that in the coming days, Hellsfire."

I nodded. "I will, Master."

"Good. As soon as we're done eating, we'll restock your potions. Then we'll go."

I didn't eat more than a couple of nibbles of my food. After hearing Master Stradus's story, I just wasn't hungry anymore. My mind kept thinking about what he had said. There was so much to learn. I started to imagine all the ways I could mess things up. I sighed. I had to trust in my training to take over when I needed it, as it had when I was buried in the bog. I couldn't let anyone down; I couldn't let anyone die. These thoughts weighed me down.

Finally, I gave up on breakfast. My stomach wouldn't stop churning. Master Stradus had said for me to gather my things while he got the potions that had set overnight, and then meet him out front. I hurried, wanting to see Cynder alone.

Cynder was in the largest cave, practicing aerial maneuvers in the limited space. He dodged invisible enemies and weapons. When he saw me, he paused in midflight, hovering.

"What do you want, little human?" Cynder asked. "Can't you see I'm busy?"

"Doesn't look like you're busy to me. Looks like you're just flying around."

Cynder snorted smoke. "I'm getting ready for battle, just like you should be." He landed right beside me, his massive body looming over me. "Lucky for you, our master will be there to help you. What do you want?"

There wasn't much Master Stradus hadn't told me about what to expect, but there was a question I hadn't asked. It was something I thought he was no longer able to relate to, and the fact that we were about to leave had pushed it to the forefront of my mind. "I've come to ask you a question."

"As I've told you a thousand times, I don't know why the gods made you bipedal creatures so ugly. I suppose they had a reason for making you soft and without scales. After all, not every creature can be great and beautiful, like us dragons." Cynder craned his neck and grinned.

I was serious for once, but he didn't seem to be. "Forget it." I turned and started to walk away.

"Wait," Cynder said. "Ask your question."

I stopped and stared into his red eyes. Seeing the seriousness in them, I took a deep breath. "All right. You dragons live so long, yet you're not immortal. I wanted to know if you're scared of dying."

Cynder paused and seemed to consider this. "I do not fear what does not exist."

I scratched my head, trying to see if this was another riddle of his. The lack of a smile told me it wasn't. "You don't believe in death? Does that mean you believe in an afterlife?"

Cynder shook his elongated head. "That's not it. You don't understand because—"

"I'm a human."

"It's about time you learned that." Cynder laughed. I didn't even smile. He stopped and became serious again. "Dragons are the pinnacle of the gods' creations. We learn what we can in this life, and when we pass on, we ascend and become part of everything."

"What about us humans?"

Cynder gave the dragon equivalent of a shrug. "I'm not a god or one of your priests. Maybe there is an afterlife for you, or maybe something else entirely happens to wizards." He gave a dragon smile when he looked at my face. "Is that what you're worried about? Dying?"

"It's one of the things."

"What are the others?"

I hesitated for a moment. Cynder might be a pain, he might make fun of me and get me into trouble, but he was also a friend. I stared into his red eyes, seeing the ancient wisdom and perspective a dragon had. I told him what I had recently told our master—my fears of not being ready, not being strong enough, of letting people down.

"That's good," Cynder said after I was finished.

"Good?"

"Yes. Fear can push you. You, being young and a human, have a lot of fears. Just focus on one and let it guide you. Don't fail your friends. Fight for the princess." Cynder stretched his long neck and winked. I had told him too much.

"That's it?"

"Yes."

"But Master Stradus said—"

"Yes, yes, I know. I'm not saying to do it as a wizard. Be you. Humans can do amazing things with or without magic."

I stood there, thinking about his words. As much as I hated to admit it, he was right. I couldn't worry about dying. I had to worry about my friends, and let my fears for their safety drive me to use my magic correctly.

Cynder blew smoke in my face. I coughed, trying to clear my lungs. I frowned at him. "What'd you do that for?"

"You were getting all serious on me, with that thoughtful, sad look on your face. Let's play before our master comes. It might be our last time."

"Are you worried you might die too?"

Cynder snorted. "Hardly." He put a talon to his chest and said, "I'm not one of you soft creatures. Don't worry, little Hellsfire, the master and I won't let you die. If anyone is going to kill you, it's going to be me." Cynder grinned, showing off his rows of pointy teeth.

"Thanks for the advice, Cynder. I appreciate it."

"I *am* a dragon. There's no wiser creature. Even wizards bow to our wisdom." Cynder raised his tail and swung at me. The massive armored tail could have killed me, but he slowed it at the last second and gently tapped me on the head with the diamond-shaped tip. "Tag. You're it." Cynder took off and flew over my head, heading into the other parts of the caves.

I smiled, pushing aside the thought that this might be the last time we got to play together, and chased after him.

I reached the entrance of the caves, letting the cold air wash over me. I bent over with my hands on my knees, gasping for air. That oversized dragon was faster than he appeared.

Cynder had his back to me, staring at the landscape below. He craned his long neck towards Alexandria. As soon as I recovered, I tip-toed across the snowy ground, sneaking closer to him. I had to be careful. I'd done this before and he always moved at the last second. If he did that this time, I could go falling right off the mountain. I was just about to touch his swaying tail when I was interrupted.

"Are you two ready?" Master Stradus asked. I froze. "Hellsfire, come here and take some of these potions."

I nodded, taking the potions from him and putting them in my purse.

"Looks like today is going to be a nice day," I said to myself, peering past the constant winter storm of the White Mountain.

"Whenever there's warfare, it's never a nice day," Master Stradus said as he climbed on top of Cynder.

"Agreed," Cynder said. "Prepare yourself, Hellsfire. Today, you will see how your race really is."

"What's that supposed to mean?"

"You'll find out soon enough."

"Cynder, enough," Master Stradus said. "Let him be. I'm sure you remember what it was like the first time you went to war."

Cynder said in a sad and quiet voice. "A dragon never forgets."

My joy and lightheartedness from playing with Cynder disappeared. I couldn't help but imagine the fallen bodies of elves, dwarves, and humans, covered in bloody wounds. Limbs broken and twisted. Premier stood on top of the bodies, cradling the *Book of Shazul* in one hand. He laughed while the incredible power he held wrapped around him.

I didn't know how much of a chance my master and I stood, but I wasn't going to let my fears come true.

"Let me help you up, my son," said Master Stradus. I took his hand, and he pulled me onto Cynder's back. "Come now, Cynder. Take flight and lead us to Alexandria."

"Yes, Master."

It was time for my final lesson—war.

CHAPTER 21

CYNDER RAISED HIS great wings and, with one swoop, took to the sky. He lit up like the sun, his body blazing red in the early morning light. It felt marvelous being in the sky, the wind flowing through my hair. From up here, everything seemed so much smaller. It was as if everyone on the ground was a tiny ant, oblivious to the greater world. It was no wonder Cynder was arrogant. With his power armored body looking down from this perspective, who wouldn't be?

The plain south of Alexandria was littered with troops. Thousands upon thousands of elves and dwarves had gathered, and now they marveled at Cynder as if he were a god of some sort. In ancient times, some people had actually worshipped dragons as gods. Cynder said he always got a kick out of that. The elves' encampment was different shades of green—a forest moving and shifting with the breeze. The dwarves' earth tones of browns, reds, and grays made them look like tiny pebbles.

"Over there!" Master Stradus said, his voice piercing the wind. He pointed at an empty space in between the two great armies. "Land right there!"

Cynder nodded and dove. He must have looked like a great red fireball about to crash into the ground. Just before he touched down, he backwinged and landed gently, right between two very large tents. A far cry from what he'd do if it were only me riding him. Both armies closed in on us. I hopped off of Cynder. Some friendly faces came into view.

I took a moment to look around at all my new friends: Prastian, Demay, Behast, and Jastillian. I had never had many friends growing up in Sedah. Now I did. I was surprised that, in such a short time, I had met so many people I could trust and who were willing to lay their lives on the line for me, as I would for them.

While I could tell by my friends' faces that they were both relieved to see my master, and a bit in awe of him, they were even more so of Cynder. Cynder basked in all the attention. Master Stradus told Cynder to stay in the landing area and not let it all go to his head.

"Please come inside the command tent," Prastian said, after introductions were made. "We're working on some final details and could use your expertise, Wizard Stradus."

My master nodded, and we followed Prastian to the tent. Just outside stood King Sharald and Lenora Rammalong. "Who is that old man with the unusual crutch?" King Sharald asked loudly.

Master Stradus's face brightened when he recognized Sharald. "Old? Why, I hardly feel a day over two hundred. Besides, you don't look too youthful yourself, little Sharald."

"That may be true, but compared to you, I'm still a baby." Sharald gave Master Stradus a hug. As soon as I saw those two side by side, I knew Master Stradus was the one in the portrait I had seen in Sharald's palace. "Stradus, this is Lenora from the Rammalong House, leader of the dwarves of Erlam."

Master Stradus grasped Lenora's forearm. She said, "I'm honored to go into battle with you, Wizard Stradus."

"And I with you, ma'am. It's been ages since I last fought alongside your people. It was an honorable experience."

"Thank you. Come inside, and we'll fill you in on our battle plan."

I was the last to walk into the tent. When I got inside, my stomach clenched and my heart stopped. Krystal stood next to a map-filled table. Here! I couldn't believe the princess was alive and safe. Seeing her banished one fear—that Premier would hurt her when we attacked. My first impulse was to rush to her and throw my arms around her. I held myself in check.

"I'm so glad to see you're all right, Your Highness," I said, walking closer. "I was afraid something might have happened to you."

The princess gave me a small smile. "You came, and brought help, as you said you would."

I opened my mouth to reply, but as she moved her head, I saw the bruise that covered the left side of her face. She saw me staring and moved her hair to cover it.

"What happened to you, Princess?"

"Now's not the time."

"Premier." I said, feeling my anger rise. I stared at the bruise, imagining what other things he might have done to her. She wore loose peasant clothes, so I couldn't see if she was wounded anywhere else. I thought of Master Stradus's story and of how Premier used to love the ladies. My anger exploded. All the candles in the tent went out.

"Hellsfire!" Master Stradus said, his stern gaze resting on me. I couldn't believe I had let my emotions get the best of me. I was glad the tent had darkened so no one would see how embarrassed I was.

"Forgive me, everyone," I said, and reignited the candles.

"It's quite all right," Krystal said. The others didn't seem to think anything of it, except for my master, who frowned at me. "You're the one who trained Hellsfire?" Krystal said to my master. "On behalf of Alexandria, it is an honor to meet you. I appreciate your coming here. We can use all the help we can get."

"I'm glad to be of service, Your Highness. I'm Stradus. We'll do all we can to stop Premier."

"Thank you." The princess took a seat at the table, and everyone else followed suit. She looked around the table. "Thank you all for coming. Alexandria is in your debt. Wizard Stradus, since you are here and you brought a dragon, we may need to change our plans a bit."

"That's fine, but first, may I ask how you escaped Premier, Your Highness? I had thought you were taken with the city."

"I was." The princess looked at the others. "I know you've heard this before, so forgive me."

"It's quite all right, Highness," Lenora said. "The two wizards should know."

"Very well, but I'll try to make it short." Krystal took a deep breath before starting. "A week after Hellsfire's departure, Premier's army of Wasteland creatures came to Alexandria. There were too few soldiers to resist, and Premier used his magic on those who stood against him. He quickly seized the city and promised no one would get hurt if we did what he wanted."

My master stroked his beard and asked, "What did he want, Princess?"

"Knowledge."

"Knowledge?" I asked. What could a thousand-year-old wizard with the *Book of Shazul* want with any knowledge Alexandria could have? I looked at my master and could tell he was thinking the same thing.

Krystal nodded. "Over the centuries, Alexandria has acquired certain…items."

"Items?" I asked.

"I can't get into what they are, Hellsfire. Some of the items are from the War of the Wizards—others have been found in the Wastelands. A few are dangerous, especially if they fall into the wrong hands. Premier wanted these, and only those with Alexander's bloodline have access to them."

"Did you give these to him, Princess?" Stradus asked.

She shook her head. "When Premier first came to power and began to influence my father, I took and hid those items I deemed the most valuable—or dangerous." Her strong violet eyes met my master's, and for a second, they wavered. "When Premier finally showed his true colors and took over the city, he came to me and demanded to know where I had hidden the items he sought. I held out for as long as I could. He threatened to hurt my father, but I knew my father would give his life to protect Alexandria, and I didn't give in. Premier then had one of his minions beat me."

Krystal's eyes shimmered on the verge of tears, even though the rest of her face was stoic. Her bodily wounds must have been worse than I thought. I had to control myself not to let my rage take over my body and unleash my fire.

"It was only when he started executing my people, did I finally relent," she said. "Premier was cold in his executions. He didn't care about the people he slaughtered. To him, they were merely a means to an end. So, I gave him what he wanted."

Stradus bowed his head. "You did what you had to do, Princess," my master said.

Krystal gave a small, satisfied smile. "I gave him worthless scrolls and artifacts. Things that once had power, but didn't any longer. I knew I had to be gone before he realized what I had done. As much as it pained me to leave my people at his mercy, I couldn't let him have anything that would increase his power."

I tried to read her face, but it was impossible to break through that royal mask. I wondered what would happen to her people now—if, in his anger at her escape, Premier would kill more of them. I didn't want to make her feel worse by bringing it up, but Krystal seemed to read the question in my eyes.

"I can't let any of those items fall into Premier's hands. If I did, he would be unstoppable and none of Northern Shala would be safe." She paused. "You must understand," she said carefully. "For centuries, Alexandria has dedicated itself to protecting Northern Shala from the consequences of Renak's evil. That includes not just fighting the Wasteland creatures, but collecting objects of power and making sure that they never again fall into the hands of wizards who might use them for harm. Every citizen of Alexandria would give his or her life to keep that from happening. And, if necessary, it is my responsibility to decide when to risk those lives."

I stared at her, amazed and frightened by her words. I didn't know if I could make the same decision. I'd had a hard enough time leaving Alexandria without at least trying to warn her. She was braver than I.

"We'll avenge your people, Your Highness," Jastillian said.

"We might not have to," Sharald said. "Premier has not sent any messengers or shown us any bodies. Once the princess was gone, Premier might have decided it was unnecessary to kill anyone else."

"Gentlemen, I thank you for your concern," the princess said, "but right now we have more urgent things to worry about. Premier also let it slip that the bulk of his forces will arrive soon."

I sighed at this news. Just how many more creatures could there be? My master wasn't as surprised by the information as I was.

"How did you escape Premier, Your Highness?" Master Stradus asked.

"I was worried that Premier might have used a spell to bind or track me, but I had to risk it. I thought your arrival was more than enough to keep Premier occupied. He had imprisoned me in my chambers, with two ogres to guard me. However, he only gave my rooms a cursory search for weapons." She gave a small smile. "He seemed to forget that I am the descendant of a thousand years of warrior kings and queens. All the royal chambers are fitted with numerous secret compartments where we keep hidden weapons." The smile grew wider. "The ogres were very sorry that Premier had not searched more thoroughly. At least, they were when I killed them."

I stared at her in awe. Having gone up against an ogre myself, I knew how tough they were—and I had magic. The princess had nothing but her wits and sword. And she was wounded.

"But how were you able to get past the castle walls and all the creatures?" I asked.

"Easily. There are secret passages throughout the castle and the city that only a few are privy to. I escaped through one of them and made my way here."

"We'll need to work together to win back Alexandria," Master Stradus said. "Princess, do you know if Premier's creatures outnumber us?"

"Judging from what I've seen and been told, our forces roughly equal theirs," Krystal said. "This includes all three armies, which means those in the city."

"We must get those inside the city to attack," Lenora said. "Premier is in the best defensive position. We don't have time to properly siege and storm the city before Premier's reinforcements come."

"A direct attack would be foolhardy," Sharald agreed. "Alexandria can withstand months of siege."

"The problem isn't numbers or defenses," Krystal said. "The problem is that Premier has the creatures organized and disciplined." She sighed. "As we've found out to our sorrow."

I looked around at everyone. They all had more experience at this. No one wanted to fight a losing battle, and no one wanted to lose any more people than they had to without a good chance of success.

Lenora shifted the map of Alexandria on the table. It detailed the city, the castle, and the surrounding area. Different colored stones represented the three forces. The black stones were Premier's forces. There were far too many of his stones, and they were all inside Alexandria.

"Wizard Stradus," Lenora said, "we were going to send a group inside Alexandria to help free the loyal guardsman locked in the dungeons and rally the people to fight. Tonight. The main attack begins at dawn. My people can see just as well as those foul creatures in the dark, and King Sharald's people can compensate with their excellent hearing.

"That strike force is vital. We need one of you to go with them. We expect there to be little resistance, since we'll be keeping the bulk of Premier's forces busy on the southern walls. We need a wizard to boost their chances of success."

My master's blue eyes gleamed while he played with his beard. "It's a good plan. I'm just not sure about one of us going into Alexandria."

"What do you mean, Stradus?" Sharald asked.

"Neither of us would be able to use our magic once we reached the city—Premier would detect it and pinpoint the location of the strike force immediately. We could only use our power to fight Premier himself, if we happened to stumble over him. Premier is much more likely to engage those attacking the city. My magic will be needed to counteract his. And even if that shining force of yours does run into Premier, I don't know that having Hellsfire with them will save them." He looked at me apologetically. "Hellsfire lacks the experience to fight Premier on his own."

I clenched my fists. "That doesn't mean I won't try."

"No," Master Stradus said. A strong breeze filled the room. "You will remain with me on the battlefield: observing, learning, helping. I can't risk you confronting Premier again. There are still more important things for you to do."

"Master, if we fail here, then what happens later won't matter."

"I said no. The risk is too great."

I wanted to argue with him, but held my tongue. It wouldn't do to argue in front of everyone. I would have to try to change his mind later.

"My old friend," Sharald said, "we need one of you to help in this. Once we attack, Premier will be far too busy to detect magic inside the walls."

Master Stradus's face softened. "I understand your position, but there are things I've seen that none of you could understand. We *will* beat Premier, but it must be together." His ancient gaze moved to each of them in turn, and they gave up the debate.

"Then it's settled," the princess said. She looked at the others. "We'll start the assault under cover of darkness. I'll join your troops later tonight, and we'll go into Alexandria."

"You're going, Your Highness?" I asked.

"Someone has to lead the troops through the city. No one here knows the tunnels."

Krystal's bravery and determination shamed me. She had been through so much and was still willing to put more on the line. Her father, her life, her people—there was no end to her sacrifices. I couldn't sit back and do nothing. I couldn't let anything happen to her.

"I'll be right there with you, Princess," I said.

"Hellsfire—" Master Stradus said.

"Master, you don't need my help, but she—they—do."

Jastillian leaned forward and said, "Don't worry, Wizard Stradus. I'll go too, and make sure nothing happens to the lad here. I still owe him for rescuing me."

"We'll also watch Hellsfire," Prastian said. "The dwarves are not the only ones whom Hellsfire has helped. Right, Demay and Behast?"

"Of course!" Demay said.

Behast nodded.

Master Stradus's ancient, magical eyes hardened to ice. His powerful gaze rested on me. "You are a stubborn apprentice, Hellsfire. You must learn to master your emotions, or they will get you killed." Master Stradus sighed, before giving a tight-lipped smile and a slight nod. "You may go. I see that with so many friends, you will not need my protection, but all the same, you must be careful. Do not, I repeat do *not*, under any circumstances, fight Premier without me."

I hid my smile. "I will do as you say, Master."

"May we fight well and die harder," Lenora said to everyone before leaving. Jastillian followed her.

"It's good to see you again, old man," Sharald said.

"It's good to see you too, old friend," Master Stradus said. "I wish it were under better circumstances."

"Me too." Sharald smiled at his friend before leaving. The other elves followed.

Just Krystal, Master Stradus, and myself were left.

"Master, what would you like me to do until the strike force assembles?" I asked.

"You, my apprentice, may have the hardest job of all."

"What would that be?"

"I want you to walk around and experience what the dwarves and elves are going through. I want you to feel their anxiety and hear their hearts beating as they sing battle songs and prepare for war. I want you to understand all that goes into warfare, so you won't thirst for it like those who came before you." Master Stradus's eyes became clouded, much like the globe on his staff. "See the faces and listen to the stories. Remember, war is a terrible thing, unless you're fighting for what's truly right instead of what you believe is right."

"I will do as you say, Master."

He departed, and it was just me and the princess left. I turned to her, about to tell her how happy I was that she was safe. Then she spoke in a hard, distant voice.

"Thank you for bringing allies and for coming to the aid of my people, Hellsfire, but I don't need you constantly watching over me. I've managed without you fine so far."

I stared at her, my mouth hanging open. "I don't get it. What did I do?"

The princess's violet eyes turned stormy. "Next time you leave me at the mercy of a mad wizard who is planning to conquer the world, do you think you could warn me?"

So that's what this was about. "I never got the chance to, Princess. Jastillian needed my help, and when Premier caught us escaping, the only thing my spells did was slow him down. I couldn't get to you without the entire castle knowing."

Princess Krystal didn't say a word. She simply stared at me, her face still furious. My own anger rose at the look, and I couldn't stop the flood of words. "Don't you think I wanted to warn you, Princess? Don't you think I knew how much danger you were in? If it had been up to me, I would have taken you with me when I left. You have no idea how I felt, leaving you there. All this time, I've done nothing but worry about you and ride the countryside, getting the help you needed. Even when I found it, I didn't know whether we'd make it in time. You don't know what I've been through."

"*You've* been through? My kingdom has been taken. My people are starving and dying. My father is still in there—sickened and imprisoned by an evil wizard! And you have the audacity to say I don't know what *you've* been through!"

"You're impossible!" I threw my hands up in frustration. "I gathered two armies for *you*. I'm trying to help you get back your kingdom, Princess. I'm doing everything I thought you'd want me to. I'm doing all of this for you!"

Her violet eyes blazed with fire. "You have no idea what I want! Now leave!"

I raised my finger and opened my mouth. Angry words rushed through my mind, yet I couldn't get any of them out of my mouth. The power within built up, aching to be released. This woman was infuriating. Fire seeped from my pores, encircling me.

The princess wasn't afraid of my magic. She stormed over to me and jabbed a finger in my chest. "I said leave. Now!"

"Fine!"

I punched the tent flaps, not even caring that they didn't open completely. They smacked me in the face as I pushed through.

"Impossible woman," I muttered loud enough so she could hear me. "After all the things I've done."

I strode off, trying my best to push aside my thoughts of the princess and do what Master Stradus wanted me to—learn about war. I couldn't. I summoned my power into a fireball and sent it crashing into the ground, creating a little crater. That helped. A little.

King Sharald appeared beside me and placed his hand on my arm. "Princess Krystal isn't telling you everything, Hellsfire. She was in very bad shape when we found her. She was lucky to make it this far. Our healers did everything they could, but she really shouldn't even be walking around. Be easy on her, Hellsfire. She's in a lot of pain—and I don't mean just physical." He patted my arm, then walked away before I could answer him. If I had even known what to say.

My anger cooled a bit at his words, and I was able to do what Master Stradus had asked. The first thing that struck me was how young a lot of the soldiers were, in both the dwarves' and elves' camps. I had expected them to be grizzled veterans like Prastian, Behast, and Jastillian. They weren't. They were like me. They had young, smooth faces free of hair, and no scars showing. But it was the looks on their faces that got to me.

They were scared. They acted brave and put on a good front with their boasting to each other, but their eyes gave them away. I noticed that older ones kept the young soldiers busy, barking orders and making them sharpen weapons, carry supplies, or drill formations.

I wondered if I had the same expression as I walked around the camp. In a way, I envied them. They had something to keep them occupied. I didn't. I was trapped with my thoughts and worries for these people willing to risk their lives for Alexandria. If only Master Stradus had me do some magical drills.

I stopped when I reached the hospital tents. They were clean and empty now, but I couldn't help but imagine how many people would fill them after the battle. Some would never leave again. Others would leave with missing limbs or horrendous scars. Blood would flow everywhere, and groans would ring throughout the night. I said a prayer to the gods and tore myself away from imagining what it would be like.

I continued to walk, trying not to see death on people's faces. If it were up to me, they would all come back alive. If I had defeated Premier when I rescued Jastillian, we wouldn't even be here now.

As my melancholy thoughts took over, I realized that Master Stradus was right. My emotions were going to get in the way of my ability to do my part in this fight. But just as I was determined not to let that happen, my heart betrayed me.

Krystal was alone in an open space, practicing with her sword. She danced as she spun, stabbing and slicing at some imagined monster. Her movements weren't fluid or perfect. Whenever she tried to use her left side, she winced, and once or twice her left hand went to her ribs before she could stop herself. I winced with her. She still kept at it, pushing past the pain, trying not to favor her wounded side. The sweat glistened from her body, and she breathed heavily.

My frustration and anger melted away. She was right, and I was a fool. I didn't know or understand the things she'd been through. I couldn't. She'd had to deal with these life-altering decisions her entire life, for her entire kingdom. I'd only had to worry about myself and my mother. And if we failed here, she would lose more than just her life. Yet she didn't appear afraid of Premier or death. How did she handle it?

The princess composed herself, holding her sword out in front of her, her still form deep in concentration. With startling speed, she broke out of her stance, lunged, and thrust. She cried out in pain and fell to the ground. I wanted to run to her and make sure she was all right. I didn't. I knew she wouldn't want my help. Krystal pulled herself off the ground and performed the same move. This time she succeeded. I couldn't help but give her a quiet cheer.

When the sun sank to the horizon, painting the sky in deep purples and pinks, I returned to the tent where I thought Master Stradus would be. Instead, I found the princess.

She was bent over the map, scrutinizing the drawing of her kingdom and the stone pieces on the board. She glanced up, and our eyes met. This was my chance to apologize and to tell her how I felt. Instead, I froze.

She didn't say anything. She stood up, ignoring the map, and watched me.

"Forgive me, Your Highness," I said, breaking the silence. "I was looking for my master." I bowed, then turned and walked to the entrance. "I'll leave you alone."

"Hellsfire."

I stopped. Suddenly, I realized what a coward I was being. I turned around. "I'm sorry for what I said earlier. You have a kingdom to think of. I have to remember that. It was just so hard to leave you there, with Premier, and I was terrified something would happen to you before I had a chance to bring help. And if anything were to happen to you…I don't know what I'd do."

The princess didn't say anything. She walked closer. Her being so close made me nervous, and my fire disappeared. I held my breath, afraid to even breathe on her. I had forgotten how tall she was. "But you did come. And you did bring help."

"I keep my promises, Your Highness."

"We're alone. You may call me Krystal."

I nodded, not trusting myself not to say something stupid again.

"If we survive this," she said, "Alexandria will owe you a great deal. You'll be richly awarded."

I shook my head. "I didn't do this for money or power."

"Then why did you do it?"

This was an echo of our very first conversation, in the woods near Sedah. And the answer was still the same. "Because it was the right thing to do, and…for you."

I met her violet eyes and smiled. She smiled back. I saw the remains of tears on her cheeks, as though she'd been crying before I came in. I took a chance and gently put my hand to her face, wiping them away. Her eyes filled, and more tears spilled over. Despite her vulnerability, she looked stronger—not weaker—when she cried.

If she were anyone else but a princess, I would have kissed her. I wanted to—needed to. I let my hand fall and took a step back. In a surprising move, she took a step closer, her warm body brushing mine.

I cleared my throat and whispered, "Krystal, Princess, what are you doing?" I tried to lean back, but any farther and I was going to fall.

"Be quiet, hero," Krystal said, leaning closer and putting her fingers against my lips. She ran her fingers slowly through my hair. I shivered. She pulled me closer until our bodies pressed together. She groaned softly from the pain in her side.

"Krystal! Are you all right?" She held on tighter.

"I'm fine. You worry too much."

Krystal moved closer and brushed her lips on mine. Everything slowed. It was stronger than any magic I had ever experienced. Emotions flowed through my body as I returned the soft kiss. I was drawn into our own little world, where I only wanted to be with her. Nothing else mattered. As unexpectedly as it had begun, the kiss ended. Krystal released me and stepped back. I stood there, dumbfounded, my eyes still closed, dwelling on that magical kiss. Finally, I blinked and shook my head.

"Wha-wha-what was that for?" I asked, my voice barely a whisper.

"For luck, hero." Krystal kissed me on the cheek and smiled one last time before she glided out of the tent.

I stared after her. I couldn't believe that the princess of Alexandria had kissed me. If I survived the battle, perhaps things might not be so bad. Perhaps a simple farm boy could be more.

But I couldn't think about the future now. I first had to make sure that Krystal survived and Premier died. It all came down to that. Too much rode on today—far too much for a wizard-in-training and a young man from Sedah. I gazed up, praying the gods would walk with us.

CHAPTER 22

I MET EVERYONE at the edge of camp. I walked past the fifty elves and dwarves that had been chosen for this mission. Unlike those I had seen earlier, these elves and dwarves were older and had bodies full of scars. Their faces were grim and their eyes were hard.

I went to the front of the group, where my friends were. Cynder towered over all, letting everyone marvel at him; Master Stradus, a bucket of water at his feet, was talking to Sharald; and Jastillian, Prastian, Behast, Demay, and Krystal were busy discussing the attack.

"Sure took you long enough," Cynder said and snorted. "We don't have all night."

"Forgive me, everyone," I said. "But I can't fly like some creatures here."

"Not yet, you can't," Master Stradus said. "Not yet." Everyone laughed, releasing our tension.

I stopped laughing. I took a deep breath and said, "I'm ready."

"Plans have changed, Hellsfire," Master Stradus said.

"Oh," I said, hoping that he hadn't changed his mind about me going with the team into Alexandria.

Master Stradus looked at the night sky. "Unfortunately, the clear night is going to cause a problem. The creatures will spot you before you get to the walls. We're going to fix that and provide adequate cover. Pick up the bucket and let's be on our way. We'll be back in an hour or so." He started to walk towards Alexandria.

I grabbed the bucket and picked up my pace to catch up to Master Stradus.

"Good luck," Krystal said. I turned around, and she gave me a warm smile.

We left the camp and walked north over the rough, barren terrain. We stopped when we saw the city walls.

I squinted. "Think they can see us from here, Master?"

"No, but this is far enough. I want you to create fog, and you will do so by using the water in this bucket. I will bring the clouds towards us so that they will blanket the area and shut out the light. You do know how to go about it, don't you?"

I nodded.

"Good."

"Will Premier be able to figure out who's behind this?"

Master Stradus smiled. "He's going to think you're behind this, and he'd be right."

"What if he decides to undo the spell and they spot us?"

"He won't. If I know him, his overconfidence won't allow him to. He won't see the point of it. He's in a position of strength. Us hiding our troop positions won't worry him."

"If you say so, Master."

Master Stradus walked away, and I sat down cross-legged in front of the bucket. Since fog is a combination of air and water, those were the mana I had to use. I closed my eyes and reached out to the fierce wind and water.

"May the cold air guide this water into fog. May the cold air guide this water into fog." I repeated the incantation in Caleea over and over. The cold air rose from behind me and flowed all around my body, numbing my hands and face. I wasn't sure how long it would take to create enough fog to blanket the entire field, so I kept repeating the words. Goose bumps popped on my body. This was much different from sitting on the ledge of the White Mountain. I wasn't using my fire mana, and without it, the power of the cold overwhelmed me, making my body shiver. I forced myself to stay awake and finish the job.

"Hellsfire," a sleepy voice said. "Hellsfire, come out of your trance." I opened my heavy eyes. "Good job, my boy. Hurry, we must get back to the others."

I wobbled to my feet. At first, I thought my eyes were fuzzy because of the deep trance I had been in, but the mist blanketed everything. I waved my arm through the ocean of fog. Everything looked unreal.

"Make haste and lead the way back to camp," he said.

I took a step forward, then stopped. I turned my head to the left and then to the right. "Master, I'm not sure which way that is."

"It's that way," he said, and pointed. "Would you like me to provide some light, or would you like to do that?"

"I'll be more than happy to." I released the inner fire that dwelled in me. The heat coursed through my body and filled me with life. I let out a sigh of enjoyment. I made a ball of fire that stayed in my hand. "I feel soooo much better, Master. Let's go."

It took us longer to go back to the encampment than it had to leave. I wanted to take it nice and slow so I wouldn't veer off and get us lost. However, I soon heard voices and continued to walk us in that direction until I was able to see who was talking.

"We're glad you're back," King Sharald said.

There were multiple torches surrounding him, so I extinguished my little ball of fire.

"Is everything ready?" Lenora asked.

"As you can see, we have provided everyone with adequate cover," Master Stradus said. "As soon as they leave, I'll work on a counterspell to this." He looked at the princess. "You have one hour to make it to the walls before you'll lose your cover." He turned his attention back to Lenora and Sharald. "Is your army ready?"

"Aye," Lenora said.

"Are your elves ready, Prastian?" Jastillian asked.

"Yes. We can depart as soon as *your* dwarves are ready." Prastian smiled.

Jastillian laughed and clapped him hard on the back. He put a helm over his head. "Then let's be on our way. Your Highness, if you please."

"Good luck, my son, and please be careful," Master Stradus said. "And heed my words—*don't* fight Premier without me."

"I won't." I didn't want to face Premier by myself. He did have the *Book of Shazul.* I walked over to Krystal. "Ready, Your Highness?"

She nodded.

I created a condensed and focused fireball, making it provide more light than heat.

"May the gods walk with you," Sharald said.

"Fight well and die harder," Lenora said.

Krystal and I led the group, the rest falling in behind. My heart pounded, ready to explode. I exhaled and said quietly, "This is it."

Krystal's hand brushed my arm. Her purple eyes stared into mine, calming me.

While we walked, I parted the fog around us just slightly so the princess could see better, though I was careful to keep it thick enough that we were invisible from a distance. She navigated the level terrain easily, only pausing now and then to correct our direction.

To my ears, the light clattering of weapons and armor sounded far too loud. I kept glancing at those rattling chainmail or clattering quivers of arrows. The soldiers fingering their weapon hilts or scratching their beards added to the noise. Even the sound of their soft footsteps in the patches of grass on the flat ground rang in my ears. I tried not to think about such things and focused on the task at hand.

When we arrived at the city's walls, I let out a breath, thankful that we hadn't been spotted so far. I craned my neck at the towering walls, hearing the constant movement from the heavy creatures patrolling. Worried that they might see us, I drew the fog around us.

"Please put out the flame," the princess said. She walked along the wall. Her eyes scanned for something while her fingers danced on the stones. She slowed down to a crawl, then stopped. "Here it is."

Krystal pressed one of the stone blocks. A small opening appeared in the wall. She stepped in, and I followed her. The others poured in past us, into the dark hallway. After we were all inside, Krystal pushed another stone on the inside of the entrance. The doorway closed, sealing us in the small, cramped, pitch-black hallway. It smelt stale and stuffy.

Even though the city walls were deep, it was too small inside the passage, especially with so many people. I hadn't thought it would be like this. The space was only two people wide, and all the warm bodies made me feel trapped. I leaned on one of the walls, my hand tracing the lines in the stone. My chest heaved, and I closed my eyes and clenched my teeth. My heart vibrated through my ears. My breathing seemed louder than the entire force.

"Hellsfire," Krystal said, keeping her voice low. "Hellsfire, are you all right?" She reached out from the darkness and grasped my shoulder.

I took a deep breath, trying to breathe normally. I remembered all the people outside who had far harder things to do than I did. "Forgive me. I'm...fine, Your Highness."

I squashed my emotions and focused on my magic. It was hard to use only a small portion of it. The need to use more almost overwhelmed me, but my fear of hurting the others controlled it.

I created a fireball in my hand, illuminating the hallway. Monstrous shadows danced on the walls. Their pupil-less eyes forever watched us. That's one of the main reasons I hate small spaces—your mind plays tricks on you.

The princess led me past the others to the head of the line, and we moved out. Although we were inside the wall, there were a lot of twists as well as branching passageways. They must have been put there to confuse people, or perhaps they led to other places in Alexandria.

A long time passed, and no one said a word. Only the scurrying of rats, the dripping of water, and the sound of the fire in my hand accompanied the tread of our feet.

My thoughts kept straying to those outside these walls. As much as I worried for them, I was thankful for something to occupy my mind. Thoughts of their well-being kept me distracted from the cramped corridor.

The corridor slanted steeply down and opened up, big enough for a cart and horses to travel through. The ceiling was much higher; I couldn't even see it in the darkness above. The princess stopped. We all huddled around her. The stone had disappeared. We now seemed to be underground, and the tunnels were dirt shored up by timbers. Unlike the section we had just walked through, unlit torches hung on the sides of the walls.

"We're underneath Alexandria and close to the castle," the princess said. "Watch your step from here on out, and don't touch anything. You may trigger a trap."

Everyone moved uneasily. "Traps?" I asked. I didn't like the sound of that. "Can you disarm them?"

"Unfortunately, no."

I raised my hand. The flame left it, bouncing along the torches, reigniting them. That small bit of mana wouldn't be enough for Premier to detect.

The princess led us closer to the castle and our destination. She paused every so often, peering through the dim light at the tunnel walls or the ground.

The princess stopped suddenly, and I almost bumped into her. There was a slight clicking noise.

"Down!" she yelled.

She fell to the ground, grabbing my robes and pulling me with her. I barely had time to put my hands out in front of me before my face hit the tunnel floor. Something whirled through the air above us like birds in flight.

We heard thuds and grunting as elves and dwarves flung themselves to the ground. One landed on top of us and didn't move. The whirring echoed down the passageway, deadly in its quiet tune.

"Princess, what is it?" I asked.

"Quiet!"

The whirring noise stopped. None of us moved until the princess rose again. Two dwarves and an elf had fallen with tiny needles sticking out of their faces, necks, and arms. Their eyes bulged and their mouths were open. Their veins stuck out of their bodies, as if trying to leave their skin. Poison. Krystal's face grew tight.

We were just starting to move the bodies to the side of the passageway until we could return to claim them, when a low rumbling noise surrounded us. The elves moved their ears, trying to pinpoint the sound. It sounded like it came from above.

"What—"

A stone the size of an ogre's head crashed down on the elf standing next to me. I heard his skull crunch, and green blood splattered my face. Part of the stone chipped off and hit my forehead, causing a deep scratch. Stunned, I reached up to wipe the blood out of my eye.

"No time!" the princess said. "Run!" She pulled at my arm, forcing me out of my shock. She sprinted down the tunnels, and we followed.

The ceiling kept dropping stones. It sounded like the growling of a thousand monsters. The princess was barely ahead of the tide. Rocks landed near me, forcing me to dodge and leap them. The soldiers behind us had the worst of it. Their heavy armor provided them little protection from the rocks, and it slowed them down. As much as they darted and weaved, not all of them were able to avoid the rocks. Behind us, we heard deep dwarven grunts, and the higher-pitched yelps of elves. I wished I could use my magic, but it was impossible while on the run. The rocks fell too fast and too erratically, and my control of earth mana wasn't strong enough to manipulate this many without stillness and concentration.

After a few minutes that seemed like hours, the princess reached a smaller passageway and turned off. The others funneled in behind us, and we waited, panting, as the deadly rain poured down in the main tunnel. We heard faint cries from those left behind. I winced with every one, until they went silent. The soldiers stared straight ahead, stony-faced, as did the princess.

Finally, it was over. Krystal held her left side and panted. All of us breathed hard in the stale air. The sweat ran down my face, mingling with the blood from my forehead. I ignored it, creating a fire so everyone could see.

"What happened?" Demay asked, leaning over with his hands on his knees.

Krystal's eyes narrowed. "Someone tripped one of the traps."

"How many did we lose?" Jastillian asked.

"Three to the poison darts," the princess said. "I don't know how many to the rocks."

We did a quick count. Out of the fifty we had started with, fifteen were missing. Jastillian and Prastian went back down the tunnel to check for survivors.

Blood and sweat ran into my left eye, and I wiped it aside.

"Hellsfire, you're hurt," the princess said. She ripped off a piece of her tunic and wiped the blood from my face. She tied the cloth around my forehead.

"Thank you, Your Highness."

Prastian and Jastillian returned, looking grim. Prastian caught the princess's eye and shook his head once. No survivors. All fifteen missing were dead.

"Can the rest of your elves and dwarves continue?" Krystal asked.

"We can, Your Highness."

"I'm glad," she said. "This is going to put us behind." She peered down the tunnels. "We must press on, but we can no longer take the shortest route." She looked back at the rubble. "Please watch yourselves, and do not touch the walls. I don't want to run into any more traps."

We continued our journey through the tunnels, hurrying to make up for the lost time. Everyone hugged their weapons close to their bodies so they wouldn't scrape against the walls. We made sure we didn't touch anything but each other. I even wrapped my loose wizards robes closer to my body. The princess insisted on leading the way, so that everyone could follow in her exact footsteps. I didn't like letting her go on alone, but she was in charge of this expedition, so I obeyed her.

We traveled like this until we reached a door.

"Past this door, we're in the castle," Krystal whispered. "There are no more traps and people shouldn't hear or see us unless they know of the hiding places. Be quiet, though. I don't know what or who is in the castle. Hellsfire, I'm going to need you to shrink your fireball so the light doesn't give us away. "

"As you wish." The fire in my hand compressed, leaving those farther away in total darkness.

The princess opened the door. We once more faced a narrow stone passageway, in which only two of us could stand side by side. I stood by her, being her human torch. The way inclined, at times turning into flights of steps. Passageways branched off. At one intersection, Krystal paused for a second before choosing one.

The floor leveled out, and we began to occasionally pass holes in the stone walls, where people could spy on what was happening in the rooms or corridors on the other side. Light seeped through them, and the hallways began to lighten. Dawn had broken. The rest of the army was going to commence the attack, whether or not we freed the imprisoned Guardsmen and raised the city. I looked at those around me. They clenched their teeth and kept glancing at the spyholes, as if looking through them would allow them to see the battle. It was impossible, but they did it anyway. So did I.

We continued our silent trek. I wanted to ask Krystal how much longer until we were freed from these suffocating tunnels, but I refrained.

"We're here," Krystal said.

"Thank the gods," I said under my breath.

The princess bent down and pushed three stones in an order known only to her. The wall moved, and another opening appeared.

She was about to go through when Jastillian said, "Princess, allow us."

She nodded, and Jastillian and half of the others went through the opening. I stayed behind to guard the princess, my magic at the ready. After a few tense seconds, we were given the all-clear to come through.

The rest of us exited the tomblike passageway and poured into the room. My entire body relaxed as soon as I stepped out, glad to breathe fresh air and escape the oppression of the tunnels. Krystal leaned down and pushed a stone, sealing up the entrance once more.

We were in a library. It was three times as big as Master Stradus's library, and much fancier, with carved shelves and expensive rugs, but I doubted it contained anything like the information he possessed. The strike force began to fan out to check the exits. I started to follow, when my back straightened and my shoulders tensed. Something was wrong. I felt something…magical. Not Premier—at least, not a spell he was actively casting. It was far too weak to be a direct threat. Still, I didn't like it.

"Wait," I said.

"Hellsfire, what is it?" Krystal asked.

"I'm not sure. Give me a second."

I closed my eyes and focused my magical senses. I let the faint magic guide me, slowly and carefully, lest it was a trap and pulled me into it. I opened my eyes and saw the door. A web. I turned to the other doors and saw webs on them too. I walked closer to the first one, getting a better look. What bothered me wasn't that the webs were there. I was bothered by the type of webs they were. They weren't meant for detection, entrapping, or killing. They were meant for concealment.

That was when we found out what was behind them.

CHAPTER 23

CREATURES FROM THE WASTELANDS poured into the dim-lit library from behind the concealment webs. Everyone drew their weapons, backing away from them and forming a ring, protecting each others' backs. We stood as one, but the creatures had us surrounded and outnumbered.

A large ogre came forth and snarled. He pointed a long, jagged sword at Krystal. "By the Wizard's orders, surrender or die."

The princess held her head high. There was only one option.

The creatures sensed this. The goblins, smaller than elves, slobbered and bounced in their packs. If not for the huge ogres in front of them, holding them back, the goblins would have attacked. Square-headed trolls wore twisted smiles. Their bulky muscles tensed and twitched in anticipation.

I didn't see Premier. He could still be behind the webs, watching and directing everything, not wanting to get his hands dirty. On the other hand, it was possible that he had simply left guards at every exit from the tunnels, just in case. If he was here, I would reach that crossroads when he appeared. Like Master Stradus said, I had to focus on the now.

While the ogre waited for Krystal's answer, I acted. I lit all the torches in the library and every candle on the tables. They exploded into great balls of fire.

It stunned and blinded everyone but me. My hope was that it would cause the creatures more difficulty. They had excellent eyesight at night, but like other animals, I gambled on their eyesight being sensitive to light.

It was.

Our forces understood. They attacked before the creatures could recover. I hoped it would be enough to make up for the losses we suffered earlier.

Fire swirled into my hands until it became great and deadly balls. I slung them, guiding them to the creatures' scarred, twisted, ugly bodies. One struck an ogre, igniting his side. Another ogre dodged in time. The ball smashed into a hanging tapestry and incinerated it.

I guarded Krystal's weakened left side. The crowded room forced me to be careful with my spells; otherwise, I could harm our own side. When the small fireballs hit the creatures, they roared in pain. Two trolls advanced towards me. The fire exploded in my hand, tripling in size. They froze. Three dwarves led by Jastillian cut down the monsters, hacking them with their axes.

Three ogres charged at me, crashing through tables and crushing the books beneath them. They knew I was their biggest threat. They even killed some of the smaller goblins on their way, but they didn't seem to care. I couldn't stop them with the weak and easy spells I was using. I had to risk a bigger one.

I pushed my hands out in front of me. The trio of ogres trampled two elves. The lead one then rammed his sword through a dwarf, lifting him high into the air before he flung him off.

I built up the fire inside of me, waiting until they were close enough and all my allies were free from their rampaging destruction. There was one dwarf in the way, but he fell to a troll's massive club. He toppled over with half of his face smashed in. The three ogres were still coming.

I put my hands up and released the thermal blast. The flames smothered the ogres. The carpets and tables around them caught fire. One ogre slammed to the stone floor, shrieking as his skin crisped and blacked. Another followed.

The last ogre burst out of my inferno. In his burning rage, he moved too fast for me to stop my spell and get out the way. The beast roared, lifting his rusted sword towards me. Before he could bring it down, Krystal ran him through, pushing him out of the way. She pulled her black-soaked sword free, and the flaming carcass collapsed to the ground.

I panted, "Thank you."

Before she could respond, a group of tightly bunched goblins charged her. I grabbed the princess's arm and pushed her behind me before hurling wind mana at the frenzied goblins. The rushing wind knocked them off their feet and sent them smashing against the bookshelves. Krystal sent me a quick smile before lifting her sword and resuming the fight.

I glanced around at the chaos in the once pristine room. We were holding our own, but the sheer numbers and recklessness of the creatures had begun to take their toll.

Despite my well-armed allies, the mindless creatures didn't hesitate. All the goblins lacked any sort of armor—their fighting strategy was to stay in groups and mob people, killing them with their filthy teeth and claws. Two dozen goblins buried a trio of elves. A troll used his tremendous strength to club a dwarf until the red blood bathed his hands. Only the ogres had some restraint. Their dented, ill-fitting armor and unsharpened swords helped. However, that made them more deadly killers. We were losing too many people.

A fallen bookshelf was the tombstone of two elves. A dwarf lay as broken as the table he sprawled across. An ogre and a dwarf were locked in a lover's embrace, a fallen tapestry blanketing them.

I had to do something.

The lit torches and candles that hadn't fallen over or burned out gave me an idea.

"Princess, I need you to guard me. This ends now."

Krystal nodded, and with one fluid movement slashed one green goblin and finished another with her backswing. She corralled a couple of dwarves and elves. They surrounded me, taking the brunt of the attacks while I slid into a trance.

I focused on all the fires that still burned, feeding my power into them. They blazed and burned as bright as the sun. I opened my eyes, and the flames danced straight up, moving to an unseen force.

The creatures didn't flinch. They pushed their advantage. My friends and allies took defensive measures. They slashed and cut the creatures' arms—any opening that was exposed. Dark blood sprayed everywhere. The disciplined soldiers made no move to lunge for the finishing kill.

They didn't have any shields, but the dwarves took the brunt of the creatures' assault. A young dwarf blocked an ogre's sword. She swiped the sword away then rammed the pointed end of her axe up and through the ogre's chin.

The elves in the center of the circle sheathed their swords and pulled their bows, showering death over our heads at the taller creatures. Prastian and Demay shared a smile, each trying to outdo the other. They loosed their arrows and struck a troll's eyes.

The noose around our collective neck got tighter. A dwarf cried out as his arm was cut through. The goblin frenzy was like a never-ending tidal wave. An elf screamed while being dragged away. Another fell over from a fatal bite to the neck.

It was now or never.

I stopped drawing in magic. I lifted my hand. Streams of fire twisted and turned in the dim room. They hovered over our heads, mesmerizing everyone. Everyone gazed up and stopped fighting. That's when I brought them down.

The waves of fire plummeted, splashing over and through the creatures. I guided the blazes to engulf only the monsters. Their bodies burned and cooked. Their disfigured skin blistered, then blackened. The horrific smell of rancid roast pork filled the room. I forced myself to block out their chorus of agony, remembering that I was doing this for the princess and the people of Alexandria.

Groups of goblins collapsed. Their small bodies twitched. The heat drove the ogres and trolls insane. They struck and crushed their own people, trying in vain to put out the flames. Bodies of trolls and ogres toppled over like an avalanche. They crashed into the floor, igniting up the remaining carpets.

I could no longer contain or control all that magic. I sent a tiny bit of the fire back to the torches; the rest dissipated into nothingness. The flames on the corpses popped and crackled.

I bent over, putting my hands on my knees, and panted. The sweat rolled down my face. I sucked in as much air as I could. Dwarves and elves moved around the room, finishing off those creatures still living with expert cuts of their swords and axes.

"Hellsfire, are you all right?" the princess asked, placing a hand on my hunched back.

I wiped a drop of sweat from the corner of my eye and shook my head.

"Is there anything we can do for you?"

I waved my hand, trying to speak. My mouth moved, but no sound came out. I took one gigantic gulp of air. Then I rose, reached into my purse, and downed a rejuvenation potion. My strength came back to me bit by bit.

"I'm all right, Your Highness. Thank you."

I stood on guard. Premier could have sensed my magic and be on his way, or he could have been behind those webs all along. I doubted the latter. Even with the lack of regard he showed his creatures, not even he would have wanted so many to be killed when he was so close to victory.

"Nice job, lad," Jastillian said. He flicked some dark entrails from his bushy beard. "And my foolish brother didn't believe you had it in you." He laughed, and I couldn't help but grin.

"How could we have missed them?" someone asked in frustration. "The doors are wide open, and we saw nothing!"

"Concealment webs," I said, staring at the illusion of empty hallways created by the webs. "Premier must have known about the tunnels and set a trap in case Princess Krystal returned. I need some of you to cover me while I take down the webs."

I undid the webs. It was sloppy and messy, but fast. I would have walked through them, but didn't want to take the chance that Premier had more surprises in store, or was just standing right there. I breathed easier when I saw Premier wasn't there and that there wasn't another trap.

"We can't keep taking losses like this," Jastillian said.

"What's the count?" I asked.

"Fourteen dead and four seriously wounded. More than half our people are gone."

"We've got to hurry," Prastian said.

"The dungeons aren't far from here," Krystal said.

"Let's hope we don't run into any more surprises," Behast said.

We left the wounded concealed in the secret passage, with a dwarf and an elf to guard them. The library was on the castle's first floor—as close as the princess could get us to the dungeons. We jogged through the hallways, heading for the lower levels and keeping an eye out for any more traps or surprises.

We neared our destination and stopped. Krystal and I scouted the entrance to the dungeons. Two trolls and four goblins guarded them. I peeked from our hiding place and scanned the area for any magic. There were no webs or enchantments I could feel. It wasn't the strong magic that worried me. It was the subtle magic I might not be able to detect.

We returned to the others and told them what we'd found. They decided to attack directly, since there was no other way to get to the dungeons. I would stay behind, watching for magic and guarding the princess.

Our forces rushed out. From a distance, the elves were able to get a few of their remaining arrows off. One troll had five arrows sticking out of his chest. Black blood ran down his chest, and he fell to the ground. Two more arrows pinned a goblin against the wall. As he slid to the floor, his dark blood left a slimy trail. The other goblins moved quickly, running towards us before more arrows could be released. The second troll had an arrow piercing his shoulder, but it barely slowed him down.

The dwarves and Behast followed the arrows. The dwarves' axes found their marks and hacked away. Even if a creature blocked one, someone else's axe took its place, until the creature lost a limb and eventually its head.

This battle was far different from the previous one. There were no casualties on our side, and the only injuries were minor scratches and bruises.

Everyone went through the arch and filed down to the dungeons. The dwarves went first, in case there were more creatures below. I hurried to catch up to them, but stopped when something caught the corner of my eye. I turned my head, but saw nothing. The hair on my neck rose, but I didn't sense any magic. Krystal pulled at my arm, and I followed her to the dungeons. I made sure she went down the steps before I followed, still looking over my shoulder.

The humidity and stale air in the stairwell made me feel trapped once more. My stomach twisted into a knot. I couldn't be sure if it was my nerves, or if it was something else.

When I reached the bottom, the strike force already had the cell doors open, and the prisoners were filing out. I pushed my way through all the people, making my way to the front by Krystal's side.

The Royal Guardsmen of Alexandria were nearly naked, wearing dirty rags that barely covered them. They stank and were undernourished. Ardimus was in the worst condition. He leaned more than stood. Dark bruises encircled his face, and blood was crusted on his swollen lips. Lacerations and cuts marred his arms. Even in his condition, when he saw the princess his smile was full of love and warmth.

No matter what ragged condition they were in, their angry eyes spoke volumes, saying they were ready for battle.

"There's one bloody fight ahead of us," Jastillian said. "Are you and your men with us, Ardimus?"

"I'm always willing to kill as many of those creatures as I can; however, my first duty lies with the princess." Ardimus turned to Krystal. "May I be allowed to leave your side and save our fair city, Princess?"

"No, you may not," Krystal said. "I'm going to need you. You're to come with me while we find my father."

He bowed. "As you command, Princess. My men and I are going to need weapons. I believe Premier had our weapons taken to the armory. Gods willing, his despicable creatures won't have ransacked it. I believe he promised to give them to his favorites as prizes after the battle." He gazed into the faces his men. "Does everyone know what to do?" he asked. "You are to help our friends take back what is ours! For Alexandria!"

The Guardsmen of Alexandria ignored their wounds and raised their fists in the air. They stood straighter, their pride and dignity showing through their rags.

"If Her Highness will lead the way," Ardimus said. "Make way! Make way!"

I was the last to leave the dungeon's depths. I was anxious for battle, but I wasn't craving it like they were. I wasn't a warrior. I just wanted to be rid of the creatures and Premier. I didn't want to see any more of the good people of Alexandria, Erlam, or Sharald die.

As I walked towards the armory, I couldn't shake the feeling that we were being followed. I kept checking behind me and around the corners, but there was no one. Prastian sensed my uneasiness

"Is something the matter, Hellsfire?" Prastian said.

"Something *is* wrong," I said. "I don't know what it is. But I can't shake the feeling of danger." I shrugged. "I haven't seen anything. Have you or any of the other elves heard anything?"

Prastian's long ears twitched in different directions. "Nothing."

"I pray you're right."

We soon arrived at the armory. Prastian left me and went inside with the Guardsmen of Alexandria. I stood outside the entrance as guard, along with the dwarves and elves. I glanced from side to side, but saw nothing, so I peered inside the armory, curious.

The armory was larger than I expected—a long room bristling with weapons. Arrows were bundled and leaned against the walls. Wooden racks held swords of all sizes, from short swords and longswords to huge broadswords. Light gleamed off their deadly, sharpened edges, slicing through the air. Crossbows and longbows hung on the walls. Wooden dummies wore helms, armor, and shields. The polished steel shone, and the red dragon emblems gleamed like rubies. Even though I wasn't skilled with a weapon, that deadly beauty was entrancing.

The men and women of Alexandria wasted no time. They strapped on body armor and breastplates. One woman tucked her ragged hair under a helm. Another man strapped the gauntlets on his arm. A shorter woman picked up a heavy axe and swung it through the air, testing its balance. A man restrung a bow and plucked the string. He nodded, satisfied.

Their transformation was complete in a matter of minutes. They worked in silence, the only noises the hiss of swords into sheaths and the soft clink of chainmail. A nod here, a look there, was all they needed to communicate.

All the ragged, dirty-looking guards from the dungeon had recovered their armor, their weapons, and more importantly, their pride. With the dragon symbol emblazoned on their chests, they now looked like those heroic Guardsmen of Alexandria I had heard stories about. In front of them stood Ardimus, his chainmail gleaming and his sharpened scimitar at his side.

The Guardsmen's faces became grim and their eyes gleamed with an angry fire. Blood and battle was on their minds. Gods help whoever stood in their way.

Ardimus walked towards me. "This is where we part ways," he said. "Be careful, Hellsfire. I still owe you."

"I will," I said.

I turned towards Krystal and gave her my full attention. There were so many things I wanted to say to her, but all the words were inadequate.

"I'll be back to get you, Your Highness, once we see how the battle is going," I said. "Please be careful."

"You too, hero."

She turned to walk away when I stopped her, "Wait!"

"Yes, Hellsfire?"

"Take this."

I pulled my dagger from underneath my robes. I clasped it in my hands, enchanting it with minor, temporary magic. My hands glowed and transferred power to it.

"Here," I said, handing it to her. "I doubt you'll need it but if you do, unsheathe it the slightest bit and you'll activate its magic. I'll know you're in trouble and where you are."

"Still looking out for me?"

"Always."

We shared a smile before departing.

We ran toward the entrance. I pushed thoughts of the princess's safety out of my mind so I could focus on the upcoming battle. As soon as we were out of the castle, the blinding daylight struck us, disorientating us for a moment. Then we picked up the pace. The weight of the soldiers' gear didn't slow any of them down. They hungered to lighten the load by burying their blades and arrows into Premier's creatures.

The keep had emptied out—the main battle was at the wall by the city's south gate. As we ran through the courtyard, two giant shadows passed over us, and we heard an inhuman scream. I stopped and looked up. Cynder was overhead, locked in a battle with a giant bird of some sort. It must have been Premier's own guardian. The bird's sharp talons dug into Cynder's flesh, and he cried out. Cynder stretched his long, reptilian neck, snapping at the bird's feathery side until he was free. I wanted to help my friend, but there was nothing I could do for him. I prayed the dragon would survive.

We passed through the castle gate. It was unnerving to see the silent temple and the streets so empty of people when there were crowds the last time I had passed through. Even the beggars and prostitutes would have been a welcome sight.

We ran down the hill, heading for the square where Alexander's statue stood, when the magic hit me like a sledgehammer to the head. I wobbled, nearly toppling over. I put my fingertips to my forehead, and the throbbing pain settled until it became a buzzing haze. I looked back at the castle.

The princess was in trouble.

Most of the Guardsmen were still running, but my friends stopped. "Hellsfire, what is it?" Prastian asked.

"I've got to go back to the castle. The princess is in trouble."

"Then I'll go with you," Jastillian said. "I promised Wizard Stradus I'd watch your back."

"And we'll go, too," one of the women of Alexandria said. "She's our princess."

I shook my head. "No. I'll be faster alone." I pointed to the southern walls where the battle raged. "The princess needs you to help with that."

From our height, across the city, it was hard to see what was going on. The fire and smoke obscured most of the battle. But what I saw was enough.

Tiny silhouettes fought hard on the wall. Our forces had climbed sections of the wall, but were bottled up. The creatures' hulking forms pushed our forces back. On one section of the wall, the creatures were like a dragon's mouth, swallowing our soldiers whole.

"Alexandria is more than just the crown," I said. "The princess knows that. Do your duty. Rally the people. Open the gates. I'll go back to the castle."

"What about you?" Prastian asked. "What about your duty and what you promised Wizard Stradus?"

"My duty lies with the princess."

I turned and ran back to the castle. The fire building inside of me became hard to contain. It oozed out of my hand and through my eyes, the more I thought about Krystal. I left a fiery trail behind me. If any harm had befallen her, it would be all my fault.

CHAPTER 24

I SPRINTED into the castle. I followed the magic in my dagger, the haze lessening the closer I got to it. The princess still had it with her. I hoped one of the creatures lurked nearby so I could vent my anger. I didn't find any. I found something much worse.

Inside the keep, at the top of the main staircase, were the bodies of Krystal's guards. One man lay on his stomach, his neck twisted so that his vacant eyes stared at the ceiling. Another guard's face was so charred and blackened I could see half her skull.

I crept to the nearest body. She slumped against the wall, leaving a bloody trail against it. There was a fist-sized hole in her chest. I bent down and put my fingers to the blood. It was still warm. Whatever caused it could lurk nearby.

I worried that Krystal was amongst these bodies, even though the magic I felt wasn't near here. It was off towards the end of the corridor. But the dagger could have been taken from her. I checked the bodies, and they all wore the armor of Alexandria.

I kept my guard up and crept forward, stepping over the dead bodies. Something moved. I created a very hot and hungry fireball in my hand.

"Help me," said a weak voice. It was coming from one of the hunched, shadowy bodies. He tried to move again, and cried out in pain.

I crept toward the voice, still scanning the area. It could be a trap waiting to spring when I helped the wounded soldier.

"The princess…you must help her." My heart beat fast at that. That meant she was still alive.

I rushed to the man, ignoring the possible trap. I had to find out what he knew. It was Ardimus. Fresh cuts and bruises marked his face, and blood trailed from a large gash in his right arm, dripping into a puddle on the floor.

"Are you all right?" I asked, keeping my voice low.

"No, but I'll live."

My eyes scanned the shadows and open doors. There were far too many hiding places. "Is there anyone else here?"

Ardimus shook his head.

I ripped off a fallen soldier's tunic and tied it tightly around his open wound. The cloth darkened with red. It wasn't enough, but it would have to do. I helped Ardimus up, taking his left hand. He grunted in pain and touched a hand to his right side. It came back with more blood.

"What happened here? Where's the princess?"

"Premier came. He attacked us with magic and took her." Ardimus shook his head in shame. "I failed."

Ardimus's clothes had disintegrated over his chest, but his chainmail remained intact. I sensed magic coming from the chainmail. I latched onto some mana and touched it. It hummed in response.

"How did you—"

"My chainmail and sword are enchanted. They were a gift, long ago, and provided some protection." Ardimus squirmed in pain. "But they weren't enough." He looked at the dead bodies strewn across the floor. "My people…the princess. We've got to help her."

"No, I will find her."

"But—"

"You're in no shape to fight Premier. If you weren't hurt, I would be honored to have you by my side. I need you—no, the princess needs you to guard King Furlong. Will you do that?"

"I will follow her orders," he said, the embers in his eyes growing into flames. "Please give me my sword."

I walked a few paces away and picked up his scimitar. Magical power lurked within. I handed Ardimus his sword. He drew himself erect and proud, even though it hurt him to do so.

"Make him pay dearly for what he's done, Hellsfire."

"You have my word." I left Ardimus and called the wind to help me in my race.

I followed the magic, running through the empty hallways and down another flight of stairs. It was strange to be inside the castle with no guards or servants. The enchantment led me down familiar corridors until I realized there was only one place Premier would have taken her—his tower.

When I arrived at the northwest tower and stepped through the doorway, I had my magic at the ready. I didn't summon any mana in case Premier could sense it, but it lurked just under the surface. I prayed Premier would be alone. I didn't want to have to worry about that damn ogre of his.

I expected they would be down in his workroom, but my spell pulled me upstairs. I crept up the stairs and hid at the top, peeking around the corner. The haze in my head disappeared when I saw them. Premier and Krystal stood in a large, spacious room. Parts of the stone walls were cracked, bits of them scattered on the floor. Black scorch marks spotted the walls. There was no furniture. The starkness and condition of the room reminded me of the training room in the White Mountain. The princess still had the dagger; I could sense the hidden weapon.

"For the last time, I will not give you what you want!" the princess said.

Her hands were bound, but she stood tall and proud before Premier.

Premier turned to the side, a thoughtful look on his face. "I underestimated you. I had thought you weak. Who would have thought that the blood of Alexander would run so strong in a girl?"

In a calm but deadly voice he continued, "If you don't give me what I want, the line of Alexandria ends here. The creatures of the Wastelands will be free to wreak havoc on Northern Shala. That will be your legacy, princess. That will be what people remember. But before that happens, your people will die, your father will die, and I will turn this entire city into a barren wasteland. I will force you to watch, and then I will kill you."

Krystal's violet eyes were full of fire and anger. If looks could kill, Premier would have dropped dead. I prayed she didn't do anything that would anger him further.

She did. She spat in his face. Premier calmly wiped his face before backhanding her. Krystal fell to the ground. She stood up again, blood trickling from her nose. I focused, suppressing my rage and my fire.

"That's unbecoming of you, Your Highness," Premier said.

I had to figure out how I could attack Premier without hurting Krystal. I thought of a quick and easy spell, one I wouldn't need too much mana to perform. Then we could escape, or she could, while I faced Premier alone.

I waited until Premier's back was turned, then darted out of my hiding place, sprinting as fast as my long legs would carry me. The distance wasn't far, but it seemed to take forever. I gathered in wind mana, preparing to unleash it on Premier.

Without looking at me, Premier reached out and grabbed Krystal by the neck. "Tell me, boy, have you ever forced the manas upon someone? I have. It's fascinating. Though it appears to be a very painful way to die."

I froze in my tracks.

"They say it shreds the soul, while destroying the body. It doesn't work on those like you and me, but the princess can't perform magic, can she?" Premier squeezed her throat even tighter. I felt him gathering mana.

"Stop," I said. "Leave her alone."

Premier squeezed once more, then dropped Krystal. She fell, gasping for air. The magic Premier had summoned vanished.

He turned to face me and said, "You're beginning to become an annoyance, boy. First the elves, then the dwarf, and now this." Premier closed his eyes and put his fingertips to his temple. He opened them again. "What I don't understand is why."

I met his dark gaze. "It's the right thing to do."

Premier studied me, his expression incredulous. "You're serious?" Premier chuckled, then gave a full-blown laugh. "Such heroic nonsense."

I watched the princess struggle to rise. Premier's gazed followed mine. He kicked her hands out from under her. I took a step forward and narrowed my eyes at him.

"Ah, that's why you're doing this," Premier said. "Not because of some silly moral code. Because of her." Premier gave the princess and me an evil smile. "You may yet be of use to me, boy."

"It ends here," I said, finding my words surprisingly steady. And if I failed, there would always be Master Stradus.

"Boy, I have centuries on you. You couldn't comprehend the things I've learned and the sort of power I have." He focused on Krystal. "One last chance, Princess. Give me what I want or he dies."

Krystal's eyes met mine. Hard and full of fury against Premier, they softened when she looked at me. Sadness and guilt lurked in them. She shook her head, strands of her sun-streaked hair flying.

She said quietly, "I can't. Forgive me, Hellsfire."

"There's nothing to forgive," I said.

"Ah, youth," Premier said. "How sweet."

Without warning, Premier summoned a torrent of black mana, casting it with lightning speed.

The last thing I saw was Krystal, still on the ground, shouting, "Hellsfire!"

Then the darkness engulfed me. Premier and Krystal disappeared, and there was nothing but the pure blackness. I had used black mana before, but never felt its touch like this. It was as icy and cold as death. I collapsed under its oppressive weight.

I tried to summon white mana to counteract it, but I couldn't grasp it. It flickered and sparked but wouldn't come. I sank lower to the floor, gasping for air. The magic was crushing me. I reached out, trying to break free. I couldn't do it without the proper magic. I was enclosed by invisible darkness, pressing against me until it suffocated me.

The darkness lifted. The princess had thrown herself at Premier, breaking his concentration. Premier snapped his fingers, summoning a wind that pushed her away. She flew into the wall, her head hitting the stone hard. She collapsed on the floor.

"Krystal!"

I tried to get up. Premier's attention re-focused on me. The black mana hit me like the touch of a feather, but with the force of an avalanche, sending me back into the darkness.

I couldn't get the princess out of my mind. That head wound might have killed her. I pushed aside my fears, letting the darkness and my rage fuel my magic.

My greatest strength—fire—came out to battle the blackness, though. I knew it would be useless against Premier's black mana. I needed the mana of life. I thought the fire would be devoured as it pushed out against the shadows. It wasn't.

Instead of trying to overcome the darkness with its own light, the fire absorbed it. It swayed and roared with power, sucking the black mana within itself. The room spun into view again. I slowly got up, calming the fire and forcing it back within myself.

Krystal lay on the floor, very still. I ached to go to her, but it would be suicide. I thought I saw her take a shallow breath before I turned my attention to Premier.

"How did you do that?" Premier asked, taking a few steps closer. He seemed to have forgotten all about the princess. "That spell is far too advanced for a whelp like you."

I had no idea how I'd done it, but I wasn't going to tell him that. "I told you. I'm going to stop you."

The curiosity left Premier's face. Good. I wanted to anger him, so his complete attention would be focused on me instead of the princess. I circled around him. Premier countered my move. When he was safely away from Krystal and before he realized what I was doing, I attacked.

I summoned a small portion of my fire and tossed it at Premier in the form of a fireball. He deflected it easily, and it bounced off the wall and dispersed. The next time, I used both hands. Premier knocked aside the fireballs as if he were swatting flies.

"You showed promise with your counterspell earlier," Premier said. "Don't disappoint me now with these simple spells."

I performed the same spell again. Right before Premier deflected it, I split each ball into two. He blocked the first two as I had expected, but the other ones broke through, heading straight for his head. I thought they were going to hit him, but he dissipated them without even blinking.

I sped up my attack, trying to take him off guard. I let out a shout, creating a scattershot of fireballs. They sped out of my hands, swooping towards Premier. He stood calm, blocking them or absorbing them. He wrapped himself with air mana, using it as a shield. The air diffused my spells. Then he extended his shield and blasted my fireballs and me. I stumbled backwards, breaking my concentration.

"Is that all, boy?" Premier asked, with a bored expression on his face.

I punched the air and used the force of my punch to guide the air towards him, as if I was close enough to hit him. Premier tilted his head to the side, dodging it. The force of the air caused pieces of the stone to break off the wall behind him. I swung my left arm. He dodged again. However, those stones gave me an idea—something to work with in this stark environment.

While I loosed more fireballs at Premier, I channeled earth mana into the stones. They trembled in response. I prayed my fireballs were enough to distract Premier. He continued to block them. I summoned air to hurl the stones at the back of Premier's head. I thought I had him, but he sidestepped at the last moment. I barely had enough time to dodge them. They whizzed by my head and struck the opposite wall.

Premier's constant smirk infuriated me. He toyed with me, making no move to attack me. At most, he countered my spells. His eyes reminded me of Master Stradus's, the way he studied me and my spells. They focused on every move I made, unwavering. Unlike Master Stradus, though, Premier wasn't going to give me any feedback. I expected him to attack me any minute. My spells just weren't powerful enough. I needed more time. The question was, would he give it to me?

Judging from the smug look on his face, he just might.

I gathered in water mana. As I hoped, Premier didn't attack me. He stood, waiting to see what spell I had in mind. I wiped the sweat from my brow, flinging it to the ground. I gathered as much water mana as I could, until I became dehydrated and my dry mouth pleaded for water. I fed the mana into my drops of sweat. My skin shriveled and caved in. My spell ballooned and multiplied.

Water sprang up beneath my feet and swelled, rising until it nearly touched the ceiling. The salty water formed into a tidal wave, and I brought it down at Premier with as much force as I could. Premier didn't make any move to stop it. He just looked at the wave and smiled.

It crashed into him with tremendous speed. The backwash covered me to my neck in the warm water. With horror, I realized I had forgotten Krystal. She floated face down. I swam over to her and turned her over, trying to get her to breathe again. She sputtered and coughed up water, but she was still unconscious. I held onto her, making sure she wouldn't drown.

I didn't see Premier break the surface for air. The water level went down as he worked his magic. I held onto the princess but still concentrated on my magic. If I didn't stop Premier here, we were dead.

I grasped water and air mana and said in Caleea, *"From the water comes the clouds and may the clouds fill the top of the room."* Wisps of water floated into the air, becoming dark clouds that filled the ceiling, rolling and flashing with magic. Within moments, the water from the room was gone.

And there stood Premier with that smug, ugly smile I hated. I laid the princess down and walked away from her. Premier's eyes went to the princess. He didn't notice or care about the clouds. I worried that he would attack her, but he didn't. He smiled as if he could kill her at any time. Puddles still dotted the room. Premier stood in quite a large one. That gave me an idea.

"I tire of your beginner's magic," Premier said. "I thought you might make things interesting. You started off so promisingly. Now I find you wanting."

"How about this!"

I released the magic from the clouds, summoning a flash of lightning. It streaked toward Premier.

Premier shook his head like he was disappointed. He did what I expected him to: he raised his hand to the lightning, summoning a spell to deflect it. He succeeded, and the sizzling bolt crashed into the large puddle underneath him.

Aided by the water, the bolt of lightning coursed through him. Anger and pain surged across his face. The lightning seared his muscles and bones, making him look transparent. Premier's steaming body crumpled to the floor.

My muscles relaxed, and I breathed again. It was over. I stared at Premier's corpse. The emotions of battle had drained me. I was glad I lived and that Krystal and I were safe, but part of me was sad I'd had to kill Premier, even after all he'd done. From what Master Stradus had told me, Premier was once a good man, who became corrupted by power. Yet Premier had to die. Too many people had been hurt and killed because of him. I glanced at the one who he'd hurt most of all.

The princess was finally safe. Premier's own arrogance and cockiness had aided me. I wasn't sure how I would have dealt with his spells had he decided to attack me. He was right about one thing. I had done all this because of her. I would do it again.

I walked over to the princess. She was drenched in water, but when I leaned close to her pale face I heard her breathing normally. I lifted her head, feeling to see if any blood came from her head wound. There was none, but she did have a great, swollen lump. I took off the bandage she had made me and used it as a pillow for her. It wasn't much, but it was all I had. I needed to get her to a healer, and soon.

I wasn't sure if I could carry her. I was exhausted and thirsty. Using all that magic had taken its toll on me. I took off my purse and was reaching inside for my last revitalization potion when a great gust of wind hit me.

I screamed in pain and surprise as I flew into the wall. The wind had edges to it. It tore at me, scratching my face and hands. Premier stood in the middle of the room. His wind ripped my purse from my hands, sending it tumbling across the room and down the stairs. He pinned me up against the wall, my feet hovering not far from the ground.

"Impossible," I said. "You should be dead."

I channeled the air around me, trying to wrest myself from his invisible grip. I couldn't move. It wasn't that Premier's magic kept countering mine. It was so strong, it simply crushed whatever spell I tried to perform. Underneath the air, black mana lurked. It gave the air an unholy, yet powerful feel to it. The strange spell weakened me.

"You don't have the power to kill me, boy," Premier said. The amusement in his face was gone, and his lip curled in anger. I might not have killed him, but I had hurt him.

I squirmed, but his spell drained me. I tried incantations, but all my spells failed. Nothing would weaken his hold.

"Don't waste your energy. There's no escaping my grasp." Premier lifted his hand and squeezed. The invisible force bruised and battered my body. His pure black eyes moved and swirled. "The time for your annoyance is at an end. Perhaps in the next life you'll learn to use magic properly.

"The God of Death I beseech you. You have allowed me to live for centuries and now I give to you a wizard in return. Sort of." Premier raised his hand. Black mana engulfed it. Death was on his hand, and he was about to give it to me. "Goodbye, Hellsfire."

"No!" I said as the cold overtook me.

I summoned all my strength to break free of his grasp, drawing mana from myself and the environment, pushing past the weariness brought on by his spell. This wasn't the time to hold back and worry about the damage I was going to do to myself.

My own magic was a storm, shredding me from the inside. I wasn't trying to do any sort of spell, just break free from Premier's grasp. That much energy and power needed a release. Premier stopped me from finding one, so it raged against my body. Premier couldn't lock down my magic completely. It wormed its way through a small opening. I focused it against Premier's spell, widening the gap until it struck against him.

The two powerful magics clashed. Premier's had the upper hand, but my sheer, uncontrollable magic lashed against his, turning the tide. Premier struggled to maintain the spell that bound me and the one in his hand. His face twisted in concentration. He needed to choose one spell to strengthen; he could lose his grip on both. The burden on his mind, spirit, and body were great. He was a few steps away from me. He had only to touch me to kill me, yet each step he took looked like his feet were mired in mud.

I struggled to lift my arms. I needed them to channel my spell. I clenched my fists, and my forearms bulged. I yelled, using both magic and my physical strength to break free. My right arm was loose from Premier's binding spell. My clenched fist almost smacked me in the face when I pulled it free.

I stretched my arm at Premier. Instead of fighting his spell and trying to break it, I let loose the pent-up magic that was eating me from the inside. The elemental magic blitzed Premier. Rainbow colors sparked and sizzled through the air. Because I shifted the magic and ignored his spell, his binding spell on me renewed. My body twisted in agony. I pushed aside the pain and weariness, using my emotions to fuel my magic. I had to end it here. For Krystal's sake, for Alexandria, and for my friends.

Premier's mastery of magic was incredible. He maintained the binding spell, the death spell, and put up a defense against my onslaught of magic. My elemental magic clashed against his invisible shield. The bright colors swirled around him, yet they never did him any harm. His spell had weakened, but he continued to move closer.

My feet hovered above the ground. I was still pinned, but I was able to bring my left arm up. I let loose even more magic at him. Blood trickled out of my nose. The noise and pain in my head grew louder as my life force left me. It slipped away along with the magic I cast. The neverending abyss called out to me. Although I didn't want them to, pieces of my soul went towards it.

I was dying.

I was using too much of my own mana to fuel my blast at Premier. The fire within me wavered and flickered, dimming with each second. Coldness crept into my skin. Goose bumps ravaged my body. I had to fight to stay conscious and focus my raging magic at Premier.

My magic wasn't enough. Premier kept taking one small step after another. I poured more mana into it, making the pain in my head even worse. The blood from my nose was like a river. My eyes started to bleed.

It was no use. Premier was in front of me.

"Die, boy!"

CHAPTER 25

PREMIER BROUGHT HIS hand down, bringing death with it. Before he could touch me, a huge gust of wind sent him flying towards the opposite wall, slamming him down hard. His concentration broke. He released me from his grip, and I slid to the floor. I barely had enough energy to look up.

Master Stradus stood over me, bathed in blue mana. "Are you all right, my boy?"

I lifted my tired head and wiped the blood from my nose and cheeks. I blinked several times, trying to bring the world back into clear view. I forced a painful smile. "I'll manage. Thanks for saving me, Master. How did you get here?"

"We've breached the gates."

He sighed, and I sensed Master Stradus had used up some of his power to help those outside. I wished he hadn't. We were going to need all the strength we could muster. If only we could get to my potions and restore our strength.

"What in the Pit made you come in here and fight Premier alone against my wishes?"

I motioned to the princess's still body with my head. "Her."

Master Stradus nodded and gave a tight-lipped smile. "I understand. We'd better hurry up and get her to safety. We haven't much time."

We were out of time.

Premier rose and faced us. His robes were singed and tattered. His face was scratched and bruised. He didn't seem to notice. His black spell was still in his hand. I thought he would have let that go when he let me go, but he had somehow held on to it. He narrowed his eyes at my master.

Master Stradus helped me up, never taking his eyes off of Premier.

"I know you," Premier said.

"You did once, a long time ago."

Premier was quiet as he thought about it. "That wind felt…familiar." His dark eyes gleamed with recognition. "Stradus, is it?"

My master nodded. "I see you've taken the egocentric name of Premier. And I thought you were just joking."

"Yes, and you still have your head in the clouds, Stradus." The spell ate Premier's own hand, and he didn't care. Master Stradus was right. Premier had lost his mind. I could make out only madness in his pure black eyes.

Master Stradus studied Premier, fiddling with his long, white beard. "I see time hasn't been good to you."

I stared at my master, wondering why we weren't attacking. I was exhausted and needed the breather, but standing here was also giving Premier a chance to recover. What were we waiting for?

Then I felt it. Master Stradus was using this time to gather in energy. I had to do the same thing.

I stopped gasping for air and drew in mana from the life all around us. Master Stradus gave me a subtle nod. I looked at the princess still on the ground, praying she would wake up and escape.

Premier chuckled. "If only you knew. I'm not the only one, Stradus. But I do like that beard you have going for you. That and all your white hair makes you look like one of those so-called wise fools on the Council."

The globe on my master's staff swirled as he gathered energy. "Thank you."

"And a staff, too. I don't need a useless tool to focus my power. I may be old, but I'm not a weakling like you."

Master Stradus ignored Premier's taunts, continuing to draw in energy.

Premier glanced at me. "Quite an apprentice you have there, Stradus. He has potential. It's too bad he's never going to reach it. I'm going to kill him, and then I'm going to kill you."

"You mean you're going to try, old friend."

"Always the *hopeful* one, I see."

"And still the *mad* one, I see."

The two wizards stared at each other, filling the room with powerful energy. It thickened the air, leaving its touch on everything and everyone. The ancient, dense magic made the hairs on my body rise. Even the princess stirred, but she didn't wake. I wished she would so she could escape. If it was dangerous in here before, it was going to get a lot more dangerous now. All that power ached to be released.

Our magic came out based on our strongest mana. A strong breeze circled the room. My fire surfaced to my hand. Premier's Art was the black mana he tapped into.

Premier drew power from himself. The spell around his hand consumed it. His skin peeled back until I saw the muscles. Then they disappeared until there was nothing but bone. With each horrific change, the spell grew stronger. He didn't cry out in agony, nor did his face twitch in pain.

Master Stradus's face scrunched up, and his eyes were squinted. He studied Premier's hand like he would study me when I performed magic. I wished he had the chance to tell me what he knew about Premier's magic.

A thunderous silence filled the room while we studied each other and debated who would make the first move.

Premier smiled in his arrogant way. "Suppose I get rid of your apprentice, and it can be like old times?"

Premier released his now chest-sized death ball and flung it in my direction. By instinct, I raised my hand to deflect it with my fire.

"No! You can't affect it with elemental magic!" Master Stradus said, pushing me out of the way. I knew that. I should have remembered it.

I dove to the floor, grunted, and released a fireball at Premier. It didn't touch him. Premier stood there with his eyes closed, as a barrier of magic protected him. "Premier's up to something. He's in a trance."

"Watch out!" Master Stradus yelled. We leaped out of the way just as the ball went flying past. The ball moaned, aching to kill something. The sound sent a shiver to my soul.

"What do you want me to do, master?"

"Damn him. He didn't give me enough time to gather in mana. I'm going to work on that. I'll be invisible to him. Attack him directly. He'll be vulnerable once you get past his defenses."

Master Stradus walked away and stopped on the other side of the room. He released the power he had been holding, until a white light glowed around his body like a firefly. His eyes became pure white.

Premier's spell stopped moving. His head turned, and his eyes shifted around the room, passing over my master as if he wasn't there. "Stradus, where did you go?" His black eyes focused on me. "No matter."

The black ball of death started its descent again, flying and spinning through the air until it was almost upon me. I swayed like a cat, getting ready to jump. I was too tense. I jumped too soon. Instead of me fooling the ball, it changed direction, heading right for me. I conquered a gust of wind and pushed myself in the opposite direction. The ball skittered past and went off the other way, wailing in disappointment. This was my best chance to attack Premier.

I rushed to tackle him. I was exhausted from the magic I had performed earlier, and hoped his shield only applied to magic. It didn't. I yelled out in pain as I collided with the magical shield. I tried to punch him, throwing all my weight behind it. The shield seared my hand. My knuckles burned. I thought that at least Premier couldn't perform any more magic while he worked these two.

I was wrong.

Premier's human hand slung a fireball at me. I deflected it. He cast more. I had no problem blocking these weak and easy spells. He frowned in concentration, which meant he was hurt, tired, and not all-powerful. I deflected some of the spells back at him, but they did no harm. He continued to cast them. I didn't realize his misdirection until it was almost too late.

I dodged the death ball at the last possible second. Its musical death passed by and the spell went straight towards Premier. He tried to change the spell's direction. It clashed against his barrier. Premier struggled, lifting his arms and grunting to push the spell away. He succeeded, but his protection flickered; the magic waned. That's when I saw my chance.

I rolled up my sleeves and gathered my strength, remembering the first rule: only magic can defeat magic. *"Wind and fire unite, cause great harm to this parasite."*

Fire spewed out of me, combining with the wind. I hurled it at Premier, putting all my strength into it. It consumed Premier in a wall of fiery wind that shot up to the ceiling, slashing and burning him through his shield. I tried my best to keep the wall as solid as I could, but the spell put a great strain on my mind and spirit. I had already used up too much power against Premier.

I glanced at the death ball to see if it might be slowing down. It was, but only a little. It still headed in my direction with the same furious appetite it showed earlier. I fueled my spell with more mana, feeling Premier's shield weaken even more. It wasn't enough. His hungry spell came. I breathed heavily, not sure if I could move fast enough to dodge the death ball. It got closer, moaning incessantly, scratching at my mind and soul. I cursed and released the spell, diving onto the hard floor. My shoulder recoiled from the pain.

Looking up from the floor, I saw her move with cat-like grace. The princess had my dagger in her hand, and darted behind Premier. She brought her hand down to strike. Premier saw her too. He twisted in time to avoid her death blow. She struck him in the shoulder.

Premier yelled, "Bitch!" He propelled her back with a blast of wind. He held her in place, drawing the air from her lungs. She clawed at the invisible force and gasped for air that wouldn't come. He stretched out his hand. "Goodbye, Your Highness."

I got up and ran. I used my own magic to cut off the spell he used to hold her. He had another spell ready. I reached her in time and caught her unconscious body.

Fire sprang from Premier's fingertips, and I cradled the princess and shielded her with my own. I summoned up what little magic I could, keeping the flame from hurting her. The intense heat screamed to burn me. My exposed neck scorched as the flames brushed against it. I pushed against his magic with my mind, willing the fire to die down. Blood dripped from my nose once more, and I crumpled. How could this simple spell be hurting me so much? I focused, remembering that fire was *my* element. Not his.

I didn't have the power to stop or deflect his spell. As I looked inside the spell, I saw the magic Premier used to fuel it. It was difficult to stop magic at its source. One had to bypass the wizard's defenses and touch the person's soul. I used the fire as a conduit, traveling within to its wondrous heart. I reached out to Premier's mana, crushing it and extinguishing the fire.

My sweat-drenched body throbbed. Every sore muscle cried out in pain. I saw the princess, unconscious but unharmed. At least she was safe for now.

"Bravo," Premier said. His death spell hovered in front of him. "But it was all for naught."

Premier's spell flew towards me. I didn't have any more magic, and even if my body could move, I wouldn't. If I did, he would kill the princess. I held onto Krystal's body, praying I would take the brunt of the attack and that Master Stradus would have the time he needed to defeat Premier.

I stared into the ball, seeing my reflection gazing back at me in its smooth, icy surface. It was calm and peaceful for something so dangerous, coming to devour me.

"Let him be!" Master Stradus said. He jumped in front of me and pushed his ancient staff towards the death ball.

The white light around his body transferred to his staff. He shoved it in front of him, pushing all his will and might into it. The staff came alive, moving and hissing. When the death ball came into contact with the snake, the two powerful energies struggled, each one vying to be the winner in the deadly contest. Master Stradus's body wrinkled and cringed, but he held fast.

"Stradus! It's time to finish this!"

"You will *not* win, Premier. Do you hear me? You will not win!" Master Stradus said it with such ferocity, it shook my heart.

Blinding light flashed everywhere, stinging my eyes. The life and death that came from both my master and Premier shook the foundation of the castle. The trembling tower felt as if it would fall apart at any second. Premier and Master Stradus's high-pitched yells pulsated through my head, shattering my ears. Magical tidal waves splashed me, brushing against my soul. Premier's cold magic made me want to give up and die. Master Stradus's magic filled me with energy, making me want to live. Feeling them fight each other was akin to being burned, then frozen alive—not my body, but my soul.

I hunched over the sleeping princess, trying to protect her from all this. My meager body wasn't enough. I took the brunt of the spells, yet she stirred and squirmed in my arms. Her body wasn't trained to deal with these magical forces. I wished I could shield her from this with my magic. I had none. By the gods, why didn't she leave when she had the chance, instead of trying to kill Premier?

Because she wouldn't have left. This was her kingdom, these were her people, and she would fight until she succeeded or there was nothing left. This was as much her fight as it was mine or Master Stradus's. Maybe more so. I would help her carry the load as much as I could.

Master Stradus glowed as bright as a polished coin and as pure as the freshest milk. He wasn't going to lose; he couldn't lose, not with all this power and years of experience.

But Premier's power was greater than I thought. He made one final press. It was enough. Master Stradus gave one heartrending cry as Premier's dark magic overtook him.

The death ball entered Master Stradus, and I could only watch.

CHAPTER 26

"**MASTER!**" **I CRIED,** reaching out to catch him. I was too late. The death ball burrowed inside him, and he collapsed to the ground. His staff became motionless and snapped. I had failed him. The backlash of the magic crushed me. I screamed until the magic scattered and disappeared.

I laid the princess's body on the ground and rose. I could do nothing but stare at Master Stradus's lifeless body. I couldn't believe he was dead. It was all my fault. He came here because of me. He fought because of me. He died because of me.

"Goodbye, old friend," Premier said, gazing at Master Stradus's corpse. "It was…good to see you after all these years." Premier's black eyes focused on me.

One of the first things Master Stradus had taught me was that in learning to control my powers, I had to hold back. If I relaxed too much or if my emotions overwhelmed me, I would lose control of my magic. I remembered the family I had traveled with and the harm I caused them. But this was no time to hold back. Premier had countered or survived all the spells I had cast. There was only one move left. Krystal would want me to do this. I had to defeat Premier, for the good of the people. I couldn't worry about my own safety, or even hers. She had taught me that Alexandria was more than just her.

My eyes met Premier's. "No more!"

I went against all of my training, letting my emotions overwhelm me and fuel my magic. I thought about all of the people that had suffered and died because of Premier. From the little starving boy in the street to the king and to the people who were dying right now. Each one of them was on my mind. Lastly, I thought of how much pain Premier caused the princess, and how he killed my master.

My anger swelled over the pain and grief. It boiled and splashed throughout my body. The power begged to be released. It wasn't enough.

I thought of how the children in Sedah, especially Nathan, teased and bullied me; how my father died before I ever got to know him; how poor my mother and I were. Every time I had been wronged, embarrassed, or shamed came to my mind. Tears poured from my eyes from all the hurtful memories that came. The streams of water burst into flames.

This was all a game to Premier. He didn't care about these people. He didn't care about anything. Everyone was just a pawn to be used. It didn't matter if it was the creatures of the Wastelands or the people of Alexandria. He only cared about himself. He would destroy anyone that got in his way.

The flames crept out from every pore in my body, surrounding me in an aura of fire. The emotional storm threatened to suffocate and smother me. That's when I risked doing what I had been trained never to do.

I let it all go.

The fire spewed out of my body, saturating the entire room. It burned everything, leaving only the princess and Master Stradus unharmed. The elemental magic headed for Premier. He put up a counterspell. The flames clashed against his shield, never touching him.

Premier smiled in triumph. He knew what I did was a last-ditch effort. All wizards could let their strongest mana come out of their body, yet it had no focus, no control. It wasn't a spell; it was more of a deathspell.

My fires weren't hot enough. Premier couldn't attack me, but he didn't have to. I couldn't keep this up forever. I needed to get past his defenses. I needed to give it everything I had until there was nothing left. Even if it cost me my life. It was all or nothing—there was no in between.

I dug deep into my soul. Deeper than I realized was possible, and to a place few had ever gone before.

It was there I found the strength I needed.

I clenched my fists and screamed. The flames burned faster, brighter, and hotter. Premier struggled to maintain his shield. The searing flames transformed, becoming black and more powerful. The black flames made me feel like I could do anything. Nothing would stand in my way. I could barely control the magic. It was enough not to explode. My body ached until it burned and I became fire.

The otherworldly fire smashed into Premier's defenses and shattered them, enveloping Premier.

Premier tried to counter my magic, but he couldn't. His incantations failed. All the magic he used burned away. Premier screamed while the dark fire ate him. Blisters and boils popped, then peeled away. The black fire savored his flesh. Premier continued to cast spell after spell even while being burned alive. My fire ate his spells, using them as fuel for the fire.

Premier exploded in a dark swirl of red and black light. The tower rocked on its foundations. I fell to my knees. I thought I had no strength left. But I did.

Wherever I had gone to, I had found power. Tremendous power. It called out to me. Beckoned me. It was a whisper at first. The voice grew louder. I couldn't ignore it. In fact, I wanted to answer it. Oh, how I wanted to answer it. It said I could rule all. That I could restore peace. That I could do whatever I wanted.

I clutched my heart and toppled over. The fires burned even brighter and darker than before. What I could do with this. All my desires, cravings, wants, wishes, could be granted if I said yes. No one could stop me if I gave in. It would be mine to command.

I saw Krystal's sleeping form next to me. Her transparent, heavenly glow made her look like the angels my mother told me about growing up. The princess reminded me I had a duty to the people, to the wizards that came before me, to her. I didn't want the world. I didn't want the power to rule over people.

With all my concentration and will, I took a deep breath and forced the fires to stop. I used the relaxation techniques Master Stradus had taught me. I pictured the Peaceful Pond and how I would lie in the soft grass, watching the ducks swim by. I remembered how the princess's kiss made me feel.

The dark fires were reluctant to go. They pushed and fought me every step of the way, as if they had a mind of their own. The black flames died, and along with them the voice in my mind.

Sweat drenched my entire body, and I gasped for air. A moment ago, I had the power to change the world. Now, with the power gone, I had the strength of a newborn kitten. The warm stone floor embraced me into unconsciousness.

"Hellsfire," a gentle voice said. "Hellsfire, please wake up."

I moaned and forced my eyes open. The room and everything in it was dry; the walls were scorched and blackened. My body screamed for more rest. I smiled when I saw who was speaking, and that she was safe. "Princess, are you all right?"

"I'm fine, thanks to you." She rubbed her sore wrists, now free from their bonds. "There's someone you should talk to before it's too late."

"Hellsfire," a very weak voice said. It was Master Stradus. I strained my ears to hear him. His voice was a whisper.

I trembled with shock, crawling over to him. He still lived. I took his cold hand within my own. "Master."

"Very good job…Wizard Hellsfire," he said, managing a weak smile.

When he gave me my title, my power grew. My inner fire, while weakened and tired like I was, brightened. I nodded, understanding the lessons I once studied. New possibilities crept into my mind. I was now a wizard, one of the few who were bound to all living things. My former master's wind mana died down.

"I should go," the princess said.

I reached out and grabbed her hand before she could leave. "Please. Stay."

She nodded and squeezed my hand. I squeezed back.

Stradus smiled, seeing our hands. He said to her, "He's going to need you, Princess. More than you know. Please watch out for him."

"I will."

Stradus's aura flickered and faded. "What can I do to help you?" I asked.

"No…it's too late. The spell is still…eating me. My magic countered it…for as long as it could. It's just a matter of…time." He coughed and spat blood. The life in his eyes faded.

"Please, don't talk like that. There must be something I can do. Some kind of potion or spell." I frantically looked around for my pouch.

"There's…nothing you can do for me…but there is one last thing you can do."

"Anything. Just name it."

"Stop…Premier."

"I thought I just did?"

Stradus's blue eyes flickered. "No. That wasn't him. People don't…blow up like that when getting burned." Stradus laughed, coughing up more blood onto his face. I wiped the blood and spit away. "Thank…you. That was…an avatar."

"Avatar?"

"Yes…" He gulped for air, and I moved to help him sit up. He was thinner and lighter now, as Premier's spell ate him from the inside. "Please…my time is short." Stradus focused, his eyes radiating with white mana. His voice became full of strength and life again. "I see it now." He stared through me at something else.

"An avatar is a projection of sorts, involving a very powerful ritual," Stradus said. "If you succeed, you can project yourself elsewhere. It's very hard to pull off one that enables you to interact with your environment to such an extent, be hard to detect, and still not deal with the pain or bodily functions that one normally has to go through. I couldn't pick up on it until you defeated him."

That would explain why Premier's skin didn't look altogether human and seemed to sag off him, and why he never ate or drank.

"You've got to stop Premier, Hellsfire. If he was able to pull this off, then there's no telling what he's capable of. He's not going to let this rest. I know."

"I wouldn't know where to start."

Stradus's was about to say something more, but his eyes lost their life. The energy around his body collapsed, and he slumped in my arms. Focusing his mana had sped up the spell. The black mana of death encompassed his body, about to claim him.

I clasped my hands onto Stradus's. "I call upon the gods to transfer my energy into his."

The different manas inside me flowed from me to him—fire being the most dominant. I put as much of myself into him as I could without fainting from exhaustion. Stradus smiled, his eyes turning a clear blue with a hint of red.

"I've traced Premier's spell. He's in Masep, Renak's old place of rule, located deep in the Wastelands. I want you to get the book from him. Tread carefully. You have two months before he will fully recover. And don't kill him."

The princess gasped at this, and so did I. "Why not? After all the pain and suffering he's caused, why shouldn't I kill him?"

"He still plays an intricate part in what's to come."

I gazed into Stradus's glazed eyes, trying to figure out the future. What role could Premier possibly play? A storm swirled in Krystal's eyes. She didn't agree with letting Premier live.

Stradus coughed up some more blood and squeezed my hand tighter. His eyes faded, becoming dilated. He looked towards the afterlife. "Bury my ashes in the…garden."

"Yes, Master…I mean Stradus," Once someone was declared a wizard, they no longer called their former teacher master.

Stradus smiled. "Good, Wizard Hellsfire, good. I always thought of you…as a son. Take care, my…" The pressure from his hand faded. His whole body caved in as the spell finished its feast.

Memories flooded my mind, forcing tears to well up. I remembered the times he taught me how to make potions in his garden. I made a rejuvenation potion wrong, and it ended up bitter. Master Stradus couldn't stop laughing when he saw the expression on my face and how frantically I tried to spit the stuff out.

He was also gentle. There were countless times when I saw him tending to the plants in his garden with the softest touch. I even saw him singing and talking to the plants on occasion. I questioned him about that, but he always denied it. King Sharald would have been proud to see him continue what he learned from his elven friends.

My magic would always be associated with him. Master Stradus taught me what I wanted to learn the most—how to control the fire within me. But that's not all he taught me, or even the most important thing. He showed me how beautiful magic could be. How when used properly, it connected a person with everything, and those things were connected to him. He taught me that it wasn't about power or control, it was about being alive. I thought my magic was a curse because of the harm I caused. Now I didn't think I could live without my magic. It was all because of him.

And now he was dead.

"You were the closest thing to a father I had. I will do as you ask. Mother was right. You truly were an angel."

I swept my hands over his face and closed his eyes. I leaned in and kissed him on the forehead. I got up, staring at his lifeless corpse. This was my fault. If only I hadn't disobeyed him, if only we had attacked Premier together at full strength. We could have beaten him together. *Book of Shazul* or no, Stradus was the stronger wizard.

"Hellsfire," the princess said, startling me. I had forgotten she was there.

"Yeah?"

"Come here."

I let myself be swept up by her. Krystal reeled me in until our bodies pressed together. When I looked into her gentle, purple eyes, that's when I lost it.

I wept for my former master's death, I wept for the people who had died, and I wept for the pain the survivors would go through. The princess didn't interrupt me. She held me in a warm embrace and let me cry on her shoulder. It was several long minutes before all those pent-up emotions of fear, anxiety, and guilt were manageable. They were never going to leave completely, but I needed the time to let part of them go.

I stopped crying and sniffling. "I'm sorry, Your Highness. I don't know what came over me."

She made my eyes meet hers. "It's all right. I understand. What did I tell you? Call me by my name when we're alone."

"All right, Prin—Krystal."

She smiled. "Good."

I tried to return her smile, but couldn't manage to give her more than a small one. How did people constantly deal with all this fighting and death?

Krystal put her hands to my cheeks and wiped my tears away with her thumbs. "Relax, hero, it's over. Being too tense after battle is never a good thing."

"I've never been through this before. I had no idea how it feels."

Krystal leaned close to me. Unlike the first time, I made no move to stop her kiss. It was short but gentle and warm in its caress. "Feel better?"

I couldn't help but grin. "A little. Thank you, Krystal."

"No, thank *you*, hero."

Before we left, I retrieved my potions from downstairs. I downed half of a vial before offering the other half to Krystal.

"What's this?" she asked.

"It'll help restore your strength. It won't treat your wounds, but you'll feel better."

She shook her head. "Take the rest. You need it."

"No. You need it too. You've reminded me the day's not over yet."

Krystal took the vial and drank it. "Here's your dagger back. It came in handy, like you knew it would."

I nodded and took it. I put on my purse before picking up my former master. He was much lighter than he should have been. The spell had done its job well.

We left the tower and walked the quiet halls. We parted ways, as she went to check on her father. I told her I would look at him later, to see if what Premier had done to him was gone. I left the castle, carrying Stradus's body in my arms.

The bright sun blinded me as I stepped outside. I walked through the courtyard and past the castle walls until I was in the streets of Alexandria. The closer I got to the gates and the carnage, the more I had to deal with the lingering smoke. I coughed, wishing it was already dark, or that the smoke was dense enough to impair my vision.

Bodies of both the alliance and the creatures lay everywhere, twisted in a way none of them could have survived. A lot of them had the same expression on their faces. It was a look of horror and agony as they met their deaths. The thick smell of blood covered their bodies. I could almost taste the metallic liquid.

Hundreds of creatures had arrows stuck in their bodies. One ogre's gigantic corpse had sprouted so many arrows, they pinned him to the wall of a shop. Another shop's walls had caved in. A dwarf's feet poked out of the ruins. One human corpse was missing his arms. I walked by one arm a few feet later, seeing teeth marks in it.

Many of the human bodies I saw were without armor or proper weapons. One woman had a troll corpse draped over her body. Her head was nearly severed, but in her hands was one of the jagged swords the Wasteland creatures used. She had turned it on the creature, and it stuck out of its back. The Guardsmen had rallied the people of Alexandria, and had convinced them to fight even without weapons. Amazing.

People walked through the bodies to finish off the growling creatures that were too wounded to move. Some also finished off their moaning allies who were too injured to be helped. Every once in awhile, they would find someone who could be saved and treat them. That was too rare a sight.

The streets of Alexandria were no longer empty. As I passed the people of Alexandria, I read the relieved looks on their faces, even while they tended to the wounded and dying. They were glad the day was over and that they were out from under Premier's influence. The dwarves sang about their victory and boasted and bragged about how many they killed. The elves weren't as happy. When I asked why, I was taken aback.

Prastian had been mortally wounded, and even Jastillian had been badly hurt. I went out to the tent where Prastian was. I placed Stradus's body down before entering.

I nodded to Demay, who was sitting in the corner, tears running down his face. "How is he?" I asked King Sharald, as he sat next to Prastian's cot.

"The healers say if he makes it past tonight, he'll live." Sharald looked up. "I'm keeping vigil, praying to the gods that will happen. Where's Stradus? He might be able to—" Sharald caught himself when he saw my former master's body lying near the open tent flaps. He sighed heavily. "He finally died, and before me. I thought he would outlive everybody."

"He died saving my life."

"It's what he would have wanted, Hellsfire. Stradus told me you would do things that would far outweigh what he had ever done. He said you would need help. I told him that I, and my people, would be there for you."

"Thank you, Your Majesty."

Sharald turned his attention back to his younger cousin. I walked to Prastian and listened to his shallow breathing. Stradus wasn't here, but he would always be with me to guide me.

With my new wizard powers, I saw the green mana lurking within Prastian. Like Stradus's, it was fading. Even with my new powers, I was still no good with white mana. That dark place where I went to defeat Premier would be no help either. I took Prastian's hand and latched onto his mana. I fed it with all the healthy elves around me, taking their lifeforce piece by piece. Prastian's breathing eased. His heartbeat grew louder until it was strong.

Prastian slowly opened his eyes and said, "Hellsfire?"

"Brother, you're alive," Demay said, running over and hugging him.

Prastian cried out in pain.

"Sorry. Let me fetch you some water."

Prastian reached out to me. "Thank you, my friend."

"Rest."

"Thank you, Hellsfire," King Sharald said. He glanced at the other wounded elves in the tent. "Can you do the same for them as you did for Prastian?"

"I wish I could, but I can't. I didn't heal his wounds."

"I understand."

I walked out of the tent, trying not to look at the other injured elves. I wanted to put my hands to my ears to drown out their moaning. I didn't. I deserved the guilt that lingered. I saved Prastian because he was a friend, and the next ruler of Sharald.

I went to one of the dwarves' tents next, to see if I could do something for Jastillian. I smiled when I saw I didn't have to. He was sitting upright while a healer tended to his left arm.

"Lad!" Jastillian grunted when he tried to move. The healer forced him to remain still.

"How are you?"

"My arm's sore, but I won't lose it. Thank the gods for that. How are you?"

There was no easy way to say it. I managed. "Stradus died."

"I'm sorry to hear that."

"Me too." I didn't want to hear anyone else giving me condolences over Stradus's death. Every time they said something, the tears in my eyes built up. I changed the subject. "What did I miss?"

Jastillian told me of how hard-fought the battle to open the gates had been. They did it, but not without heavy losses and serious injuries. Eventually, the combined forces and Wizard Stradus were too much for the creatures. They routed them at the south gates, but before they could secure the north gates, more creatures from the Wastelands had come.

Jastillian hadn't been sure they could win that battle. Then they saw the fire I had created in the tower when I defeated Premier. After that, the creatures were confused and disoriented. The alliance used that distraction to take out the creatures. Some still fought hard, but not as a group. Others fled back to the Wastelands. A few escaped into Northern Shala. Patrols had been sent to kill those in our land.

I left Jastillian without telling him about Premier. I let him assume he was dead. I knew I had to tell everyone, but not this moment. Krystal knew. I knew it would only be a matter of time before she was obligated to tell someone.

I carried Stradus's body to Cynder. He lay down on a hill, well away from the armies and the city walls. He slept, but didn't snore, which meant he wasn't in a deep sleep. Spots of dried blood covered Cynder, and his scales were cut and slashed. I had never thought such a thing could happen to a dragon. Thankfully, he wasn't bleeding now. I was worried that the wounds were serious, and that he slept like people did before they died. I put Stradus's body down and put my hand over Cynder's rough red scales.

Cynder flinched when I touched a wound. "What'd you do that for?"

It bothered me that he didn't snap his jaws or blow smoke at me. He might have been seriously injured in ways I couldn't comprehend. "Are you all right?"

Cynder snorted. "You're concerned about me? How touching." He laughed, but it came out raggedy. "I'm fine. I just need to rest. Stupid, freakish, and *loud* bird. I hope it's somewhere dying. I would so love it to suffer, but the screeching would drive me insane, even from here." Cynder focused his red eyes on Stradus. "So he's finally dead. After all the adventures we went through, I didn't think he *could* die. How did it happen?"

I told the dragon what had happened, and how Stradus saved my life. I even told him what he wanted me to do about Premier.

"The old man was always a bit soft when it came to lost causes," Cynder said with a smirk. "He took you in."

I chuckled at his remark. "Yeah, I guess he started being that way when he took *you* in."

Cynder grinned and snorted smoke. "What are you going to do about Premier?"

"I'm going to do what Stradus asked. The *Book of Shazul* is far too dangerous to remain in Premier's hands." I swept my arms towards the destruction and devastation he wrought. "Look at what he's done already."

Cynder was going to retort when we heard cheering. I raised my right eyebrow, and Cynder craned his long neck to see what everyone cheered about.

King Furlong and Princess Krystal walked among their people, seeing to the wounded. The sight of the rulers of Alexandria raised their people's spirits. They lifted their tired, dirty faces to smile and wave at them. The princess saw us. She spoke to one of her guards, who ran over to us.

"The princess sends her regards and wants to know if you require anything, Wizard Hellsfire," the guard said.

I told him what I needed. "And please give Her Highness my thanks."

The guard, along with a few others, came back later with a cart carrying the materials I needed to construct a pyre.

"You know, this wasn't the first time I ran into one of those annoying birds," Cynder said as I worked.

"It wasn't?"

"Nope. Years back, me and the old man ran into them. He was much younger then…"

Cynder regaled me with countless stories of him and Stradus and the adventures they'd had, while I built the pyre. Cynder had told me one or two of the stories before, but only to help with a lesson. These were different. They were him remembering an old friend. I saw why Cynder didn't think Stradus could die, with all they had survived together.

The dragon lent his strength to me with his words. I also told stories of Stradus. They weren't as entertaining or numerous as Cynder's, but I still told them. They helped me remember the man he was, and told of better times. The laughter Cynder and I shared helped hold back the tears.

I spent the rest of the day building the pyre, which consumed all of my remaining strength. Other funerals and burials went on all around me. Dusk was approaching by the time I was done. I lifted Stradus's light body onto the pyre.

"Would you like to do the honors?" I asked Cynder.

Cynder set Stradus's body ablaze with a long stream of fire. "I'm going to miss him."

"Me too. He was amazing, wasn't he?"

"He sure was, even for a wizard."

I walked closer to the fire and bowed my head. "May the gods guide him on his journey to the afterlife."

"We have company," Cynder said, and motioned with his eyes.

King Sharald walked closer to the pyre. "Goodbye, great wizard." Sharald bent down and grabbed a handful of dirt. He flung it into the flames, symbolizing Stradus's return to the earth and completion of life. "I'll see you soon, old friend." Sharald nodded at us, then left.

I stared into the roaring fire as it glistened against the violet-blue sky, consuming my former master's body. I gazed deeper into the flames, seeing the life and magic that lay there. The fire pulled me into it, and I became lost in its translucent beauty.

I enjoyed the warmth, and the flames comforted me. The power wrapped around my spiritual being as I became connected to it. The fire mana within me grew. I explored it, like Stradus would have wanted. Deep within the fire, there was something else—something dangerous. I recognized it. It was the power I had used to defeat Premier.

The powerful, ancient magic called out to me, saying it was mine to command. I wanted to reach out to it and take hold of it. I didn't want to use it, but I did want to explore it. I wanted to know more about it. Therein lay the problem.

Stradus had told me of those whose magic overpowered them and controlled them, or they became lost in it. I worried this could happen to me. Something about this magic was different. It was something I had never experienced before, or learned about in any of my lessons. It wasn't even in the books I'd read. I stared at Stradus's burning body, wishing he was here now. I needed his advice and wisdom. There was no other wizard I could turn to.

Someone touched me on the shoulder, and I jumped.

"Hellsfire, are you all right?" Krystal asked.

"I'm fine, Your Highness." I glowered at Cynder from the corner of my eye, for not warning me about her approach. He grinned. I bowed to both her and King Furlong. "Is there something I may do for you, Your Majesty?"

"No," King Furlong said. "I came over to thank you for what you did in saving my kingdom."

The princess gave her father a stern look. He looked uncomfortable. "I also came to…apologize for how I treated you earlier. I owe you a great deal, Wizard Hellsfire."

I fought to hold back a smile. In my humblest voice, I said, "Think nothing of it. You were under Premier's spell. Do you mind if I check you out to see that there are no lingering effects?"

The now healthy and vital king nodded. He was pale and thin from lack of sunlight and food, but that could easily be fixed. I extended my magical senses into King Furlong. I poked and prodded him until I had checked every part of him. He squirmed and tried not to move. I wasn't very good at being subtle, and I couldn't afford to be. I had to make sure nothing was left behind. There's something unnerving about someone probing you with magic. If you let them go deep enough, it's worse than standing in a crowd naked. It's more like baring your soul to them where there's no place to hide. I didn't immerse myself in him that way. I stopped before that.

It all seemed so simple now. His mana was damaged in a way I couldn't see before. It was weaker and had gaps in it. The gaps were filled in now, but were dangerously thin. With rest, he would recover.

"You're fine, Your Majesty. Whatever Premier did to you seems to be gone."

"Thank you, Hellsfire," Krystal said. "For everything."

"If you need anything at all," I said, staring into her eyes, "I'll be here for you." I remembered the king and cleared my throat. "For Alexandria."

King Furlong eyed me, then his daughter. He gave us both a disapproving look and let out a small sigh. "I'll keep that in mind, Wizard Hellsfire. If we ever have need of your services, I shall let you know." The king glanced at his daughter one last time before walking away.

"I'm glad to see he's feeling better," I said.

"Me too," she said. "It was all thanks to you and Wizard Stradus."

"It was my pleasure, Your Highness."

She gave me a playful smile. "What did I tell you?"

I smiled back. "Sorry, Krystal."

"Here." Krystal pulled her hand from behind her back. In it was a well-crafted wooden urn. On it were six triangles that composed the hexagram—the symbol of magic.

"This is beautiful." I took the urn and inspected it. It was old, but there was something special about it—magical even. "Where did you get this?"

"It's been in my family for generations."

"Thank you. Did you tell your father about Premier?"

She shook her head. Her face became somber, and she narrowed her eyes. "Not yet. I wanted to give him a few days to rest and recover. He also has to worry about rebuilding, and we both have to fix all the things Premier did. I didn't want to burden him even more. At least, not yet." She brushed back a lock of her hair that dangled in front of her face. "Are you really going into the Wastelands after Premier?"

I nodded. "Yes."

"It's dangerous. At least you'll have a dragon with you."

Cynder opened one eye. "Who says I'm going? I'm not *his* guardian."

"Cynder, show the princess some respect."

The dragon snorted and grumbled. "Humans. You're all beneath me. I'm the greatest of the gods' creations."

"Forgive him. It's been a long day and he's still upset that Premier's bird got the best of him."

Before Cynder could respond, the princess said, "It's quite all right. It's been centuries since we last had a dragon in Alexandria. We appreciated your services, Cynder. You gave us hope and made us even prouder to wear your insignia."

Cynder's smile was so wide it exposed all his pointy teeth.

"Stop it," I said. "You're encouraging him."

"I meant every word of what I said."

"That just makes it worse."

Cynder couldn't stop smiling, but at least he had enough sense to not talk.

"Are you going to leave soon?" she asked, her tone full of worry.

"No. I need to rest and plan. We still have time before Premier recovers. Besides, someone promised me a tour of Alexandria."

"Someone did? I'll see if I can work you into my schedule. I am a princess, you know. I'm a very busy woman."

"I'm a wizard and I'm equally busy, and my services aren't cheap, Princess. I expect to be well paid when you hire me."

I realized that despite all the death and destruction I'd seen and caused, I was more comfortable with Krystal now than I had ever been. Part of it was because I was now a wizard. While I may never have to know what ruling a kingdom is like, I had my own responsibilities—responsibilities that included others. No matter what happened, we would always share this moment, and the time when I had first met her. She would always be a part of me and my life.

"I have to go, hero," Krystal said. She brushed her hand across my arm, letting it linger. "I'll see you later. Goodbye, Cynder."

"Goodbye…Your Highness," Cynder said, opening an eye.

"Goodbye, Princess."

"Some advice?" Cynder asked, after she left.

He'd tried this before and it had usually resulted in a joke at my expense.

However, every once in a while, he's given me some insight. Seeing the serious expression on his reptilian face, I risked it.

"Sure," I said.

"I don't understand what the princess sees in you. You're ugly, you smell, you have hair on your head but not on your face." I began to regret saying yes. "But she likes you. She's a keeper, that one. Hang on to her for as long as you can. Dig your claws into her and don't let go."

I watched the princess go back into the fold of her people. "I will."

The exhaustion from the day finally hit me. Aside from all the emotions I had gone through, my body screamed for rest. I couldn't ignore it any longer. I put the urn on the ground and sat down against Cynder's rough hide. His rhythmic breathing lulled me. I forced myself to stay awake, staring at the dancing flames on the pyre while they consumed my former master's body. I didn't reach into its magic, fearful of what I might see.

There was only one thought on my mind—Premier. He was out there. And I was going to find him.

To be continued in

What Once Was One

The Passage of Hellsfire Series, Book 2

Lead by the dark wizard, Premier, the kingdom of Alexandria was almost overrun by the foul creatures from the Wastelands. With the help of his friends and neighboring kingdoms, Hellsfire was able to defeat him, but only at the cost of his mentor.

Hellsfire is now a wizard, but he must finish what he started by hunting down Premier and retrieving the *Book of Shazul.* He must venture deep into the Wastelands, bypassing his way through thousands of creatures bent on killing him.

Beating in the heart of the Wastelands, is something far more dangerous than Premier or his beasts waiting for Hellsfire. It will force Hellsfire to make a devastating choice—a choice that will have repercussions not only for the Wastelands and Northern Shala, but for the entire land and the one he loves the most.

What once was one, will then be two, and never again be as whole...

Author's Corner

Email: *marcanthonyjohnson@gmail.com.*

Facebook: *https://www.facebook.com/MarcJohnsonAuthor*

Goodreads: *http://www.goodreads.com/marcjohnson*

Twitter: *http://www.twitter.com/Hellsfire*

Website: *http://www.marcanthonyjohnson.com*

www.ingramcontent.com/pod-product-compliance
Lightning Source LLC
Chambersburg PA
CBHW051330250626
47155CB00007B/2531